Badon Hill

Part three of the
Dominic Chronicles

F J Atkinson

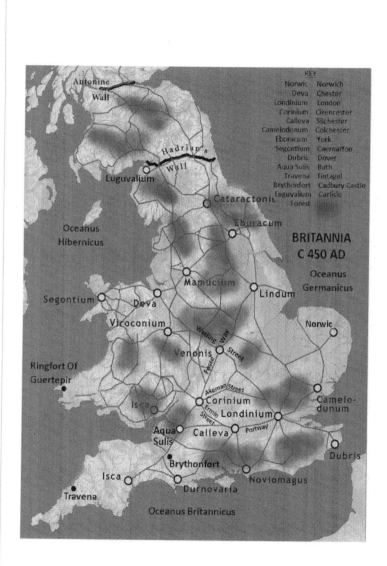

KEY

Norwic	Norwich
Deva	Chester
Londinium	London
Corinium	Cirencester
Calleva	Silchester
Camelodunum	Colchester
Eboracum	York
Segontium	Caernarfon
Dubris	Dover
Aqua Sulis	Bath
Travena	Tintagel
Brythonfort	Cadbury Castle
Luguvalium	Carlisle
Forest	

Antonine Wall

Hadrian's Wall

Luguvalium

Cataractonit

Eboracum

BRITANNIA
C 450 AD

Oceanus
Hibernicus

Oceanus
Germanicus

Mamucium

Lindum

Segontium

Deva

Viroconium

Norwic

Watling Way

Venonis

Street

Fosse Way

Ringfort Of
Guertepir

Akeman Street

Isca

Corinium

Camelo-
dunum

Ermin Street

Londinium

Aqua
Sulis

Calleva

Portway

Dubris

Brythonfort

Isca

Noviomagus

Travena

Durnovaria

Oceanus Britannicus

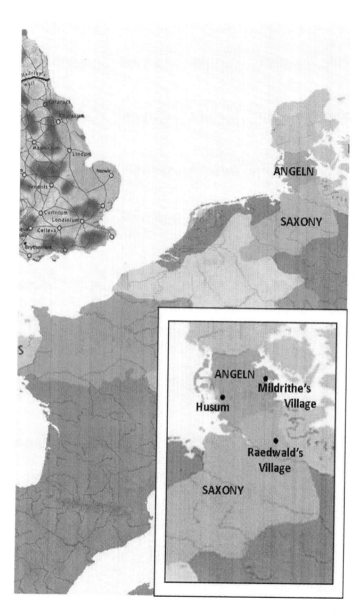

PROLOGUE

Fifth century Britannia was no place to be in mid-winter. Hanging like a rain-sodden canopy over the bleak winter fields, the sky offered a begrudging gloom, even at the zenith of day. Thin and searching winds further compounded the misery of the incarcerated, deterring even the hardiest peasant from wandering too far from the relative shelter of their draughty huts.

Occasionally, a fall of snow would serve to lift the spirits of the people—the deluge elevating the land from its grey mundaneness to a sparkling, white optimism. Yet the joy of the covering was usually short-lived, as a quick melt or stubborn freeze would often follow.

A thaw meant ankle-deep slush, which soaked into the leather boots of those lucky enough to own footwear. Others, mainly children and the destitute (and there were many of these), braved the conditions barefoot whenever need demanded they search for firewood or descend into dark root cellars.

Yet, if the snow lingered, this too would bring its own hardship. On these occasions, much of the land became impossible to traverse; leaving folk with little to do but stare at the frozen fields from wind-whispered doorways.

As such, the midwinter feast was much anticipated. After starting on midwinter's day, the celebrations would last for seven days and provide the peasants with a modicum of respite from the smothering stranglehold of winter.

Bevan welcomed a recently arrived group from a neighbouring village. He knew them all well; knew everyone, in fact, who had assembled for the feast. In all, the populations of four villages had come to make merry. Twenty in number, the latest arrivals had dragged a stout log for the winter burn, creating with it a wet furrow across the fallow fields.

To make the feasting area attractive and welcoming was the next undertaking. Evergreens, such as holly, adorned many hut doorways, over which mistletoe (fashioned to make kissing-boughs) had been placed. Much anticipated by the younger villagers, these had often served to spark into life the latent fancies of many a youth.

Clement weather, for now, blessed the gathering, and the log soon began to steam as the kindling's yellow flames danced below it, exorcising its dampness. A ring of rough log benches encircled the central fire and upon these, sixty villagers sat and luxuriated in the spreading warmth.

A second fire roasted a haunch of venison; and, already, Bevan and his sons had started to carve slices from it. Loaded on to pewter plates, the portions found their way to the waiting and salivating feasters. Most had provided several barrels of mead—the recipes of the fermentations being a source of pride and friendly rivalry. The quicker any particular mead could make a fellow fall on to his arse (and make no mistake; many a villager would do *just* that) the better it was deemed to be.

It did not take long this night for the feast to become merry and animated. Already, the gaiety had intensified, as adults, fuelled by the mead, began to jest and revel in the light of the square. Around them, thrilled children—their excitement heightened to near frenzy by the jollification—skittered and dashed between the tables.

Corran, a jovial barrel of a man, his usual ruddy complexion now intensified to crimson thanks to the toasting flames and gut-warming mead, banged his empty drinking-horn on the table in a demand for attention.

'A song!' he shouted. 'A song to do this feast proud—performed by me, the greatest songster in all of Britannia.' He accompanied the boast with an extravagant, hat-doffing bow.

The crowd cheered as Corran stood on the mead table. Another man, wielding a homemade wooden flute, was quick to join him. In a rumbling bass of a voice, Corran started to sing, nodding towards the flautist, who soon took up the tune.

> 'The winter's yolk, doth freeze my loins,
> The seasons frosts doth make me shiver,
> Oh, how I yearn for summer's breeze
> To set my cod into a quiver.'

Hoots of laughter from the men, and peals of shocked screams from the women now drowned out Corran, who, with thumbs tucked under his belt and chest thrust forward, ploughed straight into the second verse.

> 'I warm my arse by the fire's glow,
> Keep head bone-dry 'neath woolen hood,
> And when I see my true love's bumps,
> My cod is warmed by rush of blood.'

This time, the gathering—a people starved of joy and mirth since the dark onset of winter— positively erupted. Throughout the uproar,

Corran allowed himself a comical, lewd smile of contemplation. His wife could only throw her apron upwards to cover her face as her table neighbours slapped the timber in fits of laughter. Corran began the third verse.

My tunic comes down to my knees,
And up my legs I feel a breeze,
But worry not, for soon I'll feel,
The sweet, smooth skin…'

After hanging on his every word, Corran's audience were stunned to silence as his voice faded away; their concern deepening when beholding his alarmed mid-distance stare. Like he, they looked beyond the glow of the fire, where, defined as a series of dark shadows against the frosty sky, stood a great host of men.

CHAPTER ONE

Cunedda ap Edern had spent his entire life (some twenty-seven years) on the eastern fringe of Britannia in the wild land between the Roman walls of Antonine and Hadrian. His people—the *Votadini*—had earned the protection of Rome when, decades earlier, Cunedda's grandfather, Padarn Beisrudd, had agreed to keep the region free of hostile Pictish and Hibernian occupation.

As a child, Cunedda had hero-worshipped his father, Edern, and by the time he was twelve years old, Cunedda, who by now accompanied Edern on his frequent patrols, knew every mile of the two Roman walls. Fluent in Latin, Edern would often take his son into the Roman forts and the lad became popular with those garrisoned there, many of whom were now British and foreign auxiliaries. Few Romans remained; trouble back in Rome had necessitated their withdrawal from the island. Therefore, British families, including many from the Votadini with nowhere else to go, continued to reside at the forts along the wall.

In his fifteenth year, Cunedda, who by now rode alongside his cousin, Abloyc, was involved in his first skirmish. Edern had come upon a party of Picts heading for a Votadini village near to the abandoned wall of Antonine to the north of the realm. As was the way with Picts, their group comprised of wives and children as well as warriors. The engagement was short and brutal and Cunedda had killed his first Pict that day—a lad of a similar age who ran screaming and undisciplined towards him. Cunedda felt ambivalent towards the kill. Part of him swelled with pride at his father's subsequent endorsement, yet somewhere inside he nursed a deep sadness as he witnessed the boy's mother shriek over his corpse.

On that day, Cunedda saw a side to Abloyc that greatly disturbed him. As was customary, Edern ordered the killing of the remaining Picts, mostly children, women and old men. The kills would be clinical and rapid–Edern having no desire to extend the misery of the survivors; his purpose being merely to eliminate the seeds of the Pictish warriors. Cunedda had witnessed such culling before, but never taken part. Expected now to participate in the executions, he dreaded the ordeal. Before he could begin, however, a wild screaming alerted him towards Abloyc, who possessed no such scruples over such cold slaughter. In fact, Abloyc, who had already killed his first infant, was holding the child's head aloft and taunting the mother with it.

Appalled, Cunedda had stridden to Abloyc and struck him, knocking him to the ground. Abloyc, spitting with rage, went for Cunedda then, but once again found himself knocked to the ground, and this time Cunedda beat him so thoroughly that Abloyc took no part in any further killing that day. By the time Cunedda had finished with Abloyc, the rest of the killing was over, and mercifully, for that day at least, Cunedda was able to avoid a task he dreaded.

Twelve later, his father was dead, leaving Cunedda to guard and protect the land. Abloyc, who usually rode with him, sometimes led his own patrols when the Votadini had more than one attack to deal with. Free from the restraint of Cunedda, Abloyc would give full vent to his barbarity on these occasions, and the subsequent tales of his cousin's excesses inevitably filtered through to Cunedda, filling him with repulsion.

The Picts and Hibernians continued to be a threat, and Cunedda knew it was merely a matter of time before they swamped his land. He travelled south of the wall, came to the town of Deva, and saw that it was walled but not garrisoned. He decided that day that the town was right for his people. There, they could defend themselves. Better still, the town was just a short way from where the Hibernian threat—the Uí Liatháin clan—often made landfall on Britannia. Here, Cunedda and his people would be able to defend themselves from invasion; here they would have early warning of their approach. As for the Picts—they were welcome to the barren lands between the walls; could have the wild winds from the Oceanus Germanicus. As far as he was concerned, the elements could happily scourge their painted, bare bodies.

Cunedda had been a solid leader and his people respected him. He bade farewell to his wife; his six daughters; his seven sons; then left with a vanguard of fifteen hundred warriors. They travelled westwards along the wall of Hadrian until reaching the town of Luguvalium on the bleak western shore. The townsfolk had watched the approach of the fierce-looking Votadini (all carrying shield and spear) with some concern, but their anxiety was unfounded. Cunedda passed them by; having no wish to get embroiled in battle with them. Without even entering the town, he led his men southwards to travel the passable Roman road until reaching the Cilgwri peninsula. Here, he turned westward again until coming to the prominent road named Watling Street.

Now his men were hungry and weary after a long day's march, and as darkness fell, Abloyc saw the light from the village.

'Smell that,' said Abloyc. 'Venison if I'm not mistaken. I would happily kill the entire village

15

to eat freshly roasted venison … by Jupiter, I would.'

Cunedda perused his captain, aware he would do *exactly* that if left to his own devices. 'Not the wisest thing to do, Abloyc: make enemies of our neighbours, seeing how we hope to settle not six miles from here.'

'Still it would get us ready to deal with the Uí Liatháin bastards when they make landfall,' said Abloyc as he continued to gaze at the glowing village. 'Gods' know; my arms are aching and stiff; a bit of sword-play would loosen them.' In emphasis, Abloyc kneaded the knot out of his shoulder.

'No, we don't kill children; how many times must I repeat myself on the matter,' said Cunedda, eying Abloyc with some disdain. 'Save your swordplay for the Hibernians when we meet them. If you wish to loosen your shoulders you can spar with me anytime you want.'

Abloyc threw Cunedda a sardonic half-smile. 'I think not Cunedda; the last time I *sparred* with you I ended up with a bloody head.'

'Well if you insist on going at it hammer and tongue what am I supposed to do,' said Cunedda. 'My father always taught me to fight fire with fire.'

'All the same, I'd rather loosen my limbs on them,' said Abloyc as he nodded towards the villagers who were near enough now to see. Before Cunedda could reprove him again, Abloyc added: 'But I am aware you will not allow such sport, so I will hold my sword for now.'

When Corran stopped singing, Bevan looked with the others towards the gathering of men at the village edge. His mind leapt to the Saxon threat; to the scourge that had already torn across much of the south-east. But why did they merely stand and stare at them; why had they not attacked. A nervous murmuring circulated around the table. Then, a noise from behind had Bevan turn. It was Corran. He was down from the table and beside him.

'What do we do now?' asked Corran. 'Hope they go away? ... Invite them to the feast?'

'We wait for now. We have but one deer; that would nowhere near feed them, anyway.'

Their dilemma evaporated when, close enough for Bevan to see them in detail, two of the men walked into the brand-light of the clearing. They were imposing men, and Bevan guessed them both to be taller than any man at the feast. One man wore his hair long and braided. The other had a shaven head; his only facial hair being a blonde, chin beard. Both had faces studded with gold; the precious metal piercing their nostrils, earlobes and upper lips.

Still stunned to silence, Bevan and Corran waited as the larger of the two men—the braided one —approached him. The man looked at Bevan, then at the gathering of silent people who sat at the tables. By now, parents had retrieved boisterous young, and many of the bairns now sat on their mothers' laps, wide-eyed and expectant.

'You feast well; the harvest and livestock must have been kind to you this year,' said Cunedda as he swept his hand towards the gathering.

Bevan was relieved to hear the man talk in his own British tongue. At least they were not Saxon, which explained why the men had hesitated at the edge of the clearing; why they had not cut their throats. 'This is the produce of several villages,' began Bevan. 'Tonight is the start of midwinter as you doubtless know, and the feast here serves to both celebrate the solstice and help us forget its hardship for a few days.'

Cunedda nodded his comprehension to Bevan. 'We know about the winter feast, indeed celebrate it ourselves back home. Like you, we are native to this isle, and doubtless, like you, we lived well with the Romans when they walked the land.' Cunedda could feel the fear; could even *smell* it in the confines of the clearing. Behind him, stood his men—their sinister spear-burdened profile a dark shadow against the starlit sky. He shouted now towards the tables, intent on assuaging the anxiety of those who sat in trepidation. 'Worry not, we are not here to cause you harm!' He looked to Bevan again as a relieved murmur drifted from the tables. 'If you would see fit to give us water we will be on our way.'

Before Bevan could reply, the other man—the bald and bearded one—stepped beside Cunedda. He nodded towards the spit, where the venison had cooked to perfection. His voice held a hint of assertion. 'And maybe you could see fit to carve me a slice off that roast that so teases my nostrils. My belly aches with hunger after a long day on the trail.'

Bevan studied the man and liked not what he saw. Unlike the braided man, this fellow had cold eyes; humourless they were and bore into him like dagger blades. The man was daring him to refuse his request; Bevan did not doubt that.

But fortunately for Bevan, Cunedda had the measure of the situation, and before the headsman could agree to Abloyc's request (which he undoubtedly would do, for Cunedda could see that the Briton before him was not a stupid man) Cunedda stepped in. 'That will not be necessary, good fellow. My friend here,'—he gave Abloyc a sharp stare—'my friend here is never full; his belly always craves food. I can see that you have many mouths to feed, so if you would be good enough to get the water for us we will be on our way.'

'Of course.' Bevan was relieved and happy to busy himself, if not only to step away from the other who now glowered at him. Cunedda signalled towards his men at the edge of the village and some of them stepped forward with goat-hide water pouches.

With Corran's help, Bevan took the pouches to the village water supply and proceeded to fill them. When they had done, Cunedda's men took the water.

Cunedda made to leave. 'We go now to Deva,' he told Bevan. 'There we intend to stay, so we are to become your neighbours.'

Bevan considered this. He looked at the braided man and felt the power—*the sheer presence*—he radiated. How the man was accustomed to using his power (for he was undoubtedly the leader), or how he would use it in the future, Bevan could only guess. But the other man—the bald, bearded one—troubled him, because Bevan had been around long enough to recognise a black soul when he saw one.

CHAPTER TWO

Almaith walked naked through the body-littered hall. The feast had lasted three days and come to its conclusion when the last standing man had fallen to the dirt ground. Now the scene resembled the aftermath of a pitched battle, with bodies draped and limp across floor and table.

But Almaith had saved herself. Unlike the rest of them, she had placed her hand over her cup when approached by the wine bearers. Then she had watched as the assembly had become more and more raucous; more and more incapacitated; until, one by one, they had become victims of their own gluttony.

Yes; Almaith had saved herself; saved herself for the handsome merchant who now lay amongst his own vomit in a shadowy corner of the hall. Almaith's hair—long, grey and parted down the middle—fell to either side of her pockmarked face, down as far as her lumpy, sagging hips. Her pendulous and veined breasts swayed as she picked her way through snoring bodies and headed towards the youth. Standing proud of her breasts, such was her excitement now, her well-suckled nipples (the brown areola of which spread in a saucer-sized disc around them) pulsated with every beat of her racing heart. Her stomach, like her breasts, was pendent, and hung down from her like a sagging skirt; mercifully hanging low enough to hide her genitalia.

Now she grunted with the effort of removing the heavy chair which lay upturned beside the snoring merchant. The scrape of the timber did not disturb the man who lay on his back—he was long past the point where he *could be* disturbed. Almaith knelt before him and lifted his tunic.

She hoped his penis would be susceptible to her manipulation, even though the man was clearly out of his brain. She was not to be disappointed, and it did not take the man long to rise to the occasion as Almaith rolled his member between her hands, as if rubbing her palms together on the coldest of days. Salivating as the penis reached its highpoint, Almaith stooped to place it between her lips. For some moments, she sucked and gabbled to herself as she simulated copulation upon it, whilst the man, now in the grips of some somnolent erotica, mumbled and groaned below her.

As his grunts became louder, Almaith, who was careful not to wake him, nor generate the spurt that would soften his erection, reluctantly removed his member from her mouth. Now she straddled him and looked at the throbbing flesh below her. She fondled the erection with anticipation. Almost to climax herself now, she could stand it no longer and eased herself upon him.

Like riding a runaway horse, she bounced and gyrated, her movements becoming more exaggerated as her juices slopped from her. Her squeaks became squeals, the squeals then turned to screams as she felt the man release his warm outflow inside her. It was enough to bring on her climax. With abandon, she threw her head back to screech her pleasure to the rafters of the hall.

The release had woken the man, who to his utter dismay found that the curvy, voluptuous serving wench of his dream was in reality Guertepir's hag of a wife. Like the horse that Almaith had made him, he bucked in revulsion when seeing Almaith bestride his thighs. But he had no need to work too hard. Deprived of her fleshy pommel—for the man had softened at once upon seeing who sat upon him—Almaith slid from him and stood up.

The man looked down at his loins; saw they slopped with her juices as well as his own. He scrambled to a sitting position and shrank away from Almaith. 'Away from me you witch!' He pulled his tunic down to cover his manhood, then promptly vomited upon the earthen floor of the hall.

'*What* have we here!' The voice boomed and came from beyond the tables. Guertipir arrived with his man, Diarmait. He took in the scene; looked at his wife who stood hunched and naked before the cowering, young merchant. He nodded to Diarmait, who removed his woolen cloak and placed it around Almaith. 'Take her back to my rooms and make sure she takes to her bed.'

'At once, my Lord.' Diarmait, whose face held not one hint of surprise, led Almaith away.

Guertepir looked at the man below him. 'Whatever I ordered from you yesterday, double it,' he said as he extended his arm to help the man to his feet. Guertepir explained himself. 'You've saved me a gruesome job, you see. Better still you've made her happy for a while, and as long as she's happy her father sends me gold from Hibernia.' Guertepir began to laugh then; the sound hysterical and cruel as he walked from the chamber.

Two days later, he sat in the same hall, but now the place was empty apart from one other man.

Guertepir petulantly jabbed his finger into the knotty wooden table before him. '*Do not* tell me I can no longer spend on feasts and entertainment, it's not what I want to hear.'

'Perhaps not,' said Kelwin, the guardian of Guertepir's purse, 'but if you carry on as you are, you won't have a pot to piss in this time next year.'

'And what of my reserves, man. The last time I looked my vaults were stuffed with gold.'

Kelwin threw up his hands in frustration. 'The last time I saw you in the vaults was *three years ago*. Since then you have thrown lavish feasts nearly every night.' As he looked at his master, Kelwin realised that maybe the question of his finances was academic to say the least. If he continued the way he was going he would be dead within the year, anyway. Up close, Guertepir's face was blotched with drink; his enlarged, porous nose riddled with rosacea. Thick, self-indulgent lips were lavender in colour, hinting at an inner disease. He, Kelwin, liked a drink as much as any man, but knew when to stop—when to respect his body— unlike Guertepir who had no such resolve.

'What about the gold from Hibernia,' asked Guertepir, frowning. 'My wife's father is rich ... he has more cattle than any man I know. He still sends me gold, that I do know; the ships carrying it come in regularly.'

'Yes they arrive here and the gold is taken straight to the vaults, but I'm afraid it is your only major income and it's not enough. The feasts you throw cost much, far more than comes in. Quite simply, my Lord, demand is outstripping supply at the moment.'

'So you're telling me to cut down on the feasting; the enjoyment; the entertaining?'

'Either that or increase your revenue,' said Kelwin.

Guertepir's eyebrows shot up. 'And how would I do that?' he asked. 'It would be no good taxing the people round here, because just like me, as you so eloquently put it, *they don't have a pot to piss in.*'

'How you gain your funds is your own business, my Lord, but one thing I do know is this: the price for cattle is high in Hibernia at the moment, and your father in law would buy as many heads as you could supply to him. Remember, you send me to him occasionally to keep him on your side. He always yearns to increase his herd, and so his standing in the community. I believe it's important over there in that waste land.'

'I think you forget that my grandfather came from that *waste land*,' rumbled Guertipir; 'driven out by the Uí Liatháin bastards, he was. And *I* still consider myself Hibernian, so hold your tongue on the matter of my homeland or I'll have it served up as an appetiser at my next feast.' Guertipir sighed, looked at Kelwin, sighed again. 'Increase revenue … sell cattle … good in theory, but I *have* no cattle to sell, save the small herd of white longhorns that crop and tidy the castle lawns.'

'Yes, most of your vast herd are already sold to pay off your debts.' Kelwin nodded sagely, his expression telling Guertepir: *You see; it's exactly what I've been telling you; your extravagance has left you high and dry.*

The truth of it only fuelled Guertepir's anger. 'Hell and fury!' he exploded, 'what am I supposed to do, then; things have to be paid for!' He twiddled his fingers at Kelwin, inviting a response. 'Come on then, man; your supposed to be my advisor on these matters; advise me.'

'If you were to head northwards along the western coast you will see fields full of cattle,' said Kelwin. 'All the way up to Deva.'

'You're suggesting I *steal* livestock?' asked Guertepir with some incredulity.

Kelwin shrugged. 'I'm suggesting no such thing, my Lord. I'm merely pointing out the desperateness of your situation. One thing's for sure, though: the British leave the herds unguarded. Unlike your fellow Hibernians, they are complacent on the subject of cattle thievery.'

Guertepir had resumed his drumming of the table. He stared long and hard at Kelwin, chewing on his lip as he considered the covert proposal. Eventually, he made to dismiss him. Now businesslike, he said: 'Leave me now, and send me Diarmait; I have much to discuss with him.'

CHAPTER THREE

Aquae Sulis had been the jewel in the crown of Roman occupation for four centuries.

Millennia earlier, the Brythons (a folk who attributed much power and magic to water) had been the first to discover the mineral springs bubbling from the earth. Furthermore, they had found the water to be hot and stone-green in colour, and this had considerably elevated the importance of the place.

Its aura had not been lost upon the Romans. Pagans themselves, they at once recognised the divine significance of the shrine. Consequently, they had transformed it from a boiling, gravel-ringed pool, sited within a forest, to a temple dedicated to their Goddess, Minerva. A huge stone caldarium had been built to hold the emerging water, and this enabled them to actually immerse themselves within its holy embrace. Next to this huge, hot pool, they had built both a warm and cold pool—the tepidarium and frigidarium. The complex had been a magnet to pilgrims who had worshipped at the shrine of the Goddess Sulis (also identified as Minerva by the Romans). Inside the defensive walls of the town, they had also built many dwellings—these to service the needs of the pilgrims who visited what had become the most important site in the Roman world.

After the Roman withdrawal of Britannia, the town had fallen into disrepair, and seemed to be heading the same way of many such towns, which had been stripped of their stone and timber, and almost vanished from the landscape. But Aquae Sulis lay just sixty miles from Arthur's stronghold of Brythonfort, and Arthur had been aware of its importance and beauty since his childhood. He knew the town was worth saving, and for eight years had been responsible for its restoration.

He had garrisoned a small force of his knights at Aquae Sulis—their role being to protect the artisans and workers who laboured there. Cleared of their accumulated silt, the baths had been restored to their former glory, and now brimmed with stone-green water. The buildings, too, had been returned to their habitable former state, and Arthur had made sure they were equipped for permanent habitation now; an improvement on the occasional pilgrim use of before.

The final task was now underway: the rebuilding of the stone walls. Much of the material had been lost over the decades; the stone being prized and desirable for many uses; but now the walls had been built to their original specification and the town once again had a curtain wall to protect it.

The garrison of knights was under the captaincy of Erec, a weapon's instructor from Brythonfort. Along with his wife, Morgana, he had spent his last eight years living between Brythonfort and Aquae Sulis. With little to threaten them (the Saxons knew better than to travel anywhere near Arthur's lands), life had been quiet for Erec and his knights, who had often relieved their tedium by mucking in with the labourers if there was a ditch to be cleared or a stone to be shifted, and this willingness to help had served to break down the barriers between the artisans and military men.

It was in one of the renovated buildings (a wine tavern) in the narrow, main street of Aquae Sulis, that Pwyll the labourer now sat. Never the brightest of men, Pwyll was a loner who always put in a hard day's toil for his master. Honest yet diffident, Pwyll kept his own company and looked forward to the end of each day, and the cup—or two—of wine which he considered a just reward for his labours.

Now as he sat by the fire, rubbing the winter chill from his hands, he was happy to note that apart from the tavern keeper he was the room's only occupant, and this suited him just fine. Today, he would not be relentlessly teased; would not have his slow speech and languid movements mocked.

But Pwyll's tranquility was not to last. He flinched as the door opened and two men bustled into the tavern. Worse still, and to his utter dismay, Pwyll knew one of the men; knew him as Hal: a sneering bully. Pwyll turned away from them. Hunched and anonymous, he faced the fire, quietly cursing the Gods for sending Hal into this wine tavern ... on this day ... at this time. Quickly, he sipped at his wine. Maybe he could slip out unnoticed; after all, he could hear them preoccupied with the tavern keeper; could hear them laugh their clever laughs as they waited for the man to fill their cups.

After draining his own cup, Pwyll had almost reached the door when Hal's lickspittle companion—a man named Menw—spotted him. His nudge and smile to Hal said, *Look what we've got here!*

Immediately, Hal hurried to the door and blocked Pwyll's exit.

'No you don't; you don't leave without me buying you a drink my challenged friend.' Hal's pinched face was resolute, his narrow eyes cold, as he stared at Pwyll. Soon, though, the thin line of his mouth began to twitch, as the hint of a smile turned up its corners. The smirk soon became a mocking grin and, in an act of faux bonhomie, he draped his arm over Pwyll's shoulders and turned with him towards the tavern keeper. 'A large cup of your best Gaul wine for my thirsty friend, barkeeper!' he shouted.

Pwyll frowned and looked at the door. 'No ... thank you ... but no. I've had my fill and have a heavy day at the quarry tomorrow. I must be gone from here.'

Hal looked positively wounded. '*No!* my friend. How can you deprive me of your eloquence this night.' He nodded towards Menw. 'Surely you would not leave me to spend my leisure with that cock-brain.'

Menw considered Hal's slight towards him, but soon realised the joke was on the dimwit and not him. After giving a broken-toothed grin he waited in anticipation.

Hal guided Pwyll to the counter where the tavern keeper, who by now was far from happy with affairs, waited with a full cup of wine. Hal slid a coin across the counter, picked up the cup and offered it to Pwyll. His tone had now lost its affected geniality. 'Come, drink up and let's hear no more of your nonsense about working in quarries.'

Slacked mouthed and dreading whatever Hal had in store for him, Pwyll took the cup. He raised it to his lips and looked nervously at his tormentor who sternly nodded for him to continue. Pwyll took a mouthful of the wine. He swallowed it with difficulty as if swallowing sawdust. Four more such gulps emptied the cup, then three more cups followed as Hal and Menw waited in icy silence to witness Pwyll's inebriation. But Pwyll held his drink well that night ... remained sober ... too terrified anyway to be effected by the wine.

Far from pleased, Hal decided to move things along; decided it was time to hasten Pwyll's humiliation. He pursed his lips in mock contemplation as he nodded towards Pwyll's crotch. 'Is it true what they say?' he asked.

Pwyll looked puzzled—a frown creasing his troubled face. Self-consciously, he placed his wine cup on the counter and dropped his hands to his crotch. 'W-w-hat *do* they say?' he asked.

Hal turned to Menw and shot him a glance which said: *Listen to this; you're about to wet yourself.* He turned back to Pwyll, nodding again towards his crotch. 'They say this: that the Gods compensate for what's deficient between a dullard's ears by blessing him with an abundance between his legs.'

Pwyll had no idea what *compensate* or *abundance* or *deficient* meant, but he *did* know he was in trouble now. He knew Hal; knew what he liked to do. Worse still, the other man had started to laugh and that would only make things worse ... would encourage Hal.

Hal moved close to Pwyll; so close that Pwyll could smell his wine-tainted breath. Without touching him, Hal walked him towards the corner of the tavern, forcing Pwyll to walk backwards until reaching the lime-rendered wall.

Hal was still nose-to-nose with Pwyll, whose own breath now left him in panicky gasps. Over his shoulder, Hal gave Menw his instructions. 'It's no good doing this without an audience. Get some women in here off the street; they need to know what they've been missing.'

The sound of a door opening came to Pwyll as Menw left the tavern, but all Pwyll could see for now was Hal's face. His tormentor wore a lizard smile; a smile that did not reach his eyes.

'It would be better if you let me go now,' said Pwyll, determined not to let the tears that threatened to break from him become visible.

He did not want Hal to see them; did not want to give him more reason to mock him.

'And why's that?' asked Hal, his smile lingering as his gaze flickered down towards Pwyll crotch again. 'Why *should* I let you go? If I did that we would never know if the Gods were telling the truth.'

'I just want to do my day's work for my master, then have my wine at the end of each day. I do not understand what you said about the Gods. If you let me go now ...' The door opened causing a rush of cold air into the room. Female voices accompanied the gust. '...if you let me go I can get to my bed and rest for the morrow.'

Pwyll's eyes stung as he realised that Hal hadn't the slightest intention of letting him go. His tormentor saw the surfacing tears and was inwardly satisfied; tears were his currency ... what he strove to achieve. He grasped Pwyll cheeks with his right hand (the first time he had actually laid hands upon him during the entire ordeal), causing his cheeks to compress and his mouth to pucker like a bloated fish. 'Of course you can get to your bed, my challenged friend. As soon as I've de-bagged you, you can leave.'

'No you can't do that to him.' The woman's protestation gave Pwyll no hope; laced as it was with humour. She didn't mean it. He could tell. She said it merely because it was what she was supposed to say. She wanted her show — a show he would soon provide.

Hal still stood in front of Pwyll, his hand now removed from his face. Now it rested flat against his chest, pushing him against the wall. Hal turned his head to look over his shoulder at the woman who had spoken. He could see she was no older than twenty. She lingered with another of a similar age. Both had been walking home when Menw had persuaded them to enter the wine tavern with his offer. *'Just a moment of your time, girls. I promise you a sight you will never forget,'* he had told them.

The other woman — the one who had remained silent up to now — shuffled uncomfortably and frowned at her friend. But her companion just nodded at her, a small smile playing on her face. *No, let's stay a while, perhaps we can see what he has to show us*, was the consensus of the smile.

Pwyll slammed himself back against the wall and clutched at the waistband of his hose as Hal turned on him.

Hal nodded to Menw and exploded into action. 'NOW … WITH ME!' He made a grab for Pwyll's tunic, his intention to pull it upwards over his head, but Pwyll dropped to the floor and curled into a ball.

Menw fell on him and pulled him on to his back, but Pwyll brought his knees up. Whimpering with raw fear now, he bunched his body into a tight cocoon. Hal knelt beside him and began to pummel his fist into his thighs. Angry and breathless, he punched him repeatedly. 'Straighten out ... you retard ... or we'll strip you completely ... make you walk home bare-bollocked.'

The two girls stood frozen, hands to mouths in shock, not knowing whether to laugh or cry now the show had started in earnest.

An uneasy frown creased the tavern keeper's face. He knew he should do something—this could not be right—but what *could* he do? The men before him would probably do the same to *him* if he interfered; they were much younger and stronger than he. If he left to get help, the thing would be over with before he got back. They were about to humiliate Pwyll (a simple man, but a man he liked); humiliate him so badly he would never be able to show his face in Aquae Sulis again. He could see that Pwyll's strength was waning—could see that Pwyll was crying now, as Menw lay across his knees, pinning them straight.

Gasping and clench-teethed from the struggle, Hal knelt over him. He looked to the girls as he rummaged up Pwyll's tunic and searched for the top of the hose which Pwyll still clung to. He callously bent Pwyll's finger back from the hose and shot the girls a quick glance. 'I swear this has been worth your wait—' he finally got his hands around the hose rim which circled Pwyll's waist and got ready to tug hard—'just look at...'

The door opened and Augustus walked in.

Put in charge of the local quarry by Arthur, he was Pwyll's master and had decided to join him for a late drink, knowing, as he did, that Pwyll would be in the wine tavern at the end of his day. Augusrus knew the man was unobtrusive and preferred his own company, but Augustus always sought to draw him out of himself—to offer him friendship.

The tavern keeper had flinched when the giant Briton had entered, because then he knew things were about to happen. He knew all about Augustus—*who didn't?* Knew he was genial and friendly; also knew he was formidable. The rumours of what he had done in Norwic—how he had defended himself, bare handed, against two killing dogs and an armed warrior of renown—had elevated the man to legendary status. Like all tales it been exaggerated in the re-telling, and when Arthur had seconded Augustus to Aquae Sulis to help with the town's renovation, the sight of him had actually stopped people in the streets. Soon though, folk were to discover that *'big Gus'* (as he was known) was a man of the people; a man who waved away any suggestion he was in any way special. In particular, he would go out of his way to befriend the so-called *lesser men*—men such as Pwyll. But the tavern keeper *knew* that August was special; special in the way that any room he walked into was immediately enhanced and made more interesting by his booming personality and aura.

Unfortunately, though, Augustus had just walked into *his* room, *his* tavern, and that could only mean one thing. Hastily, he removed his best jugs of wine and placed them under the counter. He considered joining the jugs on the ground but his curiosity kept him standing.

Augustus was at first puzzled when he saw Pwyll in a struggle with two men. Had he had a fit? A seizure? But when the cruel eyes of Hal and Menw turned towards him (two men he could not stand), Augustus then knew. Menw was the first to his feet. Augustus stood facing him, then looked at the girls who by now had moved to the counter.

'Leave, please,' Augustus instructed them quietly. He stepped back to the door and opened it for them. As they scuttled, shame-faced through the door, he added, 'And disgrace on you.'

Hal was standing now. He knew all about Augustus—knew that he had a reputation; had heard as well that the big bastard was a bit stupid and could be reasoned with; fighting him was *definitely* out of the question, even with Menw to help him.

By now, Pwyll had scrambled to his feet and hitched up his crumpled hose. Augustus nodded towards the wine counter. 'Go behind there with the tavern keeper, Pwyll. I'll buy you a cup of wine when this is done with.' He turned back to Hal and Menw.

They exchanged glances. Hal, jittery and unsettled by Augustus' measured tone, attempted a compromise. 'We were just having a bit of fun with him. L-look at him, w-we've not harmed a hair on his head.'

'And I won't harm a hair on yours,' said Augustus. He nodded towards Menw. 'Or his.' Hal's and Menw's sigh of relief was audible to everyone in the room. They were about to thank

Augustus for his clemency when he continued. 'Now be good enough to step out of your clothes so we can get this matter dealt with.'

'Hhh?' Hal was wide-eyed and dismayed as the gravity of Augustus' command sank in. He looked at Menw, whose expression, if it were possible, was even more haunted than before.

'Yes, you heard me right,' said Augustus. 'I want you both to strip naked here before me, just as you would have stripped Pwyll naked.' To emphasise the folly of refusing his request, Augustus let his hand drop to the stonemason's hammer that hung at his belt.

Hal and Menw looked at Augustus who was two heads taller; looked at the meaty fist grasping the hammer.

They began to undress.

Moments later, they were standing naked before him, shuffling uncomfortably—their dropped hands preserving their modesty.

Augustus let out his breath in a disgusted 'phh.' He looked over to Pwyll and the tavern keeper. 'Pour two cups of wine please ... one for me ... one for Pwyll.' He looked with mock apology at Hal and Menw, as if he had committed the clumsiest of faux pas. 'Oh, I am sorry ... y-you didn't think they were for you, did you?' Hal and Menw blankly shook their heads. Augustus looked them over again, then turned to the tavern keeper, but now his tone was frosty. '*Why* were the women in here?' he asked.

The tavern keeper pointed to Hal and Menw. 'Those two wanted the women to watch Pwyll being stripped; they brought them in to laugh at him.'

Augustus nodded and pursed his lips as if enlightened. He looked back at Hal and Menw. '*Better* if there's an audience, is it?'

Hal had no idea whether to nod or shake his head. Neither action would satisfy Augustus— he knew that. Instead, he merely shrugged his bare shoulders at him.

Augustus feigned bewilderment. 'What?— you mean to tell me you *don't know*? That's strange, because you seemed pretty sure of it when I walked in.' Crowd murmurings now came from beyond the door. The expelled women had spread the word that the giant, Augustus, had caught two renowned bullies; caught them trying to humiliate a man in the wine tavern. 'Outside,' said Augustus, pointing to the door. 'You are both leaving this town and I want you to go now.'

Hal shook his head. 'No … you can't mean this. This has gone far enou—'

'OUT OF THE DOOR, I SAID!' Augustus stepped towards them, his latent fury close to eruption.

Hal and Menw shrank from him, then edged themselves towards the door. He leant before them and opened it. And there they stood; naked as the day they were born—the snickering crowd facing them. Augustus kicked firstly Menw, then Hal into the street. Both men landed on their knees amongst the crowd—a crowd which had now started to jeer them.

Augustus followed and began to kick their skinny backsides down the muddy road. Several times, they would fall to their knees; then, after waiting with folded arms for them to get to their feet, Augustus resumed his kicking as he coerced them towards the gates of the city. Eventually, Hal and Menw had had enough, and began to run in a stumbling gate down the street. The crowd followed, shouting insults and pelting stones. The gates could not come soon enough for the two men.

Erec rode up towards the city gates of Aquae Sulis with his woman Morgana by his side. Having spent the last six months at Brythonfort, training new recruits at the academy, Erec's time had come again to assume his six-month tenure as steward of Aquae Sulis. Morgana's saddle had been adapted to hold their three-year-old son, Girard, firmly in place—a wise move that had been partially successful in restricting the youngster's boisterousness on the sixty mile journey from Brythonfort. Now as they neared the open gates, the infant's keen eyes had spotted movement beyond the open gates of the city.

He turned to his father. 'Papa … men are running towards us. They come to say hello.'

Erec could see for himself now, and bade Morgana to stop. He squinted into the distance, still not sure what was happening. 'Stay here, please,' he said as he spurred his horse into a trot towards the gates.

The son of a peasant, Erec had inherited his father's genes, and when still only fourteen towered above the tallest man in his village. His athleticism was not lost on Arthur's scouts, who, as well as checking that the lands around Brythonfort held no threat from Saxon incursion, looked out for boys of Erec's stature. His parents agreed for him to go to Brythonfort (indeed it was deemed a considerable honour for any family to have a son selected for training with Arthur's militia) and at the age of fifteen Erec left his village to take up his lodgings at the bastion.

Arthur's faith in Erec had not been misplaced and the boy took easily and naturally to his tutorage. He excelled in all aspects of his training, and at the age of twenty-one was trusted to lead his first patrol from the gates of Brythonfort. They came upon a Saxon war party, intent on striking deep into the western lands. The party had strayed into Arthur's protectorate and needed to dealt with. Under Erec's leadership, and employing the Roman techniques utilised by Arthur's standing army, Erec and his knights had ruthlessly sliced through the Saxon threat that day, leaving not one Germanic warrior alive.

Erec led many more patrols, and the result was always the same: total annihilation of his adversaries. The quality of Erec's field craft was such, that he was asked by Arthur to take up the role of weapons instructor in the academy when only twenty-five years old. Erec had proven to be a tough but fair trainer. Five years had passed since that day, during which time many youths and men had graduated through the academy.

At about the same time Erec took up his post at the academy, the girl, Morgana (then twenty years old) began her employment as a cook. Her role was to assist the older women and ensure that the trainees' *hunger was satisfied at the end of each day. She soon caught Erec's eye, and after a slow and awkward beginning—Erec having spent all his years since adolescence either training or fighting, and Morgana never having developed any romantic attachments, such was her age—they had fallen deeply in love. After a short courtship they had wed, and one year after that, Morgana gave birth to a son whom they named Girard, after Morgana's late father.*

Now as he approached the city, Erec thought of his son and considered the infant's vulnerability in the uncertainty of the post-Roman world. Anything could happen at any time, he knew that. For now, Arthur had secured the western lands, but Erec was shrewd enough to realise that Britannia was volatile and always open to Saxon dominance—especially if the barbaric war bands came to realise that their fragmented approach to warfare had its limitations. Already there was rumour of troop movement, *from the north of all places*, causing Arthur to dispatch Dominic and Tomas at once to scout the situation.

The jeering crowd ended Erec's contemplations and brought him back to the present. The people of Aquae Sulis seemed to be at unrest and that worried him.

As Hal and Menw ran from the gates, Augustus, with the throng behind him, boomed after them. 'If I see you two here again I'll strip you of your skin as well of your clothes. Get under the stones from which you crawled, you worthless...'

Augustus voice trailed away as he saw Erec, and, not for the first time, was impressed by what he saw. Only slightly shorter than he, but just as imposing, Erec was a handsome man, whose blonde braided hair fell to his jawline. A full beard covered his angular face; a face now full of concern.

Glad to see Augustus apparently in charge of *God-knew-what*, Erec shouted: 'What gives here, Gus?' He watched Hal and Menw run away from the city.

Augustus scratched at the curly hair that grew from the back of his neck. 'Nothing worth much of a mention,' he replied. 'Just two bullies with nowhere to live anymore and without a shred of clothing to wear.'

Erec cast an indifferent glance towards the now-distant exiles. 'Hmm ... never liked them anyway ... too smart for their own good.' He slid from his horse and embraced Augustus as the crowd dispersed. 'Good to see you, man, but it's not the best of news; word is out that Guertepir has gone northwards in numbers. *And* ... listen to this, my friend; it's also been reported that some tribe from beyond Hadrian's wall—most likely the Votadini—have travelled to Deva. It seems that things are about to get interesting.'

CHAPTER FOUR

As soon as the traveller had arrived at Brythonfort with news of Guertepir's journey northwards up the western peninsula, Arthur had dispatched Dominic and Tomas upon the road.

Two day's travel saw the pair bypass Aquae Sulis and reach Corinium. From there, they took the network of lesser roads, westwards, until reaching the shoreline of the western peninsula—the route taken by Guertepir. For two further days, they stuck to the road as it passed through wood, field and marsh. Whenever passing a homestead or small village, they took care to blend into the adjacent countryside, having no wish to endure any lengthy conversations or explanations of why they were on the road. Although they expected no problems from the folk living on the western peninsular, many of who were Desi exiles of Hibernia, they nevertheless knew them to be curious folk when seeing strangers.

It was the bellowing of cattle that first alerted Dominic and Tomas to the movement ahead of them. Garbed in russet cloaks of broken weave, both rangers had no trouble blending into the shrub cover that pushed shoulder-high from the ground twenty paces from the road.

'That sounds like *a lot* of cattle,' said Dominic, as he lay on his belly below a twisted winter bramble.

'Far too many for any of the small farmsteads *we've* passed,' said Tomas, nodding towards a cluster of buildings that lay within a fold of ground nearby. 'That family yonder can only have twenty cows at the most, and that seems fairly typical.'

As they watched, a billowing of dust rolled up the road. The first of the cow herders rode through the miasma, emerging as if creatures spawned from a desert land. Their presence caused Dominic and Tomas to shrink a little further into the shrub cover.

'Under all that shit, they're Guertepir's men,' Dominic said. 'I can tell by their bearing on those horses ... typical Hibernian riding style.'

'So, they're here to herd cattle?'

'More likely to steal them. It's what Hibernians do when scraping for gold. Looks like Guertepir's extravagances have caught up with him'—he gripped Tomas' arm and pointed to the nearby smallholding—'maybe we're about to find out.'

As they watched, a larger group of horsemen emerged from the swirling cloud and made for the homestead. Dominic, who had been to Guertepir's ringfort recently, strained to recognise them; strained to recognise Guertepir. But he could not recognise any man before him, the dust was far too thick for that.

At the farm, the riders were met by three men and two boys—probably a father and sons, thought Dominic. Arms were raised as a squabble ensued, then the man fell to the ground. As his sons stooped to attend him, a thin reedy scream sounded above the lowing of encroaching cattle. 'The bastards have killed the father,' said Tomas. 'Look ... the mother has arrived.'

Tomas made to gain his feet, but Dominic put a restraining hand upon him. 'No! Stay hidden. There's nothing we can do here; not against so many men.'

Released from their pen by the riders, the twenty cows from the homestead had already blended with the main body of cattle and begun to move with the herd.

An unending movement of cattle and men continued to amble past Dominic and Tomas. Dominic squinted as he peered through the dust and attempted to count the riders. Such were their numbers that the procession continued for much of the morning. Dominic frequently exchanged looks of astonishment with Tomas as the extent of the cattle theft became apparent. When the last of them finally passed by, another large body of men emerged from the dust.

'What the...' began Dominic.

'They're not Guertepir's men. Even I can tell that,' said Tomas.

'No, *they are not*; they are Britons from beyond the wall; I've seen their horses and livery before when I worked for Rome. Will also rode with me then, and we ventured northwards with the legions as far as the Antonine wall. Their shields bear the sign of the juniper and that makes them Votadini, but what in hell's name are they doing this far south?'

Dominic counted seven hundred riders (again all well-armed) following the cows. Eventually, the last of them passed by, leaving Dominic and Tomas watching the empty road. When the dust finally settled, they got to their feet and ventured from the shrubbery. Southwards, in the distance, they could see the dust cloud that followed the mass movement of men and cattle.

Dominic sighed resignedly as he nodded towards the farmstead. 'Looks like Guertepir has changed *their* lives forever.' Fifty paces from them, a woman wept at the side of the fallen man. Dominic and Tomas went to them. The woman shrank back as they approached, whilst the sons sprang to their feet.

Dominic held up his palms in non-aggression. 'Do not be hasty. We are not with the raiders, but we saw what they did.'

The woman's wretched face was an amalgam of dust and tears. She looked at Dominic, then beyond him. 'And who is he who rides with you?'

Startled, Tomas and Dominic looked behind them. Sat upon a mule, bumping down the track towards them, was a monk.

Dominic's mouth was agape. Chance meetings with past acquaintances were rare in Britannia, but Dominic *actually knew* the youth who now approached him; knew him as Ingle, the young monk from Hibernia.

Ingle's own face rivalled Dominic's in incredulity as he got close enough to recognise him. 'What in the Lord's name are you ... ' His voice faded to silence when he saw the group of homesteaders surrounding the dead man. By now, his sons had lifted him from the road and started to carry him back to their hut. The woman, too preoccupied with her grief now, turned from Dominic's group and followed her sons.

'The raiders killed him,' said Dominic in response to Ingle's questioning look. 'He wouldn't give up his cattle so they just killed him; there's nothing we can do for them now.'

Ingle slid from his mule and embraced Dominic, his voice respectably subdued such was the gravitas of the scene. 'Well-met Dom, believe it or not but I was seeking you out ... well, seeking out Brythonfort anyway.'

Dominic turned towards Tomas. 'This is my companion, his name's Tom. We were sent to watch proceedings here.' Ingle and Tomas (two youths of a similar age) exchanged nods. Dominic continued. 'Now perhaps you can tell me what the hell possesses a monk from Hibernia to ride alone in the middle of nowhere this day?' Before Ingle attempted to reply, Dominic noticed him glance at the sack that lay over the rump of Tomas' horse. It occurred to him then that Ingle looked half-starved. 'No don't answer me yet. We'll eat first. You can tell me what happened when your belly's full.'

Ingle began his story after the meal, telling of how he had come to Britannia; one of a group of eight monks led by Rodric—an admirable man known to Dominic from his trip to Hibernia. Their mission was to convert the pagan people of Deva and its surrounding countryside. It was Ingle's second trip to Britannia in two years and one he had greatly looked forward to. At first things went well, and Ingle enjoyed his incursions into the green lands around Deva, meeting people whom he came to regard as friends. He was popular amongst them such was his cheery disposition and mischievous sense of fun. Consequently, was able to convert many of them to Christianity. *They are reluctant to offend you by saying no*, Rodric had laughed.

Ingle told Dominic and Tomas how life had been austere but pleasing for the monks at Deva, until the arrival of Cunedda and the Votadini, that was. With no garrison or militia to defend their town, the people were left with little choice but to accept the inflow of men from the northern lands. No blood was spilt and the men took up residence in a quarter of the city that was mostly ruinous and weather distressed. Indeed, when their leader visited the monks on his second morning, Ingle had found him to be stern yet unthreatening. The man—a pagan—insisted the monks did not bother them with the nonsense of Christianity and Rodric had readily agreed to this, knowing that conversion often took months or even years to achieve. But another man who walked with the leader—the one named Abloyc—really bothered Ingle; troubled him to the extent that he voiced his concerns to Rodric. Rodric, a shrewd and clever man, also felt the bad energy radiating from Abloyc, and counselled caution as far as the man was concerned.

Then things changed. Another group of men turned up at Deva, these having approached from the west, along the northern shoreline of the peninsula. Ingle feared that a savage battle was about to erupt, but Cunedda, the leader of the Votadini, left the city and went to parley with an envoy of the newly arrived men. When Cunedda returned he met with Abloyc and debated with him late into the night. Ingle witnessed Cunedda leave with much of his army the next day. Curiously, he had joined with the other force and travelled behind them, westwards, along the northern coastline of the peninsula.

But to his dismay Ingle bumped into Abloyc later that morning. Cunedda had left him behind with five hundred of his men to retain a presence in the city. It took Abloyc very little time before he approached the monks, and that was when things started to go wrong for them. Now free of Cunedda's restraining hand, Abloyc began to push the monks around, deriding them for their *"nonsensical creed"* and *"mad hair and skirts."* He forbade them to leave Deva, and one morning when they met for prayers, Rodric was not with them. Abloyc struck Ingle for his insolence when he enquired of the whereabouts of Rodric, and later that morning they found him cut, tortured and dead by the city walls. The distraught monks lifted him and buried his body at a small gravesite inside the city.

After this, things became far worse. Abloyc insisted they report to his quarters every day and wait on his every need. Always, they were derided and belittled by him and his circle of lackeys, and one by one the monks disappeared. In the four days since Cunedda had left the city, Abloyc had reduced the monk's numbers by six, until only Ingle and an older monk named Constance remained.

Ingle knew it was time to get out or die. Under cover of darkness, he waited with two mules beside the walls of the city. But

Constance, who had been serving Abloyc that night, did not show. Ingle feared the worst and decided to leave without him, knowing that his own life was very expendable at that moment. His intention was to travel westwards along the northern coast until reaching the port at Segontium from where he hoped to find a boat to take him back to Hibernia, but when reaching the port he was forced to hide when learning that Cunedda, who had passed that way, was gone. Three hundred of his men remained at the port to act as a blockade against invasion from Hibernia.

Therefore, Ingle found himself in a dilemma. He could not go back to Deva, for there he would be surely killed, and now he could not home. He thought of Maewyn, the boy from Britannia who now trained as a monk in Hibernia. The boy had told him many tales of his life in Britannia; told him of Brythonfort and its safe haven and strong king. Indeed, Ingle had already met three worthy men from Brythonfort: Dominic, Withred and Flint. He decided to travel south along the road that led from the port. His intention was to somehow reach Brythonfort and find sanctuary there. He soon realised the road was the same one taken by the two armies, and after two days travel he saw a swirling dust cloud before him. He also noticed the empty fields beside the road where cattle had once so obviously grazed. The armies had been amassing a herd as they headed south; that was apparent to him, and soon he could actually smell the cattle as he caught up with the slow moving mass of men and cows before him. From then on, he had been extra careful to remain at an unseen distance from them.

'And then you saw us,' said Dominic, who had listened intrigued and without interruption to Ingle's story.

'And what a totally unexpected and astounding sight for sore eyes you are,' said Ingle.

Tomas lay propped on one elbow on the floor as he chewed on a hard tack biscuit from his pack. 'You did well to get away when you did,' he said. 'I too was under the yoke of a wicked man; for a full two years he beat and abused me before I found Dominic in the woods and escaped.'

Ingle looked at Tomas and liked what he saw. He guessed his age to be sixteen and could see he was confident yet unassuming. Enveloped in his dusky cloak, he looked every inch the young tracker; a smaller (far less wrinkled) version of Dominic, in fact. And his eyes were striking ... so striking. Penetrating and intelligent as they were, they also had a hollow depth to them. Ingle could tell that Tomas would never forget his two years of servitude. What he had endured he, Ingle, could only imagine.

'I don't think I would have lasted two days, let alone two years, with Abloyc at Deva,' said Ingle. 'I suspect I'm the only monk who survived. I'm not sure if he disliked monks or just liked killing.'

Dominic got to his feet and looked at the sky. 'I've a feeling we might find that out before long, but for now we still have half a day of daylight before us. Time is important now and we need to get back to Brythonfort and report this. *Any* movement of armies is bad news in these troubled times.'

'You know who leads the armies, then?' asked Ingle.

'Yes, now I do. The cattle thievery points to Guertepir, and the juniper emblazoned shields to the Votadini from above the Wall. What they are doing together is a mystery, but worrying nonetheless.' He looked at Tomas as the youth climbed onto his horse. 'Troubled times lie ahead, lad. Only the Gods know what this will lead to. Looks like we're going to be in the saddle for some time yet.'

CHAPTER FIVE

Raedwald was the tainted, bastard seed of
Egbert. For nineteen years, he had spent his life
in Saxony, reared by a bitter mother who
harboured no love for him. Egbert had raped
her when she was barely into puberty, and from
the moment Raedwald entered the world she
saw her son as nothing more than an Ebert-
inflicted disease.

In his early years, Raedwald endured many
beatings and scoldings from his mother, and the
abuse was not been lost upon others. Soon the
other boys from the village, who saw him as a
pariah, began to tease and mock him
mercilessly.

Raedwald, feeling isolated, took to walking
the woods alone, where he began to trap birds
and other small creatures that scuttled through
the forest undergrowth. These he tortured to
slow deaths, blaming them for all the ills in his
life.

Eventually, the day had come when he grew
big enough to say, *"no more!"* to his mother.
Then, he had beaten her; beaten her so badly he
had broken her teeth and imploded her nose.

Consequently, Raedwald had become the
dominant figure in his household, and his

standing in the village soared accordingly. Now it was his mother's turn to be treated like a beast of the fields.

As for his father, Raedwald had always hero-worshiped him, seeing him as the mysterious avenger of Saxony on the dark isle of Britannia, having no idea of Egbert's actual black depravity. Not that it would have made any difference because Raedwald himself was now corrupt—bad genes and a brutal upbringing had seen to that.

When news came to him that his father was dead (worse still, dead at the hands of the renowned but traitorous Angle, Withred) Raedwald had gone berserk.

He had killed his mother that night. After dragging her into the forest, he had cut her throat, blaming her for his father's absence. Then he had scraped a mound of leaves over her, and returned to his hut. There, he had screamed his misery to the thatch until the insipid morn had found him exhausted and wretched.

A year passed over and Raedwald's hate for Withred still festered within. He imagined a multitude of ways to get back at him; ways to kill him slowly and painfully. To go to Britannia and seek him out was his intention, but he did not possess the gold needed to pay for his passage across the Oceanus Germanicus to Camulodunum on the eastern seaboard of Britannia. If he was ever to get there, he would have to steal the gold, he knew that, but no one in his village *possessed* any gold.

It was a chance meeting with a gnarled Angle, recently returned from Britannia, which finally set Raedwald into motion. After Raedwald told the Angle he was Egbert's son (a fact he bragged about at every opportunity), the man whistled and remarked how Raedwald must yearn to cut Withred's throat. Raedwald concurred, and then became excited when the old warrior, during the course of his general chit-chat, told him of Withred's aunt, a renowned herbalist, who resided in Angeln on the White Sea shore. Furthermore, the man was able to describe the route to the village, telling Raedwald that four days travel on a good pony would get him there.

Two days later, Raedwald (intent on gaining revenge against Withred in any way he could) set out to Angeln. With him rode a sickly individual named Eadwig; the only youth in the village gullible enough to believe Raedwald's hastily assembled story of an abandoned gold mine on the banks of the White Sea—one which had been worked clean, but would still provide them with enough scraps of gold to get them to Britannia.

But after four days of rough travel—two of them through the unforgiving marshes and forests of Angeln—a trail-weary Raedwald had become weary, and ready to give up his quest for vengeance.

'Miserable bogs and trees, that's all we've seen for the last two days; no wonder the Romans left this place alone,' grumbled Raedwald, as he now stood pulling at his pony's reins. Once again, the beast had become stuck in the mud.

Eadwig, whose own pony was knee-deep in the mire, mirrored Raedwald as he dealt with his own problem. 'I thought you said this would be an *easy* trip,' he said. 'All we've done up to now is *walk* with the ponies. What I'd give to actually *ride* upon mine.'

'Over there,' said Raedwald. 'There's a track. The ground looks more solid over there; we must get to it ... and shut your bellyaching or I'll cut your tongue out.'

Eadwig fell silent then, knowing the folly of disobeying Raedwald when his eyes became hollow and bleak.

Another bout of pulling and cursing saw them on the track. One hour later, a curl of smoke in the distance evidenced the location of a settlement. Raedwald knew it must be the village of Withred's aunt. The Angle's description of the huge deeply-etched oaks that lined the route to the village had been precise, right down to the lightening-struck tree which was scarred with a deep rebate from canopy to root.

Raedwald knew it was time to tell Eadwig the real reason for the trip. The lad was weak and slow so would be easily won over. 'We need to be careful ahead. I've been told a witch resides in the village.' he said.

'Then why do we ride towards it?'

'Because like all witches she has a cache of gold. Gold that will get us to Britannia.'

'And what of the gold mine? I thought we were to get our gold from the mine by the shore.'

'Would you rather spend another five days striking through this wretched mud, then? Because that will happen if we head for the gold mine.'

'Better that than fight with a witch. I hear they can turn you into toads.'

Raedwald looked at Eadwig as if were completely mad. *'Turn you into toads.* Whoever told you that. No ... I have a plan. Listen to me, it's quite easy really...'

Mildrithe was sad after attending to Lufe. The man was old, had lived fifty-seven long years, but now his life was ending. A chill resided in his chest, setting it to an all-too-familiar rattle, but at least Mildrithe knew his end would be gentle—the chest malady always took them gently. *Nerthus* herself knew there were many worse ways to die. She thought then of Withred and wondered if *he* still lived. Often, she thought of her nephew; considered his new-found committal to the British cause, but this did not worry her. She knew him to have a good soul, so he must have abandoned the war bands out of decency.

A stranger, distraught, on the edge of the village startled her. Strangers were rare in Angeln and this one looked as if he had been through a battle. Of medium height with a wispy, ginger beard, a youth of nineteen held out his hand in supplication. But Mildrithe noticed a disturbing cast to the youth's eyes which made her uneasy. She looked around for support, but for now she was the only person standing out in the open—the men were in the fields and the women at their chores.

'My friend is hurt; he fell under his pony back down the trail,' said Raedwald. 'I was told that a woman lives nearby; a woman who can heal. I seek this woman, though I fear it may be too late now to help my friend.'

Mildrithe's unease immediately dispersed as she heard Raedwald's plea. A man was hurt and she would help him because that was her role in life. 'Did he break any bones?' she asked Raedwald as she hurried back to her hut. 'I will need to set them securely if that is the case.'

'I don't think so,' said Raedwald as he followed Mildrithe to her hut. 'He is holding his belly as if something strikes him there.'

Mildrithe pushed a bunch of dried herbs and a jar of salve into the voluminous pocket of her dress and brushed past Raedwald who was standing in the doorway. 'Come, take me to him. I'll see what I can do.'

As Mildrithe bustled past him, Raedwald noticed the necklace that hung from her neck. Heavy and pendulous, it seemed to be made of quality stones and had a gilding of yellow metal; gold most probably. Even more fervent now, Raedwald took the lead and walked from the hut. 'Follow me, frau. My friend is but a short way down the trail.'

Mildrithe's short legs were hard pushed to keep up with the hurrying Raedwald as he hastened away from the village towards the thicker woodland which adjoined the track half a mile away. He looked back to Mildrithe, giving her a half-smile as he furtively checked over her shoulder to ensure no one from the village had seen them leave. After five hundred paces, he stopped and pointed into the trees beside the track. 'His pony bolted into the woods,' said Raedwald as he parted a thicket of hazel and strode into the muted interior of the forest.

Mildrithe followed him and gingerly picked her way through the undergrowth. 'I thought you said it threw him onto the actual track,' she said as her unease returned.

'No, he's there, just ahead.' Raedwald pointed towards a shape on the ground nearby.

Eager to help Eadwig, Mildrithe scurried towards him but found him dead—his head crushed and brain-smitten. The rock, bloodied and adorned with Eadwig's hair, lay nearby.

At first, Mildrithe could not take it in. The youth said the man had hurt his belly, but it looked as if the prone man before her had fallen from his horse and struck his head. Of the horse, there was no sign.

As she knelt beside Eadwig and saw his injuries, an awful truth dawned on Mildrithe. *This is no accident, this is wilful murder.* She turned as Raedwald closed on her.

Moments later, he threw the rock to one side as Mildrithe fell at his feet. With her scalp cloven and gaping, she was barely conscious. 'That's for my father, you witch,' Raedwald said.

Through a dim, grey miasma, Mildrithe struggled to assemble a single coherent thought as she looked up at Raedwald. ''What have you done … why is this…' She touched her head, her eyes rolling and distant. 'What … what have you …'

'I've *hit* you,' sneered Raedwald. 'Because you're the sister of the mare who foaled Withred.'

Mildrithe, whose consciousness was beginning to fade, could only mumble a confused response.

Raedwald dropped to his knee to hang above Mildrithe. With his fury rising, he grabbed her face. 'My name is Raedwald, son of Egbert, and I have travelled four days to avenge him. Your nephew lured my father into the forest and that's what I've just done to you. I come to claim blood for blood—if not Withred's, then yours will do for now.' He shook her face as she drifted away from him. 'No—no, don't you dare go to sleep on me. Not until you've felt my dick inside you.'

Mildrithe's eyes fluttered, her voice a low whisper. 'Withred, my Withred … what have you done…'

Raedwald pushed her face to one side and lifted her dress.

When the awful deed was done, he removed the necklace from Mildrithe's throat and rolled onto his back. Propped on his elbows, he cast a quick glance at Eadwig who lay dead nearby. *Never would have gone through with it; I don't know why I even asked you to come with me.*

As Mildrithe's mumblings came to him, he realised he still had unfinished business. The woman had hardly been aware of her violation and her oblivion grieved him. He had wanted her to feel and taste all the savage thrusts he had delivered into her every orifice; hear every curse he had spat into her face. That she had been oblivious to the degradation, truly saddened him.

He gained his feet, picked up the murder rock and held it above his head. Mildrithe squirmed below him, her clothes bunched under her chin. Viciously, he slammed the rock downwards.

The necklace felt heavy in Raedwald' hand as he pulled if over Mildrithe's maimed head. Its acquisition alone had made his trip worthwhile. Just one of its stones would buy him a sea passage. Now he could go to Britannia; now he could kill Britons.

CHAPTER SIX

Three thousand men camped on the huge open space within Guertepir's ringfort. Dominic, Tomas and Ingle had shadowed the army before going their separate ways. Dominic and Ingle continued to Brythonfort, leaving Tomas behind to watch for any signs of troop movement.

Specially built to hold the seven hundred head of cattle stolen from the western peninsula, a huge corral now sprawled before the bastion. It had attracted a number of curious local people, such was its vastness, and it was amongst this crowd that Tomas was able to blend as he spent his days waiting and watching.

A rider, a man known to Tomas as Nairn, approached him as he leaned on the fence of the corral.

'Are all thirty riders in position?' asked Tomas.

'Yes, Arthur instructed it as soon as Dominic gave him the news,' said Nairn. 'One rider on a fast horse every six miles between here and Brythonfort.'

'Good; that means any news can get back to Arthur in a day.'

Nairn looked at him ... saw the tired cast to his eyes. 'Looks like you got the dung end of the stick here.'

'It had to be me,' said Tomas. 'Dominic is known to Guertepir; he would have stood out like a boil on his cock.'

Nairn pulled Tomas away from the corral's fence. A group of drovers had ridden from the castle gate 'Careful, they're moving cows out of the compound.'

'As soon as the ships come to port they take fifty cows away,' said Tomas. 'It's been going on for two days now. Guertepir is getting them over to Hibernia as quick as he can.'

'The sooner they're gone the better for him, no doubt. That way he gets his gold quickly.' Nairn watched the drovers rounding up a group of cattle. His unease grew as he looked towards the gates of the stronghold. 'Well, I'll leave you alone, it's better that way ... won't turn as many heads.' He nodded towards a spinney two hundred paces distant. 'I'll camp there beside the trees. Day or night, I'm ready to go as soon as you have any news.' He bade his goodbye and Tomas turned back to observe the ringfort.

Guertepir sat beside Almaith in the hall. Thirty of his men took up the rest of Guertepir's side of the long table. On the opposite side, Cunedda sat with his own bodyguard of thirty men.

'It won't be as easy as you think,' said Cunedda. 'Arthur is a powerful man and a fierce enemy when crossed.'

Guertepir sighed and cast a quick glance towards Almaith. 'I want Aquae Sulis for my wife; I told you that at Deva. You knew the deal before you came down here; *do not* go cold on me now.'

'I'm not going cold on you, I'm merely stating that things are about to get lively. We have four thousand men between us when the rest of my men arrive, I would rather it be six thousand.'

'Four thousand will do it,' said Guertepir. 'How many men do you think Arthur can muster for Erecura's sake? I hear his stronghold has fewer than two hundred knights.'

'Knights yes, but you are forgetting the levy.'

Guertepir sighed impatiently. 'What levy. What are you talking about, man?'

'The common men who walk the fields. He can call upon them to fight if his kingdom is threatened. Do not forget, I am British, I know how these things work.'

'Common men ... yes ... maybe.' Guertepir waved his fingers at Cunedda in dismissal. 'How many? Maybe a thousand poorly trained and ill-equipped peasants. We will fart them away, believe me.'

'They may be peasants but Arthur will have them adequately trained. He regularly sends his knights to the villages to show them how to defend themselves. It's in his interest; it takes the pressure off him if they have a measure of independence.'

'Even so, we will still heavily outnumber them,' said Guertepir, 'that's why we need to strike fast.'

'Obtaining Aquae Sulis is one thing but defending it is another,' said Cunedda. 'Do not forget there are other Celtic lords who may ride to Arthur's aid.'

'But I hear his Dumnonii brethren further west have no time for him,' said Guertepir. 'Some dispute over a woman, I believe. You Britons are too sensitive over women; you should learn to share them like the Desi. So, you see,' said Guertipir getting back to the point, 'Arthur stands alone. Just his knights and peasants against four thousand of us. Why are we even discussing this?'

'And what if they put their differences aside,' said Cunedda? 'What then? It will not be just Brythonfort we have to deal with but the fortress of Travena. A great lord resides there, and how many men he has at his disposal I can only guess. Then there's the Cornovii, further west still. I hear they're primitive but fierce. What if they decide to join Arthur?'

'And why *would* they join with Arthur,' asked Guertepir, his exasperated look of, *what other obstacles is this man going to throw at my feet!* directed towards his captain, Diarmait.

'Because an army of four thousand men would be camped on their threshold. Maybe they *just might* feel threatened themselves.' Cunedda now sighed and brought the ledges of his hands down to the table in a conciliatory gesture. 'Look, I want to work with you and I appreciate your offer to allow my men to patrol your seaboard and repel the Uí Liatháin from landing and upsetting my people in Deva. In return, I *will* give you my support on this matter—that has always been the deal, but we need to get this right. Believe me, we *need* more men. I have spent the last decade above the wall taking back land stolen from me, only to see it lost the next year because I didn't have the men to hold it.'

'All right, all right.' Guertepir's tone now demanded that Cunedda convince him. 'Let's just say I agree with you on this—that we need two thousand extra men. Tell me this, then. Where the hell are we to get them from?'

Cunedda exchanged a glance with Lieth, his advisor and bodyguard, who sat beside him. Lieth, who knew where this was going, nodded his endorsement to Cunedda. 'The Saxon you found wandering in your forest stealing game,' said Cunedda. 'I speak his tongue of a fashion and spoke to him two days ago in his cell. Do you still hold him?'

Guertepir was about to answer when Almaith squeezed his hand. He gave her a quick glance then turned to Cunedda. 'Oh, him ... yes. I would have fed him to my pigs but my wife asked for him to be spared for a few more days. Why do you ask about him?'

'He was in Camulodunum twenty days ago and told me he could get men to ride with him if we forged an alliance with them.'

Guertepir looked at Cunedda as if he had just guffed the foulest of smells into the room. 'Saxons? You're actually suggesting we encourage a large body of Saxons to get together?' He shook his head in apparent bewilderment, as if the suggestion was just too much to take in. His look to Diarmait, *can you actually believe what this cock brain has just said*, was not lost on Cunedda.

Before Guertepir could vent his incredulity, Cunedda pressed on with his argument. 'Look, I know you've had issues with the Saxons in the past but times are different now. A lot of the settlement has already happened in the southeast and they have shown they are capable of compromise. Yes, some Britons have lost their land, been murdered even, but at least the Saxons have granted them *some* concessions if the word of the travellers I have spoken to is to be believed.'

'Then *don't* believe them, said Guertepir, who looked as if he was still recovering from a kick in the groin. 'Absolutely out of the question. I've killed their fathers and grandfathers as a favour to Rome when keeping the western lands clear of their stinking spawn. They're not to be trusted, I tell you. How can you even consider this? They've killed Britons in droves, man. And *you're* a Briton for pity's sake.'

'This is *war*, Guertepir, and allegiances *have* to be forged in war. Don't forget that we Britons are tribal still. Even more since the Romans left. I see myself as Votadini not British. No doubt, Arthur sees himself as Dumnonii. Loyalties change depending on the circumstances. You yourself once rode with Arthur, now you're planning to usurp him.'

'Right, right,' said Guertepir now playing Devil's advocate. 'Let's just say we have four thousand Saxons turn up here to help us and we take Aquae Sulis, what then? We thank them for their help and they just ride away do they? Because if you believe that, I think I may have misjudged your lucidity when I offered you this deal.'

'Yes they *do* just ride away,' said Cunedda. 'They ride into the southwest. It's the southwest they want. They want Brythonfort and Travena. Above all, they want access to the southern shore. Aquae Sulis would be a small concession to them for all that. They would rule the southwest and we would have replaced rebels with allies. They would do our job for us. They would keep the land clear of insurgents.'

'*Would, would, would!*' shouted Guertepir as he brought both fists down upon the table. 'It's all conjecture, man. The perfect outcome. But life *isn't* perfect is it, Cunedda? Life is a barrel of shit that constantly topples over, and believe me we would be left with one big barrel of shit.' Guertepir sighed as his temper waned, then looked to Diarmait who sat beside him. 'What do you think, Diar? You've been quiet throughout all of this and you've killed more Saxons than any man I know. Please tell me you think this is insane.'

Diarmait glanced briefly at Guertepir then looked at Cunedda. 'Two thousand men you say? We need an extra two thousand men to make this work?'

'From my experience above the wall, yes. Six thousand men in total should do it.'

Diarmait nodded as he absorbed the numbers, then looked to Guertepir. 'That means four thousand of us and two thousand Saxons against Arthur. If you're asking me, my lord, then I think we should go with Cunedda's plan. Such would be our numerical advantage over the Saxons, it would make them think twice about any duplicity after the battle is won. And I must say to have six thousand men against Arthur has got to be better than four thousand.'

Guertepir, who had faith in Diarmait's judgment, sighed and dragged an anxious hand down across his lips and onto his chin. 'I didn't even think we'd even be discussing such madness,' he said. With a contemplative frown,

CHAPTER SEVEN

Days earlier, Raedwald had sat in the smoke-filled alehouse with the youth, Wilburh, whom he had met on the sea passage from Saxony. Together they had travelled to Camulodunum, and at that moment Wilburh was the only friend Raedwald could claim to have on the isle of Britannia.

Both men were excited at the prospect of making their mark on the island; both shared a common goal: to ride with a war band and gain riches. Raedwald told Wilburh all about Egbert, and Wilburh was impressed. Egbert's infamy was well known and his legend exaggerated. To be riding with the son of such a man, albeit a bastard son, was a source of pride for Wilburh. Together they would make a mark, he was sure of that.

As he looked at the veteran warriors and drinking men who seemed so at ease in the alehouse, Raedwald reddened as he remembered the events of the previous evening. A stocky Saxon chieftain—a man cast in the mould of many such chiefs, with his inherent arrogance and brutality—had entered the alehouse looking for men to ride with him into the forest in search of untouched villages.

Raedwald gathered with the other men, most of them seasoned warriors, as Hrodgar—a man who could really whip up a crowd—held court whilst standing atop a wooden table. Thirty men agreed to ride with Hrodgar that night, all lured by his promise of gold and slaves. It was exactly the opening that Raedwald had been waiting for. He anticipated how the man would be impressed when he told him who he was ... the possibility that his father might be despised having never occurred to him.

Hrodgar in particular had suffered rebuke and derision from Egbert when riding with him as a youth. But his hatred was not born from witnessing Egbert's debauchery and excesses on the raids, because Hrodgar himself was quite capable of such conduct—no; it was the *mocking and belittlement* dished out by Egbert that had led to his loathing of the man.

He immediately saw the opportunity of exacting retribution on Egbert's seed. There stood his son—a youth already bearing the haughty traits of his father.

Raedwald bristled with shame as he lived through the scene again. Hrodgar had hushed the room when Raedwald approached him with his offer of enlistment and disclosure of his parentage.

"Look what we've got here," Hrodgar had shouted. *"Another one of Egbert's spunk spurts."*

The crowd had roared at this—Raedwald's glowering response only making things worse. Many of the men approached and pawed at him, as if checking out a mule for the trail. Laughing at his soft arms and wispy beard, they declared to Hrodgar that he might go with them on the raid but only to carry the water and hold down the women. But Raedwald had committed their faces to memory, and one day they would laugh no more. Oh yes, one day they would pay for humiliating him.

For now, he would get his own men, just as his father had. He would be a leader, and show Hrodgar and the others he was his father's son. Even now, Wilburh was out in the town looking for any youths rejected by Hrodgar; youths who would be very happy to follow the son of the legendary Egbert.

A grunting coming from a nearby curtained stall interrupted Raedwald's unhappy musings. One of the older warriors was busy with one of the six whores who made their living at the alehouse. Again, Raedwald bristled when recalling how even the whores had laughed at him when he approached them. One had pointed at his crotch and asked if he actually had a dick down there, such was the scarcity of the bulge in his hose. He had been ready to slap the flopsie, but the innkeeper—a huge man who always made sure his girls were fit for duty—had pushed him back onto his wooden bench and threatened him with expulsion from the inn should he continue his barrage of abuse towards the woman.

The door opened, ending Raedwald's bristling, and allowing an eddy of cold January to whisper around his feet.

Wilburh entered with three young men, all of them spare of frame and hunched against the cold. 'Eldstan, Dudda, and Baldward,' said Wilburh, nodding towards them in way of introduction. 'I found them sleeping rough with some cows on a smallholding in the town.'

Raedwald looked the young men over. Their ages ranged from seventeen to twenty by the cut of them, and all looked as if they had been out in the open for several weeks. Two of them, Dudda and Baldward, looked alike—brothers Raedwald guessed. All had slicks of snot below their noses. *What a sorry bunch of downbeats,* thought Raedwald. *They actually make Wilburh look impressive and that's something.* But

Raedwald knew it was the best he could do for now, and whatever their condition he intended to leave with them and show Hrodgar and the others he was capable of leading men. He knew his reputation would soar if could successfully capture slaves and obtain gold.

Raedwald looked at the heavy looking sack grasped by Wilburh. 'What did you barter for the jewel?' he asked.

Wilburh paused. The man who had been busy with the whore parted the stall curtain and stepped out. Wilburh recognised him as one of the tough-looking men who had mocked Raedwald the night before. The man cast an amused glance over the group as he snatched tight his belt around his middle. '*What* a bunch of losers,' he laughed, before moving away to the bar.

Raedwald glowered at the man's back as he walked away. Annoyed, he nodded towards the sack. 'Let's look, then.' He shot a glance at the new boys. 'And you three—sit and make yourselves less obvious.'

As they slid onto the bench seat beside Raedwald, Wilburh emptied the contents of the sack onto the table. Three knives and two seax's fell with a clatter before Raedwald. All were rusty; all were dulled and battered.

'And that's the best you could do?' asked Raedwald, his face a mask of dismay.

'Yes, and I had to haggle hard to get the third dagger,' said Wilburh. 'I got them from a smith who was about to melt them down.'

A peal of laughter rang from the bar. Raedwald saw the man who had been with the whore cast a look over his shoulder towards them as he leaned on the counter sharing a joke with the innkeeper.

'Get them out of the way and into your belts before he sees them,' said Raedwald, sliding the daggers to the three recruits. He took the better-looking seax, leaving the other for Wilburh.

'Are the ponies still tethered at the end of the town,' asked Raedwald, his voice low now.

'Yes, and poorly guarded,' said Wilburh.

'Then we leave at dusk.'

'No one said anything about stealing ponies,' said Eldstan, at last breaking the silence of the three men. 'We'll be slain if we are caught with stolen ponies.' With eyes wide with fear, Dudda, and Baldward nodded in support of Eldstan's statement.

'That's why we're leaving at dusk you dunderhead,' said Raedwald. 'We will be in the forest and out of sight before the ponies are missed.'

'But they'll know it's us,' said Eldstan. 'How can we ever come back here, they'll string us up as soon as they see us.'

'We won't be *coming* back here,' said Raedwald, glaring at Eldstan as his limited reserves of patience drained from him. 'We take the slaves and gold then head straight to *Norwic*. From there we sale home and lie low for a year before returning for more of the same.'

Eldstan frowned and looked far from convinced as he twirled his newly acquired knife in his hand. For now, though, he had decided it prudent to keep further opinions to himself. Dudda and Baldward also looked at their knives, their expressions mirroring Eldstan's.

The theft of the ponies went smoothly, filling Raedwald with hope for the future of the mission. Seven hours later, after riding through the night along the good road that ran from Camulodunum to Londinium, they came to the forest edge. As the first suggestion of grey dawn smeared the eastern horizon, they took a rough track into the woods.

After two miles, the track petered out and they were left with no option but to push through the tangled undergrowth of the deeper forest. Dudda, Baldward and Eldstan were bare-legged, wearing no shoes. Already full of holes and distressed before they had even set out, their tunics were bramble-snagged and wretched. Grime smeared and skinny, their legs ran with the blood from a hundred scratches.

Raedwald and Wilburh, who wore hose and boots, had fared better, but still cursed in frustration as the vegetation tore at their clothing, and when mid-morning came Raedwald decided it was time to stop.

'Look, there's a small lea ahead!' he shouted. 'Time to give the beasts a rest and have a doze.'

'What if we've been followed,' said Wilburh, giving an anxious glance over his shoulder. 'They'll hang us from the trees if they come upon us now.'

'We have seven hours on them, how are they going to *come upon us now?*' asked Raedwald, rolling his eyes in supplication. 'Besides they'll never find us in this forest.'

'How much further?' asked Eldstan. 'I thought you said we would come upon homesteads soon.'

'Soon means in a few days, not *today*, you dick,' said Raedwald, his exasperation growing again. 'Just get your head down in the bracken, you'll feel better after a bit of a sleep.'

After a short rest, they pushed on through the short afternoon, and when darkness came it found them bedraggled and weary.

An uncomfortable and cold sleep through the long night did nothing to lift their spirits, and at first light they set out with a stiff reluctance deeper into the forest.

Four more days passed as they fought through the unyielding undergrowth, having brief respites whenever they came upon colonies of beech. Here the scrub was always sparse, allowing them easier passage.

It was in one of these clearings that the group sat at the end of the fifth day since leaving Camulodunum. All reclined filthy and careworn before a cooking fire—their provisions meagre, having been thrown together by Wilburh. Now all they had left was half a sack of oats.

As the porridge bubbled away, Dudda, the older of the two brothers, looked down at his feet and sulkily kicked at the forest litter. 'I never thought I'd say this, but I had a better life back at the town. The food was shit there too, but at least we got some variety.'

Raedwald gave him a contemptuous glance as he stirred at the porridge. 'Well you won't be going back to the town for a while 'cause they'll string you up if you do, so be grateful for what you've got. At least you're not starving.'

Dudda lifted his tunic to his chest to display a hollow stomach and ribs that stuck out like latticework. 'If this isn't starving then what is?'

Raedwald waved for Dudda to lower his tunic. 'If you'll just get your dick out of my face and realise that this'—he pointed to the porridge—'is just to get us through the trip. Once we've taken slaves and received payment for them, you'll have a fancy tunic and hose and boots, and as much swine and beef as you can eat.'

Baldward—Dudda's brother—spoke now. 'You make it sound easy. We just ride into a village and help ourselves to the children who will fetch a good price at the slave markets. Their parents will just let us take them, will they? ... I don't think so.' With a sceptical, 'Huhh' he followed his brother's example and stared moodily into the fire.

Raedwald was aware the brothers and Eldstan were probably not killers. Had *never* killed before. When the time came to do it, he hoped they would deliver, but for now he knew he had to tread carefully around the matter. 'First of all,' he began, 'we do not enter any villages. That would be madness; there are only five of us. No ... we find a homestead. There, we will be against fewer people, and we are armed, don't forget that.'

'So we just chase the parents away with our rusty daggers and swords do we?' said Baldward, still sceptical.

'No we overcome them and lock them in a hut,' said Raedwald. 'Then we put a day's travel between us and them.'

'And come back through this stinking forest, no doubt. Where in Woden's name are we anyway. Does anyone actually know whether we are heading north, south, east or west?'

Raedwald, who had not the slightest idea where he was, felt his forbearance leaving him. 'Of course I know where we are, you miserable scarecrow,' he lied. 'We are about to leave the forest and find a homestead.' He slopped a gloop of porridge into a bowl and thrust it at Baldward. 'Now if you've finally emptied your belly of aches, then fill it with this.'

Three days later, they were still in the forest and their food had almost gone. By now, Baldward, Dudda and Eldstan were ready to desert. Only their fear of Raedwald, and the question of where they could actually *desert* too, kept them with Raedwald and Wilburh.

Raedwald, by now, had become desperate and spent much of his time slashing at the undergrowth with his seax and cursing wildly at the trees around him. It was the early afternoon of their eighth day in the forest when he noticed brighter light ahead. His hope grew as the trees thinned around him and soon he rode through scrubland with fewer trees. Here, swathes of ferns grew healthy and strong in the unrestricted light of a huge glade. Beyond the glade the tree line suddenly stopped.

He turned to the others, weary but triumphant. 'Look, we're through it. I told you I'd get you to the other side.'

They heeled their ponies to where the trees stopped. The land before them seemed to be coarse pastureland—the sound of sheep sounding in the distance giving credence to this. The undulating nature of the landscape before them restricted their view, but it was clear they had come to a definite end of the forest and not just some clearing in the trees.

Wilburh, who rode beside Raedwald, suddenly grabbed his shoulder and pointed to a faint track that ran through the pasture. Beyond the track, rising from the horizon, a languid curl of grey smoke spiraled into the thin January air.

Bradan's morning, as ever, had been tough and uncompromising after labouring to grub up two deeply-rooted shrubs from his new field. Come the spring, he hoped the field would be ready to plant with barley.

Three years earlier, many of his fellow villagers had expressed their concerns when Bradan had stated his wish to go it alone and form an independent homestead on the very edge of Arthur's protectorate.

Still living with his peers in the village, he had spent every moment of his spare time travelling to and repairing the hut at the abandoned homestead, as well as clearing the overgrown field that lay fallow nearby. In his second year, he had sewn his first trial crop and waited. The small harvest had been a success, and Braden guessed it would have been enough to feed his small family throughout the winter had he been resident at the homestead. He was then confident that he and his family could survive alone. His trial run over, the following year he moved permanently to the homestead with his wife and girl, along with his three sheep and two pigs.

The day was quiet and mild for January as Seren, Braden's wife, sat before a cooking fire outside the hut where she stirred a pot of Barley and root vegetables.

'The sheep have done a good job of cropping the grass down to short stubble in the new field,' said Braden as he approached Seren. On his shoulders sat Cara, his infant daughter. He lifted her down and sat beside Seren. She handed him a wooden bowl and spoon.

A frown creased Seren's smooth face as she ladled a measure of broth into Braden's bowl. 'You work too hard; you're going to be worn down to a greasy spot before this winter's out.'

Braden lifted his daughter upon his knee. He smiled at her as he guided a spoonful of his broth towards her open mouth. 'I *have* to work hard so that this little lady has a full belly.'

Cara dutifully opened her mouth to accept the broth. Braden took a spoonful himself and looked at his wife as she continued to stir the pot. As far as he was concerned, she was still the pretty girl he had married. A little older and slightly more careworn, *maybe*, but still, she was radiant and precious to him.

He was about to tell her to stop stirring and start eating when the grunt of a pony had him look towards the fields.

Fifty paces away, a group of five ragged youths sat on five miserable ponies. The ponies had started to feed on the rough pasture beneath them and seemed to have no intent to move any further. One by one, the five youths dismounted.

When two of them took short swords from their belts, Braden bundled Cara to his wife. His instruction to her was rapid and urgent. 'Go into the hut and stay there until I've dealt with this.' Seren wavered as she looked anxiously from Braden to the youths. 'Please girl, get inside the hut,' repeated Braden as his gaze flickered to the adze at his feet, thankful now he had retained the tool when returning from the fields. Seren turned towards the hut, but still she hesitated. 'Get inside, now!' hissed Braden as the two youths with swords, who had been involved in a heated conversation with their three companions, began to saunter towards him.

Wilburh had been the first to see the small group feeding beside the hut. Raedwald had soon joined him and inwardly rejoiced when seeing the family. He turned to look back at Baldward, Dudda and Eldstan who had spent the last two miles grumbling and bouncing uncomfortably upon their ponies.

'There, I told you we would find folk if we continued through the forest,' he said. 'And these look like British folk not Saxon. So, you see, we've come into land that hasn't been raided.'

Eldstan seemed less than happy now that things were ready to happen. 'What do you propose to do now, then,' he asked Raedwald.

'Take the child of course; we'll get a fortune for her in Norwic.'

'What about the father?' asked Eldstan. 'He's ready to fight by the look of it.'

'Then we'll have to deal with him.'

'W-what, tie him up and put him in the hut like you said?'

Raedwald shot Wilburh a *now's as good a time as any to tell them* look. 'No, we don't tie him up,' he said. 'Not now he's armed himself with the adze. We need to kill him, it's the only way.'

Eldstan held up his palms in rejection and backed away as if confronted by his most feared nemesis. 'No ... you didn't say anything back in Camulodunum about killing anybody. *"We find a homestead, steal a child and return to Norwic,"* you told us.' He turned to Baldward and Dudda for support, their nods conveying to Raedwald, *Yes, he's right … that's what you said.*

'So you think that raiding parties come out here, then find slaves, then maybe shout harsh words at them to get them to hand over their children … Oh, come on!' Exasperated, Raedwald looked to Wilburh, then cast a quick glance back towards the hut. 'Look—we need to get this done. The woman has gone inside with the girl, and the man needs to be taken care of.'

But now it was obvious to Raedwald, as he looked at Eldstan, Baldward and Dudda (who had grouped together in a mutual huddle of rejection) that they would never kill. He pointed back towards the forest. 'RIGHT!' he exploded. 'Get yourselves back into that forest and die there, because only a gibbet awaits you in Camulodunum!'

The three shrank away from the heat of Raedwald's outburst. Dudda was the one who eventually summoned the courage to respond to him. 'I for one *will* leave for the forest; I no longer want to be any part of this. I'll take my chances in Camulodunum, maybe even go to Norwic.'

Raedwald could tell that all three were of the same mind. He raged at them. 'Away with you and go then!' Yearning to slay them but not having the time, he turned to Wilburh and saw that he too was hesitant. 'And you ... get your sword out ... what's *wrong* with you, man?'

Wilburh darted a nervous look towards the Briton who was standing his ground in front of the hut. Slowly, he took up his sword.

The others had turned away and led their ponies into the forest, unwilling even to witness the oncoming fight.

Raedwald's onrushing lunge at Braden was immediate and clumsy and the homesteader was easily able to avoid the seax strike. In terms of reach, Braden's adze had the advantage over the short swords of Raedwald and Wilburh, but his first hack with it missed Raedwald.

Wilburh, who had hung back, now saw Braden wrong-footed. His slash at him was even more inexpert than Raedwald's but somehow his seax hit the mark, splitting Braden's scalp from ear to crown.

The Briton staggered and brought his hand to his head as his vision began to blur. He removed the hand and saw it smeared in his own blood.

'With me, finish him!' Raedwald screamed his instruction to Wilburh as he sensed Braden's incapacity. This time, Raedwald's heavy, horizontal swipe ripped Braden's bicep to the bone, causing him to drop the adze. Again, Wilburh seized upon the opportunity to lunge at Braden unopposed. Ham-fistedly, he thrust the point of his sword into Braden's stomach.

As soon as Braden fell, Raedwald and Wilburh were upon him as their bloodlust erupted. Braden rolled onto his back using his arms as a fleshy shield as they slashed and stabbed at him. Soon he sprawled dead and torn, his arms shredded.

Panting and splattered in Braden's blood, the Saxons finally stopped stabbing at him — exhaustion rather than an abatement of savagery being the reason for the curtailment of their assault. Raedwald looked to the hut.

Seren emerged with Cara in her arms. She saw what they had done to Braden and began to scream. She took a hesitant step towards him then realised it would take her closer to the killers. Thinking of Seren and possible escape she looked towards the distant tree line, but wavering and aghast, remained unmoving.

Raedwald wiped his sword on the grass at his feet then moved towards Cara. 'Help me here,' he said. 'Grab the sprat while I deal with the woman.'

'No—no! Get away from her!' Seren's scream rang hollow and awful as she stepped back into the hut. She was prepared to scratch and bite like a vixen to protect Cara, but the pommel of Wilburh's seax, delivered with force upon her forehead, ended her fight before it could begin. Wilburh grabbed Cara as Seren dropped to the reed-strewn floor of the hut.

'Take the child outside,' said Raedwald. 'I'll deal with the woman and make sure she doesn't hinder us.'

Wilburh still pumped with battle-fever, his earlier reluctance a distant memory. He read Raedwald's intent. 'Yes, I'll hold the brat but don't kill the woman until I've had my go with her.'

Seren's eyes rolled as Raedwald dragged her to the back of the hut and began to tear at her dress. *Another one not quite with it*, he thought as he pulled his hose down to his knees.

Flint was one hour south of Corinium on his way back to Brythonfort. The town, like many others, had gone into decline after the withdrawal of Rome. However, an industrious local man had utilised the cleared area of the old amphitheater and erected a huge timber building upon the grounds there. Here, his pottery business thrived, supplying much of the local area with their needs. Such was the renown of his products that many Britons now journeyed miles to obtain them.

Flint and eight knights travelled beside a covered wagon packed with wares as it headed back to Brythonfort. Their presence beside the wagon had been of dual purpose: to ensure the wagon was untroubled by robbers, as well as checking out the country beyond the northern limits of Arthur's protectorate.

A curl of smoke coming from beyond a low hillock to the right of the track alerted Flint to a possible habitation—the first he had come across for several miles. He looked to Emrys, a young knight of promise who was on his first patrol for Arthur. 'Think we should take a look, Em?' he asked. 'Get a flavour of what's been happening in these parts?'

'Well, that's what we're here to do,' replied Emrys. 'Just me and you on this one is it?'

'Yes, no need to take the rest of the men.' Flint wheeled his horse around to face the others. 'Stay with the wagon,' he instructed. 'I'm taking Em with me to chew the fat with some locals.'

The wagon creaked to a halt and the men dismounted, glad to have a rest from the saddle.

Flint and Emrys rode at a trot on the rutted track that led to the homestead. Emrys was the first to get sight of the dwelling as he rounded the knoll, his abrupt stop immediately alerting his companion.

Flint looked at a ragged man holding a hysterical child. He flicked a rapid glance to Emrys, *there's something not right here*, as he noticed a look of fear slide down the face of the man.

Now he feared the worst and was tense and ready as he walked his horse forward. 'What's upset the child and what's your name, fellow?' he asked. 'Maybe I can help with the babe.'

The man, whose expression had changed from elation to despair upon seeing the knights, attempted to mumble a reply as he placed the child to the ground.

'SAXON!' shouted Flint upon hearing the Germanic tongue. 'See to him, Emrys, I'll take the trail and follow the pony tracks, they may have taken slaves away.'

Inside the hut, Raedwald's blood turned from fire to ice upon hearing the cry. He rolled off Seren and arranged his disheveled clothing as he realised something was amiss. Events were happening outside. A horse rattled by the hut and Wilburh had given off an alarmed cry. He knew he had to get out, knew it was his only chance. They would be in the hut soon and that would be the end of him. He cast a quick glance at Seren who still moaned in her concussion. She could not be allowed to talk to the Britons when her senses returned.

He groped about in the dim light of the hut feeling for his seax. He found it and slicked the blade across Seren's throat—her moans becoming a gurgle as her blood drained into the rush matting beneath her.

He looked at the door, knowing the Britons for now were preoccupied. But the door was not an option for him ... outside the door death lurked. He turned towards the back wall of the hut and jabbed the point of his sword into the wattle frame. The willow split and he tugged at it until he could see a layer of daubed and cracked mud; a thin barrier between him and the outside. He punched out and the mud collapsed to leave a shoulder-width hole. Raedwald dragged himself through the hole and jumped to his feet.

Ahead, lay a series of low hills. Hearing nothing now from beyond the hut, he ran in a stumbling gait towards the first hill. He crested it, then he half-fell, half-ran, down its slope. Thanking the Gods for his escape, he came to a thin stream and began running along its stony shore, heading for the spinney growing in a curve away from the banking. A steep dell clogged with thick brush, ran along the entire length of the spinney. Exhausted, Raedwald slid into the dell and lay panting beneath the shrubbery.

Emrys was in no doubt what to do as he rode towards Wilburh. Arthur's edict on the matter of Saxons caught within the confines of British habitation was quite clear: his instruction called for immediate execution.

After Flint heeled his horse into a gallop away from the hut and along the track that led to the forest, Emrys carefully steered his own horse around the child who crawled towards the door of the hut. A slight delay allowed the Saxon to make his escape along the same track Flint had taken. Emrys, unconcerned, goaded his horse into a quick trot.

Wilburh nursed a vague hope the Briton bearing down on him might have compassion in his soul. He turned to beg for mercy as Emrys' shadow engulfed him, but a grey blur accompanied by the hiss of cold steel through even colder air, was Wilburh's last sensation as Emrys cleanly decapitated him.

Emrys dismounted to pick up the head, just as Flint returned from up trail. Strung together and tied to the back of his saddle, bounced three more heads—Eldstan's, Baldward's and Dudda's.

'No mercy,' stated Flint, 'for any Saxon found in the protectorate in the vicinity of a homestead.'

'No mercy,' concurred Emrys as he lifted Wilburh's head for Flint to see.

After studying the head for a moment, a look of alarm slid over Flint's features. 'The child,' he said.

'The hut,' replied Emrys, his own look mirroring Flint's.

Both men ran down the track to the hut and were able to get there before Cara could enter. Emrys picked her up as Flint went in. Moments later he emerged, his face set pale and grim. 'Take the child to the wagon,' he said as Cara buried her head into Emrys' shoulder. He dropped his voice so it was barely above a whisper. 'Looks like we've got another orphan for Augustus and Modlen to look after.' His haunted look and shake of the head told Emrys all he needed to know.

Raedwald shivered as nighttime found him still in the ditch. In fear of pursuit, he had crouched hidden for half of the day, but had worried needlessly. Unknown to him, Flint had assumed the hole in the hut wall was due to natural decay rather than forced exit, having seen many such huts whilst on the trail.

Raedwald decided to move under cover of darkness and take his rests during the day until he reached the concealment of the forest again. Then he would make for Norwic and find a ship to take him to Saxony. He still had the necklace and it still hung with many semi-precious stones, one of which would pay for his passage home.

For three days and nights, an increasingly weakening Raedwald stuck to his plan: stumbling throughout the nights, drinking water from the muddy puddles which lay everywhere, and sleeping fitfully by day. He was lost, he knew that now; knew he should have reached the forest days ago.

As the fourth day dawned, he at last saw the trees before him. Unbeknown to him, it was the wrong forest—the western Dobunni forest—yet a desperate Raedwald entered it with hope, convincing himself he had found the eastern woods. Close to collapse, he squelched through puddles of silver rain, occasionally falling to his knees to drink from them as his strength ebbed away. By midday, he feared he would die. His belly was hollow and his energy depleted. Kneeling against a gnarled and ancient ash, he fell immediately to sleep, his contorted, slavering face pressed against the grey bark.

'Whaa—' He awoke with a start when kicked from the tree.

'Why have you entered this forest?'

A man dressed as a hunter and carrying a stout stick had delivered the question in Celtic.

Raedwald sat on the forest floor and blinked away his confusion as he looked upwards to the man. Behind the man stood two others, similarly attired.

'I ... I ... do not understand your language,' uttered Raedwald. 'I am not of these—'

On hearing his tongue, the men became noisy and animated, drowning out the rest of his reply. They looked down on him—their faces betraying anger.

They dragged him upwards. Raedwald guessed his end was near when a tensioned bow was thrust a finger's width from his face.

He winced as he awaited the arrow's delivery, but the first man was to stay the archer's arm.

Again, a lively discourse ranged between the men, and Raedwald sensed they had different ideas about how to deal with him. Eventually, he was dragged away from the tree and his arms bound behind him. One of the men went to his pack and removed a piece of dried salmon from it. He thrust the fish into Raedwald's mouth.

Three days passed as Raedwald was pushed before the men, firstly through the forest then along the stony roads of the cleared land beyond. Midway through the morning of the fourth day the ringfort came into view. Spread beyond it was the grey sea. Raedwald now knew that he was on the wrong side of Britannia.

Four further days were to pass as Raedwald lived on his nerves in his cell in the ringfort. On his first day, they had attempted to clean him somewhat and thrown buckets of cold water over him. Rough sacking had been his towel, and Raedwald had nursed the hope that if they wanted him clean, they wanted him alive. Later that morning the reason for their clemency became apparent when a hag of a woman entered the cell. With her were two guards who insisted he lay down and undressed. Raedwald had complied, knowing he had no choice. The woman had then told the men to leave and had lifted her dress and sat upon him. In spite of himself Raedwald had become hard and the woman had ridden him to orgasm, both hers and his.

Raedwald had flinched when the door had opened again. This time, though, it was a tall and imposing Briton who entered. The man spoke the Saxon tongue to him and asked him about Camulodunum. In particular, he inquired about his connections in the town. Raedwald had been unable to resist boasting of his importance and influence and the man had gone away pensive, yet seemingly satisfied.

Almaith was to visit him five more times during the next two days and nights. Then, on the fifth morning of his imprisonment he was taken from his cell and marched into the hall of the ringfort.

Guertepir now looked at him as if he had just crawled out of the ringfort's cesspit. Two guards grasped Raedwald's bound arms, immobilizing him. Guertepir waved the guards to take a step backwards.

'That's better,' said Guertepir, his nose wrinkled in disgust. 'Perhaps I'll be able to keep my wine down now.' He looked to Cunedda who was standing nearby. 'I'll talk to him through you. How good is your Saxon?'

'Good enough,' said Cunedda. 'We did trade with Saxony when I lived above the wall. I could get by then, I can get by now.'

Guertepir nodded, satisfied, then looked Raedwald directly in the eye. 'Cunedda tells me you have connections in Camulodunum, is that right?'

Raedwald nodded his acquiescence. 'Yes, my father was a fearless and respected leader and this gives me standing and influence in the town.'

'And your father was?'

'Egbert ... Egbert was his name.'

Guertepir pursed his lips and frowned in the manner of a man trying to remember something. 'Nah ... never heard of him,' he said after a moment's contemplation. 'But no matter ... carry on.'

'A warlord named Hrodgar was in the town when I left and he was gathering men for a raid into the lands beyond the ancient forest.'

'How many men?'

'Usually between forty of fifty for a slave raid.'

Guertepir threw up his hand in exasperation as if to say *forty or fifty, what good is that?* He spoke directly to Cunedda. '*Two thousand* would help us, you said. That didn't sound like two thousand to me.'

'Keep with me on this,' said Cunedda, who had been translating. He turned to Raedwald. 'When we spoke the other day you said you would be able to persuade the warlords in Camulodunum to raise the quota we require for this war. Why do you now talk in such low numbers?'

'I talk only of the numbers used on a small raid. Once you lure them with the promise of land in the southwest they'll flock to you in droves.'

'And you're sure of this?'

Raedwald, who had bought himself time and possibly his life with his promise, now played his trump card. 'Yes, but only upon my introduction. By all means, show a presence to demonstrate you're serious, but it would be madness for a British warlord to ride into Camulodunum without Saxon endorsement ... without *my* endorsement. At the very best you would be laughed out of town, at the very worst you would never leave the town.'

'No. It seems more likely that *you* would be laughed out of town. Look at you, covered in grime and of obvious low status.'

'You forget, my lord, that I would have you, and'—he nodded towards the impressive Diarmait who was standing beside Guertepir—'him beside me to boost my status.'

Guertepir, who had become impatient and hungry for news as he listened to the Germanic staccato, grabbed Cunedda's arm. 'Well?' he pressed. 'Stop gabbling in that devil's tongue and tell me what he says.'

Cunedda looked disdainfully at Guertepir's hand upon his sleeve. He tugged his arm away and let his gaze linger a moment longer upon him, before relating his conversation with Raedwald.

When Cunedda had finished, Guertepir sighed, nodded slowly, then sighed again. 'I just hope we are not kicking over a basket of vipers, but I will go with your plan. The extra two thousand men *will* make a difference, but that must be it: two thousand only; if more of the bastards come they'll want everything.'

'I'll leave tomorrow then?'

'Yes, and take a hundred of your men with you. Go well-armed; you must have the capability to protect yourselves; you're riding into hostile country. But do not daub yourselves in that brash, blue dye. Remember, we need to recruit them, not scare them shitless. Diarmait will go with you with a similar number of my men.' He looked at Raedwald. 'Ah, yes. I'll get him cleaned up and provide him with decent livery.' He turned to the door and gave a little smile as Almaith walked in. 'And no doubt my good wife will check him from top to toe to make sure he's fit for purpose before he leaves.'

The next morning, Tomas watched as two hundred men left the ringfort and took the eastern road towards Corinium. It was the first significant movement since he had arrived, and set him in a trot towards the coppice where Nairn had his camp.

As Tomas approached, Nairn knew his time to ride had come. Immediately, he was on his horse.

'Two hundred men going eastwards. Probably an envoy; Hibernians and Votadini. Arthur needs to know, today,' shouted Tomas as Nairn wheeled his horse towards Brythonfort.

CHAPTER EIGHT

The final fast horse arrived at Brythonfort just before dusk. Arthur, who had been hungry for more information since Dominic had arrived days earlier with the news of the Hibernian and Votadini allegiance, had since taken to pacing the ramparts of Brythonfort. His woman, Heledd, was beside him, and shared his look of concern as the rider rushed through the gates of the bastion. The rider ran to Arthur while his horse, panting and slick with sweat, was led to stable.

He addressed the king. 'An envoy has left Guertepir's, my lord; Hibernian and Votadini. Two hundred men. They travel eastwards; their road takes them towards Corinium. Further along the road will take them to Londinium.'

'Londinium,' mused Arthur, frowning. 'Why would they go there, the place is falling to ruin.' He grasped the rider by his shoulders, his eyes intense with urgency. 'Do me one last service before you rest, and find Gherwan and ask him to call an assembly to the hall immediately.'

Arthur turned to Heledd, his hand instinctively dropping onto his sword, *Skullcleft*, as the rider left them. 'This doesn't bode well,' he said. 'They'll pass close to Aquae Sulis but it should be safe for now—two hundred riders will not trouble a fortified town. But why Londinium?'

Heledd was thoughtful a moment. 'Maybe the road to Londinium will take them past the town; towards another place ... Camulodunum perhaps.'

Arthur's face took on a grave cast. 'That's what I feared, also,' he said. 'Come, we must get to the hall.'

Two hours later, the hall was full. As Arthur walked in with Heledd, the drone of conversation died to a hush. Arthur allowed Heledd to sit down, but he remained standing before his place at the table. He took in the three, huge round tables in the hall; all populated by formidable men. His captains, Flint, Gherwan and Erec, sat on his own table along with other high ranking knights. Similarly, men of mutual trade or interest had grouped together on their own tables. The artisan Robert sat with his team of craftsmen, including Simon from the eastern forest.

Dominic, too, had his long-standing friends around him: Will the tracker; Augustus (who, like Erec, had returned from Aquae Sulis); Murdoc (who sat beside his woman, Martha);

and Withred, who sat brooding and dark—intimidating even to Arthur. Also sat with them was the young monk, Ingle.

Arthur looked over the impressive gathering, then began. 'Oh, that I had six thousand men of your quality to call to arms on this day. Many of you know why we are here, so I will not go over it again. What I need from you now is your speedy action.' He focused upon Dominic. 'Dom, you have seen the two armies when they passed you by. What was your count?'

The heat in the hall had risen as the fire in the iron brazier had begun to dance. Dominic, sweating now, took off his wolf hat and placed it on the table before him. He swiped a hand over his beaded face. 'Two thousand or so went past me that day, seven hundred of them Votadini. I was at Guertepir's ringfort last year as you know, and I reckon he has a standing army of two thousand men in his own right.'

'And what of the Votadini? You say seven hundred of them went past. How many more—have you any idea?'

Dominic gestured towards Ingle. 'My friend here was in Deva when the Votadini arrived, and like all monks he can count. He tells me he stood on the walls and tallied their numbers.'

Arthur turned his stern gaze towards Ingle. 'How many, young monk?' he asked.

As all the room looked at him (a room full of people the likes of which he had never seen before), Ingle's mouth suddenly felt like it was full of sand. He licked dry lips and began. 'I counted fifteen hundred, my lord. The morning they arrived ... fifteen hundred was their number ... or there abouts. Later ... two days later, I think ... one thousand of them left the town. When I escaped from the place I travelled to Segontium to get a boat back to Hibernia, but the Votadini had left a force of men there to guard the port, so I continued southwards.'

'How many men at the port?' asked Arthur.

'I would guess three hundred.'

Arthur nodded as the numbers began to make sense to him. 'Thus, leaving seven hundred to march south with Guertepir.' He looked again to Dominic. 'So that's fifteen hundred Votadini that we know about. How many more could they muster do you think?'

Dominic looked at the tabletop before him and tapped at it as he did a count in his head. 'Not that many more,' he said eventually. 'He needs to guard Deva if he has relocated to the town as I suspect. So he needs to keep a goodly sized force based there permanently. Also, as we've just heard, he's secured the port of Segontium, and will also need to garrison men there to hold it.' He paused again, fingers to lips and brow wrinkled, as he did a final count. 'Two thousand men would be my guess ... a similar force to Guertepir's.'

'So that's four thousand men mobilized,' said Arthur. 'Two hundred of them now marching to Londinium ... and who knows? ... possibly Camulodunum after that.'

A murmur of anxious conversation infused the hall as the significance of Arthur's remark was absorbed. Gherwan, who sat beside Arthur, attempted to speak above the noise. Arthur held up his hand until the drone abated.

He nodded for Gherwan to have his say. 'Camulodunum,' began Gherwan, 'is a Saxon stronghold as we all know. You say that two hundred men now march along Akeman street?'

'There or there abouts,' said Arthur.

'Too small a party to raid a town, we've established that, so why go to Camulodunum.' After a moment's contemplation, Gherwan looked at Arthur, his expression one of a dawning awareness.

Arthur gave Gherwan a nod of confirmation. 'Yes,' he said. 'My thoughts too. They go to

Camulodunum to discuss a partnership with the Saxons.'

The conversation in the hall now broke out with alacrity. Arthur allowed the tension its outlet whilst talking with Gherwan. After some moments, he banged on the table with his empty flagon, bringing the room to silence.

He looked to Dominic. 'I need you to prepare to leave in the morning. Take Will with you and follow the gathering to Londinium. If they go beyond the town and head northeast then they can only be going to Camulodunum and we know what that means. I need one of you to get back here with the news if they do head for Camulodunum. The other can follow them into the town, then follow them wherever they go after that. As soon as their intention becomes obvious, return to Brythonfort. Fast, fresh horses will be waiting on the roads between here and Camulodunum. We need to know where they intend to strike first.'

'What will you do if they continue towards Camulodunum?' asked Dominic.

'More like what I will to do *now*,' said Arthur. 'We have four thousand men to contend with as it stands. What their numbers will be if they look for a deal with the Saxons I can only guess. Six ... seven thousand, maybe.

What their intent is, we do not know, but we must be ready. First we must raise the levy.'

'How many men will answer it and come to Brythonfort?'

'A thousand if we're lucky. 'It's winter and that's in our favour; the men are not needed in the fields so they'll be available.'

'That gives us two hundred knights and a thousand men for a shieldwall—that's still far too few.'

'We need to get to Travena on the rocky shore southwest,' said Gherwan. 'If we are threatened then so is Ffodor and his trading stronghold.'

'How many men can he provide?' asked Dominic.

Gherwan exchanged a telling look with Arthur. The exchange told Dominic that getting men from Ffodor would not be straightforward. 'Four hundred cavalry, some of them charioteers,' said Gherwan after a pause. 'In addition he could levy maybe sixteen hundred men for the shields.

Arthur nodded resignedly, his expression neutral. 'We can but try,' he said. He looked to Gherwan. 'You must leave tomorrow and travel to Travena; Ffodor has respect for you and may see sense on this.'

Withred spoke now, breaking his silence. 'That gives us barely three thousand men, although you seem unsure if this Ffodor will come to the cause.' He let his words hang awhile, hoping to promote an explanation from Arthur.

Arthur gave a quick glance towards Flint, who shifted uncomfortably. 'Let's just say there are complications with Ffodor, but hopefully nothing which cannot be resolved under the circumstances.'

Withred sensed that Arthur was holding something back, but now was not the time to press him. 'Even if these *complications* as you call them *are* resolved,' continued Withred, 'then we will still have just three thousand men against six thousand or possibly more. Are there no more tribes to the north who will help you?'

'There are Silures, Dubunni, Atribates,' said Arthur, 'but all have trade connections with Guertepir who controls the port.'

'So Ffodor is your only option then?'

'No, there are the Cornovii further west still, but they are a mysterious folk who keep themselves to themselves; they cannot be counted upon.'

Withred looked to Augustus who sat beside him. Augustus nod to him—*put it forward Withred; now's the time*—was all the endorsement he needed.

'I can help ... I think,' said Withred. 'I may be able to get more men to fight for our cause.'

'More men ... from where?' queried Arthur.

'From my homeland ... from Angeln. There are many who wish to leave the bog and forest there; many still who would welcome new land.'

An extraordinary expression, half scepticism, half surprise, came to Arthur's face upon hearing Withred's proposal. 'You're suggesting we invite raiders to Britannia? Men who would take British villages by force and enslave its people?'

'Except that the people I bring over would be men who until now have resisted the lure of the campaign. We could offer them the prize they desire the most: we could offer them land.'

'But I have no land to offer.' said Arthur perplexed. 'Apart from the most unforgiving wilderness, all the land around here is settled and under the plough. What empty land there is—the lands of the Levels—is unpeopled and for a reason: it's flooded for most of the year.'

'You are forgetting about the territory above the wall,' said Withred. 'Dominic tells me, the Votadini who march with Guertepir come from above the wall.' He cast a quick glance towards Ingle. 'And Ingle reckons they intended to settle in Deva and forsake their northern lands.'

'And so they'll leave fields and pastures ready to settle above the wall,' said Arthur, as Withred's proposal started to make sense to him. 'But why would they want such land if the Votadini are so eager to leave it?'

'Because all land is coveted on this isle,' said Withred. 'Especially empty land that can be colonised quickly.'

'So you would go to Angeln—you, a man who is seen as a traitor to his own people—and expect them to come over to the British cause?'

'Yes, because they desire land above everything else. With respect, my lord, you do not understand what motivates the men of Angeln. They live in a land of floods and famine which even the Romans left alone.'

Arthur looked to Gherwan. 'Help me out here. What do you think of this?'

'That we are not in a position to refuse *any* help,' said Gherwan simply. 'If Guertepir's force was to come at us now we would be finished, pure and simple.'

Arthur sighed, resigned now, and turned back to Withred. 'It seems that we have no choice but to give this a go. How long will it take for you to put this together?'

'Providing I can get men to come over, then I could be there and back in thirty days.'

Arthur seemed surprised. 'So soon?'

'Yes, twelve days or so to get from Brythonfort to Angeln, six days or so to recruit a force of men, then twelve days to get back here.'

'And who would you take with you?'

Withred looked towards Augustus. 'I can think of no one better than this man to accompany me, if he would consent to the journey.'

'Why not,' said Augustus. 'I dwelled for thirty-five years never venturing from my village and in the last two years I have crossed the breadth of this land twice. I might as well do it a third time, *and* sail the sea as well.' He took in Withred's swarthy visage; his shaven head; his chest-length beard; his glittering eyes. 'And like I once said: my friend here would make Grendel shit its pants, so I am in safe hands.'

'You don't look like a man who *needs* a safe pair of hands,' smiled Arthur as he appraised

Augustus' gigantic frame. 'The sight of the pair of you would make a *legion* of Grendels shit their pants.'

'Then we'll leave at first light tomorrow,' said Withred, his voice cutting through the ripple of laughter. 'We have no time to waste on this.'

'That's it then ... All will have to leave tomorrow,' said Arthur. 'Dominic and Will to follow Guertepir's group; Gherwan to Travena, and Gus and Withred to Angeln.'

Now he turned his attention to Robert, Simon and the rest of the artisans who sat together nearby. 'There's much to do,' he began. 'If war indeed comes to us then we must meet it with brains as well as force. Sixty miles from here, near Calleva, there is a field where the Romans dumped their broken artillery— ballistae and the like— before they left our isle. The last time I was there, some eight years back, the field had grown through most of the weaponry and some of the wood had been taken from the field—probably to frame a hut or to use as firewood. Still, there may be enough machinery left to get an idea as to its construction. Robert—and Simon too if you're up to it—I want you to travel to Calleva and find the field and glean what you can from whatever remains.'

Emrys, Flint's companion from the trip to Corinium, spoke now. 'If I may, high lord ... I know of the field of which you speak. I come from a village near Calleva. As boys we played upon the weapons and fought many a battle there in our childlike way.'

'Then you shall go with them, Emrys. You and a company of six knights can take the artisans straight to the site as well as protect them.'

'Is our renovation of Aquae Sulis to be suspended, then?'

'Not completely ... a small team can continue for now. The town walls are finished and that's something. I'll send thirty knights to show a presence and boost the morale of those remaining at the town—they're bound to have heard the recent news.'

Robert looked dismayed. 'You think they may attack the town, then? Attack Aquae Sulis?'

'Who knows. One thing's for sure, though: Guertepir loves to feast ... loves to entertain; and he's aware of Aquae Sulis; aware of its restored opulence. If he intends to make war, then Aquae Sulis would be a significant capture for him. It would also be an easier target than Brythonfort. He would serve to draw us to him by taking the town.' Arthur again turned to Dominic and Will. 'It looks like you're going to be saddle-sore before this plays out, fellows. As soon as one of you gets back here with the news that I fear you'll carry, we need to be planning for the next occurrence. If I can *indeed* raise an army then I need to know where to send it.'

He looked at Flint who sat beside Emrys. 'As for you Flint, I want you to start the levy at first light tomorrow. I want as many men as possible here at the fort within six days so that Erec can start to show them the finer points of brute force.'

CHAPTER NINE

Godwine and Hild were up to their knees in the cold waters of the Tamesa as they gathered their net towards them. On the shoreline lay Udela, their daughter, lost in her child's game as she chattered away to the driftwood shards that had become her dolls.

The previous year, the Saxon family had been gaunt and hollow-cheeked from impending starvation, but all that had changed when Augustus had arrived with the fishing net. Before his arrival, they had lived by scavenging the shoreline for anything they could use or barter. Pickings had become lean and the family had consequently suffered. Now, though, they could catch fish. Such was the richness of the Tamesa that they often had surplus to barter. In exchange, they procured firewood and utensils—items to make life more comfortable in their rough shack beside the city walls of Londinium. Now Hild was with child again and the future looked brighter for Godwine and his family.

'I'll take the weight of it now,' said Godwine as the end of the net, ensnaring its one fish, came into view. 'Just a small salmon this time, but that will do for today. Go and sit with Udela while I tidy the net away.'

Hild slid her hand down Godwine's arm as she left, her look leaving him in no doubt of her love. Smiling, he removed the parr, then threw it onto the rocky shoreline where it flopped and twisted its way back down to the water. Squealing, Udela jumped to her bare feet and ran to stop the parr's liberation from the cooking fire.

Behind the family stood the stark backdrop of Londinium. Its one impressive feature was its wall. Tall and thick, the structure was still complete, having been the last major construction project accomplished by the Romans. The rest of the town, though, was in the process of slow decay. Most of the population, British and Roman, were by now long gone, leaving just a few Saxon families to populate the town. The Roman layout of streets, now defined by low-lying, broken walls that were lichen-grey and stained with red, was still plain for any traveller to see, but years of looting and reclamation had removed the roofs and significant sections of wall from the structures. The result was a town that looked victim to an earthquake. Now, goats bleated, and hardy little pigs grubbed amongst the rubble, feeding on scraps and plant growth that had colonized the streets. All the animals wore the mark of their owners; all were a vital source of milk and meat.

The hollow sound of hooves upon the river's one timber pile bridge had Godwine look up from the net he was unraveling. On the south bank, a host of men had started to traverse the bridge. Godwine immediately called Udela and Hild towards him as the procession of armed warriors filed across the bridge amidst a clatter of hooves and snorting horses. An impressive-looking man with braided hair—his shield emblazoned with the symbol of the juniper bush; his ears and lips studded with Celtic gold— reached the northern shore of the Tamesa and cast a brief look towards him. To Godwine's relief, the man—who by his bearing and stature *had* to be the leader of the first group of men—turned from him and shouted at two of his charges who had broken from the line and seemed intent on making mischief towards Godwine and his family. The men checked their progress and rejoined the main group.

To Godwine's utter amazement the man had spoken the British tongue, not in itself unusual: but what was rare—*unknown in fact*—was to see

Britons armed and in numbers in Saxon territory.

As the Britons passed over the bridge, Godwine's eyes widened further when seeing another group of riders (this time decorated with the sign of the white bull) follow in their wake. Again, Godwine could hear their shouts as they continued to file over the bridge and through the city; and again their shouts were British—albeit of a different dialect.

He held Udela, her blue eyes awash with January grey as, open-mouthed, she watched the biggest procession she had ever seen. Godwine turned to Hild who was standing beside him, her arm encircling his waist. 'Come,' he said, 'the world seems to be moving again; let us retire to our hut and cook the fish.'

Dominic and Will had flanked Cunedda's envoy and now watched as the Votadini chief led the company out of Londinium and headed for the Camulodunum road. Earlier, Augustus and Withred—who had ridden with Dominic and Will as far as Londinium—had left them and continued up the Camulodunum road; their destination Norwic and the sea.

'Their troop didn't even rest up in the town,' said Dominic. 'Their task must be pressing to continue without even looking at the place. But here they come, get down…'

Below them, Cunedda led his men along the broken Roman road, northeast towards Camulodunum. With Cunedda was Guertepir's man, Diarmait. Both radiated an aura of power and leadership. 'I know that man,' whispered Dominic; 'the one at the front; the captain with the white bull sign on his shield.'

'Humourless looking shit,' commented Will.

'He's Guertepir's man, Diarmait. I met him last year when in Dyfed on the western peninsula. 'Holds a lot of clout with Guertepir's army; the men would follow him through a forest fire if he asked them to.'

'And the man who rides with him?'

Dominic's face was a mask of disdain. 'He's of the Votadini tribe; so he's British for Jupiter's sake. He must be Cunedda.'

'He's not the first man to be a traitor to his own people,' said Will thinking about Irvine, the British scout who had perished alongside his Saxon master, Ranulf, the previous year, 'and he won't be the last.'

It did not take long for the two hundred riders to file past. When the last of the men had gone from sight, Dominic sat up. He looked down to Will who had rolled onto his elbow and lounged upon the turf banking. 'This is where we part company Will, it's what Arthur wants.'

Will nodded. 'I'll follow them to Camulodunum; you go back to Arthur, that's what we agreed.'

They stood and took their horses. 'It's hard riding for me now,' Dominic said. 'Arthur has had fast horses and grooms follow us here. They string the route every six miles from here back to Brythonfort—twenty horses or so. They should get me back in a day.' He regarded Will with mild concern. 'You can only go at their pace from now on and make sure you're not seen.' Will climbed onto his horse. Roman fashion, he gripped forearms with Dominic as they prepared to part, Dominic's expression betraying his unease. 'Be careful Will, that's all I'm saying. If you enter Camulodunum be extra careful.'

Will laughed it off, although feeling anything other than comfortable with his role. 'I'll be alright, Dom. Remember the scrapes we survived when scouting for Rome; this is but a stroll in the woods in comparison—a mere spying mission.'

'Spying can be fraught with danger,' warned Dominic as he nodded up the track towards

Camulodunum. 'And don't forget, that place is a viper's nest.'

Two days travel along the northeastern Roman road saw Cunedda and Diarmait reach Camulodunum. Their journey had been uneventful; their passage promoting looks of astonishment from the few travellers who were on the road. Britannia was in the grip of grey January, and British war bands were a rare sight.

Raedwald, who to Cunedda's eye looked increasingly edgy the nearer he got to Camulodunum, now rode at the front beside Diarmait. He glanced at Cunedda, then rushed his gaze back towards Camulodunum as the enormous oak gates of the town came into view. That they were open and unguarded told its own tale: quite simply, the Saxons did not fear invasion or attack, such was their dominance of south-eastern Britannia.

Raedwald spoke to Cunedda, his tone verging on the jittery. 'Only the two of us speak Saxon so you must help me out once we enter the town.'

Cunedda squinted at Raedwald, his expression curious. 'It's me who should be on edge, not you,' he said. Not waiting for a reply,

Cunedda nodded towards the gates. 'Looks like I'm about to practice my Saxon whether I like it or not.'

A party of fifty emerged from Camulodunum as Guertepir's envoy approached the gates. Raedwald inwardly recoiled as he recognised Hrodgar—the man who had ridiculed him weeks earlier

By now, Diarmait had joined Raedwald and Cunedda at the front of the British group. 'Fewer of them than I thought,' he said. 'Obviously fragmented and unorganized just as Raedwald would have it.'

'Their leader rides towards us,' said Cunedda. 'At least we get to talk before we fight.'

Hrodgar was arrogance itself as he brought his horse to a stop before Cunedda and Raedwald who now fronted him. Flanking Hrodgar were two tough-looking men, one of whom Raedwald recognised from the inn.

'A little birdie tells me you're British,' said Hrodgar, as he insolently appraised Cunedda. He looked scornfully at Raedwald, then addressed Cunedda again. 'So what are you doing riding with this little spunk spurt?' The two men beside Hrodgar tittered brutally. 'And a horse thief to boot,' continued Hrodgar.

'Could it be you've ridden all this way to deliver him back here so that we can pull him apart between two oxen? ... A death befitting a horse thief, I think.'

'No it's for a greater purpose we travel here,' said Cunedda. 'Not to deliver a horse thief to you'—he shot Raedwald a *you kept that quiet* look—'but to offer you the kingship of south-west Britannia.'

Now the Saxons positively roared their hilarity at Cunedda. Hrodgar was genuinely unable to talk such was his mirth, as his gaze alternated between his riding companions and Cunedda, who sat stock still and serious before him. 'Oh ... oh my ... oh, Woden's balls ... I don't know which is the funniest ... your sorry British accent, or ... or what you've just said,' he snorted.

'We have four thousand men ready and waiting to go to war in the west,' said Cunedda. 'We will ride against Arthur with or without you. We ask that you provide two thousand men only. Does that still sound funny to you? Six thousand men to ride against Arthur? Six thousand men to end his dominance in the west, once and for all.'

Cunedda's words did not completely mute the Saxon's laughter. Rather, they merely served to slow it to a halt. Hrodgar wiped his eyes and nose with the sleeve of his tunic. Slightly breathless, he addressed Cunedda, the residual smile from his hysterics still lingering upon his face. Interested, in spite of himself, he asked: 'Four thousand men you say. Where in Woden's name have you got four thousand men from in the west? More importantly, where have you got four thousand men from who are prepared to turn against Arthur?'

'That can wait for now,' said Cunedda, his tone leaving Hrodgar in no doubt that this had gone far enough. 'One thing I do know is that Saxon courtesy is piss poor. We have ridden far to offer your warriors an opportunity which will not be repeated ever again. Now do you invite us into your town and hear what we have to say, or do I turn round now with my men and return to Aquae Sulis and take the town without you?'

Cunedda felt satisfaction as the Saxon group fell silent. He knew Aquae Sulis was well known; knew it held a legendary status amongst the Saxon community; was also aware that rumours of the city's beauty and magical waters had fostered its own mythology.

Hrodgar nodded towards the city gates and addressed Cunedda. 'You'—he pointed to

Raedwald—'and him, and ten others—no more. We will hear you out. Maybe I'll get another chance to piss my pants. As for the rest of your men—they camp outside the town until we've decided what to do.'

CHAPTER TEN

Three days after bypassing Camulodunum, Withred and Augustus viewed the unmistakable sea-blue sky of the eastern horizon. Though still twelve miles from Norwic, Withred noticed a definite mood change in Augustus. He stopped his pony. 'Are we near the place it happened?' he asked.

Augustus' expression was bleak as he gestured ahead towards a low hill. 'Yes we'll see it as soon as we round yonder knoll.'

Withred was aware of Augustus' epic struggle at the abandoned arena the previous year. He was also conscious that it was something he rarely talked about; and that told its own tale, because Augustus would talk about anything: the weather; the state of the road; the wind in his guts; the cut of Withred's beard. Just about anything. He would also frequently boom out his baritone laugh after baiting Withred. That he had done none of these things for the last eight miles of their journey, told Withred that the man was troubled; more precisely that he was concerned over what had happened in the arena.

As they rounded the hill, the outer broken walls of the old amphitheater came into view. A shadow-filled archway led into the bowels of the stadium. Painted in red beside the tunnel was the word: *Færgryre*. Augustus shivered. 'I walked from there, bloody and dying,' he said. 'How I got onto my pony and sought out Griff's villa after the struggle I went through in there—that I'll never know.' He peered at the inscription, but not being a man of letters turned to Withred. 'What does it say?' he asked

'Just some nonsense written by a Saxon wizard,' replied Withred, who knew it would be folly to tell Augustus that the symbol read, *'awful horror,'*—a warning to any passersby to keep out; advice he knew must have been heeded by the superstitious Saxon folk. Hardheaded and anything but superstitious himself, Withred had an idea. 'Like to take a look inside again, Gus?' he asked.

Augustus was taken by surprise. 'What? Go back inside the arena? Why, man?'

To get it out of your system. To stop it plaguing you, maybe. 'I would like to see the place,' said Withred instead. 'It won't take long to have a look. Roman antiquity interests me ... it always has.' He affected concern for Augustus. 'Oh ... I'm sorry, Gus. I know the memory of what happened in there mustn't be easy to bear, so I'll go alone if you like.' Before Augustus could respond, Withred set his pony into a trot down the hill. He called back over his shoulder. 'Won't be long. I'll take a peep and come straight out.'

Augustus frowned, anxious, as his companion rode away. Indeed, Withred had hit the nail on the head. It was *not* easy for him. In fact, the place had infested his dreams since the day he had walked from it. The sight of it made his skin crawl. Yet the thought of Withred disappearing into the arena tunnel and not coming out was far worse. 'Hold on!' he shouted. 'Steady your scrawny Angle arse a moment; I'm coming with you.' Withred's smile was borderline smug as he continued to ride towards the ruin.

The arched roof brushed against Augustus' bald head as he followed Withred down twenty paces of darkness. When they reached the arena floor, Withred stopped to take in the depleted grandeur of the inner combat area. Behind him, a full head taller, Augustus felt a cold trickle of sweat worm down his back as he took in a scene that frequently inhabited his sleeping hours. 'Christian Jesus hanging on his cross,' he muttered. 'The covered wagon's still here.'

Withred gave him a questioning look, before stepping into the open. Thirty paces away, the wagon stood, weather beaten and dilapidated. 'Ah ... the same wagon you climbed on,' said Withred, realising now. He had heard the story from Dominic who was the only living man to have heard the tale from Augustus himself.

'Yes, still here, just as I left it ... more or less.' Augustus strolled towards the wain as wind-blown dead leaves skittered at his feet. As well as leaves, bones—human bones picked clean—cluttered the arena floor.

Withred saw the change in Augustus. He viewed his ashen face with concern. 'Maybe we should leave,' he said. 'I've seen all I want to.'

'No. Now I'm here I need to look around ... replace my thoughts with real images and hope they go away.'

'What? The images or the thoughts?'

'Both—perhaps then I'll get a good nights...' His voice trailed away as he neared the wagon. 'Shit ... oh Jesus,' he whispered. 'The wagon door's still secured by the rope I tied it with.' He walked to the door, fingered the knot, then began to work it loose. 'I left one of Griff's dogs in here, it will just be a heap of bones...' He fell silent as he pulled open the door. A clutter of stripped human bones and a skull met his stare. Of the dog, nothing remained.

Withred joined him at the door and took in the scene. 'Nerthus,' he murmured. 'The dog really had it in for that fellow.' He raised his head. 'And it looks like it made its escape after feeding on him.'

Augustus perused the hole he had smashed in the roof the previous year. Again, he shivered as he revisited his ordeal. He turned away from the wagon to look at the broken terracing encircling the arena. Absently, he said: 'I once heard the Romans used this place for theatre and plays; but it took a Briton'—he looked at Withred, disgust now lacing his tone—'can you believe ... it took a *Briton* to blood this floor.' Hollow eyed, he went on. 'Fed them to his dogs, he did. Let them rip the life out—'

Withred gripped his sleeve, silencing him. 'Over there, Gus, in the shadow of the wall.'

At first, he struggled to see anything. Withred, aware, pointed to a section of low wall overhung by a tangle of leafless clematis. As they watched, a black mastiff emerged from the shrub, gave a slavering yawn, then dropped to its chest as it stretched the stiffness out of its back.

'Shit, it's Griff's dog,' said Augustus. 'The one I threw into the wagon.'

Withred peered at the animal, ready to move should it come at them. He removed his dagger. Augustus did the same. Withred kicked at some small rib bones at his feet. 'It must feed on rabbits and the like that wander in through the tunnel.'

'And now *we've* wandered in through the bastard tunnel,' said Augustus. He started to back away. 'Look, it's seen us, get ready to run or fight.'

'No sudden movement, Gus,' said Withred, his voice surprisingly steady. 'I hunted with dogs similar to this when I was a boy in Angeln; I think I know what to do here.' He removed his pack from his shoulder and took out a piece of dried fish.

'What ... are you mad?' Augustus looked at Withred (who had gone down on one knee, holding the fish out at arm's length, trying to entice the dog) as if he had indeed gone out of his mind. 'Stand up man! I killed its sister for pity's sake. Leave it be. We need to leave.'

But it was too late; the dog had sauntered towards them. However, this was no mad, snarling rush—if anything the dog looked nervy as it approached. 'Come ... come boy.' Withred, ignoring Augustus, enticed it nearer. When within reach, he threw it the morsel. The dog caught it with a hollow snap of its jaws and gulped it. To Augustus' utter surprise, the mastiff then sat down, brought up its hind leg, and proceeded to scratch at its ear.

'See ... it just needs a bit of love and attention,' said Withred, distractedly, as he rummaged in his bag for another scrap.

Augustus crouched beside Withred, all the better to get his attention. He touched his shoulder and Withred looked at him. Augustus gave him a faint, incredulous smile. 'Withred, I've seen what this thing is trained to do. It's trained to *eat ... people ... alive.*' He emphasised the last three words with an awed whisper as if talking to a dullard, then continued. 'Now stop this tomfoolery and let's get on with our journey.'

In response, Withred nodded towards the animal. By now it had dropped to its belly; its head resting upon its paws; its amber eyes inquisitive and trusting—the very epitome of the faithful dog yearning attention from its master. He threw it another morsel, and again the mastiff caught it mid-flight—the maneuver requiring only a slight movement of its head. Withred looked at Augustus and saw he had relaxed a little. *Maybe if you see the animal as a dog and not the demon that plagues you, then you might sleep better tonight*. He stood up and offered his arm to Augustus, who still sat on his haunches. 'Come then, Gus, as you wish, we'll get on with our journey.' When eye-to-eye with Augustus, he said: 'It's just a dog, man; its master turned it into a demon, but now he's gone.'

Augustus, far from won over, replied: 'Yes, I know, I cut off his master's head ... remember.' He pointed at the mastiff which continued to look at them with trusting eyes. 'And that vicious fiend probably ate him.'

'Come, then, we'll leave,' said Withred, hoping their visit to the amphitheater had somehow helped Augustus.

Outside, they mounted their horses and continued down the track towards Norwic. Augustus was at first contemplative and lugubrious as he rode beside Withred, but his silence was short lived. 'Now look what you've done,' he said, as he tilted his head back to the track behind them.

Loping along twenty paces to their rear, the dog had decided its fortunes would be better served, *its belly better filled*, by latching on to the two travellers.

Withred could only smile. 'At least it doesn't want to eat us, Gus. Leave it be, it wishes us no harm. The exercise will do it good and we'll soon leave it behind.'

Augustus gave a sceptical grunt and heeled his pony into a fast trot. Withred reciprocated, and soon Griff's villa came into view. From a distance, it looked no different from the place Augustus had ridden from a year earlier.

'Two women—Griff's servants—patched me up after I returned here after my struggle,' said Augustus. 'They told me they would survive without Griff, but I've often wondered what became of them.'

'Maybe they still dwell here,' said Withred. 'The place *certainly* looks habitable. We may as well take a look while we're passing.'

'Why not,' said Augustus as he tore down the track. 'It seems you intend to drag me to every place of my nightmares.'

As he neared the villa, Augustus realised its pristine condition had suffered noticeably since his last visit. The gates, always kept shut by Griff, now hung agape. One of them, having come off its lower hinge, had dropped to the floor and jammed into the mud, becoming immovable. Vegetation, stripped of its summer foliage, grew from cracks in the rendered walls—something the fastidious Griff would never have tolerated. With instincts prickling, the men halted before the gateway.

'Better if we enter quietly,' cautioned Withred as he dismounted, '... leave the horses outside.'

Their feet had just touched the ground when the dog arrived. '*Quiet* might not be possible with this around our ankles,' grumbled Augustus. 'Stay here!' He pointed his command at the mastiff. The dog sat, its ears pricked, its body attentive, as it awaited further instruction.

'Looks like it's got a new master,' said Withred as he took in the scene. 'Come ... let's see if the women still live here, but let's have our wits about us.'

His call for a cautious approach proved wise. The villa consisted of a perfect square of buildings which surrounded an inner courtyard. Augustus and Withred lingered at the gates, looking into the inner space with its backdrop of buildings. Across a dusty, leaf-strewn square, stood six Saxon ponies.

A woman's scream came from a room Augustus guessed to be Griff's one-time opulent apartment. Withred made to move forward.

Augustus immediately read his intent. 'No! We don't have the time and those ponies tell me we're outnumbered.'

Withred paused and peered into the courtyard. He grudgingly shrugged his agreement. 'I suppose not. We're no use to Arthur killed or wounded.'

'Quietly then; on your mount and let's get away from here.' Augustus moved from the gate and led his horse from the villa. He noticed the mastiff still sitting to command awaiting his instruction. 'And you ... you piss off!' He passed it by and when ten paces from the villa, pulled himself onto his pony. Withred was beside him instantly. At a slow trot, *and with the dog following*, they headed towards the Norwic road. Before they had gone any distance, a child's scream sounded from the villa.

Both turned in their saddles. Augustus looked at Withred, Withred at Augustus. 'I can't ride away from this,' said Withred. 'It's not me.'

'Me neither,' said Augustus as he halted his horse.

Ohtrad had become bored with winter and yearned for the raiding season to begin again. He was also bored with the whores of Norwic.

Consequently, he had persuaded four of his friends—had *dared* them, even—to travel with him to the old amphitheater. The place was haunted, he knew that, but being *scared* shitless was better than being *bored* shitless as far as he was concerned.

As for his companions: they were a worthless bunch on the periphery of Angle society. They were men content to follow others as long as they got a reasonable share of the spoils, and a second or third go at the women on the raids.

Their journey to the amphitheater took them past the villa. Ohtrad was aware of the tale. Griff, as well as his champion, had been found dead on the floor of the arena. Their ghosts were said to haunt the place, adding a further thrill to the adventure.

It was Swithulf, an unkempt man of dubious personal hygiene, who first saw the woman outside the villa gates. Olive skinned and dark haired, she had left the courtyard to empty a jar of laundry water into a swath of shrubbery outside the gates. Swithulf had immediately grabbed Ohtrad's tunic sleeve and pointed her out.

Ohtrad then decided upon a change of plan. Unlike the worn-out whores of Norwic and Camulodunum, this woman was a beauty—a

Roman beauty by the look of her. He decided to abandon the trip to the amphitheater. Instead, they would ride into the villa and see what mischief they could make. He was aware he needed be cautious because what lay beyond the opening was anybody's guess. He led his rag-tag group down to the gates, halted, and looked into the inner courtyard. Inside, he saw an old wagon hitched to a mule—a farmers rig by the look of it. Confident that no nasty surprises awaited them, he had entered compound.

To his surprise, *and delight,* he discovered the woman was not alone. Another of similar beauty also resided at the villa. Both had nervously approached his group asking the nature of their business. Still cautious, Ohtrad lied to her, telling her his party required water. The women, visibly relieved, headed for the villa's well.

Meanwhile, Swithulf dismounted and sauntered to the mule and wagon. Beyond the rig, he saw an open door ... heard voices. Furtively, he had sidled up to the ingress and looked inside. Within the room, a peasant sat with his wife and daughter; the girl being no older than thirteen years. Swithulf had given

Ohtrad the nod, then—the signal telling him it was time to act.

As the Angles whooped their spontaneous cry of delight and anticipation, the olive-skinned women ran to the gates, but Penda and Waldhere (two more of Ohtrad's cohorts) were soon to catch them. Upon hearing the commotion, the farmer—a Briton who had broken his journey to Norwic market to receive hospitality from the women—had edged outside to investigate the disturbance. Ohtrad, who by now realised just how he intended to spend the next few days, saw the farmer as nothing other than a hindrance. Callously, he had slid from his horse, run to the man, and stabbed him repeatedly with his dagger.

Ohtrad, with the help of Swithulf and the fifth man, Frethi, had then turned his attention to the farmer's wife and daughter who had emerged from Griff's apartment to find their loved one bled out and lifeless. Screaming out their grief and fear, their stricken looks wavered between his dead form and the men who approached them.

Ohtrad, Swithulf and Frethi had manhandled them back into the room just as Penda and Waldhere arrived with the other two terrified women. Ohtrad had secured the door and sat down against the outer wall of the room.

Three days passed, during which time the Angles raped and beat the females. Always drunk from their own ale, as well as the jugs of Gaul wine they found at the villa, the men had defiled the women in every imaginable way until their liquor-sodden bodies had become spent of their seed. Then, they slept, but upon awakening began the abuse all over again.

Bare-chested and wearing just his filthy hose, Swithulf now lurched towards the door that adjoined his room. He said: 'The young wench, I think I'll have the young wench next; she tickles my fancy she does.'

Waldhere, who lay slumped against the back wall of the apartment nursing a jug of wine, snorted his derision at Swithulf. 'Tickles your fancy because there's no struggle in her, that's why.' He belched and looked towards the adjoining door as Swithulf opened it. 'Come to think of it,' he slurred, 'they've *all* lost their fight now … they just look at you with those dead eyes, they do … gives me the shivers, it does.'

Against the opposite wall, Ohtrad, Frethi and Penda, who were having a break from their relentless assaults on the women, directed their bleary gaze towards Waldhere.

Ohtrad then grunted to his knees, ready to gain his feet and follow Swithulf. 'Glad they don't fight it anymore,' he mumbled. 'Don't think I've the strength left to fight back.'

A disparaging cackle came from Frethi, who slapped the wall and pointed at Ohtrad. 'Ha ... Ha, Ha ... too weak to fight a woman ... what chance would you have against Arthur and his Britons.'

Swithulf left the drunken exchange in his wake as he stumbled into the adjoining room. Before him, the four women, naked and filthy, shrank against the wall. Seeing Swithulf make towards her daughter again, the mother screamed at him. 'NO!—NO MORE! Haven't you had enough. Leave her be. She is already torn and bleeding. What use can she be to you!'

Swithulf met the woman as she rose to meet him. He grabbed her wrists as she came at him, struggling briefly with her. After disentangling himself, he delivered a slap across her jaw; a clout delivered with all the venom he could muster.

As the woman fell stunned onto the floor, the other two women formed a protective cocoon around the girl.

'What the ...' Ohtrad had entered the room, ready to resume his depravity. He took in the scene. Swithulf was standing in front of the crouching women, his hose down to his knees as he masturbated before them. Ohtrad pushed him to one side. 'Lazy bastard — scared of a bit of a struggle.' he muttered. Now he ogled the girl, who shrank from him. He threw his next remark over his shoulder at Swithulf. 'Watch ... and don't squirt over me or I'll cut your cock off.' He crouched and grabbed the girl's arm. 'Let me show you how it's —'

Spontaneously, the women screamed as Withred slipped into the room from the outer door. Without preamble, he was upon Ohtrad, who had stopped mid-crouch and let go of the girl. Anticipating a fight at close quarters, Withred had armed himself with his dagger before entering. He thrust it into Ohtrad's gaping mouth.

As quickly as the knife was in, he removed it and turned to Swithulf who was standing transfixed as an alarming pounding and snarling came from the other room. Such was the speed of his next attack, that Withred struck Swithulf before Ohtrad had fallen dead on the floor behind him.

Dispassionately, Withred thrust his dagger under Swithulf's sternum and into his heart— the power of the movement raising the abuser from his feet. He removed the blade, allowing Swithulf to drop beside Ohtrad. Seething, he strode to the adjoining door.

Earlier, Withred and Augustus had decided to take one room each. A furtive look into most of the rooms surrounding the courtyard, had left them with just two rooms to search. Augustus, aware of the layout of the villa from his previous visit, guessed the remaining room to be Griff's adjoining apartment. He had silently signalled Withred to take the right-hand door.

As Augustus took the other door, a movement at his thigh caused him to look down. Beside him stood the dog, sniffing out the room, unsure of its role. A hasty look around made it clear he had taken the room's three occupants entirely by surprise.

Frethi was wide-eyed with fear as he viewed the giant looming over him. He looked towards the adjoining door as if to escape through it. Augustus remembered the dog. 'KILL!' he snapped, and pointed at Frethi. Now fully aware of its role, the dog went to work on him, and as the snarling and tearing began,

Augustus turned to Waldhere and Penda who had risen to meet him.

Penda, still drunk, fumbled for his knife. Augustus, who was weaponless, lost no time in meeting him. His powerful slap, landed palm first against Penda's face, slammed his head into the wall. Penda slid down it, unconscious.

Meanwhile Waldhere, intimidated by Augustus, had decided to run. He managed to slip past him and reach the door. Aware his man was getting away, Augustus reached down and pulled the dog from Frethi's face. He pushed it towards the door recently departed by Waldhere. This time the mastiff needed no instruction from Augustus and bounded outside. In was upon Waldhere in five strides, knocking him to the ground.

Augustus turned to the adjoining door just as Withred stepped through it. The Angle's hollow look told its own tale, prompting Augustus to peer into the room. He saw the women, naked and wretched. Then he saw what they had done to the girl. He hitched his breath at the sight, just as Penda's groan evinced his returning consciousness.

Ashen, Augustus turned to him. 'A man are you?' he snarled. Grabbing Penda's neck, he dragged him upright as if weightless. His voice now poured from him like ice melt from a fissure. 'Makes you feel good'—he slammed Penda's head against the wall—'treating women like offal'—again, he slammed the head—'stripping them naked'—three more slams and Penda's head started to split—'and leaving them to spend the rest of their lives'—four more and Penda's head came apart—'with only'—slam—'your ugly face'— slam—'left in their memories.'

'I think he's dead, Gus; his brains are all over the wall.' Withred pulled at Augustus' thick arm. Augustus glanced at him, then dropped what was left of Penda.

'I'm ashamed to say they are Angles like me,' added Withred. My folk have started to settle the lands north of Camulodunum and many now reside in Norwic.'

'Not like you at all,' said Augustus, still breathless after his raging demolition of Penda. 'No … these were lowlifes … renegades; I'm sure many good people reside amongst the settlers, just as there are simple Saxon folk just wanting to get on with their lives. Just like Godwine and his family in Londinium?'

'Aye, I do,' said Withred smiling at the recollection. 'Pity we didn't have the time to look them up when—'

A movement from behind had them turn. Naked and filthy from his debauchery, Frethi was still alive. The dog had opened his face, leaving a meaty mish-mash of skin flaps. His exposed teeth grinned strangely at them from his lipless mouth. He turned his remaining eye—the other being glutinous and shredded— towards them. He attempted a sentence, but only a 'gheesh,' sound came from him.

'I guess he wants us to finish him,' deduced Withred.

Augustus thought of how many children men like him had orphaned. 'What ... and deprive him of his new role as a beggar on the streets of Norwic where he'll be pissed, spat and shat on. No. I think not, my friend.'

Withred grabbed Frethi under his armpit and hauled him outside. 'First things first, then,' he said. 'Can't show him to the women, though. They don't need to see this.' He dragged Frethi, who had barely the strength to stand, across the courtyard. There, he observed the dog; saw it feeding upon Waldhere. 'Gus,' he shouted as he passed the mauling. 'Your dog's eating fresh meat out here. Perhaps you'd like to take it in hand; make sure it doesn't go looking for a second course.'

My dog, thought Augustus with some exasperation. *Since when did that killer become* my *dog?*

Withred continued with Frethi until he reached the gate. 'Out with you,' he said as he pushed him on to the track outside the villa. 'Keep going until you get to Norwic. If anyone asks what happened to you, and you can manage a reply, tell them you're a fiend and that you got your comeuppance.'

Frethi stumbled away and Withred returned to the courtyard. 'I'll attend to the women,' he said to Augustus, who was kneeling by the dog having dragged it from its feast. A blood-soaked linen sheet lay over Waldhere.

Withred stuck his head inside the room containing the women. Terrified, they still crouched, huddled and naked. With deference to their modesty, he averted his gaze as he addressed them. 'We mean you no harm,' he reassured. 'You have no need to fear me or my companion. Indeed, two of you already know the fellow. Now I will find you clothes to wear. Then you can go to the bathhouse. I have no doubt you desire to wash away the filth of those men.'

Two hours later, Augustus and Withred were able to sit with the women. Having no desire to return to the room of their ordeal, they had settled in the apartment previously used by Griff's man, Ambrosius.

Augustus sat with his arms around the shoulders of Cassia and Junia, the two women from Rome—the same women who had helped dress his wounds the previous year when he suffered his trial at the arena. Augustus knew they needed *his* help now; realised they could no longer live at the villa. There, they would be exposed to other wayward men; other Ohtrad's and the like.

The farmer's wife and daughter sat with Withred. The Angle had taken the girl's hands in his and spoken softly to her. He had explained to her that not all men were bad. He had reminded her of her father whom they had removed from the courtyard and who now lay swathed in a clean linen sheet awaiting his burial. *"Judge men by him, not by the people who have hurt you,"* he had whispered. The mother, too, he had comforted, taking her head upon his shoulder as her grief poured outwards.

Augustus glanced at Withred and considered the man; reflected on what a riddle he was. That he was capable of love and compassion was obvious; he could see that for himself that very moment. Yet, a fiercer or more adept adversary he had never seen. The man was cold, brutal and cynical when faced with an antagonist. Why such a man had once ridden with the raiders, he would never know, but Augustus had to agree with Dominic's assessment on the matter. He had put it: "*Better to have Withred inside your cave pissing out, than outside your cave pissing in.*"

Withred touched Augustus' arm, ending his ponderings. 'Gus, we must leave. We have a sea journey and task ahead of us, and time is running out.'

Augustus' nod and glance to Withred conveyed both acceptance and concern. He took Junia's hand in his. 'Outside, my love, are Saxon ponies, provisioned for two weeks. Remember my directions. Twelve days should get you to Brythonfort if all goes well. There, you will meet a man named Arthur, the same man who some people in these parts talk about as if he is a God. Listen to me Junia'—she met Augustus' eyes as he pulled her hand to his chest—'Arthur is not a God but he *is* a good man; a little stern, but good nonetheless. Tell him who you are. Tell him you are the women who saved Gus when he came to you injured last year. Tell him what happened here and explain that Withred and Gus are well and on their way to Angeln. Then he will let you into Brythonfort where you will be given shelter.'

Provisioned for the journey to Brythonfort, the Saxon ponies stamped and snorted in the courtyard. The sad assembly went to them, and after a brief and emotional farewell the three women and girl rode through the gates of the villa.

Augustus and Withred pulled themselves up on to their own well-provisioned horses and took one last look around. Titon was standing at the feet of Augustus' horse, for Titon was the dog's name—that he had learned from Junia. 'I don't think I ever want to come to this place again,' he said.

'Me neither. Let's hope the rest of our journey isn't as lively,' said Withred as he heeled his horse into a trot out of the compound and headed for the port of Norwic.

CHAPTER ELEVEN

Gherwan and Murdoc rode over the elevated wooden boarding on their journey to Travena. To persuade Ffodor and his eighteen hundred men to join Arthur's cause would be their task. Two days earlier, they had left Brythonfort and since then clattered over many such causeways—the wide network of structures providing dry footing for the horses over the sodden ground of the Levels. Indeed, the causeways were a common feature of the land, and crisscrossed it and provided raised passageways between the outcrops of higher ground.

These islands, which stood proud of the terrain, were the site of random habitations in the area. Here, the local people, who supported themselves by hunting and fishing in the marshes, were friendly to both Arthur and Ffodor. Most were happy to live on land governed by the two renowned lords, aware that their proximity to them meant protection.

As the low sun dipped to the horizon, marking the end of their second day, Gherwan and Murdoc eased their horses off the causeway and on to dry ground. Gherwan surveyed the topography ahead of him. 'There should be no more marshes now,' he said. 'By this time tomorrow we'll have reached Travena.'

Murdoc drew himself deeper into his hooded cloak as the thin wind threw its grey February drizzle at them. 'And I for one will be glad to arrive at the place,' he said as he peered up at the darkening sky. 'We need to make camp now, though, before this rain soaks us through.'

Later, an orange fire hissed beside them as they sat upon their bed packs beneath an outcrop of hazel. Murdoc had entwined the branches above them, just as Dominic had taught him, forming a canopy which served to protect them from the worst of the downpour.

Occasionally, a drip of silver rain would find its way through the tangled wickerwork and fall upon Gherwan's shoulder-length, grey hair. Murdoc regarded him as he warmed his hands on the fire. As Arthur's oldest captain, the warrior commanded extensive respect from all in south-west Britannia. Eloquent and tactful, he had been that natural choice to tackle the tricky diplomacy expected at Travena. Like Arthur, he had ridden for Rome and fought the Saxons and other invaders on countless occasions. Murdoc had heard many tales of Gherwan's exploits on the battlefield. *Fifty years old you may be*, he thought, *but still I should not like to cross you.*

Gherwan, who could sense Murdoc's scrutiny, turned to him. 'You seem distracted, Mur. Do you worry about tomorrow?'

Murdoc distractedly threw a twig into the fire, and stared at its bright, yellow flame. 'Not worried so much; more fearful that Ffodor's grudge doesn't stop him sending help to Brythonfort.'

One year gone, Ffodor had travelled to Brythonfort with his daughter, Marcia. Named after the wife of a Roman general he once knew, Marcia was the apple of Ffodor's eye. As far as he was concerned, she could do no wrong. However, years of overindulgence and spoiling had ruined her, resulting in the development of a petulant and demanding young woman. Ffodor's guards, especially his handsome captain, Rogan, were often disturbed from their sleep by Marcia, because as well as having an appetite for fine wines, golden ornamentation and expensive clothing of the Roman style—and Ffodor made sure she was not lacking in any of these—Marcia also had a taste (a voracious appetite, in fact) for sex; and much to his exhaustion and utter dismay Rogan was soon to discover this.

He dreaded the night visits from Marcia because she was a plain, unclean girl—her love of feasting and drinking having transformed her from a slender adolescent, to an overweight frump of a woman. Her father's genes had ensured her face would never adorn a Greek vase, and even in an age of grubby bodies, her reluctance to enter clean water meant that anyone in her company would discretely turn away and silently gag.

Yet Rogan had no choice but to service her, Marcia having made it clear that if he refused she would tell her father he had entered her chambers in the night and forcibly taken her.

So when she arrived at Brythonfort, Marcia was already carrying a child—most probably Rogan's if the frequency of her nocturnal visits was anything to go by. At the fort, she had noticed Flint and immediately forgotten about Rogan. In fact, she had become besotted with him, although he was haplessly unaware of it. But as the days passed, the zealous Flint, who was preoccupied with his duties and patrols for Arthur, could not help but become aware that Marcia always sought his attention, whether alone or in a crowd. Yet Flint felt no attraction at all towards Marcia, always making his excuses when cornered by her.

Inevitably, she had become cross with him. She was accustomed to having her own way, but here in

Brythonfort people behaved differently. One night she decided to enter Flint's sleeping quarters. There, she slipped naked under his sheets as he slept. Flint had awoken astounded and horrified, and shoved her from his bed. Covering her with his gown, he guided her to his door. From there, she ran screaming towards her father's bedroom. A disturbance erupted and a furious Ffodor summoned Arthur. Arthur sent for Flint and listened as Marcia accused Flint of wrongdoing. Flint vehemently denied Marcia's accusation of rape, facing up to Ffodor who was intent on retribution. Ffodor called for his guards, Arthur for his, and a standoff occurred.

Arthur took Flint to one side, away from the commotion, and spoke to him alone. He told his version and Arthur believed him. He knew his man, having worked closely with him since his arrival at Brythonfort as a raw-boned adolescent; knew Flint to be sound of character and true to his word. Besides, Flint had already told Arthur of Marcia's unwanted attention towards him and although they laughed over this at the time, Arthur had advised him to keep his distance.

After his conversation with Flint, Arthur returned to Ffodor, who still seethed and demanded action over the matter. Arthur told him that as far as he was concerned Flint was innocent of any wrongdoing, and in his opinion Marcia was acting *out of spite because Flint had spurned her. Unable to accept that his daughter was capable of such bad behaviour, Ffodor was outraged and again demanded punishment—even execution—for Flint. Arthur was having none of it, and after another hour of arguing and threats, Ffodor had stormed from Brythonfort with his entourage.*

Gherwan was pursed-lipped and thoughtful as he looked into the dancing flames. After a moment, he said: 'Aye, it would be a grim outcome if Ffodor decides to let personal matters guide him on his decision.' He studied Murdoc, who still stared, transfixed, into the fire. He felt that Arthur had been wise to choose the Trinovantian for this trip—the man having witnessed the destruction of his village and the slaughter of his loved ones. Murdoc knew what the Saxons were capable of. If anyone could persuade Ffodor to put personal differences aside for a greater cause, then Murdoc could.

The next day, the cold rain, helped along by a gusting wind, needled straight into their faces. By mid-afternoon they sat soaked in their saddles. '*Damn* this winter,' grumbled Gherwan, hand to brow, straining to see through the wall of water. 'The marshes were bad enough, but at least we were dry most of the time. I've never know a season as wet as—'

'Ahead,' interrupted Murdoc, whose younger eyes had the better of Gherwan's. 'There! Atop the headland.'

Gherwan, squinting and grimacing, soon recognised the shape of a huge wooden palisade. 'That's it, I'm certain it is,' he shouted. 'Travena is before us; I'm as sure as I can be in this murk.'

Another half mile of wet travel confirmed Gherwan's assurance. As they approached from the south-east, Travena towered high above them, its loftiness accentuated by the rocky outcrop upon which it sat. Towering spikes of timber, fashioned from entire trees, formed the walls of the hillfort. Wet, dripping and massive, they projected an air of sombre impenetrability. Soon they approached the entrance where, huddled within the sheltered passageway between the inner and outer gates, two sentinels stood.

'Seem an indifferent bunch,' said Murdoc as he noticed how their arrival had only stirred mild interest from the guards.

'That's years of living under the protection of Rome for you, then years of not having been troubled further,' said Gherwan as he slid from his horse to meet Ffodor's men who now sauntered towards them.

'Your business here?' demanded the first guard.

'To meet with your lord, Ffodor,' said Gherwan. 'Tell him Gherwan has arrived to speak with him.'

The guard's eyebrows shot up upon hearing the name. Like most of the people of the southwestern peninsular he had grown up with tales of Arthur and his knights, many of whom (Gherwan included) had assumed a legendary status. Without preamble, he left to convey his news to Ffodor.

'What? He sends his lackey? He has not the grace to come himself! The temerity of the man!' Ffodor's dark eyes blazed under his bushy, unkempt eyebrows as he stamped across the hall. Beside the hall's timber table, sat the rooms only other occupant: a plump young woman of nineteen who was preoccupied with breast-feeding her baby.

Marcia looked up moodily as the snuffling baby continued to gnaw at her breast. 'For God's sake, papa, get them in and listen to what they have to say.'

'The dungeons—I've a good mind to have them thrown into the dungeons,' shouted Ffodor. 'After what Arthur's bastard knight did to you, they deserve to wallow in the shit of the caves of Travena.'

'Just get them in here,' repeated the girl, weary now. 'Perhaps they bring news that will please you.'

'Please me, I very much doubt it.' He tapped his beaky nose conspiratorially and gave a crafty wink. 'If I know Arthur, he'll want something. Oh, yes, he's sent them because he wants my help.' He fingered the twisted-gold torque around his neck as he paused for thought, then turned to the guard who lingered outside the hall. 'Well? Why do you stand there? Get them,' he snapped. 'Oh, and tell your companion to get some of my men in here while you're at it.'

The son of a wealthy merchant, Ffodor had spent his childhood in the trading town of Isca, some sixty miles east of Travena. Originally, a Roman port, the town still held a position of strategic importance, providing, as it did, the main ingress into the southwestern lands of Britannia. Consequently, Ffodor was to enjoy an upbringing of privilege as his family became wealthy upon the trade flowing through the town. Marcius, Ffodor's father, had ensured his only son would want for nothing, and when aged only seven, the boy was put under the pupilage of Justus—a Roman Legatus and accomplished warrior.

Marcius paid Justus much gold to teach his son the art of Roman warfare. His wealth also financed a mall force of local men and youths, and he formed his own militia in the town. Ffodor and the other recruits were to meet several times a week by the open spaces of the dockyard, where Justin, along with twenty of his legionaries, would put them through vigorous training—both individually and as a group. For five years the drills continued until the small British force had no equal in the area.

When Ffodor came of age, he led his men, alongside Roman scouting parties, throughout Southeastern Britannia to meet the increasing upsurge of invaders from the continent. For ten years he fought Saxon, Angle and Jute, often standing beside Arthur. In 410 AD Rome finally withdrew from Britannia and Ffodor and Arthur returned to their southwestern lands.

When back at Isca, Ffodor, a serious and industrious man, yearned for his independence from his father and approached him asking to relocate and set up his own trading outlet. Marcius agreed, and after a quest for a suitable site, they found a village on a headland on the northern coast of the southwest peninsular. Named Travena meaning village on a mountain, the promontory would be easy to defend, and adaptable as a port from where Ffodor could amass his own personal wealth. Along with his small army, he relocated to Travena and began to build its high timber walls.

It did not take long before Ffodor had to repel his first attack from the Cornovii tribe from the deep southwest of the peninsular. Not surprisingly, Ffodor's army, fighting the Roman way, was able to fend off the fierce woad-daubed Cornovii—a territorial people who took exception to strangers relocating near their lands. From that day, Ffodor, who knew never to underestimate an enemy, had held the Cornovii in respect. Although tactically naïve compared to his own force, they had nevertheless fought with extreme courage and resilience.

The defeat of the Cornovii brought respite to Ffodor and he was able to finish off the strengthening of Travena. Now he was a Lord, and his revenue began to pour through the dockside of the port sprawled below his cliffs. To the people of the surrounding villages he became a welcome addition. As a high Lord he would protect them as they went about their daily lives. A firm but fair man as well—

one who listened with patience to any disputes and ruled accordingly.

Ffodor's prosperity had then grown, along with his army, until he commanded a force big enough to repel potential attacks from the Saxon hordes.

Gherwan and Murdoc now followed the guard across the open space between the gates and the hall. Against the huge wall to their right, a large lean-to provided shelter to a group of seventy horses. In front of this, a number of men sparred in the failing light. The shouting of an instructor echoed around the inner compound, his cries reverberant and solitary.

'He appears to keep his men in good shape,' said Gherwan. 'I was afraid complacency may have settled after the peaceful years they've had down here.' He turned his attention from the knights and lowered his voice an octave as they neared the doors. 'Remember to show deference to him,' he advised. 'Do not forget that Ffodor is as great a king as Arthur, although without Arthur's common touch. Unlike Arthur, this man expects reverence and attention. When we enter the hall, do as—'

They paused as the compound became silent. The drill instructor had stopped his shouting. Looking across, they could see why. The other guard had approached him and after a hurried conversation, the trainer and twelve other men ran across the open ground towards them.

'Seems like he wants his men around him,' mused Murdoc. 'Wants to show us a bit of force, maybe.'

They reached the doors and the guard led them into the brand-lit hall. Murdoc coughed a little as he inhaled the oily smoke. Before him, standing with his hand on the shoulder of a young woman who sat before him, stood a tall commanding man. Vulture-like, with his beady, piercing eyes and prominent nose, Ffodor was dressed in an ankle-length, brocade tunic. A black bearskin covered his shoulders, complimenting the lightweight, fur stole of the woman before him.

'With me,' said Gherwan as he grabbed Murdoc's sleeve and dropped to one knee before Ffodor.

Ffodor gave his daughter a knowing little smile, then left her side and approached the crouching men. 'I never thought I'd witness the day when Arthur's people would have the cheek to come here and bow before me,' was his only greeting. He let his gaze linger upon them a moment. The quiet was broken when Rogan, Ffodor's instructor and champion, entered the room with his men. Ffodor glanced at the guard before turning his attention back to Gherwan and Murdoc. 'Lift your heads and stand up,' he instructed. 'Whatever you've to say had better please me, or you're going to my caves.'

As Rogan strode to Ffodor's side, Gherwan and Murdoc got to their feet. Murdoc gave a quick glance towards Marcia who stroked the cheek of her baby. Both of her breasts were on show as the infant nuzzled at her—a situation that concerned her not at all. She noticed Murdoc's brief attention, noticed he had penetrating, green eyes and a handsome head. She flickered a coquettish smile towards him before casting her eyes downwards to the baby again. Murdoc averted his gaze and looked to Gherwan.

'Our news is grim, indeed, high lord,' said Gherwan in the way of introduction. 'Men gather in numbers to the north and east; men intent of breaking the peace that lies upon these lands.'

'So Arthur has sent you to elicit my help, I take it,' said Ffodor, glancing to his man, Rogan, who reciprocated his expression of astonishment. 'The same man who stands up for the worthless knight who impregnated my daughter has the temerity to send his people here.' He gave an incredulous little chuckle. Rogan, ever keen to please his lord, responded likewise.

'If you'll hear me out, high lord,' said Gherwan, aware that his diplomatic skills were about to be put to their severest test, 'then I feel you would at least understand why we travelled so far to reach your impressive stronghold.'

Ffodor paused a moment as he took in Gherwan's statement, then said emphatically: 'More like *why* Arthur has not had the grace to come himself.' Before Gherwan could respond, Ffodor waggled his fingers at him with some impatience. 'No ... never mind. Just tell your tale, so I can either send you on your way like whipped curs or put you in chains for having the gall to ask me for help.'

Gherwan continued. He told of the gathering of Hibernian and British forces. Of the suspected allegiance they sought with the Saxon invaders in the east. How between four and six thousand men were expected to swarm into the western peninsular. He speculated that Aquae Sulis was the natural target and the gateway into the protected lands. That Arthur would be outnumbered was inevitable. Ffodor and his resources had to help, reasoned Gherwan. This was not just Arthur's fight.

Inscrutable, Ffodor listened to Gherwan without interruption. When his account came to its conclusion, Ffodor walked back to the long timber table and sat on its edge, his hands behind him as he looked, pursed lipped and thoughtful, at the knight.

After some moments, he said: 'It seems you'll be well and truly outnumbered without my help—by two-to-one or thereabouts.'

'Aye, that is true,' conceded Gherwan. 'But if they outnumber us, they'll come here and outnumber you, so doesn't it make sense to meet them together?'

'No—it does not. Their numbers will be fewer by the time they get to me. Arthur's intervention and the sucking marshes will see to that. Here, I'll be fresh, whilst they'll be weak.'

'They'll also be battle-hardened and keen,' pushed Gherwan.

Ffodor ignored Gherwan's observation. Instead, he turned to Murdoc. 'And what of you? What is your role here?'

'My role, high lord,' said Murdoc quietly, disliking the man's tone, 'is to explain to you what can happen when Saxon ambition is left unchecked.'

'You think I don't know what they can do? Do not forget I killed the bastards when riding for Rome.'

'And in doing so, you sheltered the isle from them. But Rome has gone, and because the eastern lands lacked a champion they fell to the Saxons, just as these lands will fall if the lords become complacent.'

'Become complacent,' spat Ffodor. He glanced at Rogan again, the look conveying, *Listen to this peasant, he comes to my hall and tries to tell me how to govern my lands*! In response, Rogan shook his head with disbelieving dismay. '*You* are telling *me* I'm complacent; *you* who stand there, from God-knows-where ... from some guttersnipe tribe from the eastern lands.'

'I come from a village flattened by them,' said Murdoc hotly. 'I was the only survivor along with my daughter! So, yes, I come from nowhere, great Lord—NOWHERE! Because my home has been taken from me.'

Gherwan shot a warning look towards Murdoc. Having noticed Ffodor's reaction, he was aware his companion's outburst had made an impact, but now was the time to tone down his address. The glance was not lost upon Murdoc, who continued with less heat. 'You see, because we had no Lord to protect us, we were left open to attack. I fled to the vast eastern woods with my child, and we would have perished if not found by Dominic.'

Rogan spoke for the first time. '*His* name has become famous, even here. An accomplished woodsman, I am told, who helped defeat a raiding party in the woods some two years ago.'

'Yes, that is he. I rode with him and we were able to kill them all because of Dominic's guile and Withred's tactical expertise.'

'Again, you utter a name known to us. A man said to be brutal in combat, yet a traitor to his own people.'

'A traitor to rape and torture, rather,' defended Murdoc. 'Yes ... he is brutal to wrongdoers, but he is also a man of good character, and a man unquestioningly loyal to Arthur.'

Ffodor spoke. 'So you've already proven you can defeat them'—a disdainful curl came to his lip—'even with help from *one of them* it seems. Back then, you had no Lord to protect you. Now you have Arthur, so should be invincible. Why bother *me* with this?'

'Because we defeated no more than thirty men that day and met them on equal terms. Now we could be crushed. You've already said we'd be in trouble without you, and be outnumbered by two-to-one.'

'Well?' said Ffodor. 'What of it?'

'This lord: The Saxon raiders are a vicious pack who will not stop until they reach the southwestern coast. Then their occupation of the south will be complete. In taking these lands, they'll leave no village untouched. That's what they do: they strike fear into the people and drive them away; the lucky ones, that is — the souls who are not killed or enslaved.' Murdoc's eyes blazed with a fervent passion as he again recalled his ordeal. 'I was such a man, I got away, and sometimes I wish I had not. What they did to my wife I will not even try to tell you, and it happened before my eyes, and *God help me* before the eyes of my infant child. If it were not for her I would have ended my own life that day, but I didn't' — he cast a glance at Marcia; a look not lost upon Ffodor — 'because my little girl needed me, just as all daughters need the protection of their fathers.'

'And I will protect mine ... when the time comes,' said Ffodor emphasising every word.

Gherwan, who had allowed the impact of Murdoc's passionate address to fall upon the room, sensed a change in Ffodor; but before he could add weight to the argument and win him over, Marcia spoke.

'Why *should* you help them, father?' She drew the infant from her and pulled the Roman stola she wore across her exposed breasts. All turned to her. 'Do not forget how Arthur treated you—*treated me!*' She looked to the side, her nod summoning a nursewoman from the shadows. The woman took the baby from her and left the hall. Marcia stood and joined the group who lingered beside the table. She shrugged further into the stola and fastened its silver-corded belt around her waist. 'If he's such a magnificent king then he will be able to handle this without help from us,' she continued. 'Do *not* go to him; he insulted me and now he clicks his fingers'—in emphasis, she clicked her own fingers—'and expects us to gallop to his aid with an entire army.' She turned to Rogan, her air defying him to disagree with her. 'What say you, champion? Do you think your Lord should run to Arthur?'

'You ask me ... want my—' Rogan quavered. Having been won over by Gherwan and Murdoc, and accepting the core of their argument, Rogan had intended to offer his advice to Ffodor—to counsel him to help Arthur. Now, though, things had changed. Marcia's stare had left him in no doubt she would make life difficult for him if he flouted her. What she had accused Flint of, she could also level at *him*, though this time it would be true. How she would do it and still get her father to abandon Arthur he did not know, but the threat was enough. He had no wish to be castigated and forced to leave Ffodor's household.

'*Well?*' said Ffodor with strained patience. 'Are you awake, Rogan? As my champion, I value your advice. Now spit it out, man!'

'I—I—think it wise not to act hastily,' he replied. 'We don't even know if these forces are hostile. But if they do come to attack Arthur, then let *him* meet them. Regardless of your past differences with him—for I think those should not have a bearing on this—Arthur must be left to cope with his own matters, like we dealt with ours recently.' He had referred to an outbreak of unrest that had led to the far-western Cornovii tribe attacking some of Ffodor's farmsteads and villages. Ffodor had contained the rebellion and driven the Cornovii back to their own territory.

Gherwan intervened, speaking directly to Rogan. 'You cannot compare a tribal dispute with what's about to happen now,' he reasoned. 'A few savages bloodying the nose of Ffodor, your Lord, bears no resemblance to the carnage ready to erupt.'

'See, father—the insults continue,' burst in Marcia. 'He demeans your achievements and would have it that your victory over the Cornovii was worthless.'

'Enough—enough of this,' said Ffodor, wandering over half a dozen things at once. 'We are going round in circles when the answer has been plain from the start,' He turned to Rogan. 'You were right when you said Arthur should be left to deal with his own matters, but wrong when you said our past difference have no bearing on this—for they indeed *do* matter to me.' He regarded Murdoc now. 'I listened to what you said, and your account was indeed harrowing. The tale served its purpose—the purpose being I will not now throw the pair of you into my caves, for I think that you, man, have suffered enough, and never let it be said that Ffodor lacks in magnanimity.'

'*Not throw us in your caves*,' said Gherwan exasperated. 'It's the best you can do? The land is threatened and you think this will be resolved by not throwing us in your caves. What about helping us defend the liberty of Britannia.' Gherwan's tone now became pleading. 'Ffodor, I beseech you; forget this— this personal dispute—there is much more at stake here.'

Indignant, Ffodor replied: 'NO! I am wronged and demand satisfaction on the matter before I will even consider raising the levy and sending men to Arthur.'

'And meanwhile the armies march and prepare to move on us while we can muster only half their numbers. And ... *satisfaction on the matter* ... what satisfaction do you seek?'

'It's simple. Send me the scoundrel who made me a grandfather. Send him here to Travena to accept his duties to my daughter and I might just spare him his head.'

Gherwan was dismissive. 'Out of the question. Flint is important to Arthur, and Arthur believes he has done no wrong and will not abandon him. Besides, the man is one of Arthur's best knights and it would be madness to remove this man from the field in times such as these.'

Ffodor's demeanor became resolute. 'Then I cannot help you. If Arthur is stupid enough to turn down my support because of his misplaced faith in one man, then so be it, this conversation is over.' Ffodor's twelve knights still stood by the door. He addressed them. 'Take these men from Travena and get them on the road back to the Levels.'

Gherwan attempted one last appeal. Looking at Rogan, he said: 'I know you; we met briefly on a campaign, and I believe you to be a man of sound reason. Surely, you know what's happening here.' He flashed his eyes towards Marcia, aware that somehow she had influenced Rogan earlier. 'Do not let others cloud your judgment, speak to your Lord. Try to persuade him on this.'

Rogan, uncomfortable, remained silent as Marcia's eyes bore into him. The guards approached Gherwan, took his arm, and started to pull him towards the door. Snatching it free, he blistered: 'Hands off, I will go freely!' Surrounded by the men, Gherwan and Murdoc walked from the hall.

Ffodor shooed them away with his hands. 'Out!—Out!—Get on your way and do not return. Tell Arthur that Ffodor does not easily forgive those who do him wrong. Those who call his child a liar.'

As he was pushed through the door, Gherwan again appealed to Rogan. He turned and shouted: 'Make him see sense, man. I know in your heart you are with us on this. Make him see sense!'

Then they were outside and into the cold night. Their horses had been readied from them, and they left Travena bitter and frustrated.

CHAPTER TWELVE

Cunedda, Diarmait and Raedwald had lingered within the walls of Camulodunum for five days awaiting the arrival of the three Germanic chiefs. Along with Hrodgar, the captains would listen to Cunedda's appeal for a union and provide four hundred men each if convinced. Needful of keeping the Saxons of Camulodunum on their side, Cunedda and Diarmait had agreed to the garrisoning of their main body of men outside the town.

Raedwald rested his elbows upon the sill of the window opening as he looked out at a dreary February morning. As he watched, a group of riders entered the town. 'Here,' he said. 'The Jute has arrived from Cantiaci. That should be the last of them. Now we'll get the chance to talk at last.'

Cunedda moved to the ingress and nudged Raedwald aside. 'Yes, it must be the man they call Wigstan.' He turned to Diarmait, his eyes betraying his intimation. 'It'll be good to finally get out of here.'

The expression was not lost on Diarmait, who, like Cunedda, had found his enforced proximity to Raedwald testing to say the least. The Saxon, who could count on no friends in the town, had badgered Cunedda and Diarmait to share their billet with him. During their journey to Camulodunum, the two leaders had become excessively tired of the overblown, blustering youth, so it was with no small measure of foreboding that they agreed. Since then, having done nothing to endear himself to the two hard-nosed veterans, they had grown to detest him. His invented tales of courage in combat, they recognised as pure lies, and his boastfulness over the matter of reprisal, they found distasteful; being, as they were, fathers of large families and men averse to gratuitous destruction.

'So we need to convince four of them that this endeavor is worth their while,' said Diarmait. 'Wigstan, Hrodgar, Cenhelm and— and—'

'Osbeorn,' burst in Raedwald. 'His brother, Bealdwine, rode with my father and was the best scout this isle has ever seen, and also a fierce warrior with no equal in hand-to-hand combat.'

In spite of his reluctance to endure another of Raedwald's diatribes, Diarmait's interest had been sparked. '*Was*, you say. So I take it this Bealdwine is not in Camulodunum. What happened to him?'

Raedwald's face darkened. 'Ambushed in the forest, he was. By the coward, Dominic, no doubt. Probably sneaked up behind him—his corpse found hanging from a tree upside down some months later. They knew it was Bealdwine by his tunic; his head was missing.'

'No equal in combat, you said. Seems he found one in Dominic. The man's fame has spread, along with his other cohorts: Murdoc, Augustus and Withred. Heard of *them*, have you?'

'Heard of them and intend to kill them all.'

Diarmait regarded Raedwald and wondered what in the name of Christ he was doing in the man's company. Having been Guertepir's master of the guard for some fifteen years, Diarmait had seen men come and go. Many, like the Saxon puppy who stood bristling before him, were loose in the mouth and usually loose in the bowels whenever things got tough.

Diarmait had spent his early childhood in Hibernia. When eleven years old, and one of twelve children, he had seen his father killed as he defended the herd of twenty cows that kept his family fed and free from poverty. Left to care for her brood without any means of support, Diarmait's mother had no option but to send her children away. Diarmait went to live with an aunt on the isle of Britannia in the kingdom of Dyfed. The woman's husband was a pitiless man who regularly struck Diarmait for the slightest transgression. His aunt, too terrified of the brute to intervene, had watched, impotent, as Diarmait had been forced to endure the man's ill nature.

By now, Diarmait viewed the world with cynicism and bitterness and his demeanor became taciturn and grim. His life as a virtual slave on his uncle's smallholding continued loveless and arduous. Five years passed and Diarmait grew into a loose-limbed, athletic adolescent. One day, after a minor lapse, his uncle struck him across the head with a knotted cord. Diarmait realised he could take no more and a crimson rage had flooded him.

His aunt's screaming had filtered into his consciousness ending his frenzy, but it was too late. Diarmait's uncle lay dead on the ground, his body battered and his head crushed flat from Diarmait's stamping. Pushing his aunt away and rebuking her for allowing his abuse to continue for so long, he had stumbled, confused yet strangely fulfilled, from the homestead. For a year, he survived by earning food for labour, his wanderings taking him ever closer to Guertepir's ringfort. There, he found a position as a herdsman, where his impressive physique and cold eyes grabbed the attention of Coirpre—the captain of Guertepir's guard. Guertepir had seen his potential, *and like all prospective recruits, Diarmait went straight to Guertepir's wife, Almaith. Diarmait emerged after three days — his virginity a distant memory. He had passed his first test.*

Five more years were to pass, and Diarmait got used to killing Saxons for Rome as he roamed Dyfed routing out rebels. His prowess soon caught the eye of Guertepir with whom he rode. On one bleak March day, after a messy and difficult engagement with a determined Saxon raiding party, Coirpre had fallen. Diarmait's actions that day — he had turned defeat into victory and savagely defended Guertepir — earned him his promotion to the captain of Guertepir's guard.

Grim and uncompromising, Diarmait had been shaped by his life. Little wonder he was singularly unimpressed by the Saxon youth before him now. His tone was an amalgam of scepticism and light ridicule as he addressed Raedwald. 'Kill this Dominic would you. And how would you do it? I believe he is —'

Hrodgar entered the hut, saving Diarmait the agony of having to listen to Raedwald's fanciful response. Brusquely, he snapped: 'To the alehouse — now! — the three of you. We are ready to consider your proposal. Tell the others what you have told me and you may get our support on this.' He stood at the door as, first, Cunedda, then Diarmait, went by him.

Hrodgar eyed Diarmait arrogantly, reinforcing the Hibernian's dislike of him. He had killed many like him when in the employ of Rome—had seen the glitter of egotism fade from their eyes as they bled out. A slight twitch of Hrodgar's face and an intensification of his stare dared Diarmait to respond as he passed. Diarmait met the action with a dismissive smile.

Lastly, Raedwald came to Hrodgar. Placing a gold-encircled arm across the doorway, Hrodgar stopped the youth in his tracks. 'You've done well to remain in possession of your cock and balls after stealing the horses,' he said with a twist to his lip. He nodded towards Cunedda and Diarmait who waited outside the hut. 'It's lucky you've got those two looking after you; by Woden it is!'

Raedwald looked to Diarmait for support, but the Hibernian seemed happy to let Raedwald squirm and sort the situation out for himself.

'See,' said Hrodgar with a lopsided half-grin, 'even your fellow lodgers have had enough of you.'

At that very moment, Raedwald decided he would dearly love to kill Hrodgar. Instead, he said: 'I think it would be better if we went to the meeting.' He fought to keep the tremor out of his voice. 'The sooner we can get on the trail, the sooner I can prove myself to you.'

Hrodgar said nothing, merely looked through Raedwald. He let his gaze linger a while, then dropped his arm. Giving a mocking, little grunt of a laugh, he waved Raedwald past him.

Three days earlier Will had entered Camulodunum with some trepidation. At first, he feared he would stand out in the Saxon stronghold but the worry proved groundless. A good scattering of opportunist Britons, ready to trade with the Saxons, now resided in the bustling town, so one more native did not register with anyone.

As he looked around, he saw the decaying bones of the former Roman stronghold. Courtyards, once resplendent with mosaics, now lay cracked and decaying. Fallen roofs, ruinous towers and the dilapidated gatehouse hinted at the town's past splendor. Everywhere, old brick structures pushed brokenly from the ground. Overlaying all of this was the indelible, pragmatic stamp of Saxony. Plank-built, thatched houses, noisy, clanging workshops and corals of ponies, spread across the broken topography of the place. At regular intervals, languid curls of smoke issued from the thatched roofs of numerous alehouses, brothels and lodging houses.

As Will sidled down a narrow, dim street, his senses were assailed by a myriad of sights and odours. The stench of human excrement and urine was everywhere, seemingly unnoticed by the bustling throngs who elbowed their way through even the smallest alleyways. To Will, a man who had spent most of his life in the languid forests, the place seemed to be nothing more than a cauldron of shouting and pushing.

A door burst open before him and a cursing harlot spilled into the street. A boot appeared from the doorway and connected firmly with the woman's backside, sending her sprawling onto the litter-strewn floor. Instinctively, Will stooped to aid her, but the woman—spiting with rage—snatched her arm from his grasp. Mercifully, her expletive-laden Germanic outburst was lost upon him. He held up his hands, happy to demonstrate his intention let her be.

Relieved to pass her by, he walked from the alleyway and entered one of the many eroded, bustling plazas. The place had long since lost the ambiance of a peaceful, fountain-adorned Roman backwater; now it was a boisterous collection of stalls and noisy merchants. Will winced when hearing their barking shouts, as they competed to attract the patronage of the milling crowds. Needing air and relief from the bombardment upon his every sense, he made for the open central area of the town.

Here a commotion had broken out as a body of men filed in through the gates. It was the third such arrival Will had witnessed in as many days. A squat Saxon led the newcomers to a coral. The crowd parted as the riders passed, the smell of sweat and leather, cloying and intense.

The Saxon went to a daubed hut that seemed ready to fall down, and stood at its door. As Cunedda, then Diarmait stepped out, Will became aware a situation was beginning to develop. Shortly after, he watched as a younger, ruffled-looking man emerged.

He followed discretely, as all walked from the square and into the bowels of the town. After passing through a confusing, twisting warren of alleyways, the men reached a tavern. Above its door swung a huge drinking horn. Cut from a massive white-horned bull, the symbol removed any doubt, if indeed any still lingered in the mind of the casual passer-by, that this was *the* place to be in Camulodunum. Furthermore, a lurid phallic symbol, painted in red upon the establishment's door, informed that ale was merely one pleasure the place had to offer.

When twenty paces from the entrance and some ten paces behind Cunedda's entourage, Will heard the unmistakable mass-murmuring of a room packed with people. Two no-nonsense Saxons stood guard. They nodded to the squat man who led Cunedda, Diarmait and the youth towards them. Will had gone far enough. The meeting was about to happen and he would not get through the door. As the men went into the room, he turned and walked back down the alleyway—his intention now, to leave town and return to his camp half a mile away. He would wait for them to complete their business.

Hrodgar had assumed his self-appointed role as master of ceremonies and took his place at the centre of the planked tables that formed a line across the back of the room. On his right sat the three men he had sent for: Wigstan the Jute, Cenhelm the Saxon, and Osbeorn, another

Saxon. On his left sat Cunedda, Diarmait and Raedwald.

For the previous five days, the feeling that something big was about to happen had swept through Camulodunum like a forest fire. The news had soon left the town and rushed through the taken lands until petering out along the coastal strips and forests. The rumours of a large envoy of British and Hibernian warriors arriving at Camulodunum had created a stir, adding to the consensus that moves were indeed afoot in Britannia.

Consequently, the alehouse was standing-room only, with many of the men forced to climb upon tables and benches to get a better view. The room now hummed with expectant, enthused conversation.

Hrodgar looked to Wigstan, Cenhelm and Osbeorn. They nodded and he stood. The sound of benches scraping against stone sounded as men climbed high to see. Hrodgar banged his fist upon his table. A tense silence fell.

'I see here many followers of mine,' he began. 'Men who I know to be worthy of the task put forward by the Britons and Hibernians who have travelled to this town.' A hush blanketed the room. 'Also, in this alehouse, I see Wigstan's men; Cenhelm's men; Osbeorn's men. No doubt you all know what this meeting is about.'

'Raping Britons, taking their land and shitting on their turf!' came a shout from a wag at the back of the room.

Hrodgar allowed himself a little nod and half smile as he waited for the laughter to abate. 'Yes, that's what it usually turns out to be,' he continued, 'but this man here'—he nodded towards Cunedda—'has plans to make your toes curl.' He extended his arm towards the Briton, inviting him to stand.

Cunedda took to his feet and looked around. Saxon expressions in the room ranged from curiosity to downright hostility. A glance downwards to the four Saxon commanders, confirmed Cunedda's conviction that the night would not be an easy one for him. He had already worked on Hrodgar and felt he had partially convinced him of the benefits of the alliance. The other three, though, appeared anything *but* won over.

Wigstan the Jute, whose blond hair was slicked with goose fat and spiked upwards, glowered at him and lightly and impatiently chopped the table with the ledge of his hand, waiting for Cunedda to begin. Cenhelm and Osbeorn wore similar scowls. Cenhelm's moustache was plaited and hung below his chin, and this he twisted between his forefinger and thumb as he took in Cunedda. Osbeorn was the brother of Bealdwine—the man killed by Dominic in the eastern forest. Osbeorn hated all Britons and, like his brother, possessed a hooked nose and narrow, animal eyes. He bore them into Cunedda now as if trying to pierce his brain.

Unperturbed, Cunedda began. 'With or without you I will march upon Arthur and lay his lands to ruin.' He allowed his statement a few seconds to sink in as glances became exchanged and a low muttering began. 'Yes ... I will march with four thousand men against Arthur. If you choose not to accept the offer I am about to put to this room, we will march without you.'

'Four thousand you say,' Wigstan regarded him with scepticism. 'The British tribes are too scattered to amass such a number.' He took a quaff from his horn and belched dismissively at Cunedda.

A ripple of laughter swept the tavern. Cunedda ignored it. 'Then you know naught of my tribe and the treaty we have already forged with Guertepir, the Hibernian king.'

'Then you must educate me on the matter,' said Wigstan, his smile still laced with doubt.

'Very well,' said Cunedda. He began to explain the finer points of the alliance; giving specific details about numbers. The room was silent as he spoke—occasional coughs and fidgeting his only interruption.

Towards the end, he introduced Diarmait to the assembly. 'This man can vouch for everything I have told you,' Cunedda said. He is Guertepir's man and is the captain of his army. He speaks not your tongue but will answer any question through me.'

'What do you want from us,' interjected Osbeorn suddenly. 'Why do Britons—people who we have driven into the dust and a people I hate with every sinew of my body—come to us now for help.' His eyes blazed at Cunedda, demanding an answer.

'Quite simple, Saxon lord,' said Cunedda. 'We want two thousand of your men to join us to ensure there's no doubt over the outcome of the forthcoming war with Arthur. For that you get what Arthur has kept from you till now: southwestern Britannia and its ports.'

Cunedda let his words sink in as the room erupted with conversation. Hrodgar, who already knew some of the details, removed his dagger and banged its hilt upon the scarred planking before him. 'Quiet!—QUIET!' His cry went unheeded so he climbed up on the table and again screamed for order. His voice was lost amongst the furore. Cunedda joined Hrodgar on the table. He raised his arms beseechingly above his head. Slowly, the room fell to silence again.

'Yes—yes,' he shouted. 'You will get ALL the southwestern lands and ALL the gold that lies therein, and I have been told the Britons dig it in cartloads from the very earth beneath their feet.'

Cunedda jumped down and sat beside Diarmait again. 'Let them exhaust their zest,' he said above a new outburst of noise. 'I told you these people liked gold—will do anything to get their hands on it—listen to the noise they make, does it not tell you I was right all along.'

Diarmait coldly eyed the Saxon leaders who were having their own vigorous conversation. He gave a slight nod towards them. 'That may be so, but they will be difficult to control, let alone their men.'

Slowly and with a stubborn, rhythmic persistence, Hrodgar began to bang on the table. The place fell to a stuttering silence.

Cenhelm, who had worn a contemplative frown and twirled his moustache throughout most of the uproar, now stood and directly addressed Diarmait. 'Like me'—Cenhelm wafted his hands across his torso; an invitation for Diarmait to take in his gold-bedecked person—'Guertepir has a fondness for gold. What's to stop him marching his men into the southwest and taking it for himself?'

Cunedda translated Cenhelm's question. Diarmait had his answer ready. 'Yes, I cannot deny it, my master covets gold also, but the prize he seeks is not the southwest; his army would be stretched too far; he already rules most of the western peninsular and that is enough for him. What my master wants is Aquae Sulis, for there he intends to set up a pleasure palace for his wife.'

Cenhelm absently fingered the golden torque at his neck. 'I hear the town is crammed with treasure. It would be worth the grind of the campaign just to see the place.' He turned his attention to Cunedda. 'And what of you, Briton? You, who are prepared to ride against your own people. Why would you do such a thing if not to obtain more land for your tribe?'

'My ambitions do not extend to Arthur's province,' Cunedda said. 'I seek alliance with

Guertepir and the freedom to patrol *his* lands—
territory that provides landfall for my enemies.
That's my reason for standing here tonight. As I
speak, Votadini people are on the move to Deva
and the surrounding country—that is our new
home. Guertepir's friendship ensures we will be
protected from the raiders of Hibernia.'

'So let me get this right,' came in Osbeorn.
'All you want is Aquae Sulis and the security of
the country north of it. And for that we get to
scourge Arthur's lands until we come to the
sea.'

'Yes—two thousand of your best men when
added to our four thousand should be enough
to overcome Arthur and his allies.

Exasperated, Osbeorn threw up his hands.
'Two thousand! Two thousand! You keep
mentioning two thousand! Why not ask for four
thousand and get this finished with quickly?'

*Because you're Saxons and would want
everything—Aquae Sulis, Northern Britannia the
western peninsular—everything!—should you
match us in numbers,* thought Cunedda. He and
Diarmait had already spoken to Hrodgar over
the matter, and found him to be an unlikely if
arrogant ally. So he decided to let the Saxon
answer. 'Hrodgar,' Cunedda invited. 'Perhaps
you can explain this to Osbeorn.'

All turned to him.

'I asked you here, Osbeorn,' said Hrodgar, 'along with Wigstan and Cenhelm, because I know the number of men you can call upon. And — yes — with my warriors that comes to the two thousand men the Briton and Hibernian need.'

'But why such a *specific number*?' pressed Osbeorn.

'Are you listening to me, man,' said Hrodgar, his patience waning. 'If it's just the four of us we get a bigger share of the taken lands, and the four of us can only muster two thousand men between us. Think of it, we will be able to quarter the kingdom. If we bring in more chiefs our tracts are bound to shrink in size.'

'And no need to worry about your northern border,' burst in Cunedda. 'Guertepir and my Votadini will keep it free from unwanted invaders. If they approach you they must travel through our lands as well.'

Hrodgar nodded his endorsement. 'Yes, I know it seems an unlikely alliance; I was also doubtful the first time these people approached me, but the more I've thought about it the more sense it makes. We want different things — they want security in the north and west, we want Arthur's lands and beyond. Oh, and listen to this'—Hrodgar looked directly at Osbeorn—'you get to meet Dominic; the man who removed your brother's head and let him bleed out like a stuck swine.'

Osbeorn blanched at the name, such was his depth of his hatred for Dominic. 'You mean he rides with Arthur?'

'Scouts for him, mainly, but he'll certainly be on the field of battle—wolf's hat and all—so he'll be hard to miss.'

'Six hundred of my men—Gedriht, Geoguth, and Duguth. Also whoever I can raise from the fyrd; as soon as I can get them here, they're yours,' said Osbeorn. 'The chance to slowly skin that wretched coward alive is worth it alone.'

'And I will raise about four hundred,' shouted Hrodgar, enthused now. 'We're half way there already.'

Whoops and shouts broke out in the room as followers of Hrodgar and Osbeorn, who had pushed to the front as they strained to hear the debate, became boisterous. Bare chested and riding upon the shoulders of companions, many of the younger men—the Geoguths—now punched at the air as they shouted their encouragement to the crowd.

Raedwald, ever mindful that his input to the discussion would attract the wrong sort of attention from Hrodgar, had remained quiet throughout, but as the atmosphere in the room became infectious he found himself up on his feet as he clapped in rhythm to emergent chanting.

Hrodgar addressed Wigstan and Cenhelm, who watched as the scenes of revelry escalated. 'Well?' he shouted, as he fought to make himself heard. 'Will you add to it? With the Britons, we already number five thousand, a formidable gathering you must agree, and I for one intend to go ... with or without you!'

Wigstan's ice-blue eyes glittered beneath his flamboyantly spiked hair. 'And split the kingdom two ways instead of four ... I think not! My people have been crowded into Cantiaci for long enough, I pledge my five hundred men!'

'And *I* pledge my *seven hundred*!' shouted Cenhelm above the clamour. 'The best shieldwall this island has ever seen will crush the life out of the dogs.' Standing, he raised his arms, his golden armlets and wristbands dropping down to his inked biceps. He threw back his head and took in the roar.

Cunedda exchanged a glance with Diarmait as the wall of noise enveloped them. He had planted the seed and the tree had burst from the ground. Now they could plan for invasion.

CHAPTER THIRTEEN

Dominic's return to Brythonfort had been brief. As soon as he forwarded the news of Cunedda's continuation to Camulodunum, Arthur had dispatched him to Corinium. Here, he would watch the northern road for troop movement from Deva. Cunedda's man, Abloyc, would undoubtedly take the direct road through Corinium should he decide to march south.

Dominic stopped at Nila's village. The mother of Aiden, Flint and Maewyn, she lived half a day's ride from Brythonfort.

Eighteen months had passed since the Saxon raider, Ranulf, had burned her world down to the scorched earth and killed her husband, Bran. On the day of the raid she had been at Brythonfort visiting her son, Flint, and so had survived. Furthermore, Ranulf had stolen her children—the abduction moving Arthur to send Dominic, Augustus, Murdoc, Withred and Flint on a quest to find them. Sadly, the party returned without Aiden—the lad having drowned in Hibernia.

For many months Nila had been inconsolable, but eventually she settled into her new life as a cook for a nearby fort. Flint operated from the outpost and she was able to see him when his duties brought him back. As for her other son, Maewyn, he was now a novice monk in Hibernia.

Desiring to be within the reach of a tract of forest one day's ride away, Dominic had moved from Brythonfort to Nila's village. Since then, he had often spent the evenings with her around his night fire speaking at length about his quest to find her sons. He was aware of how Nila gained comfort from talking about the search; it was her way of coping with the loss of Aiden and Bran. And so he was happy to tell her all he could remember.

But one thing bothered Dominic. Except that *bother* was too mild a word—*tortured* would be nearer the mark. Dominic was tortured because he felt a deep fondness towards Nila. Indeed, he had begun to spend less time in the forests and more time in the village such was the depth of his feelings, and for Dominic this was unheard of. His first thought upon awakening and his last image before falling asleep was always sad, beautiful Nila.

The crisis threatening to rip Britannia apart had almost come as a relief to Dominic. Now he could consider matters more pressing, except to Dominic nothing was more pressing than the chance to cast his eyes upon the woman who constantly inhabited his thoughts. Not that Dominic was a stranger to women.

When scouting for Rome he had become well-known throughout Britannia, from the wall of Hadrian to the southern Cantiaci coast. He knew almost every town in Roman Britain at that time and every one of them held a woman for him. Sometimes they were kind-hearted whores whom Dominic would treat well, often leaving them with as much coin as they could earn in a month. In some towns, he took up with serving wenches and women of higher status. Drawn to him by his reputation or attracted by his magnetism, these women would watch the approach of any scouting parties with anticipation, hoping the solid little woodsman rode amongst them.

410AD came and Rome left the isle of Britannia to fight foes closer to home, leaving Dominic without a role. He returned to his village then, still a young man of twenty-two. Skilled in tracking and warfare now, Dominic was unable to settle down and often entered the ancient woods, west of Camulodunum, to set his traps. For fifteen years he endured a pastoral life, living with his widowed mother and brother, Lew. However, during Dominic's service for Rome all the younger women in the village had married, putting a premature end to Dominic's carnal experiences.

One day, his brother, Lew, a man who wrestled with his own inner demons, had walked away. Dominic tracked him into the woods but lost his trail after it entered a gravel-clogged river. Fearing the worst, he returned to his distraught mother, feeling he had failed her. For months afterwards, he would search the woods as far as was safe but he never found Lew nor his trail, and finally accepted he must have perished in the old forest. His mother died and Dominic continued to struggle to see any purpose or future for him behind the drudgery of the plough. So at the age of thirty-seven he had walked away and entered the forest, never to return.

'Dom, I didn't expect to see you; you're a sight for my sorry, sore eyes.' Nila went to Dominic as he slid from his horse.

He embraced Nila. 'I'm on my travels again, I'm afraid. I need supplies before I set out for Corinium. I've been sent to keep an eye on things up there.' He stood back a step and looked at Nila. *And I needed to see you—I so much needed to see you*, he thought.

Loosely gathered in a ponytail, her dark plaits hung to one side and fell over her shoulder. She wore a simple, azure dress, tied at the waist by a plaited belt. The dress reached to her ankles, a hooded shawl of wool embracing her shoulders and keeping out the worst of the probing wind.

Beaming, she took his hands and stood back from him. 'Make sure you come to me before you leave for Aquae Sulis, it would be nice to see you off.'

After some moments, Dominic reluctantly loosened his grasp and made to turn to his hut. 'That *I'll* certainly do. As soon as I've got my things, I'll see you then.'

Later, Dominic was stuffing supplies into his pony's pannier when he sensed Nila behind him. He turned to her. In her hand, she held a small bundle tied with a strip of hemp. She gave a dismissive little shrug as Dominic glanced appreciatively at the bundle. 'Just some bread and cheese for your journey, it was no trouble to put it together. The bread came from Brythonfort bakery this morning ... should cheer you on your way.'

'Thank you,' said Dominic taking the package. Afraid to meet Nila's gaze, such was the intensity of his emotion, he looked to the ground. 'You're very kind, you're ...'

As his voice trailed away, Nila prompted him. 'I'm what, Dom?' She gave a self-conscious little laugh. 'A witch? A burden? A pest?' She prodded him playfully. 'Come on ... What am I Dom?'

Dominic raised his head and met her eyes. Resolute but sad, he stumbled over his words. 'You're lovely, Nila ... in every way, inside and out, you're truly lovely ... that's what you are ... since you ask.' Then it poured from him. 'So lovely that even though the world threatens to fall apart, I cannot get you out of my head — day or night.' Taken aback, Nila was stunned to silence. Embarrassed and angry, Dominic threw up his hands in self-recrimination. 'There ... I've said it. But what *have* I said; you still grieve and I babble nonsense at you. It was selfish of me. I am *so* sorry. I will go now and —'

Nila placed her hand on his lips then hugged him, her warm breath against his ear. She had begun to weep. 'Don't you *dare* apologize to me. You spoke from your heart and your words were true. When you get back we can talk about this.' She rubbed her sleeve across her eyes. 'Keep safe Dom. I need you to keep safe.'

Astounded yet overjoyed by her response, and unsure of whether to hug her closer or let her go, Dominic merely stood back and took her hands again. He laughed, unable to contain his delight, as he beheld her. 'Oh, I'll keep safe, Nila. If it's the last thing I do, I'll keep really safe now.'

Nila came to him and they embraced again, this time with less inhibition. When Dominic could finally let her go he walked elated to his horse.

CHAPTER FOURTEEN

Half a day after making landfall on Angeln, Withred was still the colour of driven snow. He turned and dry retched as Augustus chewed a hunk of bread, open-mouthed, before him. Titon, aware that something was going on between the two men, began to bound and yap around them.

'What?' laughed Augustus as he clapped Withred upon his back. 'Do you so begrudge me my pleasures that the sight of me enjoying myself makes you want to puke?'

Withred, whose fragility at sea had often been the source of much joking at Brythonfort, waved Augustus away. Hands on knees and coughing, he refused to look at Augustus who had crouched before him. 'No ... no, I mean it Gus, it's not funny anymore. Get away from me; bugger off, you're going to make me throw up again.'

Augustus fell back on his backside and chortled his booming laugh, sending showers of crumbs flying. 'Ha ... ha, ha ... the best warrior I've ever seen reduced to a shrunken little boy. Just *wait* till I tell Dominic.' His tone became singsong and childlike as he mimicked Withred.

'No don't do it Gus, you're going to make me throw up. Ha, ha ... ha, ha, ha—'

Augustus stopped abruptly as the *'Yaowl'* sounded. Titon stopped bounding and turned to the woods, ears raised, a low growl rumbling from him. Withred wiped the bile from his lower lip, flicked it to the ground, and looked at Augustus. 'Wolves,' he said unnecessarily. Augustus extended his arm and Withred obligingly pulled him to his feet.

'Should've left you there on the ground you fat bastard,' said Withred, smiling ruefully as he turned and looked towards a wall of trees thirty paces away. 'That came from the woods and guess where we're going?'

'Go on … surprise me ... through the woods, perhaps. How far through them?'

'All the way, some forty miles or so; straight across the headland 'til we reach the eastern shore.'

Augustus nodded in the direction of the forest. 'What's it like in there?'

'Mostly uninhabited ... timber and bogs mainly.'

'Is there no other way to get to your Aunt's village?'

'None I'm afraid. The paths should be good though. They're well used. A lot of those heading for Britannia enter the forest from the settlements on the eastern coast. I travelled through them myself before I left for the island.'

Augustus looked back down the road. Since leaving the port of Husum, it had been rutted but passable. Approaching the woods, he saw how the road narrowed to a seldom-used track. He slung his arm over Withred's shoulder and walked him down the road towards their grazing horses. 'Come on you Angle shit,' he said. 'Calm your belly and mount up, we've a wilderness to cross.' Titon who by now had become inseparable from Augustus trotted behind them as they entered the woods.

Two swift hours passed and they progressed along the thin woodland trail with little impediment. Already dark and gloomy, the day delivered scant light within the confines of the forest and when dusk came they set up camp beside a torpid stream in a clearing of bullrushes and shallow lakes.

After feeding their fire Augustus held up a finger. 'Listen,' he said, 'can you hear?'

'Hear what?'

'Nothing … absolutely nothing since we entered the forest. Surely you've noticed it.'

Withred frowned as he snapped bullrush seed-heads apart and threw them onto the fire. 'Yes and I'm not happy about it. No noise means no game; and no game means something's scared them.'

Just visible in the gloaming, the horses stood fetlock deep in a shallow pool. Titon lapped at the water at their feet. Augustus darted a worried look towards them. 'By *something*, I take it you mean wolves?'

'Or bears,' said Withred, his chiseled features lit up devilish by the fire. 'There's no shortage of big brown bears in these woods.'

Augustus stole an anxious look beyond the halo of fire light. 'Comforting bastard aren't you,' he said.

Withred smiled thinly. 'Best not to think of beasts and demons when you're in the woods, Gus. Get down on your bed pack and sleep, man. That's the *only* way to pass the nights here.'

Four hours later, their discordant snores grated through the still air of the clearing. Titon slept beside Augustus, twitching and whimpering in his dream. The fire had died to a mere flicker before the first of the horses gave out a whinny. In accompaniment, the second horse began to snort and stamp around.

Withred was quickly upon his feet. Hushed and urgent, he awakened Augustus. 'Gus! Up man and feed the fire; something's disturbed the mounts!'

'Huh?' Augustus took a moment to clear his head then rolled to his side and reached for kindling. Titon, roused now, stood stock-still and alert beside him.

Withred reached the first horse and stroked its neck, his voice low and reassuring. 'Steady ... steady boy,' he comforted. Nervy, the beast gave a low, vibrant whinny and stamped into the soft earth.

When the growling started, Withred strained to see into the darkness beyond the camp. A series of dark shapes confirmed what he had feared. Augustus stoked the fire again, its orange light reflecting in the eyes of the wolves. Twenty or so, guessed Withred. He chanced a quick glance to Augustus, now alert and holding on to Titon. 'Gus, light two brands and bring them here—big ones, we need plenty of flame. First tie up the dog. He's no use to us here; he'll only set the wolves into frenzy.'

Moments later Augustus stood at Withred's elbow. He handed him a brand. Withred took the flame without taking his eyes from the wolves. Behind them Titon whimpered in fear.

'They've not moved,' said Withred, still staring ahead. 'They're just watching us for now.' A breeze caught the torches, causing them to snap and ripple. Withred nudged Augustus. 'Move forward slowly with me,' he breathed.

As they advanced the orange eyes began to vanish. Withred stopped and grabbed Augustus' sleeve. 'They're drifting back into the thicker forest; hold your ground for now.'

Augustus rubbed his hand over his stomach where the scar tissue from a past injury pushed against the fabric of his tunic. 'They say all dogs come from wolves,' he said distantly. 'And just one dog nearly finished me off.' He nodded towards Titon. 'His sister it was. Gods help us if they decide to rush us.'

Withred drew his seax from his belt. 'We must be ready for them if they do. But I think they've lost interest for now — that or we scared them.'

Augustus retrieved his ax from his sleeping place. He scratched at Titon's skull and checked the integrity of the knot securing him. 'I'll keep the fire fed. There's no more sleep in *me* tonight so if you can sleep then get on with it, as for me, I've just had a reminder of the worst day of my life.'

The night dragged on, tense but without further disturbance, and they continued eastwards as soon as the first insipid light of dawn filtered through the trees. The day was arduous but uneventful, and two hours before dusk Withred appraised their progress. 'We need to plough on and stick to the trail. Half a day's travel tomorrow should get us to the eastern shore, and soon after that we'll come to my village. Then I can see my aunt again.'

'How many years since you last met?' asked Augustus, aware of Withred's deep love for the woman.

'Eight,' he replied. A recollection made him smile. 'Gave me a bundle of food for my journey she did. Had to hide it quickly in case the other men noticed the package and called me a mollycoddle.'

Augustus gave a little chuckle. 'Sounds more like a mother than an aunt.'

'That's *exactly* what she is to me.' Withred leaned back in his saddle and eased his horse down a steep riverbank and into a shallow river. With Augustus beside him, he headed eastwards—the shingle bottom of the river affording them an easier passage than the tangled woodland path. 'My parents were both killed when I was a young boy,' continued Withred. 'Without Mildrithe, Nerthus herself knows what would have become of me. Many love her, you know. Most of the villages along the coast go to her for help. She tends to the sick ... the dying ... the troubled. She even ...' His voice trailed away as he looked ahead up the river. Titon had been splashing along occasionally pausing and looking back to Augustus. Now he stopped and dropped his stumpy tail downwards.

The behaviour was not lost on Augustus. 'Something's spooked him,' he said. The dog turned and scurried back. Augustus dismounted, stooped to him, then ruffled its neck and ears. 'What are you telling us, eh? eh?'

'Could be a bear ahead ... anything.' Withred had dismounted and joined Augustus, ankle deep in the water. His feet were barely wet before his horse let out a frightened whinny and reared upwards. He grabbed for its rein as the wolves attacked.

Augustus bear-hugged the neck of his own horse, steadying it. Withred's horse had bolted. He was about to give chase when Augustus' shout stopped him. 'NO! Leave it! We must stick together! Let them have it!' The main body of the pack had followed the free horse, leaving eight wolves for them to deal with.

Two went for the mastiff. The dog took the fight to them. A savage amalgam of snarling and snapping ensued as Titon twisted and slithered between flurries of bites.

Withred managed to remove his seax just as a wolf jumped at him. Its sternum met the blade. Pierced through the heart, it fell dead. Immediately, another grabbed his arm. He staggered backwards as it attempted to pull him to ground.

Augustus let go of his steed and dragged his ax from its saddle. 'Keep on your feet. For Christ's sake keep on your feet!' he shouted. His horse, untouched for now, ran to the riverbank seeking escape. Augustus hefted his ax as he met his first wolf. Cold iron bit into its snout and the animal fell at his feet. He lurched forward as another attacked him from behind. Turning quickly and swinging his ax as he spun, he caught the wolf mid-leap. It dropped, its shoulder riven, its bones exposed.

Augustus turned to Withred who fought to keep his footing. Having grabbed his arm, one wolf strained to pull him to the ground, whilst another (an albino) leapt at his face. A third wolf rushed in and bit at the same arm. Their combined weight took Withred to his knees. The albino snapped at him just as Augustus arrived. Again, his ax bit, shattering the beast's midriff. The third wolf let go of Withred and with teeth exposed and lips drawn went for Augustus. It fell to another of his ax swipes. He kicked at the remaining wolf which fled towards the main pack. Augustus pulled a disheveled Withred to his feet.

A yelp had them turn to Titon. The dog tore at the throat of a wolf pinned beneath it. Another had sunk its teeth into Titon's back. Untroubled by this, the mastiff continued to gnash at the animal below it. Augustus stepped towards the melee and buried his ax into the upper wolf's soft underbelly, leaving Titon free to tear out the throat of the animal beneath it.

A distance away, the main pack had started to devour Withred's horse. Augustus grabbed Titon's collar as it turned towards them. 'No you don't you mad bastard, were getting out of here.' Panting, Titon looked up at him. Its right ear had gone, ripped off by one of the wolves. The dog was oblivious to the wound.

Withred, spent and wheezing, joined Augustus. 'We've got to climb up ... climb up from the river ...' He paused for breath as he stooped, holding up his arm. 'Over there'—

hardly able to lift his head, he turned to the river bank, where a slick of disturbed mud ran up its wall—'the horse went that way. It has half our supplies on it.'

Augustus gathered Titon's twisted leash and secured him. Weary himself, he cast an anxious glance down the river towards the scene of snarling and feeding. 'Let's get out of here, then, while the wolves are busy with that poor beast. You all right, Withred?'

'I'll live,' said Withred, somewhat recovered, as he scuffed through the water. 'Come—you're right—we need to get away.'

One hour later, they found the horse. The animal grazed from the sparse winter grasses beneath a beech outcrop as if it had just spent a peaceful day in the meadow. Knowing the importance of finding the horse and its supplies, Augustus and Withred had followed its obvious trail through the diverse flora of the Angeln headland. For the first time since their encounter with the wolves they were then able to take stock of their wounds.

Apart from shallow scratches, Augustus was surprisingly untouched by the encounter. Withred pulled his jerkin over his head and appraised his damaged arm. Augustus took hold of the limb and peered at the wound.

He attempted to make light of the injury. 'Just a couple of fang holes ... you'll live.' Withred gingerly prodded at the punctures as Augustus went to the horse. He returned with a bunch of sage. 'I got this from Rozen at Brythonfort. I was saving the stuff to cheer up your cooking but now it'll have to do as a dressing for the bite.' He twisted the herb in his hands, bruising the foliage and releasing its oils. Withred winced as Augustus squeezed his arm promoting a blood flow. He mopped the blood with sage then pushed more of it into the holes. Withred flinched again.

Augustus frowned with concentration as he wrapped the remainder of the sage around Withred's arm. 'Rozen reckons this stuff stops wounds from going bad.' He tore a strip of linen from Withred's shirt and tied the fabric tightly around the poultice. 'There ... the job's done; the oils should help you heal. Can't have your pleasure arm dropping off. Can we now?'

Withred gave a dry little laugh as he ducked back into his tunic. 'Listen,' he said as his head emerged from the garment's neck. 'Gulls are above us, we must be near the shore.'

'The eastward one I hope,' said Augustus. 'God knows which direction we blundered in when we ran away.'

'Has to be the eastern shore,' said Withred as he sniffed the air. 'We're too far from the west for it to be otherwise.'

Augustus peered upwards through the skeletal canopy of beech. 'Let's hope so, because I've had enough of this wolves' pantry and the sky's beginning to darken again. I'll get some firewood.'

That night, the fire burned high and bright as Withred and Augustus took turns at watch. Exhausted after the trials of the past days, both men had no trouble plummeting straight into bouts of deep sleep when their turn came.

Next day, the morning sky held the shade of the nearby sea. They followed a faint trail, ever upwards, until coming to the rim of a headland. Below them, the ground fell away to a brutal, swamp-infested plain. A tattered shroud of mist overlay the primordial surface of the swamp. Through the miasma, drifted an eerie amalgam of hoots, croaks and whistles. Beyond the plain lay the White Sea—silver and sparkling under a low sun. Neither habitation nor boat was visible

Augustus was lost for words as he absorbed the primeval splendor beneath him. Withred could not help but smile as he took in Augustus' astonishment. 'Now you know why the Romans didn't come,' he said. 'They would never have tamed this ... never.' Feeling very small, they were silent a while.

Eventually Withred spoke again. 'Fear not, Gus, I know where we are, and I can get us through the swamps and to the shore,' he said.

They snaked down to the level of the wetlands. Leaving Augustus and Titon to wait, Withred went to search for signs of the path he knew ran through the waterscape. An ancient alder caught his eye. He rode towards it. Tied to its lower bough was a weather-beaten cloth. He studied the earth beneath the tree and saw signs of passage. Away from the rough ground a faint trail meandered eastwards towards the morass. Satisfied he had found the route through, he beckoned to Augustus who waited with Titon five hundred paces away.

Withred met him beneath the tree. He pointed to the marshes. 'See, there's the path. I've ridden it before. I remembered the Alder. It's used as a marker.'

Augustus was not fully convinced the passage would take his weight. 'I'll stay behind you,' he said. 'If you sink up to your Angle balls, I'll know not to go that way.'

But the path held firm, and after half a day of threading his way through the swamp, Withred led Augustus on to firmer ground some half mile from the sea. 'Now we head northwards,' he said as he walked the horse towards the coastline. 'We'll keep to the shingle beach until we reach the first of the fishing villages.'

'How long before we arrive at your aunt's village?' asked Augustus.

Withred studied the sky, assessing the daylight. 'Mid-morn tomorrow, I reckon. Would've been quicker with two horses but at least we survived the wolves. Darkness isn't far away, so today is out of the question.'

'Any trouble from here on?'

'Hopefully, no. The people along this coastline are mostly friendly and treat strangers well, so we should sleep under a roof if we can reach a village I know of before sundown.'

Two hours passed as the travellers trudged leading the horse over the mud-flat and shingle beach. As the sun dipped behind the western headland, laying a slick of gold over the marshes, Augustus alerted Withred to a cluster of huts half a mile along the beach. As they got closer, they saw a fire burning in a communal area set back from the high water mark.

Aebbe looked up from her stitching as her keen ears heard the clatter of hooves upon shingle. 'People approach, Cynebald,' she said to her husband. 'Two men, a horse and a dog … a big dog.'

Holding his infant daughter, Cynebald got to his feet and strained to see through the failing light. He turned to a group of men who chatted beside the fire. 'Strangers approach,' he shouted. 'Get your spears and come with me.' He handed the girl to Aebbe and left with eight others.

Cynebald tensed as he noticed the bearing of the travellers. Confident fellows, no doubt, why else would they be on the White Sea foreshore at sundown? Sigbald, his brother, handed him a blazing brand as the group reached them. One was a colossus who snapped orders to the dog in his British tongue—the other seemed vaguely familiar.

'If I didn't know better,' he muttered, as one rider—the smaller of the two—approached him. Withred dropped his hood to reveal his features. Cynebald appraised him. Gone was the long dark hair—now the head was as bald as the sun. No longer clean-shaven—a sable beard flecked with grey grew to the man's chest. But the melancholic eyes—the positively *haunting* black eyes—as well as the sharp cheek bones chiseled upon a face which somehow managed to be both brutal and handsome, left Cynebald in no doubt that Withred had returned to Angeln.

'Wit—Withred, it is you, isn't it.' Cynebald's tone was incredulous as he squinted through the gloom at the tall, imposing man before him.

'Yes it's me, Cyn, I'm back to raise an army.'

Cynebald paused then said emphatically: 'An army!'

Withred looked towards the night fire. 'I'll tell you more as soon as we're sitting around your fire'—hunched from cold, he turned his back to the ocean—'because the wind coming off the White Sea has frozen our balls to ice.'

'Er—y—yes, yes, forgive my rudeness; it's just that you've put my head in a whirl. Come please; follow me to the warmth of the fire.' As Augustus climbed from his saddle, Cynebald's eyes grew big. Never had he seen a man as massive as the Briton who stood before him. 'Come,' he said again. 'The sooner we sit down the better.'

As the night drew on, Cynebald and the fifty men of his village became aware of all the happenings in Britannia. Withred and Augustus had learned how recent winter storms had flooded much of Angeln. Many had perished in the deluge and this saddened Withred. However, his mention of new territory to settle in Britannia had evoked much interest amongst the group, leaving Withred to think that maybe the ill winds of Angeln had blown some good upon Arthur's cause. As a courtesy to Augustus, Withred had occasionally halted the discussion and translated a summary to him.

Now, Mindful that the thorny issue of his desertion had not been mentioned at all during the discussion, Withred decided to broach the subject.

Surprisingly, Cynebald seemed unconcerned over the matter. He shrugged. 'Like all tales it is different depending upon who tells it. Some say you did it for greed, some say for a noble cause. As for me, I think I know you well enough to believe you did it for the best of reasons.'

Sigbald, Cynebald's brother, came in. 'But now we get can it from the stallion's mouth as it were. *Why* did you go over to the Britons?'—he cast a quick glance towards Augustus who sat with Titon at his feet—'not that I've anything against them personally.'

'Let's just say I didn't share Egbert's thoughts on how to treat them after a raid.' His black eyes bore into Sigbald now. 'Come on man, you should know me better than that. I don't kill children; I don't rape women.'

Sigbald shifted uncomfortably. Yet it was not Withred's piercing stare or his emotive assertion that had unsettled him—rather it was the mentioning of Egbert. He looked to his brother who appeared equally uneasy after hearing the name of a man whose name had been mentioned only days before.

Like Sigbald, Cynebald knew about the death of Withred's aunt. Knowing Withred as he did, he was also aware of what the woman meant to him. Always intending to tell him of her heartless murder and rape, he had nevertheless avoided the subject until now, preferring instead to talk of the drama unfolding across the water. But the mention of Egbert had brought to mind his meeting with a man on the shores of the White Sea some ten days gone.

The man, a Saxon, was travelling north, exchanging cooking pots for dried fish as he travelled. After Cynebald had traded with him, a general chitchat followed and during its course Cynebald told the Saxon of the callous murder of Mildrithe, the much beloved healing woman who lived north of him. Then to Cynebald's amazement he learned that the Saxon knew much more about the deed—indeed knew who had committed the outrage. The runt of Egbert, a youth named Raedwald who was known to the merchant, had crossed his path some four days earlier and boasted of the killing. The man had then spat his disgust at the deed, then left to continue his trading along the coast.

Cynebald now realised the time had come to tell Withred. In the way of broaching the subject, he asked him: 'Where are you headed after you leave in the morning?'

A fond smile played upon Withred's lips. 'To my aunt's village of course. It's eight years since I spoke with her. All this talk of war and alliances has not left room for the smaller things—the *important* things. Is she still saving lives and easing aching backs and knees?'

Cynebald cast his eyes downwards. He sighed and said: 'She's dead, Withred.' He raised his head and met Withred's startled stare. 'Slaughtered and raped by Egbert's bastard son—a lout named Raedwald.'

'W—what. Why?' asked Withred, penetrated.

'A blood killing in revenge for the death of his father.'

'But why my aunt? Whatever had she done to deserve …' And then the truth came to him. *He* was to blame. *His* treachery had spurred into action a sick and twisted mind. The mind of a man who veins coursed with Egbert's poisoned blood.

'What's the matter? What's the matter, man?' Augustus who had not understood the words but sensed they had devastated Withred, now moved closer to him. Weeping now, elbows on knees, his fisted hands pressed against his temples, Withred could only shake his head. Muffled and heavy, his sobs drifted downwards as he expelled his grief. After a while, he managed to throw Augustus a wretched look. 'My aunt's dead … I killed her, Gus. It's because of me.' He wiped the snot and tears from him but his pain came again. 'Ah, no … ah, no,' he sobbed as he fell to his knees.

Augustus looked meaningfully to Cynebald. Nodding his comprehension, the Angle stood and walked away, leaving Withred to cough his sorrow onto the earthen floor. A stark Augustus sat with him through his ordeal.

The next morning, pale and drained, Withred was ready for the trail. Cynebald came to him as he readied the horse for the journey. 'I must see her burial site,' he explained to Cynebald. 'At the very least, I need to make an offering to Nerthus beside her grave.'

Cynebald placed a consoling hand upon Withred's arm 'Yes I know, and I've found you another horse for the journey … a big one for Gus.' He stood a moment, then asked: 'And the other things we talked about last night?'

'Ah, yes. How long before your riders return with the other chiefs?'

'Two days. My men left at first light.'

Withred frowned. 'Two days … so long?' He sighed. 'Need brooks no delay, yet late is better than never. I'll see you the day after tomorrow. I'll address the chiefs on this beach.'

Augustus, who was mounted and waiting, leaned in his saddle and in way of thanks took Cynebald's arm in the Roman grasp.

At mid-morning they reached Mildrithe's village. Astounded, the villagers went to Withred and embraced him. They knew him well so he had no recrimination to fear from them. Later in a clearing beside the adjacent woods, Withred went to his aunt's grave and gave offerings to the Goddess Nerthus.

Afterwards, he spoke with Garrick, the headman of the village. He told him of the trouble in Britannia and how land was available for those willing to cross the Oceanus Germanicus and fight for Arthur. After this, he asked Garrick what he knew of his aunt's death.

'I can only tell you how we found her,' sighed Garrick, clearly troubled by the memory. Wishing to spare Withred the details of the level of atrocity meted upon her, Garrick merely told how Mildrithe had been raped before her death.

But Withred insisted Garrick tell him the full story of the savagery. Garrick broke down during his subsequent account and when he finished Withred hugged and thanked him.

Shaken and pale as death, he turned to Augustus. 'Tonight we stay here, Gus. I'll sleep beside my aunt in the grove. Tomorrow we parley with the chiefs, and if it's the last thing I do, I'll get them to follow us to Britannia.'

Next day, Withred Augustus and Garrick rode back to Cynebald's village. In total, thirty-three chiefs had assembled on the gently sloping expanse of shingle which stretched down to the White Sea.

'Better than I thought,' said Withred. 'The talk of new land has stirred their interest, no doubt.'

Augustus looked up to the sky where the sun was visible as a smudge of platinum behind an opaque sheet of cloud. 'Aye, it's not yet midday and there's already a good few here.'

Withred stood in his saddle and peered at the throng. 'And most of them I know, which should help. Come Gus, let's get down to them.'

Many on the beach were mere village headmen who had the endorsement of their people. Others were seasoned campaigners who had plied their trade in Britannia.

Some greeted Withred whilst others avoided him. The interplay was not lost upon Augustus. *"'Like all tales, it is different depending upon who tells it,'"* he said as an aside, quoting a remark made about Withred's desertion. 'Cynebald said it the other night; you translated it to me. It appears he was right; some here have already made up their minds about you.'

'That we'll learn soon,' said Withred. 'The ones who shun me are probably undecided or they wouldn't even have come. See …

Cynebald and Sigbald approach. It seems I'm about to go up in the world.'

People parted as the brothers, carrying a wooden table, stumbled through the shingle. They dropped the table before Withred. The Angle climbed upon the dais and the crowd gathered around him.

'You must already know why I've called this assembly,' he began without preamble. 'Quite simply, I intend to return to Britannia four days from now because I am needed there. Before I go, though, I hope some will see the good sense of following me.'

'Good sense. To go to Britannia and fight another man's battle. Where is the *sense* in that?' A scattered muttering of agreement permeated throughout the crowd. Hereferth, a weathered warrior—a man whose face bore a swirling design of ink—stood confidently below the table awaiting a reply to his question.

'The men you defeat will vacate land above the wall of Hadrian,' returned Withred, 'and it's a drier place than Angeln. A diverse country of forest, pasture and seashore awaits you there.'

'*And* Picts,' said Hereferth. 'You forget Withred, I once rode beyond the wall.' He pointed to his inked face. 'See ... I even got one of the Picts to put this upon me—that's one of

246

the three things they're good at. The others two
are skirmishing and making a nuisance of
themselves.'

'And I'm sure you can deal with them, just as
the Votadini have dealt with them for many
years,' retorted Withred. Not allowing
Hereferth any time to respond, he cast his gaze
over the crowd and continued. 'By my count
over thirty settlements are represented here
today. If each of you can persuade at least sixty
followers to journey to Britannia, then that's
two thousand men for Arthur. Two thousand
extra spears could make all the difference.'

'Spears,' someone shouted. 'I take it you
want men for shieldwalls. My people only
throw their weight against plough or rudder.
Why do you think they are still in Angeln? They
are a peaceful folk.'

'Aye, a peaceful folk they are,' concurred
Withred. 'Our warriors—men like me—left here
to seek their fortunes years ago, that's true
enough, but it's the *future* of our people we
must consider now. This land has become
crowded, and storms take people to the grave
every year. In Britannia, there is abundant space
and each family will be given good land.'

'But that will involve fighting Saxons if the
gossip is to be believed,' said Hereferth. 'Some

regard them as our brethren. How am I to persuade my people to go against them?'

'The gossip bears truth, but the breed of Saxon you'll be up against is no more your brethren than the wolf. These are men of greed and savagery—killers of children and wreckers of property.'

'And you think no man here has stooped to such lows,' said Hereferth. An uneasy murmur went through the crowd at this. 'I see here men who campaigned in Britannia. Men like me who did things they are not proud of.'

'Be that as it may, but we cannot allow ourselves to dwell upon past actions. None of us falls easily to sleep these days, *including me*, but war is a savage beast that touches both victor and defeated and stays with men until they die; war will not go away.'

'Your war, not ours! And what of the people you once rode with. I hear you abandoned them in the forests of Britannia.' Smala, a stout chieftain from southern Angeln, took a defiant step to the front of the crowd, his face demanding an answer.

Withred's voice cut through the ensuing expectant silence. 'I do not deny what happened, yet I am not ashamed. In fact, it is the one good deed *I did* in Britannia. I abandoned not them but their appetite for wanton destruction. And, yes, I admit I thrust my spear into Egbert's black heart, but in doing so I performed a service for all the good men of this world. I will fight to my demise—all who know me cannot doubt that—but I will not ride with men who kill the weak, the old, or the defenseless!' A silence fell as Withred's passionate invective hit home. He looked at them, their faces a sea of expectancy now. He knew he had them; knew he could play his last decisive card. He continued. 'But listen to me now; those of you who haven't heard the news already—the spirit of Egbert tragically lives on and rides with the people you would be fighting against. Raedwald is Egbert's spawn and he killed and raped Mildrithe, my aunt—a woman who many of you knew, and a woman who treated you with love and care. *That* is the type of Saxon you'll ride against. These are not the farmers and fishermen of Saxony. The Saxon raiders in Britannia are not our brethren; they are chancers who are driven by their burning lust for gold.'

Withred allowed his words to sink in as he jumped to the ground. Augustus, with Titon at his feet, was sitting against the table. 'Sounds like you stirred up a wasps' nest just then,' he said in reference to the widespread, dynamic exchanges now occurring. 'You need to fill me in on what you told them.'

Withred explained the situation to Augustus.

'You think you can sway them, then?' asked Augustus.

'Some of them at least. I'm not sure about Hereferth—he's the one with the inked face— and I really want him with us. He and his men will bring a lot of know-how. I fought alongside him once. A viscous man he is, and he has bowmen at his disposal which is unusual. Because of that, I'm sure Dominic would be glad to see him.'

'What about the little chubby bastard?' asked Augustus. 'He seemed to challenge you and speaks with this Hereferth now.'

'That's Smala, another good man and he's tight with Hereferth. They campaigned together when in Britannia.'

'So why are they back here now? Why did they not settle on British soil?'

'The land they wanted fell into Saxon hands so they returned to their villages in Angeln. Yet, they're here at this assembly, and that tells me they've grown restless again.'

Augustus nudged Withred. 'You need to get back on the table, man. They've quietened and are waiting for more.'

'Step up with me, dog and all,' said Withred. You're about to clinch this for us.'

Augustus shrugged. 'Whatever you say. Get ready to translate.'

The table bent and creaked as Augustus hauled himself upwards. Two heads taller anyway than the loftiest man in the assembly he loomed against the backdrop of milky sky. His appearance, with Titon bristling and standing menacingly beside him, stimulated an awe-laced gasp from the gripped crowd.

Withred began. 'What needed to be said has passed. Decisions now need to be made. This man'—he pointed at Augustus—'is British and will stand in our shieldwall. There're more like him—stout fellows who will not be cowed by Saxon threats or Saxon death riders seeking to intimidate.'

'Cowed by *them*, I am cowed by *him*!' shouted someone. 'Why ask for our help, just send him against them, they'll shit where they stand!'

Laughter followed and Withred turned to Augustus. 'Now's the time, Gus. Tell them why they should come over.'

Augustus stepped to the front of the table. His voice boomed across the gathering. 'I am British and dispossessed.' He let his words become absorbed as Withred translated; nodding as if to say, *Yes, even a man like me can be beaten.* Careful not to compromise his aura of invincibility, he continued. 'I fought back though and eventually defeated the Saxons who came at me ... but it was too late ... all of my friends were lying dead ... I had to abandon my village.' His tone dropped, becoming melancholic. 'So now I know how it feels to be homeless.' Silence followed. After a moment, Augustus pointed to the nearby sea. 'But for you people here, yonder ocean is your enemy. Soon it will flood you out again; take *more* lives. In Britannia you will not have such worry, and men like me'—he thumped his chest in emphasis—'big, brutal men like me will stand beside you.' He looked to Withred. 'This man is too proud to defend his reputation and so seem to be begging for acceptance, so I'll tell you this: I know him to be true and compassionate; and that is why he turned his back on those who acted as devils; that is why he now uses his skills to protect the weak, as his Goddess and yours—Nerthus—would have him do.' Augustus waited a moment as Withred translated his last statement, then he pointed at his own chest. 'And this Briton now asks *all of you* to stand beside him. Your reward will be good land and a worthy future on my blessed isle.'

Withred took over now. He looked directly at Hereferth and Smala, who had listened fascinated to Augustus. 'That's it boys. All the talking is done; I've no time to dwell much longer in Angeln. Like I said at the beginning of this meeting, I leave in four days with or without you—the time it will take you to muster your people should you decide to come with me.' He lifted his head and shouted now to the horde. 'Yes four days ... that's how long I will wait. Any man here who wishes for glory and land, be back here with your people in four days' time!'

The meeting over as far as he was concerned, Withred stepped from the table. Hereferth approached him. 'I would speak with you in private over this,' he said. 'Before I commit myself or my warriors, I will need some assurances.'

'Of course I'll speak to you,' said Withred as many more men pressed him for private discussion. 'I'll speak to you all, even if it takes me all day.'

CHAPTER FIFTEEN

Twenty-five days had passed since Arthur had held his war council. Gherwan and Murdoc had returned with news of Ffodor's rejection of aid. Dominic had been dispatched to Aquae Sulis along with thirty of Arthur's cavalry. Will was still out in the field.

Arthur walked with his woman, Heledd, beside the towering walls of Brythonfort.

'We number just one thousand men and two hundred knights,' he said. 'If they come at us now we're finished or at the very least besieged.'

'Our men watch Akeman Street for that's the Saxons' usual rout to these parts, and Dominic is up at Aquae Sulis keeping his eye on the crossroads,' reassured Heledd. 'And fast horses are ready to get any news to us within a day.'

'But still no sign of Withred and Gus,' said Arthur as he turned towards the hefty gates of Brythonfort.

Heledd slipped her hands around Arthur's arm and forced him to turn to her. 'Withred said thirty days; it's only been twenty-five, give him time my love.'

Arthur looked into Heledd's intense eyes and stroked her blonde hair. Tied as a braided band around her head, her forelocks kept the rest of her long hair from her face. Arthur imagined the sport that Guertepir or any run-of-the-mill Saxon warlord would have with her. After just a couple of months at their debauched hands, her skin, pure and unwrinkled now, would become blotched and grey; her body, plump and supple, would quickly become bone-thin and stooped. He knew this because he had seen such sights before when abused girls and women had found their way to Brythonfort. He shook the image from his head and tried to be positive. 'Yes, I know ... give them time, I really should. Listen'—he held his hand to his ear as grating shouts came from beyond the wall—'Erec's getting the men into shape as we speak.'

As she passed through the gates and entered Brythonfort with Arthur, Heledd peered up the hill. 'Sounds like Flint's been busy. How many men have you counted?

'Over nine hundred. Most of them raw, though.' A loud crash came from the drill ground. 'Hear that. They're practicing with the shields.' They passed a workshop where five men laboured at anvils. Unable to talk above the clang of metal upon metal they continued up the slope towards Erec and the recruits. As the clatter from the smithy faded, Arthur was able to speak again. 'The smiths deserve much credit. Day and night they've been forging short stabbing swords for the shieldwall—scores of them up to now. We fight as Romans and that should give us advantage.'

As they neared the exercise the clashing and shouting intensified. Watching events, sat Flint upon his white mare.

Arthur met him, patted the neck of his horse, and talked in its ear. 'There girl, what've you been up to with that useless lump on your back.' As the mare nodded and snorted its recognition, Arthur, smiling, looked up at Flint. 'Heledd reckons you've been busy. I told her you ride from here every day and find a quiet stream and fall asleep.'

'Don't believe a word of it,' said Heledd, giving Arthur a reproachful slap on the shoulder. 'He told me you'd enlisted over nine hundred men.'

'That's right Heledd, I *have* been busy, regardless of what the high lord told you.'

Arthur rubbed his shoulder in mock hurt as if Augustus himself had just slapped him. 'Seriously Flint, how're they shaping up?'

'Well ... considering this is the first morning of their training, and seeing that most of them are farmers who never held shield or a sword, pretty awful really.'

Flint's irony promoted a grunt of a laugh from Arthur. All then fell silent as they viewed Erec at work.

He had formed some of the recruits into two opposing shieldwalls, some fifty men wide. Each man held a shield and a short wooden sword. Four deep and pushed up tight against the front men stood another two hundred. Watching the drill from the flanks and awaiting their turn, stood another five hundred men.

Erec had placed himself between the two walls. He held his arms at shoulder height as if pushing back the men and barked out his instructions. 'This is your first clash so I want you to advance slowly. Keep tight to the man beside you; I don't want to see any gaps in the wall, and remember: this is to get you familiar with meeting your enemy face to face. I want no heroics here today; you are no use to me or Arthur if you take injury.' He nodded to a nearby groom who held his horse. The man brought the animal to him and he mounted. He rode slowly from between the gap. 'Not yet!' he shouted, as some of the men, trembling with anticipation, moved forward from the wall. The men went back in line. 'Bear in mind this is but a drill and you are going to practice it relentlessly until you can perform it in your sleep.' He was silent a moment as he observed the men. Keen-eyed, a swirling fog of breath rose above them as they awaited his instruction. Some were as young as fifteen, some as old as sixty. All knew they had to pay their dues to Brythonfort.

'Slowly! ... walk towards each other!' Erec's shout rang out crisply, and the opposing shieldwalls began to close the gap between them. Almost at once, the walls became jagged and broken. Several of the shield-bearing men stumbled to the ground and the men behind attempted to walk over them. 'Stop where you are. Stop NOW!' Erec played the reins of his horse steering the beast nearer to the rumpus.

Feeling rather foolish, Pwyll picked himself and his shield up from the ground. Panting with the effort of the drill, he got back in line and awaited Erec's further orders. He stole a quick glance at Arlyn, glad the fellow stood beside him. Like Pwyll, Arlyn was a simple, unassuming man. He had quickly taken to Pwyll upon arriving at Brythonfort, which in itself was rare, because men usually mocked Pwyll and his slow demeanor.

'Shoulder to shoulder remember,' said Arlyn as he pressed close. Pwyll nodded and lifted his shield. His left arm went through its leather loops; his right hand held a wooden sword.

When Flint had arrived at Aquae Sulis a week earlier looking for men, he had gone to the quarry and approached Pwyll directly. Pwyll had made up his mind to go to Brythonfort for training as soon as Augustus was mentioned. His hero would be in the shieldwall eventually and that was good enough for him, because since Augustus had saved him from humiliation in the wine shop his life had become much easier. That such an immense man looked out for him had spurred even his most dogged tormentors to leave him alone. Augustus' expulsion of Hal and Menw from Aquae Sulis was the talk of the city and Pwyll had since enjoyed his cups of wine in peace.

Pwyll first sight of Brythonfort, looming as a stranded whale on the distant horizon, made him gasp as if he had risen to the surface of the water. The enormity of the bastion was almost too much for him to take in. He had never seen anything that came anywhere near in size to the enormous buttress and its surrounding stone wall. He had exchanged an open-mouthed stare with Arlyn, who by then had befriended him. But that was merely the start of the wonder they were to experience on their first morning. When inside Brythonfort and still stunned by the magnitude of the structure, Arthur, whom neither had seen until that day, came to them and the others.

Pwyll hardly heard Arthur's stirring speech, such was the utter exuberance he experienced in the man's presence. Quite simply, Arthur radiated an aura Pwyll could *actually* feel as if it were a tangible entity. Standing nearly as tall as Augustus, Arthur was raw boned and fair of face. With eyes burning with conviction, he had walked amongst the men and actually touched Pwyll on the shoulder as he delivered his passionate address. The touch came as a lightning strike to Pwyll, who immediately realised that he, Pwyll, would run naked into the pits of hell if Arthur but asked him to.

The introduction of Erec, his instructor, did little to diminish Pwyll's awe. Another man who exuded power and authority, Erec had at first seemed harsh and uncompromising as he chivvied the raw recruits into some semblance of order. Two days were then to pass before Erec allowed anyone to touch either shield or wooden sword. These objects had remained stacked, enticing and mysterious, on the edge of the drill ground, as Erec had pummeled the rudiments of military discipline into the recruits.

Now Pwyll hefted his shield and grasped his sword as he readied himself to move forward in the wall again. Six of Erec's assistants strode through the gap between the shieldwalls checking them for trueness. One of them stood before Pwyll, and pushed and pulled at his shield. 'Good man,' he encouraged, as Pwyll held firm. 'Meet any force with an equal amount and more.' He and the others instructors went along the line throwing themselves at the shields in a test of their solidity. When satisfied the walls were steady and ready to advance again, they ran from the gap.

Erec again took over. 'At my command, move forward, this time slower and in a straight line. You men at the back, do not push unless I tell you to do so. For now just *follow* the shields.' Silence and tension ensued. 'Move now,' shouted Erec.

Pwyll shuffled forward, the clacking of wooden shield against wooden shield the prominent noise as the space between the two walls closed. In spite of Erec's instruction, Pwyll had to fight the urge to rush ahead at the opposing shieldwall.

'That's better, keep it slow and get ready to engage! Easy, easy, come together; DO NOT LOSE YOUR FORM! Come together NOW!'

A gasp left Pwyll as an earsplitting crash heralded the meeting of shields. Regardless of Erec's earlier edict, the men behind him failed to check their momentum and pressed forward in a powerful surge. A whoosh of outrushing air was expelled from the lungs of the shield carriers on both sides. Across from Pwyll, and nose to nose with him, stood his shield-carrying counterpart—a middle-aged farmer who until that day had never spoken in anger to any man, let alone glare at one as if he were some Saxon dog out to rape his wife.

'MEN AT THE BACK STOP YOUR PUSHING!' Erec slid from his horse and walked to the edge of the press. As his assistants paced behind the walls, pulling away those who had not heeded him, Erec tested the pressure upon the shields nearest. He stepped back so all could hear him. 'This gives you a flavor of how close you men at the front will be to your opponent. You will smell the ale on his breath, and as he spits out his foul curses you will see his last meal smeared on every rotten tooth in his mouth. But it will be far worse than this. They will attempt to push you back. Men will slash at your ankles ... stab at your eyes ... try to breach the wall. You will feel crushed as your own men behind lend weight to you and attempt to push the Saxon wall backwards. And while all this is happening you will be expected to cut at them with your swords.'

Erec walked behind the walls so that men at the back could hear him clearly. 'You men may not hold a shield at the moment but that is not to say your role is unimportant. On the contrary, you are part of a whole. Firstly, as soon as the shieldwalls meet, you must shove with all your might. Keep shoving and be ready to move forward to the front of the line. The reason for this is twofold. Firstly, you must be prepared to take a shield and give the shield bearers respite because—believe me—life at the front is intense. Shield bearers you will then drop to the rear and lend your weight to the shieldwall. The second reason for getting to the front will be to replace dead men.'

As Erec let his last statement hang, Pwyll gave a sideways glance and saw his own shocked expression mirrored by Arlyn. The shield-bearing farmer opposite had also stopped glaring at him. Now his eyes swam with fear and disquiet. Erec took up the thread of his instruction again. 'Yes ... this is war and some of you will die.'

Erec continued to saunter behind the walls, imparting the reality of combat to the men. Arthur, who by now viewed the exercise from the elevation of his own horse, looked grave. 'They all know there are casualties in war but that's the first time many will have heard it said in such stark terms.'

Flint spoke. 'Now we must wait and see if any desert. Until now, the newness of everything—the wonder of seeing Brythonfort and yourself, high lord—has enthralled most of them, probably to the exclusion of thoughts of their own mortality.'

'Three in ten, Flint,' said Arthur. 'That would be the usual number of desertions at training. Gods know how many of them will run from the actual battlefield.'

By now, Erec had completed his slow instructive walk around the back of the two shieldwalls. Pungent in the still air, the smell of tension had become cloying. He remounted his horse. 'Next we will feel what it's like to have many men come against your wall.' He gave a nod to his assistants and the six men ran behind one of the groups. 'Men on the right!' shouted Erec. 'At the count of three I want you to push against your opposing wall. Men on the left, you must resist the push. Hear me on this. I said RESIST! That means pushing back enough to hold position and nothing more.' He waited a moment, gave signal by eye contact with his trainers, then began. 'On three, get ready. ONE ... TWO ... THREE!'

A spontaneous roar went up from the pushing wall and immediately the men opposite began to move backwards. Peasants at the back skidded and slid on the dried mud of the drill ground as they pushed against the slide in a desperate effort to stop the retreat. Some went down, trampled underfoot.

'STOP! STOP!' Erec had been expecting the collapse. Now his instructors pulled men from the back of the advancing wall. Another shout from Erec saw the surge abate.

Pwyll by now had his face pressed firmly against his shield and stood upright only because the crush of men against him had prevented him from going to ground. Arlyn actually had his back to his shield, having lost total control of it. Both still held their swords but their arms were pinned, rendering the weapons useless.

'Stand down! Stand down!' shouted Erec. 'Give your shields to the watching men.' They broke up and the fresh men took the shields and formed two new opposing walls. The displaced men, panting and white faced, slumped to the ground to take their turn to observe.

Erec addressed the exhausted group. 'What you experienced is what will happen in battle if you do not meet force with force. Purposely, I told one wall to push and the other wall to resist. The result was there for all to see. To attempt to *merely* hold your ground is NOT GOOD ENOUGH! When you meet the Saxon wall the supporting men must push until they can push no more. Fail to do this and you will go backwards and the front men will be crushed against their shields and be of no use.' Erec smiled for the first time then, as he looked at the sea of worried faces before him. 'No doubt some of you now have flat noses.' His lighter tone engendered a ripple of laughter amongst the men, and some rubbed their noses, smiling wryly. Erec brought back a measure of gravitas and continued. 'Fail to push back with every sinew of your bodies, good men of Britannia, and you will be trampled upon and defeated—left upon the battlefield butchered and forsaken, good only to feed the crows.'

He turned to the new shieldwalls. 'This time you will both advance upon my count,' he said. 'When you meet, you will stop and push only when I tell you to do so. Then, *both* shieldwalls will heave forward with every grain of strength. Before this day is out you will all be capable of standing your ground. Above all you will have learned how to wield your swords within the press of surrounding men.'

Arthur looked at Flint and Heledd. 'Mars help us,' he said. 'Let us hope that men of such inexperience man the opposing armies also.'

CHAPTER SIXTEEN

Will had feared the worst when messengers had left Camulodunum after the meeting of the Saxon lords. Five days later, his fears were confirmed when the first of four huge gatherings of warriors approached from the southern road.

He knew these were not mere raiding parties—there were too many men for that—rather they were freemen—the *fyrd*—men enlisted by their Saxon lords. With them rode seasoned warriors equipped for a prolonged campaign. With the first arrivals came a number of covered wagons provisioned with supplies. Wives and children rode the wagons or walked beside them, and soon the open ground before the gates of Camulodunum had become alive with people.

Two more days passed, during which time Will witnessed the arrival of three more similar gatherings. Such was their count that a tented village grew on the outskirts of town. Now Will's work began in earnest as he mingled with the newly arrived and took tally of their numbers. He counted eighteen hundred men equipped for war. Within the walls of Camulodunum, another four hundred dwelt.

Alarmed, Will considered returning at once to Arthur with news of the Saxon addition of more than two thousand men to the estimated four thousand who waited at Guertepir's ringfort. But he had to be sure the swarm indeed intended to leave Camulodunum and travel westwards to join the Hibernian king.

As well as the Saxon encampment, there was still the matter of Cunedda's and Diarmait's two hundred strong envoy. As a precaution, Hrodgar had prevented the men from entering the town some twelve days earlier. Since then, they had filled their time drinking and sparring, the clang of swords and the bray of their laughter a common sound both day and night.

Will soon realised that the presence of these men—some of them Britons like himself—provided an opportunity to gather intelligence which could be invaluable to Arthur. With this in mind, he decided to undertake the risky endeavor of infiltrating the British and Hibernian camp.

During the previous days, Will had occasionally chanced the short journey to a nearby wood. Here, he had set simple twine snares near a sandy mound riddled with rabbit holes. Every day had produced at least one rabbit and these he had either eaten or traded on.

With his two latest kills, he now approached the British camp. Shucked into the hoods of their tunics as a soft rain fell around them, two Votadini sat against the crumbling town walls as they warmed themselves beside a lively campfire.

'Two coneys, caught but today; I can almost smell them roasting on your fine fire,' said Will, approaching them with the affected air of a man who is comfortable and familiar with his surroundings.

One of the group, a pallid youth whose greasy hair poked from his hood, eyed Will with disdain. 'What have we here; another trader and this one's British.' He spat into the fire.

Another, beside him, rubbed warmth into his hands and held them close to the dancing flames. In spite of himself, the man had started to salivate. He nodded towards the rabbits. 'What you want for 'em?'

'Nothing but your fire to cook them on,' said Will. 'It'll save me the job of trying to start one in this rain. For that you get to share them with me.' *Coldhands and Sallow*, thought Will as he appraised the two Britons. *Coldhands and Sallow should be your names.*

Sallow gave a dry little laugh. 'So you want nothing but the heat from our fire. Maybe we should take gold from you as well for the privilege.'

But Will, confident the men would relish fresh meat, had already crouched beside Coldhands and started to skin the rabbits. The two Votadini fell into a contemplative silence as they watched Will at work. He glanced at them as he threw the skins to one side and begun to gut and butcher the meat. 'Never seen the town as crowded,' he said. 'Rumour has it something big's about to happen.'

'So what's a Briton like you doin' in a Saxon town,' asked Coldhands, refusing to be drawn.

Will by now had pushed the meat onto skewers. He threw them into the embers of the fire. 'There ... they'll soon be done.' He turned his attention to the two Votadini. 'What? ... Me?' He faked the impression that Coldhand's question had hardly registered with him. 'Oh, I trade with the low-lifes; supply them with meat. Ignore what a set of bastards they are and you get paid well here.' He decided to go for it. 'What about you two ... you're Britons from the north by your accents. I did a bit of scouting for

271

the Romans you see ... been above the wall a few times.' He pointed at them, a knowing smile on his face. 'Let me guess'—he wagged his finger at them as if struggling to recall a name—'Votanti ... yes that's it. Votanti people you are. I never forget—'

'Votadini,' interrupted Sallow.

'Eh ... yes ... Votadini,' said Will as he turned the rabbit meat over in the fire. 'Votadini—of course. Plagued to death by Picts as I recall. That's why I was up in your territory. Ran the Picts ragged we did, me and the Romans. Did your folk a service.' He regarded the two Britons again and asked casually: 'So why're you here rubbing shoulders with these Saxon turds?'

Sallow looked to Coldhands, who shrugged back at him. Taking the gesture as an endorsement and unable to resist a little boast, Sallow said: 'We're here to escort our lord, Cunedda. Hand-picked we are—the best of our tribe.'

Will whistled appreciatively. He gave Sallow a wink and a smile. 'If I'd known that, I might have thought twice about approaching you earlier.' He threw a piece of cooked meat to Sallow and one to Coldhands. The men ate silently for a while until Will asked, 'So when do you expect to move out of Camulodunum?'

Coldhands appeared gloomy and a little anxious as he chewed on the tender rabbit meat. 'Should've been today, but the last lot of Saxons arrived too late so I expect it'll be at first light tomorrow.'

'A long trip, too,' said Will, taking a chance. 'A good twelve days for the mounted, fifteen for the foot soldiers.'

'We're on horseback, so we'll be the first to see Aquae Sulis,' blurted Sallow.

Coldhands frowned at Sallow and seemed ready to lambast him, but Will decided to get in first. 'Oh ... don't worry about me; he's not said anything I didn't already know; there are enough loose tongues in this town to pave the streets of Londinium. As long as whatever you're up to doesn't affect my trade here I couldn't care less.' He stood up and wiped his greasy hands on his buckskin pants. The youth had told him all he needed to know. Aquae Sulis was the rallying point and probably the alliance's first target. He threw his rabbit bone into the fire, ready to make his excuses and go.

His concern grew when Coldhands got to his feet.

'Not so fast,' said the Votadinite. 'You appear from shit-knows-where, give us free food, and as soon as my stupid friend reveals our purpose you make to leave.' He eyed Will suspiciously. 'Maybe it would be better if we checked you out. You say you are familiar with this town; if that's the case you can take me now to someone who can vouch for you.'

Will realised he had massively misjudged the situation; more precisely he had misjudged the man who stood threateningly before him. Should he run or face him out. A quick glance at Sallow—whose glare matched that of Coldhands—made up his mind. He laughed, as if astounded by Coldhands' mistrust. 'Of course I'll take you to someone who can speak for me, though what you think I am is beyond my—'

Leaving his words hanging, he dashed away. Knowing it was his only option, he skidded and zig-zagged through the milling crowds, scattering camp fires as he went.

'STOP THAT MAN, HE'S A SPY!' Coldhands' shout rang out behind Will as he darted through a narrow gap between two covered wagons. He half fell, half climbed, over a water barrel that blocked his way. Panting and disorientated, he picked himself up and tried to establish his bearings. Figures, shown up as shadows darting before a nearby bonfire, indicated the cry of alarm had been effective. He turned to the edge of the open ground and viewed its concealing darkness. Somewhere out there was his horse. He ran towards the gloom, but had covered only half the distance when Sallow hit him from behind. Catching him was one thing but Sallow soon realised that holding him was another—the man felt as if he were made of twisted steel. Before he knew it, he found himself on his back with Will at his neck.

The ax hit Will before he had the chance to slide his knife across Sallow's throat. Two inches of cold iron penetrated his chest, knocking him backwards. His assailant snatched the blade from his flesh and raised it above him. Will gasped and readied himself for death.

'No! Do not finish him! We need to take him to Cunedda!' The voice belonged to Coldhands, who had just arrived with a small crowd.

'Don't know why you're bothering, he won't live, anyway,' said the ax man as he watched the bubbles of dark blood emerging from Will's wound. 'I pierced his lung and Woden-knows what else.'

'Still, we need to get him to Cunedda,' said Coldhands. 'He's probably Arthur's man.'

Cunedda swept his arm across the table, clearing from it the accumulated debris of twelve days. 'Lay him down; *I'll* deal with him now.' He looked at the dying man, then turned his attention to Coldhands. 'Pumped you for information, you say?'

'Yes, before he ran off ... tried to escape when I challenged him.'

Cunedda studied Will. Something was familiar about him. 'I'd guess he's a ranger by the way he's dressed. What did you tell him?'

'Nothing, my lord ... Er ... leastways, I didn't.'

Cunedda gave the other a stern glance. '*You* didn't. Who did then? And what was he told?'

'My friend told him we were headed for Aquae Sulis, that's when he ran off.'

'Did anyone else hear this?'

'No, my lord.'

Fuming inwardly, Cunedda's stare was withering. 'Your friend could have compromised this mission, where is he now?'

'Back beside our fire, my lord.'

Cunedda gave a 'humph!' then guided Coldhands to the door by his elbow. 'Get out and tell your friend I want to see him tomorrow before we leave for the west.' He pushed

Coldhands through the door and turned to Diarmait and Raedwald.

Since the decisive meeting in the alehouse, Cunedda, Diarmait and Raedwald had lived together in the hut whilst awaiting the muster. The coming night was the last Cunedda would ever have to endure with Raedwald and both he and Diarmait could not wait for the morning. Because the Saxon youth was unpopular even with his own people, he had billeted with them since arriving in Camulodunum. But, oh, how his vacuous boasting and wondrous tales had grated upon them. Mercifully, their frequent need to liaise with the Saxon chiefs had taken them away from the hut and away from Raedwald.

As he turned from the door, Cunedda noticed Raedwald at the table. He fixed him with an amazed stare. 'What ... what are you doing?'

Raedwald, who wielded his knife, hovered over Will, hissing venom into his ear. He turned to Cunedda. 'Doing what I'm good at—getting a spy to spill his guts.' He moved the blade towards Will's chest wound. 'See ... this will get him to —'

Cunedda and Diarmait exchanged a look. Eyes aflame, Cunedda darted to Raedwald, whose mouth had shut with a snap. He pushed him away. 'What you're good at! What you're good at is expelling drivel!' His patience had finally snapped with Raedwald. '*What your good at* I have still to witness, and I'll be watching you closely on the battlefield to see if you can match your empty words with worthy deeds.' He pointed at Will, who lay oblivious and close to death. 'Put a knife to him and he'll die you idiot. Can you not see he is beyond torture.'

As Cunedda raged, Diarmait went to Will. 'You're right, his end is near. If you need to talk to him, better you do it now.'

Cunedda pushed Raedwald to the wall. 'Stay there and *don't move,*' he warned. He joined Diarmait at the table and pulled up a chair so his head was level with Will's. Pragmatic as ever, he said: 'You're going to your God, fellow, and there's nothing you or I can do about it.'

Will's head swam as he fought to retain his lucidity. The man's voice, his braided hair, the piercings on his face—all were familiar to him. Perhaps he had met him when riding above the wall scouting for Rome. He tried to speak, but the words would not come. He felt at peace and devoid of pain as his blood seeped on to the table.

'You visited my land; I've seen you before; I remember now,' continued Cunedda. He turned to Diarmait. 'The Votadini worked closely with Rome, kept the Picts from them, and in return they gave us a measure of protection. This man was a scout for Rome.'

'He's seen a life, then,' said Diarmait. 'Bet he never thought his death would come in a Saxon town with a fellow Briton and a hoary Hibernian at his bed.'

Will wheezed as his lung spat blood through the hole in his chest. The men above him talked quietly and seemed content to let him be. He thought of Britannia—of its achingly beautiful diversity. He had seen all of the land, from the southern coast to the wall of Antoine many miles north. Woods and marsh, pasture and mountain; the image was painted upon the canvas of his memory. But it was the rippling fields of barley, golden under a September sun and swelling like an inland sea, which became clear to him now. Villages, their huts thatched and nestling in the folds of the land, lay beside the barley fields. Children, enjoying the late summer sun, ran through the crops—their chatter and treble audible and lovely. And then only darkness as death came to him.

Upon hearing his final sigh, Raedwald approached the table—his look of dismay born from the realisation that the Briton had died without further torment.

Cunedda turned when sensing Raedwald beside him. Such was the Votadini chief's glare at him that Raedwald took a step back. Cunedda's voice was cold. 'You ... get someone to take this man's body to the woods and bury it.'

But Raedwald was ruffled. '*Bury* him?' Why not just feed him to the pigs. The scum would have scuttled back to Arthur and warned him.'

With an exasperated, 'huh!' Diarmait got to his feet and grabbed Raedwald by his shoulder. He guided him towards the door. 'Just do as Cunedda says. We've heard enough of the world-according-to-Raedwald for one lifetime.' He shoved him through the door and shut it.

Cunedda had covered Will's face. 'He was a worthy man'—he cast a glance towards the door—'unlike that Saxon runt.' He appraised Will again. 'This man plied an honest trade— one that got him killed in the end. In the same position, I would probably have done as he did.'

Diarmait nodded. 'Yes, he at least deserves to go into the ground now. I will personally see that his body is not despoiled before it happens.'

The month of March arrived the next morning. The four Saxon chiefs: Hrodgar, Wigstan, Cenhelm and Osbeorn, their horses caparisoned for war, rode from the gates of Camulodunum in their full splendor. Between them, they had gathered over two thousand men, half of whom owned horses or ponies. The enlisted men—the fyrd—made up the other half, and were mostly on foot. These would trail three days behind the main party as they walked with their families beside the wagons.

Whoops and shouts had begun to puncture the drone of lively conversation coming from the hordes gathered before the town gates.

Diarmait and Cunedda met the Saxon chiefs when they emerged. 'As planned, we take the road to Londinium, then the road westwards to Aquae Sulis,' said Hrodgar.

'And riders have been dispatched?' asked Cunedda.

Not familiar with being questioned over his leadership, Hrodgar was brusque. *'Of course.* Three days ago; do you think I would leave anything to chance?'

Cunedda sighed. 'No Hrodgar, but perhaps you are human like the rest of us. It does no harm to check these things.'

'Worry not, man. I told you I sent the riders. As we speak, Guertepir knows we'll meet him at Aquae Sulis in twelve days' time.' He turned to the nearby woods. 'I hear a spy was caught and killed. Pity you couldn't get some information from him before you so thoughtfully buried him between the trees.'

'It's the living ones we need to worry about,' said Cunedda. 'He was stopped before he could get back to Arthur and that's the important thing.'

'Little matter,' said Hrodgar indifferently. 'The pigs will grub him up anyway.' He looked over to Cunedda's men who were mounted and lingered nearby. 'Lead us out, I'll allow you that. Let's get this Aquae Sulis thing over. Then we can get at Arthur and enter the western lands.'

CHAPTER SEVENTEEN

Dominic was back at Brythonfort. Recalled by Arthur, after Will had failed to send any news from Camulodunum, he now dwelt in the king's hall with five anxious men. Spaced out at intervals around the huge round table sat Arthur, Gherwan, Murdoc, Flint and Erec.

'So the northern roads from Corinium were quiet when you left?' asked Arthur.

Dominic nodded in affirmation. 'Apart from the trade in pottery, the route was quiet.'

'No sight or sound of Votadini travelling down the southern roads from Deva, then?'

'None. I left Nairn there. He'll soon get news back here if anything stirs.'

'And Tomas?'

'He still watches Guertepir in the west.'

'In which case, I need you to go south again. Will hasn't shown yet. More worryingly, he's sent no word with the dispatch riders'

'No sign of Saxon movement from *them*?'

'None. Not even sight of Augustus and Withred. As I speak we have two hundred knights and a little fewer than one thousand inexperienced men to meet whatever Guertepir throws at us.'

'I'll leave in the morning and travel towards Londinium and see what I can glean,' said Dominic, '... and don't worry too much about Will. He gets absorbed in his work.'

Arthur frowned. 'I can't help it ... it's my nature. The last thing I need is to lose one of my best scouts.' He turned to Erec. 'The recruits seem to be doing well, how long before you're happy with them?'

'They're probably as good as I can get them,' said Erec. 'The only way they'll improve now is fighting for real.'

'How many desertions?'

'Surprisingly few—thirty or forty. I've impressed on them that running away only delays things. Told them they'll definitely be up against it sooner or later. Said, if they have to fight they may as well do it in a group and not alone.'

'Good, that's something at least.' Arthur paused, reflecting. He turned to Gherwan. 'Assuming we get some men—say one thousand—from Angeln, that gives us two thousand in total against the four thousand we know for sure ride alongside Guertepir. Add to that a probable two thousand Saxons. That's six thousand against us.'

Gherwan tried for optimism. 'Grim figures I can't deny, but we've held these lands for years with only two hundred well-equipped knights.'

'Yes, against war bands of no more than fifty.'

'But Brythonfort is formidable. Surely we can hold out here for many months.'

'And to what end? While we wait and starve, they'll ravish and lay waste to all the land. They'll kill and enslave every poor soul outside the protection of Brythonfort.'

'But it's six thousand against two thousand … you said it yourself. What other choice do we have?'

'To take high ground and meet them.'

Gherwan was sceptical. 'But surely they'll overwhelm us with such numbers.'

Arthur's voice betrayed his frustration. 'Yes, they probably will, but besiegement is nothing but a slow death. With full-on war at least we get a chance to hit them.'

'High ground, you say,' came in Murdoc. 'Apart from Brythonfort, the land is mostly flat around here. How do we get them to come to us, anyway?'

'We don't, Murdoc,' said Arthur, now with a glimmer of enthusiasm. '*We* go to *them*. We go to Aquae Sulis. I'm sure now the spa will be their first point of attack, lying as it does at the meeting of roads.'

'And there is high ground at Aquae Sulis?'

'Mynydd Baddon—or Mount Badon in some dialects—rears over the town.'

'You're suggesting we march to the place now?' Gherwan's tone was one of mild surprise.

'No I'm not saying that. Not even a man with my optimism can foresee any outcome other then a quick defeat if we take just one thousand farmers to meet them. No, at the very least we must wait to see what Withred and Gus turn up with. Gods!'—Arthur placed his fists against his temples in an act of frustration—'Damn Ffodor! Damn him taking things personally. Why he couldn't see that some things are above petty grievances is beyond me! With his men we would at least have a chance.'

Gherwan and Murdoc exchanged a glance. Two weeks earlier, they too had endured such frustration when trying to persuade the stubborn lord of Travena to join Arthur's cause. The best Gherwan could offer now was, 'He might yet have a change of heart and decide to ride? Who knows what drives the man.'

'Trouble is, it's all *perhaps* and *maybes*,' sighed Arthur. 'We can't fight them with guesswork. All we can do now is sit and—'

The door to the hall opened and a guard walked in with another man. The fast rider, Nairn, was recognizable to all. He burst out with his news. 'Men amass at Corinium, my lord. Guertepir's army and a force of Votadini from the northern road now move southwards towards Aquae Sulis.'

'How large an army?'

'Close to four thousand.'

'How long before they reach the city?'

'They move at walking pace so the best part of a day is my guess.'

'Do they have siege equipment—ladders, rams and the like?'

'None that I saw.

'And how long did it take you to get here on fast horses?'

'Over half a day, high lord.'

'Was Tomas with you at Aquae Sulis?'

'He was.'

'Then go back to him and continue to watch the town. If the armies move from the place then I must be told on the very day. Otherwise just watch and wait. Tremendous effort man, I thank you.'

Nairn left and a silence briefly fell over the assembly as the news sank in. A shiver like impending death passed over Erec as an awareness hit him. 'My wife,' he said. 'My Morgana—she is in the town. I must go to her.'

Arthur, thinking rapidly, dealt with Erec first. 'Yes—yes, of course; you must go at once. Thirty of my knights are there. Ride the fast messenger horses. They're stabled along the route every six miles and will get you inside the city before Guertepir and the Votadini arrive. Go now while enough daylight remains. Set Morgana and any other civilians on their way and send them back with a small escort.' Arthur turned to Flint. 'You're in charge of the recruits in Erec's absence.'

As Erec rushed from the hall, Arthur began to pace the room and collect his thoughts.

Gherwan asked: 'Should I muster the men and march to Aquae Sulis?'

Distracted and wondering over half a dozen things at once, Arthur replied. 'No, that would be folly.' A pause ensued before he came to his conclusion. 'No. We need to keep Guertepir's forces away from Brythonfort for now. That would best suit our needs.' He looked to Murdoc. 'Speak with Erec before he leaves. He must secure the gates of Aquae Sulis after he's sent the civilians on their way. Tell him to hold out there until we can get extra men and arrive in force.' He addressed Dominic. 'Dom, things have changed. You need to leave *now*. Take Murdoc with you. Get on your way down the eastern road and ride through the night if you have to. We need news of Withred … of Will … of Saxon movement. Anything!'

Dominic left the hall with Murdoc. Arthur and Gherwan remained.

'What now?' asked Gherwan.

'Wait, *damn it*, wait.' With worried eyes, he continued. 'It's all we *can* do. We don't have the men yet to go to Badon Hill. We need at least Withred, Gus, and their force of Angles before we can do that.'

'And what of Aquae Sulis? Will it hold?'

'As long as they secure the gates they should be safe. Guertepir desires the town—that is unarguable—so he'll probably lay siege, and that'll keep him away from our western lands. That's my worry Gherwan: if they head this way I don't have the men to protect my people from them. But if they *do* come we must be ready with what we've got. That's our role for now: sit and wait, and be ready to die to protect our folk.'

'And that may happen soon if Guertepir breaches Aquae Sulis.'

'We can only pray he doesn't. The newly repaired walls and gates are stronger than ever so they should keep them at bay.'

Erec made rapid progress along the thirty-five miles of good Roman road between Brythonfort and Aquae Sulis. A man waited with his final horse as he landed five miles from the town. Erec gasped his fatigue as he slid from the frothy flanks of his mare. 'Any movement from up the road?'

'Nothing, other than everyday comings and goings,' answered the groom.

He heaved himself upon the fresh steed, and another bout of fast riding took him to Aquae Sulis. Half a mile away, Guertepir's army approached the town down the northern road.

Erec spotted the sentries on the walls and realised they had not failed in their task—the gates were secure between the stone towers. He assessed his chance of reaching them unscathed. Knowing it was touch and go, his spurred his swift horse towards the city, his concern growing when he noticed five riders break from Guertepir's group and speed towards him.

When reaching the gates, Erec displayed his unicorn shield to the men on the tower. Cardew and Ferris, two knights well known to him, recognised him at once. Erec removed his broadsword as he waited. The rushing riders had halved the distance to him before he heard the sliding of stout beams behind the door. The squeak of new timber on recently-forged iron sounded, and a gap scarcely wide enough to take his horse appeared. Men waiting inside quickly secured the gates only moments before the enemy riders arrived. A hollow banging on the doors evidenced their frustration as the oak barrier checked their assault.

Abloyc jerked his horse away from the gates, then threw his iron helm to the ground. Frustrated, he dragged his hands over his shaven head, his cold eyes glittering with fury. A cohort retrieved his helm. Abloyc snatched it. 'A moment sooner and we would've had him.' He played his horse around in a circle, his blond chin beard bristling as he looked up to the tower. Two archers appeared, prompting him to ram his helm back on. 'Fall away!' he shouted as arrows began to fly.

When out of range, they checked their stride and turned to assess the magnitude of their task. 'This isn't going to be easy,' Abloyc said to the nearest man. The noise of an approaching mass of men had him turn. Ahead of the horde rode Guertepir, eager to reach Aquae Sulis before his subordinates. Abloyc threw a glare in his direction. 'S'pity the poxed whore wants the town,' he growled, 'otherwise this thing would be over with quickly. Then I could get back to my pleasures in Deva.'

A nearby rider, one of Abloyc's toadies, smirked at this. 'When Cunedda finds out how you've set yourself up there, slaves and all, he'll have your cod on a platter.'

Abloyc gave an arrogant sniff of dismissal. 'Cunedda has a battle to go through before he even gets back to Deva. Stray arrows fly from all directions in the heat of combat. Who knows what might befall him.'

'Dangerous talk,' said the toady, 'but talk I will take to my grave—that you know.'

Guertepir arrived, ending their musings. Grunting, he turned his heavy horse towards the following army, his arm signal bringing them to a slow halt. 'Locked themselves in the city have they?' he wheezed.

'Fraid so,' replied Abloyc. 'We nearly caught a rider as he entered the town, but arrived too late.'

'Any sign of Arthur's forces?'

'None yet. They can't be far away though.'

Guertepir scrutinised Aquae Sulis. He looked up to the sky. 'Night's not far off, so we'll camp before the gates.' He shook his head dejectedly as he studied the town again. 'Didn't expect to just walk in but—shit!—look at those towers ... and that gate.' He turned to a nearby captain of his troop and pointed to where the walls curved away out of sight. 'Send riders around the city, all the way and back again. Examine the walls for any weakness.'

Abloyc raised his eyebrows, murmuring. 'You really think they would be stupid enough to leave breaches in the wall?'

'No I don't,' said Guertepir, his deflated stare moving from Aquae Sulis to Abloyc, upon whom it transformed into a look of disdain. 'But these things need to be examined man. That is how we Hibernians prepare. That is why we win wars.'

Abloyc, who held no respect for Guertepir, was about to give him a sharp reply but was distracted by the approach of Votadini foot soldiers. Before them, stumbling and distraught, was a ragged man.

All turned and stared as the wretch neared them. One of the foot soldiers pushed him before Abloyc's horse. 'Came to us, my lord. He's a Briton. As soon as we stopped he appeared from nowhere.'

Abloyc dismounted and grabbed the man by his hair. He held his knife to his terrified eye. 'You had better have good reason,' he growled.

After entering Aquae Sulis, Erec went in search of Morgana. He soon found her on the main street as she walked with their infant boy, Girard. With them was Tamsyn, a woman of similar age, who had another small child at her heels.

Morgana's mouth dropped open as Girard ran delightedly to Erec. 'They closed the gates, I knew something was wrong, but I didn't expect to see you here,' she said.

They embraced and Erec told of recent happenings. He finished with: 'That's why I came … to get you out of here, but it's too late, they're already at the gates.' A shower of dread washed over Morgana. She took Girard from Erec and cocooned the boy in a protective embrace. Tamsyn mirrored Morgana as she picked up and hugged her own child.

Erec sensed their alarm. 'No … no … there is hope for you. There's a siege-passage at the back of the town; it opens onto a wooded twist in the land and is hidden from sight. It's there to get messengers in and out under cover of darkness in situations such as this. It will work just as well to get *people* in and out. You must leave tonight, both of you, along with all but the military.'

Morgana was emphatic. 'NO! I will not leave without you.'

'You are not listening, my love.' Erec's tone had become desperate. 'Go through the hidden gate and take Girard. It would not be fair to leave the boy here. They will spare nobody if they breach the walls. Believe me when I tell you that. Not one person will be spared.'

Not wishing to listen, she said: 'Tamsyn will take him, won't you Tamsyn?' Tamsyn returned a fearful nod of affirmation. 'There … it's settled. I'll stay and fight alongside you if needs be.'

'*Absolutely* not,' said Erec. 'Can't you see, there'll *be* no fighting here. Our role is to hold out until Arthur can arrive in force. You have to go … then at least one of us gets out. Would you see Girard orphaned?'

Girard stirred at this. 'What is orfaned mamma?'

Morgana brought her hand to her mouth as her tears came. She stroked Girard's fine blond hair. 'Nothing, my baby. Nothing for you to know.' The necessity of her leaving had suddenly struck her. She turned to Erec with despairing eyes. 'Yes ... as usual you speak sense. I can't chance he's left alone in this awful world. But what of you?'

'When Arthur arrives I will do the job I'm trained for. Until then I'll sneer down upon Guertepir's frustration.'

Morgana, lost for words, attempted a brave smile. She touched Erec's cheek, then took his hands and gazed at him as if it were for the last time. Moments passed before she turned to Tamsyn. 'Come, girl,' she said. 'We leave as soon as darkness falls.'

Soon after, Erec stood on the wall-walk behind the battlements. Cardew and Ferris were beside him. In total, thirty knights patrolled along the parapet overlooking Guertepir's forces in front of the town.

'They've turned up with men for shieldwalls, as well as archers and some charioteers up to now,' informed Cardew.

'Have they attempted to approach the gates again?' asked Erec.

'Once, and the first casualty of this war fell when they did.' Cardew nodded over to Ferris.

'That fellow's a talent with the bow—got him through the eye slits in his helm.'

'Trained by Dominic I take it?'

'Yes, and we'll need more men like him before this is played out.'

Erec went to a gap between the grit-stone merlons on the parapet. Below was the assembled army. His breath left him sharply. Like a giant wave which had crashed against granite cliffs only to ebb and settle at its base, the gathering was set for war. Furthermore, the force had spilled beyond the northern walls down as far as the eastern and western aspects of the city.

Troubled, Erec came away and returned to Cardew. 'Only the failing light stops them from fully encircling us. Tomorrow they'll bring out scaling ladders, that's for sure. We must get the workers and civilians away tonight while the southern siege-passage is still safe to use.'

Cardew concurred. 'Now's as good a time as any. By the time we have them ready to go it will be dark.'

Leaving the remainder of the men on the wall-walk to watch for further developments, Erec and Cardew left to muster the non-military occupants of Aquae Sulis.

One hour later, a hushed gathering assembled in a stone cellar in the bowels of the town. Foggy breath and an air of disquiet infused the damp torch-lit vault as Erec unlocked a small steel portcullis. Revealed, was a low passage twenty strides in length. Cardew walked down it towards an identical portcullis set into the outer wall.

In hushed tones, Erec addressed the crowd. 'Once through the next gate you will be outside. Morcant'—he gestured toward a felt-hatted artisan who stood beside him—'built this basement and he knows where to go when leaving it. Follow him and Cardew and *do not* lag behind. Keep perfectly quiet and communicate by touch only. Once you are across the rough ground take the southern road away from here and walk through the night. Tomorrow you are to hide in the woods until nightfall. Another night's march will get you to within sight of Brythonfort. May Fortuna watch over you all.'

As people filed by and took to the passage, Erec gave them his encouragement and farewell. Morgana was the last in line. The infant slept in her arms. Erec's gentle embrace encompassed them both, whilst Morgana's tremble evidenced her apprehension.

'Remember, keep walking until you are well away from town,' Erec said. Morgana was weeping quietly. Erec attempted to bolster her. 'Hey … hey now … this will be over soon; keep that in mind. Spring is almost here—a time for walking in the meadows under a warm sun.'

Morgana sniffled and tried a smile. 'Aye … a time to eat bread and cheese beside the Afon River while Girard runs his energy away.'

Erec took Morgana's face in his hands and tenderly kissed her tears away. Finally, he had to let her go. 'They are ready, Morgana, now we must part.'

Morgana gave one final whisper into Erec's ear. 'Stay safe—please stay safe. This world means nothing to me without you and my baby in it.' They kissed again, then Erec walked Morgana down the walkway to join those who were anxious to leave.

Cardew doused his torch, unlocked the outer gate, and strode outside. Rowan trees grew close to the walls, hiding the ingress. The faint moonlight cast an ethereal glow upon them. Cardew walked from the opening with Morcant and they took tentative steps down the dry gravel streamed that wound between the trees. Satisfied they were unseen; they turned to Erec who stood at the gate. Cardew gave his signal and Erec silently ushered the townsfolk outside.

Cardew addressed them with hushed tones as soon as they neared him. 'Follow Morcant and me. We'll take you along through the trees and up to a path. Don't lose sight of us or make the slightest noise. Move up to the road, then follow Morcant and do as he says.'

Aided by the glow of a half moon, they turned and led the company down the winding streambed as it snaked between the trees. Soon they came to a thin path and followed it until the Southern road to Brythonfort was before them.

Erec joined the refugees from behind and was immediately alert, his senses prickling. 'Listen,' he whispered. 'Can you hear it?'

Cardew and Morcant were stock-still. After a moment Cardew said: 'No. Nothing. Must've been a fox or a badger.'

Morcant agreed with Cardew. 'Me neither; could've been animals, the wind … anything.'

Uneasy now, Cardew darted quick glances around him. Satisfied that nothing lurked, he settled his gaze upon the hollow where the others waited. He whispered urgently to Erec. 'We need to move them on. Our job's done here.'

Erec beckoned to the refugees. They had barely moved when a horse snorted. 'BACK TO THE GATES!' His shout was sudden and decisive but the townsfolk froze where they stood.

From a deep ditch beside the road, a rider emerged. Ten more followed. The ditch opposite yielded yet twenty more. Abloyc fronted them. Behind him, his troop formed a semi-circle, cutting off the road in both directions. The creak of stretched yew signalled the drawing of bowstrings as a score of archers joined the mounted men.

'Go back to the gate, your escape has failed!' shouted Abloyc. He heeled his horse towards Erec and Cardew who now wielded their swords. He held out his hand. 'Keys to the hidden gates … NOW!' Erec, who held them, hesitated. He considered going for Abloyc. 'Keys and lay down your arms,' repeated Abloyc as he pointed towards the townsfolk. 'Or would you rather the *city* stood rather than these people?'

Desperate now, Erec spun as he sought a solution. Cardew looked past the Votadini horde, down to the southern road as if Arthur would suddenly appear and save the night. Both came to a quick decision: escape was impossible and fighting not an option. If they resisted, Abloyc and his men would slaughter them all.

Without preamble, Erec surrendered the keys and threw his sword to the ground. He prepared himself for immediate death. When it did not come, he turned towards the terrified shadowy crowd. He sought out Morgana and Girard. If he were to die, he would die beside them.

Yet Abloyc words were to give him hope. 'Both of you, back through the siege hole. Tell your guards on the wall to open the front gates and yield their weapons. Do this and we *will* allow these people to pass.'

'And what of my men?' asked Erec. 'What will become of *them*?'

Abloyc shook his head, the gesture giving Erec and Cardew no hope. 'This is war,' said Abloyc. 'Men die in war.'

Knowing they walked to their own deaths, Erec and Cardew slid through the weeping crowd and headed back to the dry streambed. When Erec reached Morgana, she took hold of his arm. Near to panic she pleaded with him. 'No ... don't go; there must be another way; talk to him; ask him for mercy.'

Girard had awoken by now and held out his arms. Erec touched the boy's hair but knew Abloyc would not tolerate any delay. He looked towards the Votadini chief and saw he had dispatch three men his way. 'I'm sorry but this has to be done,' he said. As Morgana's shoulders shook, he spoke rapidly in his final moments with her. 'I love you. Never forget that. Make sure Girard grows to be a good man. Tell him we will meet again in Elysium and there we'll all laugh at this fleeting moment of mortality.'

The foot soldiers reached them and pulled Morgana's desperate grip from Erec's arm. Erec turned away, his tears coursing freely as he walked with Cardew towards the tunnel. Abloyc's men followed until they reached the first gate. 'On your way,' said the nearest man as he shoved at Erec and Cardew, '… both of you.' He locked the gate then returned to Abloyc.

Abloyc removed a purse from his belt. A tumble of coins fell onto the stone sets of the Roman road. A figure emerged from the shadows and scrabbled for them. Abloyc sneered at him. 'Wretch,' he sneered. 'Betrayer of your own folk, just because you were thrown out of town naked.'

As Hal scuttled away into the darkness, Abloyc gave his orders. 'Change of plan,' he shouted. 'The woman and child who meant so much to the knight shall live. No doubt Guertepir will have sport with them *and* the knight.' He turned to the nearest rider. 'Get to our army before it enters the town. Tell them that Abloyc wishes the knight with the braided, blond hair and full beard to be spared for now.' As the rider sped away, Abloyc turned to the murmuring crowd before him. 'Pull out the woman and child and kill the rest,' he said.

CHAPTER EIGHTEEN

Dominic and Murdoc had ridden through the night upon the lower eastern road towards Calleva. When morning came they took a short rest in a spinney beside the track.

'You're sure Gus and Withred will come this way,' asked Murdoc.

'Yes—Withred assured me he would sail to Londinium before taking Portway Road to Calleva. Then he would drop southwest onto this track and continue to Brythonfort.'

'And the Saxon army?'

'They'll take Akeman Street, the higher road, to Corinium. That's the road they know. From there they'll head south to Aquae Sulis.'

'So Withred sought to avoid crossing their path?'

'Yes, he discussed it with Arthur; it makes sense when you think about it. Meet them on our terms when we are at full strength and not before. Withred needs to avoid them for now. That's why he purposed to make landfall at Londinium and not Norwic.'

'But the Saxons need to pass through Londinium as well. Surely the two forces could come together there.'

'It's risky, yes, but there's not much that can be done about that. Once out of Londinium, our people will take Portway. The Saxons will take Akeman Street.'

Murdoc became alert. 'Shh! Someone comes along the track.'

Dominic edged into the cover beside the road. Murdoc took the ponies deeper into the copse and out of sight.

Pulled by an ox, a wagon creaked towards them. Sat on the wain's high seat were Simon and Robert. Beside them rode Emrys with six other knights.'

Dominic stepped from his hiding place and stood out in full view. He watched as Emrys and the knights flinched and drew their weapons. 'Too late … too late!' he shouted. 'You would have been ambushed and killed.'

Emrys' smile broadened into a grin as he took in Dominic's cocky stance and wolf hat. 'Never,' he said as he slid from his mount and went to Dominic. 'You wouldn't have had time to fart such was the speed of our response.'

Dismissively, Dominic laughed. 'I don't think so Emrys—look behind you.' Emrys turned to see Murdoc, who had slipped quietly from cover and crept unheard behind them. He spear was pulled back and ready to throw.

Dominic gave Emrys and the other knights a smug little smile. 'Flanked you, we did'—he slid his hand across his throat in a cutting gesture—'dead as corpses, the lot of you.'

Emrys gave a wry smile 'Aye, that we would be, don't tell Arthur.'

Dominic shouted to the others. 'A lesson learned, my friends, but well-met all the same!' He went to the wagon as Murdoc and the knights exchanged greetings.

Simon climbed down from his high seat and embraced Dominic. 'As ever you're a sight for sore eyes,' he said. 'What news from Brythonfort?'

'*Forbidding* news, Si, but that can wait till later.' He peered up at the contents of the wagon. 'I see you found some Roman stuff in the field at Calleva?'

'Yes—bits of this and bits of that,' said Robert who still sat on the wagon. 'That's the trouble, though, Dom ... we found mere fragments. Bits of wood from ballistae and catapultas, bits of iron from bolt shooters. A written text on how to construct them would have been better, but of course that was never going to happen.'

'D'you think you know enough now to build a ballista?'

'We can but try.' Robert jerked his thumb back over his shoulder towards the debris in the back of the wagon. 'For every piece we take back to study, there are at least ten missing parts. But who knows; some folk at Brythonfort, you included, have seen Roman artillery in action. What we don't have here may be a memory to someone.'

Urgency meant the meeting was brief, and a little time later the Britons parted. Having learned of Guertepir's sinister arrival with the Votadini at Aquae Sulis, Simon's group had gone on their way with heavy hearts and a grim resolve.

Another day's riding brought Dominic and Murdoc to Calleva. Like a smaller version of Londinium, the place was unkempt, abandoned and largely ignored by the Saxons. The pair decided to rest up for the night and entered the crumbling town. Beside a broken wall they set up a rough camp.

Dominic soon had a fire going and lay down beside it. 'How's Martha taking all of this?' he asked.

Murdoc, who had been routing through his pack, became thoughtful and turned his gaze towards the hypnotic fire. 'Not well, Dom. She worries about me, about what will happen to Ceola, about everything that could go wrong.'

The flames danced in his green eyes, a frown creasing his fine-boned face as he mulled over the multitude of possible outcomes of the coming war. Eventually, he turned his attention from the fire and regarded Dominic. 'Yes she worries, but Christ Saviour I'm anxious *too*. That Saxons are possibly coming into this war has made me realise how they nearly took Ceola from me. Made me aware of how Martha would suffer a terrible fate in their hands.'

Thereupon a truth struck Murdoc. Dominic *himself* had someone he cared for if the rumours were to be believed. He attempted to draw Dominic out on the matter. 'That's the trouble, you see, when you love someone as much as I love Martha and Ceola all this seems far worse.' He flicked a shrewd glance at Dominic who had nodded his agreement. 'Sometimes I envy your independence. At least you've only yourself to worry about.'

They were both silent for a while then Dominic said: 'No, you're wrong actually. I *do* fret … about *everyone* I know.'

Murdoc went for it. 'Anyone in particular?'

Dominic gave him a curious little glance. 'Tongues have been wagging, I see.'

Murdoc shrugged.

Capable of love but always fighting against it, Dominic nevertheless considered opening his heart to Murdoc. The man was his best friend and doubtless he would feel unburdened if he told him how he loved the very bones of Nila. How even on such a journey as this his thoughts were always upon her. But he could not. Now was not the time. Besides, he had to respect Nila. Instead he said: 'Don't believe everything you hear Mur ... like I said, I worry for *all* the people of Brythonfort—*all* of them.'

Murdoc knew he had pushed far enough and would get no more from him. He took his sleeping place beside the fire. 'Yes, dark times, Dom,' he said as he rolled into his blanket. 'Oh, that the morning brings better news.'

The next day saw them leave the ruins of Calleva and take the old road called Portway towards Londinium. Mid-morning had barely passed when they heard the sounds of many men heading westwards towards them.

They were quickly off the road and into a ditch. The slow clatter of hooves upon stone and the whinnying of horses grew in intensity as they waited. Soon the first of the riders passed them and Dominic parted the broom plant before him and chanced a look. After his appraisal, he withdrew his head and turned to Murdoc. 'It's them,' he said in hushed tones. 'It's Withred and Gus. They've brought the Angles. Now we can return to Brythonfort and prepare for war.'

CHAPTER NINETEEN

Arthur's men, as instructed by Erec and Cardew, had opened the gates of Aquae Sulis and discarded their weapons. Abloyc's rider had arrived soon after and whispered into Guertepir's ear. The Hibernian king then entered Aquae Sulis anticipating the slaying of the guards. Stripped, bound, and forced upon their knees, all thirty of them knelt before him. Abloyc and his detachment of executioners lingered nearby.

Guertepir smiled when noticing Erec's imposing physique and countenance. He immediately had him removed from the line.

'I have fabulous plans for you my British stallion,' he said as he pushed at his broad chest, forcing him away from the impending executions.

Erec spat at him. 'That to you and your plans!' He made to go for Guertepir but was unable to shake free from the grasp of four of his guards. Unable to move anything but his head, he shoved it forward, pointing it towards the men awaiting execution. His carotid bulged like a knotted cord as he frothed with frustration. 'Put me back with them,' he spluttered. 'Death has got to be better than looking at your poxed face.'

Guertepir wiped the spit from his eye. He walked to Erec and struck him in the mouth.

Erec grimaced then turned his glittering eyes back upon Guertepir who was shaking the sting from his bejeweled hand. He spat out a tooth as blood slicked down his chin, then gave a defiant laugh. 'Ha ... ha, ha ... so that's the best you've got is it? The best you can manage upon a restrained man?'

But Guertepir would not be drawn. Instead, he pointed to the doomed men. 'Not the best, dear knight ... you are about to see something *much better* happen to them.'

Again Erec twisted in the grip of Guertepir's men as Abloyc, who stood beside Guertepir, gave the signal for his executioners to move towards the bound knights.

Cardew raised his head and looked Erec in the eyes as the men approached. 'Do not fear for me,' he shouted. 'I go to the sweet gardens where my ancestors wait.' Cardew turned his disdainful attention to the man who had closed on him. 'But for you it is hell, my friend.'

Unperturbed, Cardew's slayer went to his task. 'Lower your head and look at the earth,' he snapped as he removed the gladius from his belt. Cardew flickered the man a disdainful glance then did as he bade. The thirty who faced their own executioners did the same.

'Place your blades,' shouted Abloyc.

Brave necks felt cold iron as sword tips were rested upon them.

Abloyc paused and relished the silence of the moment. The condemned men shook and it pleased him.

Erec, his voice filled with emotion, broke in. 'Give the command you monster; what's the matter with you; is it not enough that you send them to the afterlife?'

'*You* do it,' said Abloyc unexpectedly. 'If you wish this to be over with, then *you* give the command. If not, then I'm happy to wait until they all shit themselves.'

'*That* they will never do, even if you wait all day,' said Erec, suddenly proud of his men. He paused a moment, knowing there was nothing he could do to save them. Not wishing them to linger, he gave his shout. 'Do it … use your swords you murdering bastards! You heard your beast of a captain!'

The men turned to Abloyc for approval. He nodded and swords went through flesh.

Erec face twisted as his knights fell dead to the earth.

Abloyc grabbed Erec's hair as his chin dropped to his chest, forcing him to look him in the eye. 'That was but the beginning of the show,' he hissed. 'Next, you and your lovely wife are to provide entertainment for the main event.'

An hideous truth struck Erec then. He addressed Abloyc, his voice barely above an appalled whisper. 'My wife and the others; you said you'd let them go. You have betrayed me.' He huffed out a breath of self-recrimination. 'How could I have been so foolish...' He pierced Abloyc with a hateful glare. 'But I didn't know what a rat of a man you are.' He started to shout now. 'Where is my wife! Where is my boy! What have you done with them!' Again he strained and made to break free and lunge at Abloyc, but again his efforts came to nothing. 'Spare them; *what* danger are they!' he sobbed as he was dragged away. 'And why do I live? Take *my* life. Is that not enough for you?'

Abloyc gave a reproachful look to Guertepir. 'There ... I told you he'd be trouble. Should've killed him with the rest.'

'I think not,' said Guertepir as he made to leave. 'The waters here have magical properties. They may calm his savage nature. You're coming to watch the show I take it?'

'Wouldn't miss it for anything,' said Abloyc as he walked with his arm over Guertepir's shoulders towards the baths.

Arthur's artisans had renovated the huge bathhouse to its original opulent specifications. A stone caldarium (the largest of three pools in the complex) brimmed with clear water. Emerging warm from deep underground, its visage had filled both the Hibernians and Votadini with awe and veneration. The guilt-bronze image of Sulis Minerva looked down imposingly upon all who entered the bathhouse. The smell of water and stone infused the air, adding to the unique aura of the temple.

Abloyc and thirty of his highest-ranking men now ambled between the stone pillars as they awaited the arrival of Guertepir and Almaith.

'Wait till you see his wife,' said Abloyc to Taranis, the nearest man. 'The word *hog* doesn't go near describing her.'

'A simple mare, too, by all accounts,' said Taranis.

'Yes, but with a rich Hibernian father who provides Guertepir with most of his gold.'

'So I hear ... but what's all this about? Why are we here?'

'*That*, you're not going to believe,' tittered Abloyc. 'One thing I will tell you, though, is that Guertepir's completely taken with the place. He reckons he can secure his mortality here today ... but quiet, here they come.'

Surrounded by a retinue of assistants, Guertepir and Almaith, both clad in the squirrel coats gifted to them by Dominic two years earlier, entered the temple.

'You were right—hog comes nowhere near describing her,' said Abloyc's man as he beheld Almaith. 'Even in that fine wrap she looks like something that's emerged from the bowels of the earth.'

Guertepir's druid entered the bathhouse. Dressed in a white habit, his black hair flowing from the cowl that covered his head, his long featured face a vague shadow within the hood, he chanted rhythmically whilst moving in strange, intricate steps as he carried a golden bowl. Muirecán's dance had taken him near to the pool. Inside his bowl was an amalgam of oak leaves and ox blood. As he moved forward he stirred the mixture with his hand, his invocations rising in volume. Abloyc and Taranis watched, open-mouthed, as the ceremony progressed.

As if to himself, Taranis asked: 'What in Freyja's name is he doing?'

'Serving notice to Sulis Minerva that men of this land are about to enter her realm,' answered Abloyc. 'The oak leaves represent the land, the blood the sea.'

Muirecán by now had begun to encircle the pool. As he did, he grabbed handfuls of the bloody leaves and held them before him. Reciting incantations, he dropped them in to the water. The ceremony continued until his bowl was empty.

His droning abruptly ceased when he came upon Almaith and Guertepir. They turned to him and he smeared ox blood onto their faces. He held his arms aloft, looked at them with his dark piercing eyes, then shouted his final prayers.

'She awaits your entry and is ready for your sacrifice, king,' he said as he pointed to the bubbling of water pushing upwards in the centre of the pool. 'Now she is appeased and will allow you to perform your sacred task.'

Guertipir nodded slowly and turned to Almaith. 'Are you ready to walk with me into the pool, my dear?'

Almaith, dull eyed, gave a faint nod of her head.

'Yes, I suppose you are,' murmured Guertepir stoically as he beckoned over two of his retinue. 'Take the cloaks and put them somewhere safe,' he told them.

'No ... please no,' said Abloyc with horrid fascination as the men removed the cloaks from Guertepir and Almaith. He expelled a disgusted 'huh' as their naked forms were exposed.

'They're like bloated, saggy twins,' said Taranis, his tone rivalling Abloyc's in unbridled revulsion.

Guertepir and Almaith walked down the stone steps of the caldarium until they were chest deep in the warm mineral waters. There they stood, arms floating at shoulder height as they waited. Almaith's huge saggy breast had risen to the surface and bobbed as if weightless in the ripples of the pool. Guertepir shouted to his druid. 'Have the men bring them in!'

'Now it gets *really* interesting,' said Abloyc to Taranis. 'This is where Guertepir and his hag enter the realms of immortality.'

From a shadowy recess at the far end of the bathhouse, Erec and Morgana emerged. Dressed from neck to ankle in white linen gowns, their hands bound behind and their ankles fettered, they progressed in a stumbling shuffle towards the edge of the pool. Behind them strode four of Guertepir's guards and a woman of Almaith's chamber. The woman carried Erec's infant son, Girard. She spoke soothingly to the boy and stroked his hair in an effort to placate him as he blinked wide-eyed at the overwhelming spectacle before him.

Almaith gasped as she appraised Erec's powerful physique, discernable even through the fabric of his linen shroud. Guertepir, too, seemed pleased as he beheld Morgana's svelte lines beneath her own garment.

As Erec took in the scene, things became clear to him. They were to enter the water beside the poxed Hibernian king and his rancid wife. But for what purpose he could not imagine. Muirecán approached him and began to wail an intricate incantation into his face, then turned his attention to Morgana. The chant rose in intensity until it became a shrill scream, at which point Muirecán fell to silence. Tension infused the room as he let the hush linger a moment.

At a nod from Guertepir, who had now begun to fondle himself under the water, Muirecán grasped Morgana's linen shroud and tore it from neck to waist. Morgana gasped and brought up her hands to cover herself as

Muirecán stooped and finished the task of splitting her shroud.

Erec, the whites of his eyes now dominant such was his blistering fury, attempted to bite at Muirecán, but the attack fell short thanks to the restraint of Guertepir's guards who dragged him backwards and away.

'WHAT are you DOING!' Spit flew from Erec's mouth as he twisted his head to look towards Guertepir.

But Guertepir did not respond. Instead, he nodded towards Muirecán. The druid cast a glance towards the guards who held Erec by his arms. They strengthened their grip upon him. Muirecán approached Erec and split open his gown from neck to floor.

An ecstatic 'ahh' emerged from Almaith as she studied Erec's naked form. Like Guertepir, she had begun to pleasure herself under the water, but as her juices threatened to erupt she ceased her stroking.

Livid, Erec gasped, growled and twisted in the grip of his enforcers.

'This will not do, you must stop your STRUGGLING!' Erec became still and rested his baleful glare upon Muirecán who had addressed him. 'You will enter the water now ...

both of you'—he nodded towards Guertepir and Almaith—'and do as they desire.'

Erec stole a glance towards Morgana who had none of his feistiness. Instead, she wept in the grasp of her captors and attempted to shrug herself into some semblance of modesty. She looked at the woman who held Girard. 'Why have you brought my boy in here,' she sobbed. 'He has done no harm ... he is just a baby. Please take him from this place ... he does not need to see this.'

Guertepir bellowed from the water, his shout directed at Erec. 'I see that your wife possesses all the sense in your family. While you struggle and spit your venom, your boy is at risk. Now is the time to accept your fate and enter the water. Refuse or resist further and the boy will be sacrificed to Sulis Minerva before your eyes.'

Abloyc walked over to the woman who held Girard and took him from her. The infant wriggled in his grasp, averting his head. A wailing cry came from him then—its sound heart-rending and reedy in the sparse atmosphere of the bathhouse.

Erec himself had begun to sob now. 'Let him be; sweet Jesus, how can you possibly even contemplate hurting a single hair of his head.

Send him from here ... we will enter the water. Just send him from here.'

'Ah, sense at last,' said Guertepir. 'But the boy stays. His presence will be a reminder should your liveliness return.'

Erec rested his desolate gaze upon Morgana. 'We have no choice my love. We must go in.' Morgana, her face twisted with fear and grief, gave him a despairing nod of acceptance. He turned his head sideways towards his restrainers. 'Do it then,' he said. 'Walk me into the waters.'

The guards pushed him forward onto the stone steps. Beside him was Morgana and he managed to speak to her as the warm waters crept above their knees. 'This will be over soon for both of us,' he said. 'I love you and our boy more than life itself. Keep that thought in your head, Morgana. Promise me you will.'

She wept as she was shoved towards Guertepir. 'I promise,' she said.

When close to Almaith, Erec convulsed with disgust. Daubed liberally, her rouge was smeared and greasy. Carmine grease paint, ineptly applied to her slack lips, strayed outwards to mix with the stuff on her face. She reached out and touched Erec's sword-scarred shoulders. The knight recoiled.

'Push him to me.' They were the first words Almaith had uttered since entering the water and promoted an immediate response from the guards who held Erec. Soon he was face to face with Almaith, her squashy breasts pressed against him.

Mercifully, Erec had his back Guertepir, and so was unable to see his actions towards his wife. Repulsed, Morgana had turned her face away as Guertepir pulled her knees upwards and around him.

'No ... you do not need to do this.' Her plea to him was pathetic and distraught. 'Drown me if you will. *Surely* that will appease the goddess.'

Guertepir, panting in his ardor, ran his hand down Morgana's side. 'No, it will *not* appease her,' he said. 'My druid'—he squinted towards Muirecán who had renewed his chanting at the side of the caldarium—'insists that the deity desires to witness—to *feel* even—fornication and the spilling of seed and juices into her blessed womb. *Then* you shall have your wish—*then* I will drown you—you British whore-wife.'

Abloyc had moved to the edge of the pool as he held Girard. To Erec's relief, the boy had pushed his face into Abloyc's chest, refusing to look at anything within the bathhouse. Erec implored Abloyc. 'Anything—we've told you we'll do anything—just don't touch him.'

'Then get on with it man,' smirked Abloyc. 'Do the right thing and rise to the occasion. Your water nymph is getting impatient.'

Abloyc's remark caused an eruption of laughter from his men, but no mirth from Almaith. She had worked on Erec' loins to no avail and had resorted to sliding down his knee in an effort to satisfy herself.

Erec, his head pushed back as much as he could, grimaced at the hag's close proximity as she panted and drooled into his face. But when Morgana's scream came from behind he could take no more. A crimson rage fell upon him then, and such was the strength of his muscle spasm, he was able to pull free from the men who held him. Barging Almaith away, he turned to see Guertepir grunting over Morgana as he violated her. The Hibernian's hand lay flat across her forehead as he pushed her sweet face under the waters of the pool.

Erec screamed at Guertepir as the guards made to grab him again. 'NO! Why drown her. What more do you need from her!' With elbows tied behind, Erec had few options other than push through the water and away from the men. Almaith's clammy hand fell upon his neck.

'No you don't. A wife for a wife,' growled Erec. He butted Almaith, the blow sending her sprawling backwards. He lunged at her exposed neck, his intent now to tear at her puffy flesh with his teeth. The guards stopped him. Three more had entered the water and two now helped a stunned Almaith from the pool. The third wielded a dagger.

Dead and defiled, Morgana floated before Guertepir.

Distraught and spent as his guards once more gripped his arms, Erec wept. 'No ... ah no. You had no need to kill her.'

His thoughts went to Girard. He turned to him. What had his boy witnessed? He saw that the lad still pressed his small face into Abloyc's tunic.

Erec heaved with sobs as he turned to plead with Guertepir. 'I know you're going to kill me now, but spare my boy ... he has not harmed anyone ... please spare my boy.'

'You've cost me too much gold for that you British rat,' spat Guertepir as he pushed Morgana's body away from him. 'As soon as my wife tells her father what happened in here today he will half my allowance. And yes, you're right—I *am* going to kill you.' He nodded to the man with the dagger who went to Erec and slid the blade across his neck. As Erec went limp, his guards released him, allowing his body to sink in a swirling fog of crimson to the stone floor of the pool.

Grunting with the effort of wading through the pool, Guertepir made his way to the stone steps. Impatiently, he beckoned to two of his retainers. 'Come!' he shouted to them. 'In the water and help me out. Don't just stand there with your thumbs up your arses!'

Moments later, Guertepir stood naked on the mosaic floor of the bathhouse as his servants patted him dry. He lifted his arms above his head, exposing his sides to the drying cloths, then turned his attention back to the caldarium. Discoloured by Erec's blood, the opaque water obscured the two bodies which lay on the bottom of the pool. Not far from Guertepir stood Almaith, her nose broken and bloodied from Erec's assault. Two of her women dabbed at her wound as another placed the squirrel cloak over her shoulders.

'Didn't go *quite* as I intended,' commented Guertepir as he appraised his wife.

Abloyc, who had approached with Girard, suppressed a smile. 'No ... your lady didn't seem to get the satisfaction she desired.'

Guertepir grunted his displeasure. 'Now I'll have to find some young Adonis to satisfy her.' He looked at Girard now. Face hidden, the boy whimpered and shook. Guertepir stroked the infant's blond curls as if fostering a heart-felt fondness towards him.

The nuance was not lost upon Abloyc. 'You seem taken with Erec's sprat,' he said. 'Am I to take it the court of Guertepir has a new young addition?'

Guertepir's head shot back, his smile sardonic. 'Are you mad,' he proffered. 'You know how it works Abloyc. We kill our enemies and we kill their children. This lad is the image of his father and will be *as him* one day. How would I sleep in my bed in years to come with Erec's double walking my halls?'

Abloyc's relief was palpable. 'For a moment I thought you'd gone soft,' he said. 'I shall see to the matter at once.'

Guertepir stayed Abloyc's hand as he made to remove his knife. 'No ... not with a blade.' He turned to the far wall of the bathhouse where the guilt, bronzed head of the goddess Sulis Minerva gazed down with passive eyes upon the assembly. Guertepir pointed to the icon. 'She must observe the sacrifice close up,' he said. 'Take his ankles and cast his head against the stone beneath her.'

Abloyc shrugged. 'As you command.' He turned and strode towards the wall with Girard.

The face of Sulis Minerva was inscrutable, but Guertepir had misjudged her. The Romans and Britons had known the Goddess to be life giving and nourishing, and they would interpret her stare to be one of maternal grief as she watched Abloyc's dreadful deed. With certainty, they would know that she now despaired at the very nature of man.

CHAPTER TWENTY

Days earlier, Arthur's smile was as broad as the horizon as he stood on the wall-walk of Brythonfort with Heledd. Below him, Augustus, Withred, Dominic and Murdoc had just entered the gates of Brythonfort with the men of Angeln.

'Good news ... thank Fortuna ... good news at last,' said Arthur as he gripped Heledd's hand. 'Yet, I hardly dare count their numbers.' As he overlooked the gates, the Anglii continued to file into Brythonfort below him.

He gave Heledd a swift assessment. 'Mainly footmen for the shields but mounted warriors as well.' They watched engrossed and one hour passed before the procession finally petered out. 'Two thousand,' said Arthur, as the last man went through the gates. 'Better than I expected but still woefully short of what we need.'

'They go to the hall,' said Heledd. 'There, we can hear of news from the outside.' She squeezed Arthur's hand reassuringly and peered into his troubled eyes. 'Who knows, we may be pleasantly surprised.'

Arthur, his earlier euphoria now blunted by the grim realization of the task before them, reciprocated the squeeze. 'And now I must tell them of the fall of Aquae Sulis and the probable death of one of my best men,' he said as he turned and walked from the wall.

Arthur embraced Withred and Augustus as they came to him in the hall. 'A magnificent outcome from an arduous task,' he enthused, 'and one I will not forget.' Titon padded into the hall. 'From Angeln, too?' he asked.

'It's a long story and one that can wait,' said Withred, 'but he's not from Angeln.' In the way of introduction, he turned to the two men beside him. 'Hereferth and Smala,' he said to Arthur. 'They know this land and speak British, and both are well-regarded in Angeln. It is they you can thank for the two thousand men who camp outside.'

Arthur quickly appraised the two men. Hereferth was tall and imposing with an intricate swirl of ink covering his face; Smala was compact and stout—like a young bull. Arthur grasped their hands and thanked them for their attendance. After bowing to Heledd and kissing her hand, the Angle chiefs took their seats at the war council. Heledd left the hall and Arthur briefed the gathering with the latest information—the news of the fall of

Aquae Sulis in particular creating a groan of dismay in the room.

When he had finished, all in the assembly exchanged concerned glances. In particular, Hereferth and Smala seemed less than pleased. 'We were under no illusions of the magnitude of the task before us,' said Hereferth, 'but the reward of extensive land was too much to ignore. However, what you told us of the refusal of help from this Ffodor from Travena makes the undertaking before us much, much harder.' He looked towards the door of the hall. 'Outside, my men wait to go to war. Now I must tell them they will be completely overwhelmed if they do.'

'I understand,' said Arthur with some empathy, 'but I intend to fight them from lofty ground with well-trained men. Such a combination has often overcome superior numbers in battle.'

The Anglii chief pondered Arthur's words. 'The journey here was long, yet my men remain in good spirits and ready for a fight. However, your assurance still fills me with uncertainty.' He glanced at Smala, who responded with an unhelpful shrug. Hereferth turned to Arthur again. 'Still,' he continued, 'we are here now, and may as well listen to what this assembly has to say.'

Arthur, aware the alliance could collapse at any moment, addressed Dominic, hoping he had something encouraging to add. 'What news from our fair land, Dom? ... Something good I hope.'

'Things seem quiet for now,' said Dominic. 'We got no further than Calleva ... there we met up with Withred and Gus, and they saved us the trouble of journeying beyond.'

'And why so?' asked Arthur.

Dominic glanced at Augustus, inviting him to take over. 'We had no need to seek Saxons because we had already been told a host of them had passed through Londinium two days before we reached the town,' said Augustus. 'From Londinium they took Akeman street westwards towards Corinium and Aquae Sulis, no doubt.'

Careful not to allow his inward anxiety to reach his face, Arthur responded in an even tone. 'As I fully expected; Guertepir's envoy achieved its aim.' He pressed Augustus further. 'How many men? Did they say how many?'

'Two thousand, I was told.'

'So that's it,' said Arthur, aware of the futility of trying to dress up the numbers, '... the size of our task. A total of four thousand Hibernians and Votadini, and add to that two thousand Saxons.'

Withred, unwilling to allow the meeting to take a downward turn, came in immediately. Curiously, his tone was optimistic. 'Six thousand of them and three thousand of us; much better than the numbers facing us before I left for Angeln. I am confident we can win this.'

Smala, who had remained silent until then, responded. *'Confident,* Withred? How can you be confident? Like you said, it's six thousand of them and three thousand of us ... or even fewer if I decide to leave at once and take my men back to Angeln rather than chase a lost cause.'

'I'm confident because we are blessed with something they can only dream about,' said Withred with passion. 'Something worth four thousand men.'

Smala's eyebrows shot up at this. 'And what would that be?' he asked.

Withred pointed to Arthur. *'That* would be him,' he said. 'Arthur—a man with extensive knowledge. A man who is no stranger to the disparity of numbers, yet a commander who has overcome them several times when fighting for Rome. Above all, his presence on the battlefield inspires men to fight as if possessed. I know, because I have felt his aura myself.'

Regardless of his discomfort of his elevation to an almost God-like status by Withred, Arthur, nevertheless, allowed him to continue to sing his praises. Anything … any words that would stop Hereferth and Smala leaving the hall and taking the Londinium road straight back to Angeln was fine by him.

Smala had mused over Withred's words. 'So to overcome the numbers, we are to rely upon high ground, well-trained men and an inspirational leader. Do you *really* think that will be enough?'

'We have no choice,' said Arthur simply. 'We fight or we die.'

'*You* have no choice,' corrected Smala, 'but fortunately *we* do.'

Augustus interjected now. 'You forget, I visited your country and stood on a windy beach with you, Smala. The sea floods the land constantly and eventually some of your people will need to leave. The choice is yours—help us, or go back to your sodden lands.'

Hereferth touched Smala's sleeve, then nodded towards the door. Taking up on Hereferth's hint, Smala answered Augustus. 'It has yet to be decided whether or not we *will* leave Britannia, but for now I will go from this hall with Hereferth and speak privately with him. After our talk, we'll go to our men and tell them the size of the task before us all'—he cast a quick glance to Withred—'we will also mention your endorsement of Arthur. We'll return with our decision soon.'

'As you will,' said Arthur. 'And remember your reward for this—extensive tracts of land above the wall of Hadrian.'

'Why do you think we're here in the first place,' said Smala as he stood and walked to the door with Hereferth.

An air of tension infused the hall as an anxious conversation ensued. All knew what the outcome would be if left to fend for themselves. 'If they go home we're finished,' concluded Withred to Arthur, '… even with you leading us.'

'That, I know too well,' said Arthur. 'With them, we can go to Aquae Sulis and at least take up position upon the hill and face our enemies; without them we can only withdraw to Brythonfort and sit helpless while our lands are ravished.'

'Talking of Aquae Sulis … any more news since it was taken?' asked Murdoc.

'None yet,' said Arthur. 'I have Tomas and Nairn watching the place. If Guertepir decides to take his snout from the trough and move out with the rest of them, they'll let us know.'

'And no sign at all of Erec and the knights garrisoned there?'

'Nor the people,' replied Arthur heavily. 'I fear the worst, Mur. There were many women and babies there; I should have got them out before Guertepir arrived.' Suddenly, he slapped the table in frustration, causing many to jump. 'Why *did* I let Erec go to Aquae Sulis! If we lose him it would be a sorry loss indeed.'

'What of Will? Any sign or rumour of *him* on the road?' asked Murdoc, keen to steer Arthur away from his self-recrimination.

'None,' came in Dominic. 'Perhaps he followed the Saxons as they made their way to Aquae Sulis. You know Will. Meticulous in his scouting; likes to make sure.'

'Still, I worry for him,' frowned Arthur. 'It's not like him to leave it so long without getting word back to me, somehow. But there's nothing we can do for—'

Hereferth and Smala stepped back into the hall, cutting off Arthur's words. Inscrutable, their faces betrayed no indication of their decision. Both sat and were silent a moment.

Frowning, Smala studied the tabletop. He drummed his fingers as if still mulling over his decision.

In dread of his response, Arthur asked him: 'Well, come on man; spit it out. What are you going to do?'

Instead, Hereferth answered. 'Decided we are on a fool's errand and this can only end badly,' he said. Crestfallen, Arthur's men fell to silence. Hereferth allowed the hush to linger a moment before continuing. 'But war *is* the trade of fools so we might as well get it over and done with.'

Arthur stirred as if pushed by a broom. 'You mean . . . you are saying—'

'Saying we will go to war with you, Arthur. The troop has agreed to see this out. They fear the awful trip back to Angeln more than any army—Saxon or otherwise.'

Arthur sprung to his feet and went to Hereferth. He embraced and back-slapped him. Above the outbreak of relieved murmuring, he said: 'That is so good to hear, man. Now we can fight; now I can look my enemy in the eyes instead of scanning his distant figure from the battlements of Brythonfort.'

Smala explained further. 'Our people want the land, you see. Many of the men out there were dispossessed after the recent storms and have little to show from a lifetime of heavy toil.' His attention went to Arthur. 'Also, your name is known to them; even across the sea your deeds are legendary. To fight alongside you they regard as a great honour and is the reason many of them came to Britannia, so in the end it was not hard to convince them to stay.'

Arthur gave a curious little smile. 'Convince them, you say. So you were in favour of this all along?'

'Before I left the hall I had made up my mind, Hereferth as well, but we could not speak for our men because they are volunteers.'

'Seven hundred British and Anglii mounted men, and three thousand footmen are our numbers now,' said Arthur. 'At last I have something to work with. The first thing to do is to get your mounted men used to fighting from horseback. Withred tells me the animals are used merely to get you to the point of battle, from where you dismount and fight on foot. But my knights fight the Roman way, *from the saddle*, and this will give us a steal over them. The Votadini, Saxon, and Hibernian horsemen also use the horse merely as transport, but we will force them to fight mounted, and therein lies our advantage. Your Anglii riders will receive the knowledge of how to fight as my riders, and though untested when going into battle, it will at least give you some advantage over them.'

'When do you purpose to leave,' asked Hereferth.'

Arthur turned to Flint for guidance. 'How ready is the shieldwall?' he asked.

'They're ready to fight,' said Flint matter-of-factly. 'Only real combat will improve them now.'

'And archers, Dominic. How many can we count on?'

'One hundred worthy men I took from Flint and Erec's shield fighters. All men familiar with the bow. Add the bowmen from Angeln, and I can start to prick the faces of Guertepir's rabble.'

'Archers, shield men and knights,' said Arthur, seemingly satisfied. 'A good balance of fighters to take to the enemy. One day's intensive practice for the Anglii knights—yes *knights* you will become, not mere horsemen— then two days' travel to the city. Three days from now we will stand together overlooking Aquae Sulis. Badon Hill and glory or death awaits us there.'

CHAPTER TWENTY-ONE

Tomas and Nairn looked down on Aquae Sulis from the summit of Badon Hill. Below them, at a distance of three miles, the town's northern wall stood high and imposing, its buttresses looking down upon a boundless horde of humanity. Such were their numbers that a tented settlement had set down its roots on the flood plain to the east of the river. The Afon flowed beside the towns eastern and southern walls, partly encircling and adding further protection to the ramparts.

Arthur's orders to Tomas and Nairn had been quite clear: follow Guertepir from his ringfort and send back any news of his progress eastwards. Their scouting had inevitably led them to Aquae Sulis, where, five days earlier, they had witnessed the merging of the Votadini and Hibernian armies. Nairn had sped away at once and taken the news to Arthur.

Alone that evening, Tomas had witnessed the opening of the town gates and the admittance of the enemy. The next day, Nairn had returned with another rider to learn of the capitulation of Aquae Sulis. The spare rider immediately left for Brythonfort to inform Arthur of the latest dark news.

Two days later, they witnessed the arrival of the Saxon army, when a mass of two thousand men had marched boldly up to the gates of the city.

Two further days elapsed before a convoy of wagons, wains and walking folk arrived. These, the families and camp followers, settled beside the river—their encampment now covering a broad swathe of the Afon valley in a sprawling untidy sea of white canvas.

'Do you think they'll come ... Arthur and his men, I mean?' asked Tomas as he lay on his belly, watching the activity on the fields before Aquae Sulis.

'No. Not unless Withred and Gus get enough men from Angeln,' answered Nairn. 'When I left Brythonfort, Arthur was in a sombre mood; he had only his knights and one thousand farmers in the shieldwall to count upon.'

Tomas continued to squint through the failing light. 'We are almost three miles from the town yet they stretch close enough so I can make the nearest of them out individually. There must be fifteen thousand people before us now.'

'And nearly half of those are fighting men,' mused Nairn. 'Little wonder Arthur hesitates to come and so leave Brythonfort undefended.' He strained to make out the distant gates set in the town's northern wall. 'They're arrogant bastards down there, that's for sure; they even saunter in and out through the gates as if unafraid of any reprisal. Do you think anyone got out alive?'

Tomas shivered. 'Maybe some are alive … who knows. I saw a knight—had the bearing of Erec, though I couldn't be sure—just about make it inside. He's got to be worth some concession if they decide to ransom him.'

Nairn looked unconvinced. 'Nah, I don't think so; Erec's well known in these parts; a warrior of legend; they'll kill him, trust me, and in doing so remove the biggest of thorns from their side.'

Their chat continued until darkness fell. When it did, a blaze of campfires lit the valley below like bloated dying stars in an inky universe. From near distance to afar, the lights dotted the flood plains of the Afon, their number leaving Tomas and Nairn no doubt over the size of Arthur's task should he decide to take the battle to Guertepir.

Soon, the noise of revelry and drunkenness drifted up through the chill air of the valley. Tomas shifted in his blanket. Even though it was his turn to rest, sleep would not come to him. 'Some have been pissed since they got here,' he mumbled as he sought out a good sleeping position. 'Some of those wagons were full of ale, wine and mead. I watched as they unloaded them.'

'They fight *pissed*; that's what makes them so reckless and fierce,' said Nairn.

'*And* slow, according to Flint. Arthur fines his men if they drink too much before a patrol; he reckons it takes the edge off their responses.'

'He'd do well letting the inexperienced men—the farmers and such—have their horns of mead if he ever gets them here. When faced with a jeering shieldwall of Saxons they'll need the courage drink brings to stop them shitting where they stand. Most will turn and run...' Nairn went suddenly quiet. Rapidly, he cast his blanket from him and took to his feet. 'Nemetonas' tits! How could we let this happen? Get up Tom!'

But Tomas was already beside him. Both held their knives.

'Sloppy ... I see your shadows against the lights. Both of you would wear my arrows as neck adornments were it not for your raggedy-arsed shapes telling me who you are.'

'Dominic ... you've come.' Tomas breathed his relief and relaxed.

'Aye lad, and I've brought an army with me; prepare yourself for a fight that will forge a kingdom. Tomorrow we go to war.'

THE BATTLE – DAY ONE

Dawn came and Badon Hill from any viewpoint appeared unpeopled. Arthur had been careful to place his men out of sight behind the ridge until they were grouped and organised. As tents went up, he walked with Flint, Gherwan and Withred amongst his men. The main body (the foot soldiers) occupied a sloping field that ran away from the hill's crest. Several huge tents of canvas, each roomy enough to accommodate fifty men, were laid in a grid pattern across the field. One of the many things Arthur had learned from his time with the legions was this: that a dry, well-nourished soldier was less likely to dessert than a sodden wretch with an empty stomach. Furthermore, Arthur saw his people as men of honour and dignity, and not mere puppets to dance to his tune.

He approached a group who worked together to secure guy ropes to one of the tents. 'How many's that since the sun peeked over the horizon?' he asked.

Too many to count, high lord,' said the nearest man, 'but we're seeing the last ones go up now.' It was his first sight of Arthur and his captains in the light of the new day. Their no-nonsense bearing filled him with hope.

Arthur carried his white-plumed Roman ridge helmet, allowing the man to observe his face—a visage moulded gaunt and wan with the expectation of battle. The artisan noted the hint of bridled power betrayed by a slight quiver in his king. But woe betides the enemy who interpreted the idiosyncratic event as fear. He had seen Arthur in combat; had witnessed the quiver transform into uncompromising power.

Arthur was dressed to fight from horseback; his apparel chosen for freedom of movement and rapidity. His knee length studded tunic was split to mid-thigh; its constitution of thick leather, laid over with a burnished bronze breastplate. The combination offered protection from slashing blade and errant arrow. A broad belt encircled his tunic, and from its attached scabbard protruded the long handle and silver pommel of *Skullcleft*—his renowned blade. Behind him stood his groom—a lad no older than thirteen—who held his unicorn-emblazoned shield. Flint, Gherwan and Withred were similarly attired, and all mirrored Arthur in the gauntness of their countenance.

347

Arthur moved on, giving words of encouragement to the common men who stood outside the tents; men readying themselves for the unknown experience of brutal war.

'They couldn't be better trained,' said Flint, noticing Arthur's brooding concern. 'Erec and I drilled them until their arms were rubbed raw by the shield loops.'

'Yes, I know, but war is different,' said Arthur. 'Nothing can prepare you for its stink; its noise; its rotting filth. These men are farmers, not warriors, and we are about to pit them against—'

'Probably, many other farmers,' said Withred, eager to lift Arthur. This was his leader's one weakness: his incessant anxiety over the welfare of his men. 'Do not forget the Saxon shield is made up mainly from their levy, many of whom are chancers and farmers looking to acquire new land.'

'Yes … I know … I need to relax a little,' said Arthur, aware of Withred's insight into his character. He crested the ridge. Below them lay the fields of Aquae Sulis. The four fell silent awhile as they surveyed the masses assembled below. After some moments, Arthur turned to observe his own army. A distance away, beyond the tents, Smala, Hereferth and the

Anglii laboured to establish their own camp. Further back still—beside a line of covered chuck wagons—men and women from Brythonfort had already set up tables and cooking equipment.

'We need to show ourselves by mid-afternoon,' said Arthur as he turned back to look at the Afon valley and Aquae Sulis. 'Then I can go down and talk to Guertepir or whoever's in charge down there.'

'And therein lies our problem,' said Gherwan, his tactical mind alert. 'To get them to attack uphill.'

Pragmatic as ever, Arthur responded. 'They won't. Not today … not any day; I fully expect Guertepir to laugh at us.'

'Which leaves us with Dominic's plan,' said Gherwan. 'Do you really think it'll work?'

'We've nothing to lose by trying it,' said Arthur. 'Work or not, it gives us the chance to bloody their noses before they know what's happening.'

Guertepir, in no hurry to leave the luxury of Aquae Sulis and continue with the campaign, knelt in the small temple dedicated to Sulis Minerva. He cut the hen's throat, allowing its blood to pulse into the altar bowl before him.

Since his performance in the baths four days earlier, he had persuaded himself that his skin had taken on an almost God-like glow. Frequently, he had pulled up his sleeve and rubbed his hand over his arm, convinced its smoothness was an indication of his newly acquired mortality. Surely the Goddess would reward him for the sacrifices he had made. Though why Almaith still looked a corpse puzzled him. Why had Sulis Minerva not healed the eye (now a black, puffy slit) which Erec had left her with. Indeed, why did her other eye still have its vacant look, and why did her skin remain pitted any grey? Maybe she hadn't coupled with the knight properly; maybe his seed had not entered her fat belly. His ponderings ended when an urgent Diarmait entered the temple.

'You can put it off no longer, my lord,' said his captain and champion. 'The Saxons are outside and would speak with you.'

Grunting, Guertepir got to his feet and threw the headless, fluttering chicken to the floor. 'Want to move on do they?' he said tetchily as he took a cloth from Diarmait and wiped his bloody hands clean. 'It does not surprise me; their arses have become itchy for plunder no doubt.' He jabbed his finger at Diarmait as if

350

delivering a great truth to him. 'They fear this town—believe me, Diarmait. Like all Saxons they prefer to live in their own dung, in their small settlements, that's why even their chiefs camp beyond the walls.'

'Be that as it may, but they insist you deliver your part of the bargain; they press you to move from here and take the fight to Arthur at Brythonfort. They are outside the temple awaiting you.'

With a '*hmmph*!' Guertepir kicked the fluttering chicken aside and stomped to the door.

Outside, waited the four Saxon chieftains: Hrodgar, Wigstan, Cenhelm and Osbeorn. Hrodgar got straight to the point as Guertepir emerged from the temple. 'We're ready to go; you said four days, yet five have passed.'

Guertepir blinked the low March sun from his eyes and gave Hrodgar his best winning smile. 'Of course, my friend. Like I told you before, as soon as my army and the Votadini are ready we shall leave.'

'The Votadini—this Cunedda and his rabble—seem even less inclined to leave than you do. Rumour has it they would return straight to Deva now they have your patronage—your protection down the western seaboard.' Hrodgar swept his arm behind him, inviting Guertepir to look. 'Does Cunedda's absence from this gathering not tell its own tale?'

Guertepir was aware that Cunedda had been furious with him and his own man Abloyc when learning of the killing of the infant in the temple. He knew the Votadini chief had since gone cold on the idea of taking the fight to Arthur. He attempted to placate Hrodgar. 'Cunedda will be ready to fight on the morrow, as will I.'

'So at last I can ready my men to move from this place?' asked Hrodgar, peering at Guertepir as if expecting him to add a proviso to his assurance. Instead, Guertepir gave a reluctant nod. Hrodgar continued. 'Good … Late is better than never, I suppose.' He turned to his three companions. 'Go to your men,' he instructed. 'Get them to stop drinking if you can, and tell them to be ready to move out at first light tomorrow.'

Osbeorn, who was obsessed with finding Dominic—the killer of his brother Bealdwine— was the first to turn from the assembly. 'At last,' he muttered as he pushed aside the press of people around him. He made to move towards the field beside the river where his men were camped. As he did, he looked up to the hill that reared north of the town. He froze upon seeing the spread of cavalry dotted along the hill's crest. As he watched, a long line of shields began to join the horsemen.

Behind Osbeorn, Guertepir and the rest also gawked in astonishment as the entire length of the ridge filled with Arthur's men.

Diarmait pushed to the front, his hand lifted to his forehead as a visor, as his good eyes strained to make out the distant activity. 'It seems they've saved us a journey,' he said. 'This thing can be settled here. And look ... a knight comes to parley; he carries the unicorn flag of Arthur.'

'Then get to him and hear what he has to say,' snapped Guertepir as he squinted up towards the hill.

One hour passed before Diarmait returned from his meeting with Flint. 'Hibernian, Saxon and Votadini,' said Diarmait to the amalgam of leaders who waited below the northern walls of Aquae Sulis. 'Just one of each ... the leaders,' he added. 'To meet with their envoy of three on the empty grounds before the hill.'

Arthur, now helmeted and armed, sat bestride his saddle. Alongside him, similarly caparisoned, were Flint and Gherwan.

'Guertepir, a Saxon and a Votadini,' said Arthur as he appraised the group's slow progress towards them. 'Looks like Guertepir's been quaffing wine by the barrelful since I last saw him.'

When twenty paces from them, Guertepir, Hrodgar and Cunedda halted. Arthur pressed his horse to a slow walk, followed by Flint and Gherwan. He stopped before them. He allowed the silence to linger a moment as he fixed each in turn with his penetrating stare.

His appraisal of Guertepir was contemptuous. 'Whoever thought it would come to this. For many years we lived in peace, our alliance keeping the lands free from the Saxon rabble, but it was not enough for you was it man? And did you really expect me to do nothing while you took my town?'

Guertepir gave a scornful little laugh. '*Your* town, Arthur. When did it become *your* town? Why should this most prized possession be yours. Did we not both fight for Rome; do we not both deserve the finest of rewards?'

'Men deserve what they labour and pay for,' said Arthur. 'Just as my people laboured and paid to restore Aquae Sulis. That's what gave them ownership. The sluggard's way—*your way*—is to watch while others do the work, then move in and snatch the prize after they've finished. And what of those who were within the walls before you came? The knights and the common folk. What's happened to them, Guertepir?'

'Why … I've done what any decent man would do—I've sent them on their way; got them from under my feet so I can enjoy Aquae Sulis without distraction.' He tittered now. 'And what a prize the town is. Have you actually been in there, Arthur? The place is wondrous to behold. It will give me pleasure for the rest of my very long life, for I do not intend to give it up.'

Knowing he would get no more from Guertepir on the subject of the destiny of his folk, Arthur pressed on. 'Whether I've been inside or not needn't concern you. What should worry you, though, is this: I am here to remove your head.'

Cunedda and Hrodgar immediately tensed, their hands going to their swords. Flint and Gherwan reciprocated the action.

Arthur's smile held a sneer as he looked at the three men opposing him. 'Take your hands from your swords; this is not to be settled here, you idiots.' His blistering gaze fell upon Cunedda. 'And you … you are beyond contempt. What are you thinking about? A Briton siding with Saxon and Hibernian scum; riding with the very people who would tear our land apart.'

Cunedda remained impassive, outwardly unaffected by Arthur's words. 'This meeting is to thrash out the terms of war, not to listen to your lectures or explain our actions. It's time to spit out what you want, man.'

'I've already told you what I want'—he flashed a look at Guertepir—'and his head is just the start of it.'

Hrodgar, who had none of Cunedda's poise, came in now. His expression was disparaging as he ran his gaze, head to foot, over Arthur. 'Oh, this has gone far enough. Who do you think you are? I am not willing to sit here and listen to your carping any longer.' He paused a moment as he took in Arthur. He could not deny that in looks at least, the British king lived up to his legend. His bearing, his confidence, *his sheer presence*, made him seem much bigger than he actually was—a giant almost. Regardless, Hrodgar continued with his arrogant dismissal. 'Negotiation is not an option here. I intend to dismantle your protectorate and it suits me fine that your men stand on yonder hill and leave your lands and farmsteads undefended.'

Although Hrodgar's words troubled Arthur (indeed, only a small force resided in Brythonfort along with those who had sought the bastion's sanctuary), he had nevertheless been expecting them. 'We *will not* go away, Saxon,' he said. 'You know you need to deal with us sooner or later; why else would you gather in such numbers. Now is the time for war not for talking. I meet with you now to give you my terms. Your people—families, whores, cooks and the like who travelled with you—I will allow to live, and I ask only you do the same in the unlikely event you are victorious. Any fighting men who choose to surrender to me this day will be allowed to return to their lands in the east. Of those, of course, I do not include yourselves; you are for the ax, make no mistake.'

Guertepir gave a harsh, explosive laugh. 'NO! NO! and a shit-crusted NO! to your terms.' He looked to Hrodgar who shared his resolve. 'But my apologies … I should be thanking you for saving me the journey westwards which my Saxon friend here had planned to take tomorrow. Now I can sit and wait for you to come down off the hill and fight me; because, Arthur'—he fixed the lord of Brythonfort with a knowing stare; one that said, *I know exactly what you want, do you think me so stupid*—'we are not coming up to you.'

'So you would sit and wait rather than get this thing done,' said Arthur, not surprised in the least by Guertepir's downright refusal.

'We wouldn't be sitting and waiting long though, would we?' smirked Guertepir. 'Like my Saxon ally just said—your lands are vulnerable while your main force remains here.'

Realising his faint hope of military advantage had gone, and eager to move on, Arthur decided to end the parley. 'It bothers me not whether you come to me or I come down to you. The talking is over and you have made it clear what you want, so all we can do now is fight. Get back to the town and bathe your fat body and that of your benefactor slut of a wife. Go now and cleanse yourselves for the funeral blaze.'

Guertepir, ignoring Arthur's slight, wheeled his horse around and made to leave. 'See you in front of the north wall then,' he said over his shoulder as Cunedda and Hrodgar turned away and began to trot down the hill. As if just remembering something, he put his hand to his head. 'Oh … before I forget, I brought you a gift—some friends of yours would have a quiet word with you.' From the back of his saddle, unseen until he had turned, hung a pendulous sack. Guertepir threw it to the ground, then immediately jabbed his horse into a gallop down the hill and away from Arthur, laughing as he continued towards the walls of Aquae Sulis.

Arthur, Flint and Gherwan remained frozen a moment as they eyed the sack. Flint made to dismount but Arthur stopped him. 'No,' he said. 'He was a dear friend of yours.'

Ashen and grim, Gherwan and Flint watched as Arthur jumped down and went to the bundle. He stooped to the sack and untied it. A mass of tangled hair—both blond and dark— was his first sight. He parted the hair to reveal Morgana's face. Beside her, as if inseparable even after his decapitation, was Erec. His third discovery caused Arthur to jerk his head from the sack. Gasping and ashen, he turned to Flint and Gherwan. 'They've killed the child,' he whispered distractedly as if to himself. 'For pity's sake, the bastards have dashed his brains out.'

Dominic was ready to ride at midnight. Alongside him, Tomas, Murdoc, Augustus and twenty other archers waited on the edge of the ridge. All of them wore dark clothes; all of them had mud-blackened faces. Since nightfall, they had looked down upon a vast, dark plain, punctured by twinkling campfires and specks of lamp light. But now, as the lamps went out and the fires died, the group prepared to leave.

Arthur, who restrained a leashed Titon, addressed them. 'Remember, this is a quick strike'—he tugged Titon close—'and not a task for this hellhound. Burn the tents of the military near the wall, not the civilians on the flood plain.' He turned his attention to Augustus. 'Gus, you are to do your thing then get back here; are you clear?'

'Clear as springwater, lord,' came his reply.

'The rest of you stay close,' said Dominic to the others. 'Watch where I go and follow me. When your arrows have gone, then you can split up and get back to the ridge at top speed. Do you understand?'

As they murmured their assent, Arthur had a final word with Dominic. 'Careful, Dom, we cannot afford to lose men this early. Keep your men disciplined; your plan will work if you stick to it. May Fortuna watch over you.'

He offered his arm and Dominic gripped it. Then he heeled his horse into a slow walk down the hill. Soon the group came to the edge of the civilian camp. Snores and the sound of occasional copulation came from the covered wagons as they weaved their way between them. Night fires, many of them fallen to ember, lit the wet fields with a faint glow as the riders ghosted their way towards the northern walls of Aquae Sulis.

A lone man, blanketed and huddled by a fire, stirred as the horsemen passed by. Dominic paused as the man rose to his knees and started to pee into the darkness. Dominic sought out Augustus and soon saw his large silhouette. 'Will he do, Gus?' he whispered.

'Yes. Leave me here, I'll see to it.'

Augustus noiselessly dismounted and Dominic moved on. Another period of silent approach passed until they could see the dark shapes of the military tents before the northern walls of the city. Ten fires, radiating in a rough semi-circle from wall to wall and encompassing the camp, indicated the positions of guards. Dominic turned to his men. His gesture told ten of his best archers, including Tomas and Murdoc, to dismount and approach him.

In the centre of the huddle, Dominic turned as he addressed each man individually. 'Get as close as you can and keep low to the ground. Make every arrow count. The guards must be dropped. They mustn't give warning to the camp. Do not act until you hear the owl hoot.' He went to the mounted men. 'As soon as we're done, have our horses ready and be prepared to move quickly.'

The archers fanned out, each picking out a guard. Some of the sentinels sat, whilst others stood and drank from horns of mead. Two men desiring to break the tedium of their watch, had come together to speak—their animated conversation punctuated by sporadic burst of laughter.'

'Keep your noise down; men are trying to sleep and hump in here!' The shout came from one of the tents. The guards waved the complaint away and continued their conversation.

'Tomas ... with me!' hissed Dominic. He placed his arm around the youth's shoulders and pointed towards the two talking men. '*They* are the fly in the ointment, the rest should be easy to hit, so I need your accuracy alongside mine here.' He peered through the darkness trying to see his other archers. Their crouching shadows told him they were in position. 'The men are ready to strike and I'm ready to give my signal. When I do, take the man on the left, I'll take the other. My call should serve to make the guards freeze. I've done this many times when ambushing for Rome and it always makes them freeze. But it lasts only a moment so there's no time to dawdle. Are you ready, Tom?'

Tomas, who already had his arrow nocked and his string partly tensioned, nodded his assent. He had killed men before at the *battle at the ox carts* in the eastern forest, and the story of his guile from his sniping position had earned him the name '*Merlin*' from Will—a name that most at Brythonfort called him by. That he now stood beside his hero ready to strike a blow for the good men of the world, meant everything to him.

Dominic pulled back his bowstring to the tip of his nose. Tomas did likewise and Dominic gave his signal. The singing of strings along the line followed his owl's '*hrooh,*' which was clear and authentic.

As predicted, the Saxons became still— startled by the owl call. Both fell quickly, one taking a wound to his chest, the other to his neck. Dominic and Tomas pressed their advantage and rushed them. 'Mine's already dead,' said Tomas, as Dominic ran his blade across the throat of his man.

'Mine too,' said Dominic. 'Just making sure. You do the same.'

Tomas obliged then looked across at the fires to his left where similar scenes were occurring. Dominic gripped his shoulder and pulled him to his feet. 'Come ... lets to the horses; it's time to move.'

Murdoc task had been much easier. His man, worse for wear after drinking all night, had swayed slightly as he took a huge quaff of mead. Dominic's hoot had even served to steady the sway, allowing Murdoc's subsequent arrow to find its mark. When Murdoc got to him, the Saxon lay dead, pierced through the heart.

Along with the others, he went back to Dominic. 'So far so good,' said Dominic. 'That couldn't have gone better. Now we need to burn their arses.'

The man was shaking the last drop of urine from his penis just as Augustus grabbed him from behind and lifted him off his feet. Clamping the man's mouth, he hissed into his ear. 'Stop your wriggling and this will be better for you.'

The man gave a muffled, '*mumph, mumph*' as Augustus carried him effortlessly back to his horse. Looking around to ensure his action had gone unnoticed, Augustus made to place the man upon the ground. 'Listen to me,' he warned. 'I am a giant, and I will rip you from limb to limb if you make a noise while I bind and gag you. Do you understand me?'

The Saxon twisted his head, eyes fearful and wide, as he took a sideways peek at Augustus. Upon seeing the close proximity of the big bearded face, the bald hair-encircled head and the fierce glittering eyes, he gave a frightened little nod.

'You're sure you are not going to make a noise?' repeated Augustus.

Again, the nod, and Augustus lowered him to the ground and removed his hand.

'But I'm not a soldier, I'm just a—'

'Shuush!' Augustus held a finger to his lips and the man fell silent. He nodded down at the man's crotch, where his manhood still dangled. '*Put ... it ... away,*' whispered Augustus.

Moments later, Augustus had him bound and gagged, and thrown over the back of his horse. Then, as if returning from the market with a sack of grain, he walked the horse upwards to Badon Hill.

Withred and Arthur met him when he crested the ridge. 'Good ... good,' enthused Arthur. 'Lock him away for now with the absconder. Flint will talk to him later; any information we can get from him is better than nothing.'

Augustus removed the gag from the man and pushed him through the darkness towards the holding cage.

Dominic stood in silence as he surveyed the scene before him. The ragged rain clouds had shifted, allowed a gibbous moon to cast an ethereal glow upon the walls of Aquae Sulis. Before the walls were the Saxon military tents. The campfires still burned, and beside each one lay a dead Saxon guard from the earlier attack.

The archers crowded Dominic awaiting his next instruction. 'We all need to act together on this,' he said. 'Once we move make sure you use all your fire-arrows'—he jerked his head towards the low fires still burning—'use those to light them. When you're finished it's every man for himself so get on your horses and get back up that hill.' He strained to make out his men in the darkness, looking for any who might be hesitant. Satisfied, he gave his last order. 'Right; go to it. Move now!'

Murdoc ran towards his fire clutching the first of his arrows. Its tip, wrapped in fat-soaked hemp, seemed top-heavy to him. The day before, shortly after Dominic had come up with his plan, Murdoc had practiced briefly with the flame-arrows and found them to be awkward and unpredictable. Now he hoped he could find his mark.

His ponderings ended as an arrow flew into the tents to his right. A quick glance told him that Dominic had no intention of hanging around. Murdoc lit his own arrow, let fly, then watched as its incandescent trajectory described a low arc away from him. Lower than he would have liked, the missile nevertheless shot through the side of the nearest tent. A glow immediately erupted within. Murdoc quickly lit another arrow.

All along his line of sight, shrieking flames flew skywards. Soon, he had exhausted his own supply. He turned from the walls and began his retreat as a cacophony of shouts and screams erupted from the tents behind him. Forty paces away, tied to a makeshift hitching rail, the horses awaited. Dominic's words came to him as he approached one of them. "Get on a horse *when you're done, don't worry which—any horse—just get up and ride away."*

Tomas arrived at the same time, panting and urgent. Murdoc offered his hands as a stirrup and Tomas deftly stood in them and bounced up to a snorting mare. 'Thanks, Mur,' he breathed. 'Now get yourself out of here; the beasts are becoming spooked.'

As Murdoc went to grab a nearby horse, it shied away, causing him to stumble. The hitching rail, earlier erected by one of the archers, had come away from the muddy ground, pulled out by the remaining six horses which now tossed their heads in a bid for freedom. Murdoc berated himself for his earlier hesitancy when realising that Dominic and the others were long gone.

Heat from behind had had him turn to look. In total, fifteen tents were aflame. Murdoc saw that most of the occupants had escaped death by running into the open. These, a large group of bedraggled men and harlots—some dressed, some naked, some in night apparel—milled around in apparent confusion. Soon the gates of Aquae Sulis parted and a detachment of Guertepir's riders emerged.

'Separate, and see what you can find!' Diarmait's shout sounded thin and distant to Murdoc as he

again attempted to grab the reins of the only horse remaining. The beast, eyes rolling, reared and kicked away from him—the red glint of fire on its hooves, his last sight of it as it bound and whinnied its way into the darkness.

Alone and horseless, Murdoc cast a quick glance back to the city. At least two of the riders were heading his way. Knowing his only option was to flee, he turned and headed back through the civilian camp towards the distant shadowy bulk of Badon Hill.

'Here! He's trying to get away! Over here!' Murdoc, his blackened face and dark clothing marking him out as a marauder, had caught the attention of a Saxon baker who had emerged to investigate the riot of sound outside his covered wagon. The man beckoned to one of Diarmait's men then lunged at Murdoc, but the Briton was having none of it and struck the baker, knocking him to the ground.

Murdoc cursed at the revealing fire-glow as he stumbled, fatigued, onwards and upwards. More people came from the tents and wagons and he could only push through them now. None attempted to stop him this time, and slowly he gained the open, clear fields. He welcomed the modicum of approaching shadow and could feel the churned ground beneath him. Dominic and the others were long gone—he knew that now. Girding himself for his final push up the hill, he took in a lungful of air and set off in a stumbling, exhausted run.

When the sound of pattering hooves sounded, it was sudden and unexpected. But it came from behind which meant this was no rescue. More likely, imminent death came his way. With his bow now impotent, and armed only with a knife, he turned to encounter the rider who galloped straight through him.

'No! Do not kill him!' Diarmait's shout was enough to stay the hand of his man. Having knocked Murdoc senseless with his horse, the rider had fallen upon the Briton, intending to cut his throat. As a third rider arrived, Diarmait took charge. 'Get him back to the city,' he snapped. 'Quickly before anyone rides down to look for him. A live captive is worth thirty dead men, you should know that.'

'A big bastard took hold of me when I was taking a piss,' explained Cutha to the other occupant of the wooden cage. 'Don't know what they want with me, I'm just a cook … came here to see if I could grab some land when they move westwards.'

'You should've stayed back in you rat hole back east, then,' said Liofa, the Angle. 'Come to think of it, we're both a pair of rat-brains.'

'Why's that then?'

Liofa gave an indifferent sniff and toyed sulkily with the hole in his hose. 'Because we've both ended up in this bleedin holding pen, why d'you think; and before the battle's even started.'

'But you're an Angle, listening to you. Whose side are you on anyway? I hear Angles have ridden to Arthur's cause.'

'And more fool me for doing so. As soon as I saw the numbers against us, I said, sod this, I'm off.'

'Numbers against you? What do you mean? I thought Arthur had thousands behind him.'

'He has got thousands, my friend … three thousand. Outnumbered two to one he is; why do you think I'm sat here this night. I got as far as Corinium; was going to try and make it to Norwic and sail home, but I got caught and they brought me back.'

Cutha pondered a moment as his simple brain struggled to assimilate the information. After a period of contemplative silence, he asked: 'What d'you think they'll do with us?'

'Who knows; torture us maybe.'

Cutha's eyes widened with fright as his mouth formed a shocked O shape. He then told Liofa of the rumours he had heard about the slaughter in the town. 'Killed all the women and children they did, and the knight and his wife and baby. They'll torture us for sure.'

Liofa chuckled. 'Naw, don't shit your pants just yet, we're the least of their troubles. They're waiting for reinforcements from the west. As soon as they get here they'll have the Saxons and the rest surrounded. Arthur's happy to sit here and do nothing; the last thing he wants to do at the moment is fight. This standoff suits him, even though he gave Guertepir the impression he wants him to come up the hill. His expecting help—big help—and he wants to sit pretty till it gets here.'

'Are you saying he doesn't *want* to fight yet?'

'No of course not,' laughed Liofa, astounded at Cutha's naivety. 'If they fought now, uphill battle or no uphill battle, Guertepir would kick his arse. If you ask me—'

A tumult from outside cut Liofa short. He scuttled to the bars of the cage and stuck his nose through them as he struggled to make out its cause. After sniffing ineffectively at the air he turned to Cutha. 'Sounds like *something's* ruffled their feathers,' he said. 'A load of them just flew down the hill like they've got rats up their arses. Time I sneaked off while I can—the guard's gone from the door.'

'What do y'mean, time you sneaked off,' said Cutha with an alarmed whisper. 'You can't just open the door and leave.'

Moonlight glinted off Liofa's knife as he sawed away at the twine securing the door. 'Yes I can, and this knife's my key,' he grunted as he continued to slice through the twine. 'They missed it when they put me in here … is it any wonder I ran away from the useless bastards.'

Liofa soon had the door open. He peeked outside, his head darting around like a cautious lizard as he strained to see any movement. Preparing to leave, he turned towards Cutha who had shrunk against the far wall of the cage as if terrified of the world beyond it. 'Well, I'll be on my way,' he said. 'It's off this mad island and back to the marshes of Anglii for me.' When Cutha didn't move, Liofa gave an indifferent shrug. 'Please yourself, stay there if you must, but don't be surprised if they take my escape out on you when they get back.' With that, Liofa crawled from the cage and bounded off into the darkness.

Cutha's torpidity departed him upon hearing Liofa's final words. Indeed, he would take his chances. If he ran into angry Britons then so be it. Waiting in the cage was suddenly the wrong thing to do, especially if they took their frustrations out on him when they returned. And so, seconds after Liofa's departure, Cutha ran down the hill to his own people and freedom.

THE BATTLE – DAY TWO

When dawn came, Guertepir and a small entourage rode from the protection of Aquae Sulis. Standing amongst the smoldering aftermath of Dominic's raid while they assessed the damage were Hrodgar, Wigstan, Cenhelm and Osbeorn.

'Ah, the fat bastard's here at last,' said Hrodgar as he strode out towards Guertepir. When he reached him, he jabbed his finger at the burnt out tents. 'See … *this* is what happens when you sit and wait,' he stormed. 'I lost thirty men last night—yes, it could have been worse, but it should never have happened.' He pointed up the hill. 'It's time we dealt with them and the only way to do it is to get up there and fight.'

Guertepir signalled to one of his retainers, and the man went down on his hands and knees offering his back as a stool. Grunting as he removed himself from his saddle, Guertepir climbed down, via the man's back, to stand beside Hrodgar and the others. He looked towards the charred tents and sighed … as much at Hrodgar's persistence as at the sight before him. 'Yes, they pricked our arses last night,' he conceded, 'but if that's the best they can do then we've little to worry about. I've spoken to Cunedda and Diarmait and they still think it better to wait for the Britons to come to us.'

'They may have pricked our arses this time but who knows what they have planned for tonight,' said Hrodgar, who was having none of it. 'Surely, it's madness to wait here and let them keep sending down raids. I say we get our men up that hill and meet them.'

'There's absolutely no need to be so reckless, and our wait will be short, anyway,' said Guertepir. 'How long do you think Arthur will hang around. That his people in the west are vulnerable to any chancing war band heading their way must be driving him mad. Last night was merely his attempt to draw us up towards him. And listen to you man—he's nearly succeeded in his aim. I tell you we've no need to be hasty, we are sitting pretty here … besides; things have changed since we took the captive.'

'Oh, the Briton … oh, him,' said Hrodgar, his mind still on outright attack and his interest only mildly evoked. 'What difference will he make? He's but one man. Arthur will not give concessions for the life of one man, you should know that.'

'Yes, I do know, but do not be surprised what a bit of provocation will achieve.'

'And how will you provoke him?'

'By demanding something I'm sure he will not give, and then killing his man before his eyes because he refuses me.'

'More likely you'll provoke your wife by killing him. I hear he's a handsome, athletic man; exactly the type she desires for her bedchamber.'

'I think not; he was unable to perform for her; gave him to her last night but she flew into a fury over his soft dick. Like the other, he was immune to her charms; can't imagine why.'

'Then kill him by all means,' said Hrodgar, in no mood for levity. 'Better still, torture him. Have it done now before me; it would please the men and give an edge to my appetite; why must you kill him in front of Arthur? What will that achieve?'

'Who can tell,' shrugged Guertepir. 'Maybe he'll fly into a rage and come down of that hill of his and get on with it if he sees his man slaughtered before him.'

Hrodgar was skeptical. 'You've already tried shocking him with the heads in the sack, and that didn't work.'

Osbeorn, the brother of Bealdwine (a fierce warrior scout killed by Dominic in the eastern forests two years earlier), had suddenly become interested. Like his late brother, Osbeorn was a hook-nosed, narrow-eyed, viscous killer. 'This Briton?' he asked. 'Would he be from the eastern lands or from Arthur's province?'

Guertepir chuckled and wagged a finger at Osbeorn. 'Ah … I see what you're heading towards,' he said. 'Why do you not just come right out with it and ask if the man might be a cohort of this Dominic you so obviously hate.'

'As you would hate him if he had killed your brother?' bristled Osbeorn.

'My brother—no, definitely not. I killed the bastard myself. Greedy turd he was … wanted half of my kingdom. But the answer to your question is this: yes, he is an associate of Dominic, I know because this is the second time the man has been under my lock and key. The last time was at my fort; there I held him as surety while Dominic went to Hibernia and settled an old score for me.'

Osbeorn, eyes flashing, suddenly gripped Guertepir's tunic. 'Then I must be the one to kill him,' he said. 'When it comes time, Guertepir, I must be the one to do it.'

'Look, this is getting us nowhere and the morning draws on,' snapped Hrodgar as Guertepir pulled Osbeorn grip away. 'I'm sure you *will* be the one to do it, Osbeorn. Now get the prisoner, Guertepir, for pity's sake, so we can move on this.'

Guertepir gave Osbeorn an unpleasant look then turned and nodded to one of his men. Soon, the man returned, pushing a bruised and bloody Murdoc before him.

Dominic feared for Murdoc. After returning from the night raid it had soon become clear that something was wrong. The pulsating excitement of the raiding party (all of whom were back and safe) had soon given way to anxiety when Murdoc's absence became noted. Dominic then paced the ridge, straining to look beyond the blackness towards the far glow of the fields before the city. Having waited long enough, he and ten of his men had stormed down the hill, prepared to travel even into the very midst of the enemy camp to find their man.

The discovery of his bow at the edge of the Saxon encampment, along with the telltale signs on the ground, had left Dominic in no doubt that Murdoc had been taken. Withred had come to him then. Sent by Arthur, he eventually persuaded Dominic to return to camp, reasoning that to continue the chase would only lead to his own capture or death.

A sleepless night passed, and the dawn found Dominic hollow-eyed and frantic as he scanned the tent-strewn valley below.

'Something will happen today, Dom, believe me. This will move on.'

Dominic, his face a mask of worry, turned to find Arthur. 'He wanted nothing more than to live his life in peace as a farmer,' said Dominic. 'I found him in the forest with his little girl after those bastards had wrecked his life and now they finally have him in their grasp.'

'He may still be alive,' said Arthur with scant conviction. 'He may even get away; after all *we* lost two prisoners overnight.'

Dominic had turned his attention back to the valley. 'Yes, I know, but that was a set up,' he said distractedly. 'I doubt Murdoc will get a chance like that … that's if he's still alive.'

Troubled, both walked a distance down the hill as they strained to make out the distant walls of Aquae Sulis. After a moment, Arthur put an arm around Dominic's shoulder and pointed to the open gates of the city. 'Can you see it; something's stirred them,' he said. 'It's hard to tell at this distance, but'—he turned and shouted up the slope—'can somebody up there get Flint and his good eyes down here!'

'Yes, something seems to be happening,' said Dominic. 'Maybe Flint will tell us more.'

Flint arrived, breathless and keen to help.

'How're the men faring?' asked Arthur?'

'Anxious but ready to go,' said Flint. 'Gus's with them now, making them laugh as usual. Knows what he's doing does Gus; knows the value of keeping them in good spirits.'

'And you've kept them off the ale?'

'Gave them their usual rations; though some might need a boost before they go into the shieldwall; but that seems a distant prospect at the moment.'

'And what of Liofa?'

'He's back with the men after making his "*escape*"'

'Did he feed the Saxon the shit about our waiting for an army from the west?'

'Yes, but he reckons the Saxon was a dimwit. Can't be sure the man will have the wit to go to Guertepir.'

'We can only wait for that,' said Arthur as he turned once again towards Aquae Sulis. 'Down there Flint; tell me what you can see.'

Flint brought his flat hands to his brow, squinting as he strained to interpret the movements below. 'It's a group of twelve,' he said after a moment. 'The flag of Guertepir—the white bull—is aloft. They carry the banner through the civilian camp and head this way.'

'Just twelve you say?' asked Dominic.

'Yes, that's my count.'

'Then they must come to parley.'

'In that case we need to get down there,' said Arthur. To Flint, he said: 'Get Withred, Tomas and Gherwan here with six more. We'll meet them with equal numbers and hear them out.'

Murdoc, shackled and pushed along by Osbeorn, shuffled behind the main group. Before them, Guertepir's flag billowed and snapped in the stiff breeze. The Hibernian king, who rode beside the flag bearer, turned in his saddle and shouted to Osbeorn. 'Make sure he's fit for purpose when we get him there. You'll get your chance to finish him; no need to do it now.

Osbeorn scowled up at Guertepir. Earlier he had beaten and kicked Murdoc until Diarmait had pulled him away and berated him for his stupidity. *'Don't fret,'* Osbeorn had said. *'He can walk; that's all he needs to do.'*

Guertepir turned away and dug his heels into his horse's belly as it reached the slope. 'Looks like they've seen us,' he said to Diarmait beside him. 'A group of them are on the move.'

'*This* should be interesting,' responded Diarmait.

At a point four hundred paces beyond the civilian camp, Guertepir stopped. Soon Arthur and his ensemble neared them. They stood off, a distance away.

'We've brought your man!' shouted Guertepir. 'Thought we could perhaps strike a deal.' He laughed when seeing the look of astonishment as Murdoc was pushed forward and displayed to them. 'See, I'm not such a bastard after all,' continued Guertepir. 'Allowed him to live, I did. You can have him back alive, if you agree to my terms.'

'And what would they be?' asked Arthur.

'Turn around and go home. But before you do, surrender to me one in ten of your men, because I intend to execute them. I cannot see you leave with an eager army, now can I?'

Arthur's tone was one of tired resolution. He sighed. 'Why are you wasting my time with this, Guertepir? Tell me your terms and let's get this thing done with.'

'Those *were* my terms, Arthur. Are you telling me you reject them?'

'No, I'm telling you I do not take such drivel seriously. I am going to defeat you and your rabble Guertepir—never doubt that. Give Murdoc to me now and we can discuss the terms of my clemency towards you when I do.'

Guertepir laugh was dismissive. 'And you say *my* terms are not to be taken seriously.' He turned to Osbeorn. The Saxon chief stood in blistering silence beside Murdoc. 'Cast your eyes on this fellow,' shouted Guertepir now looking towards Dominic who peered back, dark eyed and menacing from under the snout of his wolf hat. 'You killed his brother, so I am told. A fellow named Bealdwine. Beheaded and hung him up to bleed out … like a slaughtered swine by all accounts.'

'A murdering bastard who died in combat,' shouted Dominic. 'He suffered a much cleaner death that those who fell under his own cruel knife.'

Osbeorn grabbed Murdoc by the collar and pushed him forward a few steps. His other hand was furnished with his dagger, and this he held at Murdoc's throat. He rasped into Murdoc's ear. 'Talk to him, dog. Guertepir tells me the man is like a brother to you. Have your last words with him before I kill brother for brother.'

Murdoc raised his head, squinting painfully as he attempted to see beyond the purple bruises of his puffy eyes. Behind the slits, a sparkle of green still held a hint of defiance.

Through a bruised and broken mouth, he managed a response. 'Dom … this is a lost cause. They're not going to spare me … the whole meeting is … is a sham. You need to get away … away from here. Tell Martha she and Ceola were my last thoughts before—'

'No—this is not a lost cause,' shouted Dominic, near to panic. 'This is not over yet, there is still much to be bargained for here.'

'Then you agree to my terms, wolfman?' resumed Guertepir. 'If so I think you should convince your master.'

'No he does *not* agree with your terms, they are ridiculous,' came in Arthur. 'What is all this about? What you ask is beyond common sense.'

'As I thought,' said Guertepir, rolling his eyes. 'You're not prepared to listen to reason.' He nodded to a nearby retainer. The man brought Osbeorn's horse. Tied to its saddle was a rope. The retainer tied the rope around Murdoc's ankles. Guertepir wheeled his own horse towards the town and shouted over his shoulder as he made ready to depart. 'Last chance, Arthur, do you accept my terms.'

Torn, Arthur muttered: 'You know I cannot.'

Dominic tensed as Osbeorn, awaiting Guertepir's endorsement, readied himself to act. Guertepir nodded to him then kicked his horse into a fast retreat down the hill towards a large group of Hibernian riders who waited to ensure his safety.

Upon Guertepir's signal, Osbeorn actions were rapid and practiced. Bared-teethed, he flashed a look of hatred at Dominic as he cut Murdoc's throat. With fluidity, he was quickly upon his horse and away, dragging Murdoc's dying body behind him.

He had gone but thirty strides when two arrows smashed through the links of his hauberk and entered the meat of his upper back. He fell backwards over the rump of his horse and on to Murdoc, causing the beast to falter and halt.

With bows loaded and ready to use again, Dominic and Tomas ran to the tangle of bodies behind the horse. By now, a detachment of Arthur's cavalry, having seen the disparity in numbers below, had ridden down the hill. A standoff ensued. Dominic and Tomas occupied the ground between as they crouched to attend to Murdoc. A stirring and mumbled incoherence came from Osbeorn, prompting Tomas to slick his dagger across his throat. The Saxon bled out and died quickly.

Though he still lived, Murdoc's eyes rolled in oblivion as Dominic rammed his hand into the outpouring of blood pulsating from his throat. He pleaded with Murdoc as he worked on him. 'No you don't; you do not die on me; you keep with it, man … I saved your leg when you broke it, now I can save your neck … come, come, Mur, you do not get away from me so easily.'

Tomas had already begun to weep. As well as his own loss, his heart went out to Dominic—a man he loved dearly. He knew what Murdoc meant to Dominic, and Murdoc had just died before him.

No blood came from Murdoc's neck now. Dominic removed his hand. The flow had stopped. His friend lay glassy eyed and unmoving. Dominic looked up to the sky, his face pained and twisted as he screamed his grief and anger into the air above him.

After a while, Tomas, sobbing also, shook him. 'Dom, we must be gone. We need to get his body up the hill and away from this awful place.'

Dominic, his face a mask of mucus and tears, could only gaze at Murdoc's lifeless form. 'I must go to Martha,' he said. 'She's working in the field kitchens. I must be the one to tell her. Though, how I'll find the strength to do it, I do not know.'

After the slaying of Osbeorn, Hrodgar had screamed his obscenities at Ziu — the God of the sky. 'How could he sit there and watch while one of his own was taken,' he seethed, as a group of Osbeorn's men went to retrieve his body.

'Because war is war and people get killed,' said Wigstan. 'At least he didn't die a straw death on his pallet, like a woman or a crone. Now he marches in the fields of barley with Woden as his chief.'

Hrodgar shot Wigstan a dismissive half glance as he continued to brood. 'And his six hundred men, all sworn and loyal to him. Who will they march with now? What if they decide to pack up and leave now he's not here to lead them?'

'No; they're ready for battle, they won't go home,' said the Jute. 'They desire land and gold, because most of them don't have a pot to piss in; besides … they're mostly shield bearers; they can fit in with the rest.'

As Osbeorn's body was carried upon a bier at shoulder height, Hrodgar turned to Guertepir. 'Now, will you listen?' he said. 'First the tents are burnt to cinders, then one of our fiercest and most dreaded chiefs is murdered. You poke your stick into a niche of vipers and seem content to let them strike without retaliation. It's time for *us* to attack, can't you see that. We must crush the life out of the snake. We need to move, man; I'm sick of telling you.'

'Move—yes—when the time comes, but not now,' said Guertepir with strained patience. 'He will come down to us before this day is out, mark my words. And are your men ready if he does?'

'Of course they're ready,' said Hrodgar. 'They've been ready for days; though it's little wonder they're still here.'

Guertepir laughed at the absurdity of such a notion. 'But they *won't* go home will they Hrodgar. Not when they're having such fun whoring and drinking. Which reminds me; you need to make sure they're in a fit state—'

'*A man would see the chiefs*!' A messenger had arrived. All turned to him. With the man was Cutha the escapee. Guertepir went to him and stood far too close for Cutha's liking. 'Well?' asked Guertepir, hands on hips, as he scowled at him. 'What have you to say man?'

Cutha knelt and removed his cap, wringing it in his hands in a comical display of obeisance. 'This lord,' he said, keeping his eyes low. 'I escaped from Arthur's capture last night and was told news which may be useful to you.'

Hrodgar, Wigstan and Cenhelm, their curiosity now pricked, went to Guertepir's side. Guertepir, irritated by the man's slow disposition, snapped: 'Come then, spit it out, before I have you taken away and whipped for wasting my time.'

Cutha flicked a nervous look up towards the towering chiefs, then gulped and told his tale.

When he had finished Wigstan and the Saxon chiefs were elated. '*Now* will you go to war,' said Wigstan to Guertepir, who had become solemn upon hearing the news. 'Because, believe me Guertepir, if you ignore what you've just heard you are not the tactician I thought you were. Arthur has three thousand men only, and is biding his time waiting for reinforcements. Can you believe that … he was less inclined to fight than you were, and little wonder.'

Guertepir sighed and waved Cutha away. He regarded the three Saxon chiefs: Hrodgar, stocky and brooding, Wigstan with flamboyantly spiked hair and glittering blue eyes, and Cenhelm, a lover of gold and a man bedecked by his obsession. All three now bristled with expectation. A stoic sigh came from Guertepir as he turned to his man, Diarmait. 'Prepare for war,' he said. 'Tell Cunedda to ready his men, also. It seems we've no choice but to go up that shit-kicking hill today.'

A sombre mood infused Arthur's camp upon hearing of the death of Murdoc. Dominic's dreaded task had been to tell Martha, and she had collapsed with grief when he had finally imparted his news. A frantic night had already passed for her after Murdoc had not shown, but she had clung to the hope that he may have got himself lost in the dark.

Arthur, who had accompanied Dominic, managed to persuade Martha to journey home to Brythonfort, away from the impending clouds of war. Martha, who was desperate to get back to Ceola—Murdoc's little girl and her own daughter in every way but birth—had soon departed.

Looking for solace, Dominic had gone to Nila, who shared a wagon with Augustus' wife, Modlen, and Brindley's widow, Sarah. The three had earlier said goodbye to Martha and started, along with a host of other cooks, to prepare breakfast for the masses on Badon Hill.

Nila's eyes were full of empathy as she hugged Dominic. A deep sadness was upon him—a wretchedness she had never seen before. She wanted the old Dominic back—the cocky but likeable ranger.

Dominic found it difficult to meet Nila's gaze such was the complexity of his emotions. It was their first meeting since his proclamation of love towards her. Now, in his present state, he knew he was capable of saying something he might regret later.

'He was the first to die and won't be the last,' was the best he could manage as he finally looked into Nila's brimming eyes. 'Before this is done, we must all be prepared to lose someone we love—'

'As I love you,' said Nila with a sudden simplicity.

Taken aback, Dominic's words were clumsy. 'Like a brother, is that what you're saying Nila? You love me as a brother?'

Nila's smile bordered on the sad, her look conveying the thought, *Oh, you silly, silly man, do I have to write it down on a tablet of wax for you.* 'No Dom,' she said after a pause, 'I don't love you as a brother, I love you as a man.'

She came to him then and left Dominic in no doubt of the nature of her love. They kissed, and wept, and laughed, and in that moment they forgot about the brooding evil that lurked three miles away.

'What a day it's been,' said Dominic as he finally made to say his goodbye. 'I don't know whether to laugh or cry; I'll probably end up doing both before the sun sets.'

'As will I,' said Nila as she kissed him again. 'But come … this is the fourth time we've attempted to let each other go. Now you really need to get back to Arthur.'

Dominic slid his hand away and walked with a newfound lightness of step back towards the waiting crest of Badon hill.

Augustus in particular had taken the news of Murdoc's demise badly. His men (the shield bearers) were standing behind the ridge ready to form into their set unit should the call for action come. They viewed Augustus (a man they had become fiercely loyal towards as the days had passed) with concern that morning. Gone was his exuberance. He seemed faded to them now, and they knew why. As he walked along the line, many of them exchanged clumsy words of condolence with him. These, he accepted with grace and gratitude.

Also waiting to go to war, and mixed with Augustus' men, were the Angle shields under the leadership of Smala. Many of these, like the Britons, were inexperienced and anxious. Smala, for his part, also engendered a loyalty from his men. They readily accepted his tough leadership, regarding the stout Angle chief as both fair and fearless.

Flint's now strode to Augustus and Smala on the ridge, his manner telling them that the morning was about to get interesting. 'Get your men ready to defend the hill,' said Flint. 'Arthur has assembled his knights. They are'—a horn-blast from the valley below interrupted Flint mid-flow—'they are preparing for battle. Hear that, it's Saxon, they're moving at last. It's what I came to tell you. A large body of shields are marching upwards from the city.'

Augustus' smile was grim. 'So Dom's plan worked. That cunning wolf has no idea of his worth to Arthur.' He shouted to his men. 'On your feet good stockmen and farmers of

Britannia and Anglii! The time has come at last! Today you get to break Saxon heads!'

A scintillating murmur ran through the line as the men stood and took their shields. 'Keep their minds on their task and so off their bowels,' said Flint as he made to leave. He sniffed the air and wrinkled his nostrils. 'Although I fear some of them have already got rid of a respectable load.'

As Hrodgar gave his cry to arms he spotted Raedwald lingering near the north wall of Aquae Sulis. After a quick word with Wigstan and Cenhelm, he rode straight to the youth.

Amidst the shouting and chaos around him, as Saxon, Hibernian and Votadini foot solders ran between groups of assembling cavalry, Hrodgar struggled to make himself heard as he grabbed Raedwald and pushed him towards the line of shields. 'Hoping to avoid the first wave, eh, spunk spurt?' he shouted. 'Well you've just failed again; the time has come to prove yourself a man, and there's no better way to do it than to stand at the front.' He continued to push Raedwald, steering him towards the muster.

Raedwald, who had *indeed* intended to avoid the fighting, became agitated. Aware of the three Saxon chiefs' ire towards him, he had spent his time since arriving at Aquae Sulis, skulking in the shadowy corners of the ransacked wine shops. He panicked now as he realised what Hrodgar was trying to do. 'No— no! Hrodgar, I have a horse; I am to ride at the flanks with Cunedda!'

'Whose horse, you miserable thief? Did you really think I'd forget how good you are at *stealing* horses and how your father robbed me of captaincy when I was a youth? You only live to breathe this day because of the protection of your British and Hibernian captains, though rumour has it, that even they have grown sick of you and your incessant prattle! I always intended you for the pleasure of the shieldwall—another reason you still live.'

He continued to push Raedwald along until they came to the gathering. Here, combatants were linking to the wall and soon they would stand six deep behind the experienced men who held the shields on the front line. The smell of man-sweat and cow dung (for the tendency to spike their hair with the glop had become popular with the men) permeated through the still air. Hrodgar pulled the fyrd (inexperienced men who had supplied their own weapons) away from the back of the line, until he reached a shield-bearing veteran at the front. Hrodgar grabbed the fellow by the crook of his elbow and yanked him backwards, then shoved Raedwald in his place. He thrust the man's shield at him.

'There!' he laughed above the tumult, as Raedwald reluctantly took possession of the shield. 'You're in the centre of a line of eight hundred! You'll be one of the first to fight!'

Wide-eyed with fear and intending to plea his case, Raedwald looked back to Hrodgar. But it was too late … the Saxon chieftain had gone back to his business. The line closed behind Raedwald, and soon he stood pressed and immobile within it.

Arthur sat upon Storm, his mare. Beside him, were Hereferth, Withred, Flint, Gherwan and Dominic. Around them, wheeled the entire British and Anglii cavalry—some seven hundred horse. Down in the valley, the enemy shields, amidst a blaring of horns, beating of drums, and yapping of leashed war-hounds, had advanced from the shadow of Aquae Sulis and halted at the foot of the sloping field before Badon Hill.

'A line of eight hundred!' shouted Flint. 'Six deep—some five thousand men!'

Arthur's eyes were chips of granite as he assimilated Flint's information. He turned to look up the hill where Augustus, Smala and fifty other shield tacticians corralled the shieldwall into a semblance of order. There, Augustus and the others strolled before the men as they shouted their instructions to them. Augustus—who seemed a giant in his war regalia of studded leather jerkin and battered, plume-adorned helmet (the plume a token from his wife, Modlen)—hurled his considerable bulk at the shields, testing them for solidity. Titon barked and bounded around his heels as he did this, occasionally emulating its master as it jumped against the wall.

'I'm glad to see the dog joining in,' said Arthur. 'It'll give them practice for what comes later.' He surveyed the British shieldwall. 'They've spread our own men eight hundred wide, as well. There can't be any overlap, but we are left a mere three men deep along the line.'

'It will have to do,' said Withred, his oiled leather armour creaking as he turned in the saddle to watch the muster. 'We can only hope this hill cancels out their advantage.'

Arthur shouted to Hereferth, the Angle. 'Take three hundred and fifty of your men to guard the left flank and give me the rest.'

As Hereferth and a company of his riders, all bearing the lynx-emblazoned shields of their tribe, rode away along the hill, Arthur turned to Dominic. Gone was the wolf hat, replaced now with a close-fitting helmet of steel. Cheek pieces covered his craggy face and his eyes blazed out determined and brutal from under the shallow peak of his helmet. Tomas, similarly attired, sat beside him.

'Your role is a free one here, Dom,' said Arthur. 'How many archers have you?'

'One hundred and eighty men—Britons and Angles,' replied Dominic.

'Roam free and skirmish,' instructed Arthur. 'Go wherever you're needed—who knows what you'll come up against.' He surveyed the entire battlegrounds, frowning as he took in the gathered masses below him. 'Gods, we could use some back up here.'

'Any sign of Robert or Simon yet?' asked Dominic, sharing Arthur's concern.'

'No sign at all. As soon as—'

The blaring of horns from below took on a rhythmic, repetitive brashness, causing Arthur and the rest to look down the hill. Accompanied by a patterned drumbeat, a line of five riders had ridden in front of the Saxon wall where they again waited to parley.

'This should be interesting,' said Arthur. With Gherwan, Withred, Dominic, and Flint, he descended the hill to meet Guertepir and his captains.

'They're not dressed for compromise,' said Dominic to no one in particular as they neared the group. 'We should get this over with and cut the talk.'

Before them, all armoured and helmeted, sat Guertepir, Diarmait, Cunedda, Hrodgar and Cenhelm. Their shields bore the symbolism of their people: Guertepir's and Diarmait's the white bull, Cunedda's the juniper tree, Hrodgar's the rabid dog, and Cenhelm's the prancing horse.

'Your last chance, Arthur!' shouted Guertepir, his voice barely audible above the clamor. 'Pack up and go home! You are outnumbered … we know that now! Why sacrifice your men for a lost cause?'

'You have taken my city and slaughtered my people'—Arthur's face twisted in disgust—'even stooped so low as to slaughter an innocent babe, you outrage of a man. I say to you this, Guertepir: I *implore* you to send your men up the hill, because I intend to send them to Woden, Jesus or whichever other nonsense they grovel to. And when they no longer stand between you and the city, I will come down and drag you from your hiding place, for you have neither the courage or vitality to face me man to man. Then I'll send you to the hellish underworld which awaits the arrival of your twisted soul!'

A groaning and murmuring of fear came from the Saxon shieldwall as it parted to let the death riders through. Guertepir glanced at his captains, exchanging a smile with them. 'As you will,' shouted Guertepir as forty black horses trotted balefully up the hill to join him. 'The rules of combat dictate I offer you mercy and you have refused. Now it is time your men had a flavour of what they're letting themselves in for.' At this, he turned, and with the rest rode back through the approaching sinister troop.

Dominic intake of breath was sharp—driven by his repulsion at the sight before him. The others, their faces grey with fear, and horror in their eyes, were transfixed for a moment. 'They are armed and many,' said Arthur, at last able to speak. 'Let us leave this place.'

Abloyc grinned, then gagged and vomited, as he watched Arthur and his guard rush back up the hill. He was *more* than happy to act the role of death rider. With blackened face, he was covered head to foot in mud-darkened attire and wore the decaying, naked corpse of Cardew. To the Britons on the hill it appeared that a rotting ghoul now rode up towards them; and worse still, Cardew's grinning skull sat atop Abloyc's spiked helmet. Intending to display the grim spoils of war to the British shields and so break their fighting spirit, nineteen other riders, all wearing the decomposing corpses of female, child or male, rode beside Abloyc.

'It's sure to make one in three turn and run from the line. Endure the stink of the corpses and watch as they flee.' Hrodgar's words went through Abloyc's mind as he spurred his ebony horse up Badon Hill. Behind him and the other riders, the Saxon shields had also started their ascent, their progress slow but resolute. One hundred of Guertepir's horsemen had appeared on the left flank of the wall, one hundred of Cunedda's had gone to the right, their purpose for now to protect the death riders from attack by Arthur's cavalry.

As the gap narrowed between the opposing masses, Abloyc could see the British shield bearers in more detail—the vision filling him with hope. Most of them were rustics, with just a thin scattering of what appeared to be experienced fighters seeded amongst them. Some were fearful … some nauseated … most horrified … as he approached their line. A quick glance to the flanks told Abloyc that an impasse, for now, existed between the opposing cavalry; so, free to ride along the British line at will, he screamed his loyalty to Aeron, the god of slaughter, whilst tearing Cardew's body parts from him and throwing them over the palisade of British shields. The other death riders did the same, promoting a groan of repulsion and a step backwards from the shield bearers.

Augustus and the other tacticians now stood behind the wall, prowling its length and looking for weaknesses. Each of them oversaw a width of sixteen fighters. Augustus picked up a man whose abhorrence of the sight before him had caused him to jump backwards and stumble. 'On your feet man and get ready to push at the signal!' he shouted as he heaved the man back into the line. 'Save your fear for the live ones—they'll be here too soon!'

A disturbance and whinnying had him turn. Twenty paces back and spreading along behind the line, were Dominic and his archers. As he watched, they pointed their bows skywards and let fly, and so began the real battle of Badon Hill.

Abloyc's first warning of the attack was a darkening of the air above him as one hundred and eighty arrows swished a low arc over the shields. Half of the death riders went down injured or dead, victim to the first wave. Two horses also fell, pierced through head and neck. Abloyc's own horse took two arrows in its rump causing it to rear. Still uninjured and knowing he now occupied a death zone, Abloyc savagely reined his horse groundwards and made to leave. He ripped Cardew's head from above him and threw it back over his shoulder towards the British. As he heeled his horse into a gallop back down the hill, the head took a high trajectory, falling short of the shields.

As the surviving death riders fled from the field, nothing remained between the opposing forces other than a slope scarred by brook and hedge and body parts.

Flint broke from the cavalry and joined Dominic. Close by, a British trumpeter gave out three piercing blows on a goat's horn. 'The blares tell them to stand steady!' shouted Flint. 'It is but one of many signals they recognise! Shouting at them from distance is futile in this noise! For now, they await the Saxon wall, but Arthur thinks you could do something now!' He stood in his saddle, looking over the heads of the men, and pointed to the slowly approaching horde some five hundred paces distant. 'They'll break their line in a moment when they come to the hedges! Arthur and Hereferth guard the flanks against the Saxon and Hibernian cavalry but no moves have come yet!'

'Would it not be better if he attacks their wall, then, when it flounders at the hedges?' yelled Dominic

'No, they have spears ready for such a move; and spears and shields kill horses! A distant strike would be far more effective against them!'

Dominic, now aware of his next role, beckoned his archers to him and arranged them into two groups. Then they rounded the wall of

British shields and entered the killing ground between the armies.

Raedwald dithered as he trudged onwards and upwards—the press of bodies behind him leaving him in no doubt that he was in a situation beyond his control.

Having little say over his own movement, he lurched forward as he reached a ditch, his shield going to ground and slapping against the wet earth. He managed to scoop his hand through its loop as he was pushed towards a hedge. For the first time since his placement in the shieldwall, the man beside him had gone from his elbow. The line was now ragged and some of the men were on their knees as Dominic's arrows began to slap into them. Raedwald gasped as more by luck than judgment, his shield protected him from three rapid arrow strikes. The attack continued until he heard the approach of horses from behind. He turned to see Hibernian mounted archers who had ridden up to protect the advance. Soon the British bowmen began to retreat as retaliatory arrows started to fly. A quick glance along the line told Raedwald that Dominic's raid had been quick but effective. Scores of the shield had fallen, but as the last of the hedges were either climbed or trampled, the wall came together again.

Dominic cursed as he retreated from the field and headed back to his own line. 'I guess we lost twenty or so!' he shouted to Tomas who rode beside him. 'I should have got us out before their archers were in range!'

'It's war Dominic; men fall I war, you are not to blame!' shouted Tomas, wind in his hair as he rode low in his saddle. 'The raid was a success, we dropped at least sixty of them. I took out seven shield bearers myself; you must have slaughtered twice as many!'

'Still—they'll pay for killing my men!' shouted Dominic as he galloped wildly to the British flank.

Pwyll was glad to hear Augustus' voice boom out behind him. That the giant was nearby and in charge of his group comforted him. Yet Pwyll's body remained spring-tense and quivering as he watched the Saxon wall approach. The business with the corpses had repulsed him, as it had the others, but now it was over and done with he was ready to fight. His three-foot shield was made from wood and covered in metal, and bore no emblem, having been hastily constructed for purpose. Like every other man in the front line, Pwyll also carried a short stabbing sword, but these weapons were in meagre supply. Behind him in the second line, men would attack over the shields with longer swords and spears, and further back still, the supporting, pushing men carried scythes, axes, clubs and mattocks—self-supplied weapons to protect them should a breakthrough occur.

As the gap narrowed to thirty paces, the uproar intensified. Horns blasted to a new level and drums pulsated within the guts of all. Saxons had started to shout threats to the British and allegiance to their gods. Pwyll and the man next to him exchanged a fearful glance as two blares of a single horn sounded behind them—the signal instructing them to prepare for the weight of the Saxon push.

Aware of the importance of forming a continuous, solid line, Pwyll checked that his shield overlapped with the men next to him. Satisfied, he turned and peered over its rim at the Saxon wall—now only ten paces away. Like the British, the Saxons carried shields void of any heraldry, and like the British, the men who approached seemed fearful and inexperienced.

When the walls came together it seemed that hell itself had pushed up through the bloody turf of Britannia. No training in the world could have prepared Pwyll for the drive which lifted him from his feet. But the Saxons could not sustain such pressure against the steep slope of Badon Hill. Slowly, its potency ebbed, and the British wall held.

Pwyll's feet touched the ground again and he found himself a nose-width away from his opposing man—a mustachioed and gnarled hunter who snarled and spat at him. Shield to shield, both men were locked into immobility. The man behind Pwyll managed a spear thrust over the shields and was able to knock the hunter's helm to one side. Enraged, the man—a Hibernian—yelled his fury towards them, his ale-laced breath gusting into Pwyll's face.

Pwyll ducked low under his shield, away from the man's fury, just as an answering jab of steel flashed towards him from the second row of the Saxon wall. A scream behind had him turn. The spearman had taken a sword wound to his face and now bled outwards, his tongue and lower jaw razored by the strike. The man remained standing and dead, supported by the absolute weight of the press.

As the push and sway continued with no significant shift either way, Pwyll's shield parted slightly from the man's beside him. Grimacing as he attempted to free the arm that held his stabbing sword, he gave a futile push forward. After a struggle, his arm came free. Through the gap in the shields he spotted the crimson leather of the hunter's tunic. He knew the opportunity to strike at an unprotected torso would be brief, so he thrust his sword immediately through the breach. With a *'citch!'* the sword slid through the leather and into the man's gut. Pwyll followed the first lunge with three more strikes — *'citch!' 'citch!' 'citch!'* — before the coming together of shields effectively ended his attack.

The hunter screamed his agony, but still he lived. Incapacitated and of no further threat, he swayed in the grasp of the press, his eyes glazed and distant.

Augustus, meanwhile, worked frenziedly behind the line. Alarmed at the initial surge, he had feared his men would capitulate against the sheer force of numbers when, with a scintillating, metallic crash, the opposing shields had come together. Like a floating barrier riding a rolling undulation on a swelling sea, the British shield bearers had gone airborne then.

But the unit held and Augustus now fostered new hope. He stalked the wall looking for the debilitated. The initial encounter had produced five quick casualties along his thirteen-man-wide section of wall. Wading into the men as if pushing through a stand of thick gorse, he dragged the injured and dead free. His final retrieval took him to Pwyll and the dead spearman who swayed behind him. A quick tap on Pwyll's shoulder allowed Augustus to shoot him a steely-eyed look of encouragement. 'Good work!' he shouted as he noticed the incapacitated man facing him.

The pushing continued throughout the afternoon. Axes flashed and spears thrust over and below shield rims as men became exhausted to the point of nausea. Many fell on both sides. The British wall, once three men deep, slowly depleted to two.

The Saxons, harangued and screamed at by their own tacticians as they had pushed up the hill, had succumbed to utter exhaustion. The once-tight press of men had started to become detached and many stood back to recover.

Dominic was quick to spot the Saxon indiscipline. Aware he now had something to strike against, he marshalled his men for an attack. 'Hit the stragglers!' he shouted as more of the enemy pulled away from the shieldwall.

Pwyll had nothing left as he slumped against his shield—his own weight keeping him upright against the opposing wall. Drooling and slack-jawed, his cheek torn from a spear attack, he became aware of a large hand on his shoulder. 'Come away and push from the back,' said Augustus,' You have held the shield longer than any other man in this section.' Augustus, pale with exhaustion himself, took the shield. Near to collapse and barely able to stand, Pwyll went behind the wall.

Augustus stumbled over a riven body as the British wall began to gain ground against the evaporating Saxon forces. His boots squelched through faeces, urine and gore as the produce of the slaughter became uncovered. To enable them to conduct the final throes of the first defense, the other tacticians had also taken shields and spaced themselves fifteen men apart along a front still eight hundred combatants long.

Dominic's arrows flew, forcing many of Guertepir's allies to flee beyond their range. Flint arrived gasping to stand beside Augustus.

'Their wall will break at any moment!' he shouted. 'When it does we must let them go. Our men are too tired to chase and have even less energy to fight. We must keep our form. If we break now their archers will come against us and *that* will be *that*, my friend!'

'What of Arthur, Hereferth and our knights!' shouted Augustus, as he thrust his sword through a gap that appeared in the shields. The strike floundered upon the chainmail of the warrior opposite. The man shouted his defiance at Augustus but raised his head too high above his shield as he did so. In the blink of an eye, Flint spotted the lapse and pushed his seax through the man's eye. The man fell dead and another took his place.

Flint sensed the Saxon line was about to collapse. 'Arthur's been at a stalemate with Guertepir's riders!' he shouted. He raised his shield a fraction to protect his head from a Saxon spear which had been hurtled from distance. The projectile skidded from the shield and went air bound. Grimacing and through gritted teeth he continued. 'Both cavalries still guard the flanks of the shieldwalls and have barely moved. It's getting near dark now, so I reckon there's no action from *them* today.'

'So we regroup and lick our wounds that's if if we ever see the end of this day!' shouted Augustus. 'Because how much longer these men can stand steady is anybody's—'

The Saxon wall began to break. Scores of exhausted men had taken to a stumbling run down the hill.

'MEN, HOLD YOUR GROUND!' Augustus' order went along the line. The shield stood firm.

Cunedda and a body of archers had arrived and sent arrows over the heads of the retreating men, protecting them from any chase, but Dominic and his archers were still able to take many of the infantry down—their powerful bows outranging those of the Votadini.

Augustus parted his shield from the wall. He fell backwards to his rear, arms draped slackly over his knees and head hanging loosely as he gasped his utter exhaustion into the bloody ground. Now released from the intensity of battle, the entire line of shields did the same. Most of the survivors had taken wounds, but all had stood to the end. Flint sat panting beside Augustus. Now the surge of battle-energy had gone, both felt drained to the point of collapse.

Several minutes passed before Augustus could even lift his head. 'I hear horses,' he said weakly. 'Arthur and his knights, no doubt.'

Flint wearily gained his feet. Augustus took his proffered hand and dragged himself upwards. Down the hill a way, like a tumble of seaweed beached by a high tide, was the line of the dead and dying. Some of Arthur's knights searched through the sorry pile, pulling out injured Britons and slaying enemy survivors.

Arthur arrived. He was quickly off his horse. He embraced Flint then went to Augustus. Hugging him close, he kissed his bearded cheek. 'Magnificent, magnificent,' he enthused. 'Now please, to my tent. We need to talk tactics.' He looked along the line of exhausted men. 'They fought like demons,' he said. 'I must speak to them before anything else.'

Having spent the entire battle crouched and flinching behind his shield, Raedwald had survived the day. His seax—pristine and secure in its horizontal sheath—remained unused. Screamed at from behind because of his dormancy, Raedwald had remained frozen, knowing his haranguers would eventually perish and fall silent. Many pushed against him and fought above his head whilst urging him to use his blade, but Raedwald merely winced and waited as the alarming bangs, scrapes and jabs upon his shield shook him to his very core. The day passed long and hellish for him, and when it drew towards its end, he was one of the first men to run from the shieldwall.

He hid in a ditch and escaped the attention of the tacticians who were either killing the deserters or coercing them back to the shields. When Saxon archers arrived, Raedwald had a lucky break. One of the men took a British arrow through his face and fell dead nearby. Raedwald considered his options: taking the archer's place would put him back into the conflict, yet attempting to return to Aquae Sulis unnoticed was unlikely and almost certainly lead to his summary execution. Reluctantly, he took the dead archer's weapon and followed behind the main body of bowmen. His deception worked and he survived the arrow fight, which proved to be short-lived in the failing light.

Back in Aquae Sulis, he hid in an abandoned workers hut next to the west wall of the city. The battle was over for him, Raedwald was certain of that now. As long as he kept away from Hrodgar and the others—and that had to be easy to do in the confusion—he would be safe. Now he had more reason than ever to kill Hrodgar. The man had humiliated him, laughed at him, and pushed him into the line of scum at the shields. He would deal with him then ride with the victors into the western lands and have his share of women and plunder. There he could become a respected man—a warrior who had fought like a devil-possessed in the taking of the city of Aquae Sulis.

Arthur's generals stood around the long, wooden trestle. Lamps of olive oil lit his tent, giving it a dancing orange glow. Flint, Augustus, Dominic and Tomas stood at one side of the table; Withred, Arthur, Gherwan, Hereferth and Smala at the other.

Flint's did a summary and ended with the news that Arthur had lost one third of his men.

'So what do we number now?' asked Arthur.

'Sixteen hundred for the shields, seven hundred knights, and one hundred and sixty mounted archers,' replied Flint.

Arthur did a count in his head. 'That's two and a half thousand or thereabouts. And their fatalities?'

'At a rough count—one thousand. That still leaves them with five thousand—many who are fresh and unused. Not counting cavalry, they probably have around three and a half thousand men for the shieldwall. They never go less than four deep behind the shields, so tomorrow they'll come at us eight hundred wide, as today.'

Arthur tone was ironic. 'So we started the day outnumbered two to one, and finished it the same,' he said. He turned to his tactician, Gherwan. 'Any ideas how we are going to cope with them tomorrow with two and a half thousand exhausted men—less of course those who will desert tonight?'

'Thought of nothing else, lord,' said Gherwan. He went to the table and arranged a line of goblets, eight wide, upon it. Opposing them, he placed another line of eight. This is what happened today,' he said. 'They dictated the length of the line and we had to form an equal number eight hundred wide to meet them.' He raised his head, his expression grave as he looked from man to man. 'If the same happens tomorrow we are finished, do not doubt that.'

Arthur nodded, knowing the truth already. 'Our line will be too thin—just two men deep—it will quickly collapse against fresh men, hill or no hill. What's your recommendation then Gherwan?'

'This lord.' Gherwan turned his attention back to the cups. From one line he took four cups, so that eight opposed four. 'We compress our line to four-hundred-men-wide. It means the men can stand four deep behind the shields, rather than two deep. Four files all pushing at once should be more than enough to halt them on this hill.'

'But now they have an overlap two-hundred-men-wide on each flank. Surely their extra men will engulf and surround us.'

Gherwan nodded his partial agreement but pressed on. 'True … it's far from ideal, but we can only fight with what we've got.' He pointed to the extra, overlapping cups. 'These must be disrupted by our cavalry. Spears or no spears, we must go at the shields on each flank, get them to break from the line—delay them at least.'

'And be attacked by *their* cavalry while we do so,' said Arthur. He sighed and not for the first time inwardly cursed Ffodor for his disloyalty. He looked to Dominic. 'You have one hundred and sixty archers, do you think you can protect us while we attack their flank.'

'That or die trying,' said Dominic.

'And you, Gus … Flint. Can you get your men to even stand again tomorrow?'

'When I've finished talking to them they'll be ready,' said Augustus. 'And that's what I'll do now. I'll see my wife then go to them.'

When Augustus left the tent, Arthur turned to Gherwan. 'Very well,' he said, 'we will go with your plan, but now it's time to discuss the finer details.'

Stools were drawn to the table as the assembly sat with bread and cheese and goblets of wine, and readied themselves to talk until dawn.

Pwyll found Arlyn (his friend since training at Brythonfort) at the food wagon. When the battle had commenced they had stood but six men apart in the line, but they soon lost sight of each other in the ensuing chaos. At the day's end they had assumed each other dead. Clumsily now, they embraced, then joined a group of lounging men beside one of the huge fires dotting the crest of Badon Hill.

'Augustus saved me,' said Pwyll.' Just as he did in the wine shop weeks ago. Pulled me away just as I was about to drop.'

'He's a great man,' said Arlyn. 'Even gives Arthur a run for his money.'

'Yes he is. How did *you* fare today?

'Managed to stab a few and threw up a few times. Oh'—he pulled his tunic back from his shoulder—'and I took this … but it could have been worse.'

Pwyll peered at the open gash across the meat of Arlyn's shoulder. 'Need to get that seen to,' he said. 'It'll make a nice scar to show to your grandchildren.'

'I don't think any of us will see our—'

A spontaneous cheer went up as Augustus arrived at the camp. He looked down at Pwyll and laughed with delight upon seeing him still alive. After giving him a bear hug which lifted him from his feet, he placed him down, then stooped, as if a pony, inviting Pwyll to jump on to his back. Bashfully, Pwyll complied, and Augustus turned to the others with Pwyll riding high upon him. 'This is how we go tomorrow,' he boomed. 'The shitting cavalry didn't move today so we must form our own for the morning!' With that, he ran in a comical gallop into the darkness and out of sight, the roar of mirth drifting into the night sky.

Within earshot, Modlen and Nila had just served broth to some of the men. Despite their fatigue, they could not help but smile as Augustus romped off with Pwyll.

'Are you aware of how special your husband is?' asked Nila.

'Fully,' smiled Modlen. 'And I nearly lost him last year, thanks to the sister of that hound'—she nodded towards Titon who slept at her feet beneath the counter—'but Gus survived, as he will survive all of this.'

Nila studied the dog. 'Poor thing's been tied up there all day ... shook like a leaf in a breeze as soon as the battle started.'

'The noise *was* incredible,' said Modlen as she stirred the cauldron of stew before her. 'Even here, half a mile from the fighting, the ground shook.' A smile that barely lifted the corners of her mouth came to her face as she gave Nila an impish look. 'Talking of incredible men, how did yours fare today?'

'Survived, as if you need to ask,' said Nila, reciprocating the look and smile. 'He came to me before, and we talked a while, but then he had to go and talk tactics with Arthur.'

'Does Flint know what's happened between you two?'

'Not yet. The situation worries Dom, though. Worries him to think Flint will see him as stepping into Bran's shoes.'

'And you?'

'I told him there's no point even thinking about the consequences. Tomorrow may be the last day for us all.'

'Not for *us* if Arthur has anything to do with it. He wants us out and away at first light. Gus, for his part, positively *insists* I leave, not that I need any persuasion—our orphans wait at Brythonfort.'

'Art, Ula, Cate and now little Cara,' said Nila. 'They are a joy and brighten up my day when I see them.' Sadness fell upon her. 'They help me deal with the loss of my precious boy, Aiden, and the absence of Maewyn, they do.'

'Cara can come to you when we get back,' said Modlen, taking Nila's hands in hers. 'She's a sweet little thing and hasn't bonded with us yet. Gus mentioned how unfair it was to take the little dear when you have lost so much.'

The very notion made Nila smile. 'Yes ... it *would* be wonderful to care for and love such a dear child.' They were silent a moment as they thought of the children awaiting them at Brythonfort. Before long, reality rushed at Nila like a wild stampede. She dropped her head, her eyes troubled. 'But why do we even discuss this when tomorrow may bring the destruction of everything we value.'

'Because if we don't talk of normal things when surrounded with this horror we will go mad, Nila—absolutely mad.'

THE BATTLE — DAY THREE

A raggedy, low mist lingered in the Afon valley. Horrified to find that hell rather than the plough was before them that day, Arthur's men awoke to a grey dawn. Coughing and hawking resounded along the ridge as stiff bodies rose reluctantly from beds of clay and struggled into armour. A sinister tension—almost a silence—infused the air as men picked up shields and checked assorted weaponry.

Behind the hill, many defecated, some vomited, all were in fear. The sound of horses had them turn as Arthur and his entire cavalry rode up to the summit.

As the first horn-blast rose forebodingly from the valley, Arthur peered into the mist below. An outbreak of barking followed. 'They start early, Withred,' he said. 'Damn this mist. Of all mornings we could do without it.'

Withred turned in his saddle as shouts of *'Muster!'* and *'Make the wall!'* broke out behind him. 'At least we still have most of the men with us,' he said.

'How many ran into the night?'

'Fifty or so, Flint reckons.'

'We chose well it seems. Mars knows, *I* would be hard pushed to go back into that wall after the horrors of yesterday. It's a wonder they—'

An undulating, high-pitched shriek came from the valley. All became still. Men shivered as cold horror seeped through them. Horses shifted and snorted cold air from dilated nostrils. Moments later, an answering whoop sounded—eerie and nerve-jangling in the dank air of the mist. Now the valley erupted with yelps, squeals and howls.

'Druids,' growled Withred. 'First the death riders and now walking ghouls. Just what the men need—wild-haired skeletons spitting their venom at them.'

'They'll be Guertepir's,' said Arthur. 'He still believes in the old ways; not for him the uncompromising deities of Rome.'

'Nor the sweet nature of Nerthus or Jesus.'

'Pray he doesn't adopt *them*; he would turn them into a bile-spitting demons.'

Gherwan joined them. 'The men are four hundred wide and four deep as advised,' he said. 'The desertions didn't hit as hard as I feared.' He looked downwards towards Aquae Sulis. 'The mist breaks. See—they are but a half mile away.'

Below them, the miasma swirled, occasionally shifting to reveal the opaque forms of men.

'Their shieldwall is formed already from what I can see,' said Withred as he did a rough count. He shot a brief glance of admiration to Gherwan. 'And eight hundred wide or thereabouts as you anticipated.'

'Then we can approach the day as planned,' said Gherwan.

Hereferth and Smala trotted out of the mist and back up the hill. 'Thought we'd take a closer look!' shouted Hereferth. 'We Angles like to know what we're dealing with, don't we Withred?'

'As long as we don't get our heads knocked off when doing so,' chided Withred.

Hereferth gave a humourless little chuckle. '*That*, I think might happen. Many of their shields bear the sign of the juniper—Cunedda's emblem. There were few junipers yesterday, so these must be fresh and rested men.'

Guertepir sat bestride his heavy horse. With him were Cunedda and two of the Saxon chiefs. The shieldwall was before them and had started to advance. At its flanks, the cavalry lurked, led by Abloyc on the right and the gold-adorned Cenhelm on the left.

Further ahead still, beyond the shieldwall and spread out in a line as they walked into the mists, were Guertepir's caterwauling Druids. Central to the line was Muirecán wearing his ankle length, white habit. His face as ever lay hidden in the shadow of his cowl. From the hood, his dark shock of hair flew wild in the stiff breeze.

Like some parody of a Christian brotherhood, the other druids, all doppelgangers of Muirecán, chanted their incantations as they headed fearlessly upwards across the killing ground. But these gave out no enchanting madrigals to the Lord Jesus. Instead, they emitted an awful, strident cacophony of hate. No crosses did they carry. In the place of such holy relics, they held before them the body parts—heads, torsos, feet and hands—of those taken from the field of combat. Muirecán's trophy, though, was small ... almost weightless. Thrust out before him, held by its ankles, was the infant Girard's headless corpse—the cadaver's torso adorned with an intricate rune. Muirecán's screeching ululation intensified to an ear-splitting level as the rest of his acolytes took up the chant.

'Woden service me roughly from behind!' Hrodgar winced as he listened to the clamor. 'They're enough to make Grendel itself run away and shit in a ditch.'

'It'll soften the Britons up before the fight,' said Guertepir as he heeled his horse forward to keep up with the advancing shieldwall.

'Hope it has more luck than the death riders,' said Wigstan. 'We expected some of the British to run from them, but most stood firm yesterday.'

'The druids will cast their magic, that's the important thing,' said Guertepir. 'Their spells and the bodies they carry speak to the lords of the earth itself. They will bring us good fortune this day.'

'Be that as it may,' said Hrodgar with some scepticism, 'but before the sun sets the outcome of this battle needs to be decided. This can not go on to another day. Today their knights must feel the cold iron of Saxon fury.'

Cunedda, pale-faced and grim, made to ride to Abloyc. 'My best men front the shieldwall this morning so the fight *should* be brief and decisive,' he said. 'A scout tells me the British line is narrow, unable to meet us along our entire width, so this will be over quickly.' He gave Hrodgar a disparaging glance as he wheeled his horse away. 'Yes, they will fall to Saxon *and* Votadini tenacity this day.'

'And don't forget the Hibernian contribution to all of this,' said Guertepir. 'A sight to behold it will be. The engagement of our full resources at last. And just wait until we throw our winning dice, the bastards won't know what's hit them.'

Augustus, as the day before, stalked along the front of the line, shouting instruction and encouragement to the men. His humour was dark and ironic, causing many smile and titter. 'Listen to them, they must have sent their scolding wives to berate us!' he shouted in response to the approaching wall of noise coming from the druids. 'Not ones to tumble, though. These Hibernian mares are ugly enough to soften even my dick.'

A ripple of nervous laughter broke out from those in earshot, but many had started to stare beyond Augustus as the mist in the valley had thinned to a mere milky haze. Augustus turned to look down the hill. The look of confident bonhomie he had displayed to his men fell immediately from his face. As big and threatening as the day before was Guertepir's shieldwall. The druids, who walked before it, had halted. A line of arrows, sent by Dominic and his crew, stuck from the ground at their feet, indicating the limit of their safe advance. Now, unable to intimidate at close quarters, the druids shook the body parts before them and screamed out their incantations with a renewed fury.

Dominic and his archers rode past Augustus and advanced a way down the hill. 'This time we'll shut their wretched noise once and for all!' shouted Dominic, through the clamour of horns, drumbeats and shrieking. Augustus watched as the mounted bowmen, most of them armed with composite bows of tremendous power, stood in their saddles and sent a shower of death towards the druids.

Many of Guertepir's holy men fell to the first wave of arrows. The remainder turned and fled, scrambling under the shields and away from the theatre of war.

Dominic's group quickly sent another flock of arrows skywards. After describing a high, looping trajectory, the arrows fell upon the men at the back of the shieldwall. The action provoked a response from the cavalry at the flanks and a detachment peeled away towards Dominic and his men.

As the archers fled—their role being to skirmish, rather than fight head-on with armed horsemen—Augustus and the other fifty tacticians did as the Druids had done and ran towards their own wall. The shields parted, allowing them to enter and take positions at the front.

Three British horn blasts sounded (the signal to meet advancing horse), and soon spears were passed from the back of the line to stick outwards from every shield.

A detachment of sixty Votadini cavalry hurtled towards the centre section of the British wall. Two of the younger riders, driven by battle fever and eager to prove themselves, rushed at the spears. Cunedda, who led the group, attempted to check the progress of the pair but his cry was unheard in the furore.

Augustus winced as he readied himself for the collision. When it came, it sent him backwards three steps, causing his teeth to judder, but his section of wall held. His spear flew from his grasp, half its length sticking from the horse's chest. The animal reared upwards, before falling backwards and dead, its rider landing in a heap at Augustus' feet. The man next to him thrust his spear into the stricken rider, killing him. Down the line, the other horse and rider had met a similar fate.

Arthur dwelt on the right flank of the shieldwall. With him, Flint, Withred, Dominic and three hundred and fifty cavalry sat ready to go. On the opposite flank, some four hundred paces away, Gherwan, Hereferth and an equal number of riders waited. Lightly caparisoned, the cavalry wore armour made of tough fabric or leather—garb suited for mobility and freedom of movement. Shields, painted with Arthur's unicorn or Hereferth's lynx, accompanied all.

Arthur eyes blazed from the eye-slits of his plumed helm as he rode between the men. He shouted above the roar of battle. 'Remember your role is to rush the overlapping flank of their wall! DO NOT attempt to break it—their spears will put an end to you if you do! Our purpose is to draw their cavalry from the outer edges and so expose the shieldsmen there to our archers!'

He pointed to Dominic, who was addressing his men a distance away. 'They have their own role, and will be our support. Flint counts five hundred mounted Votadini, Saxon and Hibernian riders on each of their flanks, so we *will* be outnumbered! Few of them, though, are used to fighting from the saddle, and that's where we'll press our advantage!'

He looked to Withred and Flint. The pair sat pale but resolute. Withred was dressed in a black, studded leather tunic; his head enwrapped in an iron-grey helm with purple plume. Flint wore a composite bronze cuirass, consisting of breastplate and backplate. A Roman-style riveted helmet completed his armour. His arms, like Withred's and Arthur's, were bare from shoulder to fingertip. The sight of the pair filled Arthur with hope. Both nodded to him. Both were ready to go.

Arthur stood in his saddle and raised *Skullcleft*, his sword, skywards. On the opposite flank, Gherwan took up the signal and reciprocated Arthur's stance. Horses snorted, whinnied and stamped as the raw, sizzling energy of the morning infused their very bones.

A distance away Dominic had finished his parley to his mounted archers. His instructions had been clear: each group was to send death to Saxon archers, Votadini shield, and enemy riders on both flanks. Next to Dominic, bestride a piebald pony, sat Tomas. Both men (because Tomas had become a man) had ditched the helms supplied by Arthur, deeming them to cumbersome and restrictive. Now they wore their wolf heads; now they were hunters again.

The archers formed into two groups—eighty men would harass Arthur's protagonists on the right flank of the enemy shieldwall, and eighty harass Gherwan's on the left. All knew their task. All were eager to go.

'TO WAR!' Arthurs cry rang out sudden and clear. Gherwan, on the opposite flank, echoed the command.

Dominic held his archers back as the knights thundered away. He looked over to the left, where an able man named Harvey, some four hundred paces distant, awaited his signal.

Dominic watched as Arthur and Gherwan closed upon the shieldwall, prompting Guertepir's riders to break from the edges. 'It's worked,' he said. 'Now we can start to sting them.' He gave Harvey the signal to move and rode into the field of battle.

Arthur twisted in his saddle as he jerked Storm's muscular neck backwards and away from the Votadini spears that spiked from the rowan-emblazoned shields. Withred was beside him and pointed towards the approaching enemy cavalry. He shouted above the clamour. 'They come to engage and so leave their backs exposed to Dominic's arrows—so far so good!'

Arthur cast a glance behind him along the entire length of the shieldwall. 'Gherwan's troop has drawn them out as well!' he shouted. Turning back to Withred, he readied himself for the onrushing first wave of attack. 'Get ready, here they come—'

Withred's darting eyes had caught sight of the hurtling spear. Flung from the back of the shieldwall it headed for Arthur. He pushed at his lord, almost knocking him from the saddle. The shaft brushed Arthur's head as it passed.

Wheeling his horse around, Withred looked out for more hurtling steel. 'Nerthus! The bastards nearly picked our purses at the first encounter! We must get away from these shields and fight them nearer to our own line!'

Before he could respond, Arthur was forced to engage the slashing sword of a Saxon rider who had come quickly upon him. Another rider—a Hibernian, wielding an ax and holding his shield close—went for Withred. The Angle, whose preferred weapon on horse was the longsword, parried the smash with his shield. He screamed inwardly as a jolt shot up his arm, but answered the assault with a sideways slash at the Hibernian. The man barely met the parry, his shield splintering such was the power of the blow. Withred dropped his body to the neck side of his horse to avoid an immediate, retaliatory, overhead swipe from the Hibernian. The hack bit into his beast's withers causing it to rear.

With horse aloft, Withred towered above his man, and as the beast dropped to its forelegs, he timed his next attack to precision. His blade whistled as it slammed into the plumed helmet. The Hibernian's face, thus revealed, evidenced his total concussion. Withred kicked him from his saddle and swung round to Arthur.

He gasped to find that the lord of Brythonfort was already dispatching his fourth man. Arthur's words— *"Few of them, though, are used to fighting from the saddle, and that's where we can press our advantage!"* —came to him as noticed the three bodies lying dead at the busy feet of Arthur's mare. *But—Gods—man, you are not human,* he thought, as he allowed himself a fleeting glance of Arthur at work.

Arthur readied himself to strike at his fourth challenger as he skilfully and tightly guided Storm around him. Although carrying a shield, Arthur's horsemanship was such that he rarely needed to use it. His opponent, a Hibernian wielding a single-bladed battle-ax, had failed to land a single strike upon him.

Frustrated, the man screamed out his fury. 'Keep still and fight me like a man'—again he lunged and missed—'damn you, keep still and fight!'

Playing his reins through his left hand, Arthur remained impassive, his subtle signals transferring his every intention through to Storm, who danced with precision and dexterity to his tune. Soon the Hibernian was gasping. A quick glance away from Arthur, as his exasperation led him to look for help, was to be his undoing. Arthur, who had bided his time and waited for the slightest opening, met the Hibernian's renewal of attention with his slashing blade. *Skullcleft's* keen edge found the gap between the man's cheekguard and shoulder, removing his head in one swipe.

Arthur, blood splattered and breathless, turned Storm in a tight circle to assess developments. A brief respite allowed him to take in the scene. The enemy shieldwall, delayed by the mounted battle before it, had halted its synchronized march up the hill. The main body of mounted conflict (Gherwan's group having now melded with Arthur's) had edged nearer to the British shieldwall and this suited Arthur. Soon Guertepir's cavalry would be exposed to British spears. A half mile still separated the lines, and upon this ground the entire cavalries now fought.

Another rider, eager for fame after spotting Arthur's distinctive white plume, galloped towards him, but this time the British king had no need to act. The man fell from his saddle when still six horse lengths away. A glance to the edge of the battlefield revealed that Dominic's group was active and the man had fallen to one of their arrows.

Dominic had been careful to keep his men away from direct contact with Guertepir's cavalry. Whenever enemy riders rushed them, the archers would disperse, leaving the combatants frustrated and with nobody to fight.

Dominic had split his eighty men on the right flank into three groups. His best archers (some thirty men) all wielded high velocity recurved bows and these were sent to harry the two hundred strong Votadini archers who stood behind Guertepir's shieldwall. Dominic's elite archers also had their counterparts on the left flank. Both groups had the same brief: to pin down the Votadini bowmen and effectively neutralize their threat. With superior reach, the British had no fear of effective return fire from the Votadini.

Dominic's second section (again with its mirror image on the left flank) was to send a shower of death into the exposed edges of

Guertepir's shieldwall, now void of the protection of their cavalry.

The third group, meanwhile, had turned its attention to the horse fight; its task to pick off enemy riders from distance.

Tomas paused a moment as an arrow bearer came to him. Having already sent fifty arrows at the Votadini bowmen, he took a full quiver from Frysil—one of many men whose sole job was to keep the archers supplied with missiles. Frysil's own horse had full quivers of arrows hanging from several hooks and catches on its tack.

'How goes it, elsewhere?' asked Tomas.

'Goes well ... for our archers at least!' shouted Frysil above the noise. 'The edge of their shieldwall has shrunk from our arrows. By my guess its not much wider than our own now. The spare men have piled up behind it, though ... seven ... eight deep they are in in places. They'll give one almighty shove when they meet our boys!'

'And Dominic?'

'He sends hell into their riders along with twenty others; they must have taken out nearly one hundred of them!' Frysil noticed a line of arrows stuck into the ground thirty paces away.

He nodded towards them. 'I take it that's the range of the Votadini archers!'

'Yes, we're outshooting them with these bows. Have them pinned down, they can't move!'

'Well good luck, I must be gone!' shouted Frysil, his voice becoming lost in the din as he left to attend to another archer.

Augustus had taken his place at the front of the shieldwall and now watched as events unfolded below. Like an organic, single entity, the wall stood tense and ready on the ridge.

Pwyll stood beside Augustus, his small head enclosed in a round steel helmet. 'D'you think we'll get to jab at their cavalry with these spears, Gus?' he asked.

'Well, that's the plan, Pwyll,' said Augustus, his attention riveted on the action below, 'and it seems to be working up to now. The fight's coming towards us; the nearest of them can only be three hundred paces away.'

'How d'you think it's going?'

'We're holding our own and their shieldwall's lost its overlap. Shit, Pwyll, Dominic and his men are causing havoc on the flanks. It's almost as if this fight's been made for the wily bastard, he's … whoa! prepare yourself, there's a rider on his way, lift your spear!'

But it was Flint, gore-smitten and intense, who approached. He looked for Augustus in the line and soon found him. 'Their wall has enormous depth and is moving again!' he shouted. 'Our riders need to get out of the gap soon—that or be trapped. We hope to push some of their horses onto your spears before we withdraw, but nothing's certain yet!'

'Then get your scrawny arse back down there and thin them out a little before they get here!' shouted Augustus.

With a wry smile, Flint touched his helmet to Augustus, then turned and rode back into the fray.

Two hours before dawn on the third day of the battle, Raedwald had slinked away from Aquae Sulis. Not wishing to chance being seen by Hrodgar or the others, he had decided his best course was to leave the city altogether. He would head westwards towards the place named Brythonfort, and there wait for the Saxon army as it advanced. With any luck, the bastard Hrodgar might have fallen by then, saving him a job. That would enable him to blend into the army as if he'd never been away.

But instead of heading southwards as he should, Raedwald managed to get himself lost again, taking a meandering path before ending up on a road five miles east of Aquae Sulis.

Dawn was smudging the sky with its first light when he finally met the road and began to head south. Soon, a wagon rambled towards him from behind, forcing him to scuttle for cover. Raedwald cursed his luck when the dray stopped a mere twenty paces away. Astounded and hidden, he had gasped when seeing a giant of a man and another in a wolf hat. They had ridden beside the wagon and attended to the two women who rode upon it.

The wolf hat could mean but one thing— Dominic the companion of Withred, and the man partly responsible for the death of his father. The other man too was legend, as the dog tied with a long lead to the wagon reminded him. He had to be 'Augustus the giant'—the destroyer of a killer dog with his bare hands. Furthermore, he had done the same to Ambrosius, the Negro. Possessing enough rationality not to act at that moment, Raedwald decided to watch and learn.

That the women meant much to the two Britons was plain to see. Satisfied they were far enough from Aquae Sulis to continue on their way alone, the women were saying their goodbyes. No doubt fleeing out of harm's way before the battle began. Raedwald could see that the slimmer of the two was dear to the wolf man, whilst the other was cherished by the giant. He then realised that contrary to it being against him, fortune had done him a service. Before him, beside the wagon, the whores precious to the pair would soon be void of their protection. Having already settled one score—the slaughter and defilement of Withred's aunt—he now had the chance to tie up the remaining loose ends. Now he could fully avenge the death of his father. He would follow the women and slay them, but first he would have to deal with the dog.

The cavalry fight had gone well for the British. Four hundred enemy riders now lay dead on the churned ground between the shieldwalls. Arthur had lost just one hundred, leaving the number of opposing riders standing at an equal six hundred.

The fight raged nearer to the British shieldwall and the gap had reduced to three hundred strides. The Brythonfort knights; some two hundred men—specialists trained to fight in the way of the Polybian horsemen of Rome and possessing their effective weaponry and technique—had wreaked havoc upon the enemy riders. Most, like Arthur and Flint, wore cuirasses to protect both torso and back. All wielded spathas—the long swords giving them superior reach over their opponents. More importantly, they knew exactly how to use their weapons.

In contrast, the enemy equestrians had fought in a way not familiar to them. Many had preferred to carry the spear and found to their cost that the heavy weapons required two-handed use, thus leaving their horses scantily controlled. The consequences were proving dire for them, as British riders were able to avoid the spear thrusts and deliver deathblows with their spathas.

Gherwan worked his way towards the man he guessed to be Hrodgar. That the Saxon was high ranking was apparent—Gherwan knew by the way men flocked to protect him whenever he was threatened. Gherwan was sure he was the same man who had attended the parley with Arthur, but now he wore a Saxon helm, partly obscuring his features. Shrieking his allegiance to Woden, another Saxon—the last one between Hrodgar and Gherwan—came at him. Arthur's man ducked under a clumsy sideways swipe—his own counterstrike crunching against the chainmail hauberk of the Saxon, slamming him mid-torso. The man screamed out his unbridled agony as his ribs splintered beneath the ledge of the sword. Gherwan, whose horseplay matched Arthur's, guided his steed close enough to deliver a lateral dagger thrust to the man's jugular and so end the bout.

Gherwan now had Hrodgar before him. The British shieldwall, bristling with spears, stood behind them. Gherwan goaded his warhorse towards Hrodgar's, pressing him towards the spears. Hrodgar, wild eyed and aware of the move, spurred his mount forward towards Gherwan and away from the threat behind him. He screamed at Gherwan, his furious curses and oaths unheard in the tremendous noise of battle.

Their swords met, high and ringing, the resultant crucifix locked a moment skywards. Hrodgar slid his sword from the deadlock and delivered his blurring blade towards Gherwan's midriff. The blade floundered upon the bronze protection of the Briton's cuirasse. Wincing, Gherwan delivered his counterstrike. Hrodgar's horse shifted, taking the full force of the blow on its muzzle. With nostrils riven and bone exposed, the beast swung its neck away from Gherwan and fell backwards upon the spears protruding from the British shields. Hrodgar went to ground, his steed impaled.

In desperation, Hrodgar faced horse and rider. With sword gone, he lunged forward with his dagger, intent on burying it in the breast of the horse before him. Gherwan, with a play of the reins, deftly had his beast dance backwards and away. Hrodgar's helm had gone allowing Gherwan to see his gaunt features. Spittle, white and frothy, flew from his mouth as he screamed mutely at Gherwan. Unperturbed, the Briton wound up his death strike. After two swishing orbits above his head, he delivered his slice downwards into the neck of Hrodgar.

As Hrodgar's head flew high and away, Gherwan spun to face his next threat. All along the wall, he noticed that enemy horse and men lay dead, pierced by the hundreds of spears sticking from the shields. His tactical advice to Arthur had proved sound, but before he could allow himself any feelings of satisfaction, four horn blasts sounded. It was the signal to leave the field of battle. The gap had closed to a dangerous level and entrapment for all equestrians was now a real possibility.

Gherwan's steed reared high as if in defiance. Upon landing, he spurred it away and along the line as he fled the scene of slaughter.

As the mounted troops galloped from the gap, Dominic let fly his last arrow and withdrew from the flanks. He saw Tomas approach with his riders and joined him in his flight. Moments later, the archers mustered some hundred strides behind the British shieldwall.

Dominic did a quick count. 'We fared well,' he said, 'only twenty men lost; we still number one hundred and forty bowmen.'

Harvey, the man who had been in charge of the archers on the opposite flank, winced in response to the intensity of sound coming from the battlefield. 'Jesus God,' he cursed, 'Hell is about to be unleashed over there.'

Soon, the cavalry joined Dominic's group. Arthur went to him and they clasped arms. 'Hereferth fell,' said Arthur in answer to Dominic's searching appraisal of the riders. 'He died bravely but was overcome by three of them … I got there too late to save him. But I put his killers to the earth all the same.'

'Ah … that's a loss we could have done without,' said Dominic. 'The chief was an inspiration to his men. Any more captains lost?'

'None. All fought well and are bloodied but alive still.'

'What of enemy losses?'

'Many. They have fewer mounted men than us now. We lost four hundred men—more than half—but they fared much worse. Seven hundred of them, by Flint's quick count, now lie dead on the killing ground. Hrodgar went down to Gherwan. Wigstan fought well and we think he survived, though there was no sign of Guertepir as expected.' Arthur's voice now betrayed his frustration. 'Oh, that we could have continued, but we do not have fresh horses. We should be pressing our advantage, but these beasts are dead on their feet and need to rest.'

'And Cunedda and Diarmait?'

'No sign of them either. Their absence worries me.'

'As planned, we managed to kill many of their shields!' shouted Dominic as the noise intensified to a level that threatened to drown out his address. It's up to the shields now. As soon as my archers have caught their breath we'll send arrows into their flanks again!'

'Then do it soon, for they are about—' An ear-splitting roar went up and a clash that seemed to shake the very pillars of the earth muted Arthur's words. Grim faced and with horror in his eyes he looked at the wall. 'They've come together,' he muttered. 'Now this thing will be decided.'

Smala readied himself for the collision. He had briefed the men surrounding him (farmers and peasants who asked themselves not for the first time why in hell's name they had ever agreed to fight in Britannia for a foreign king) to meet the enemy advance with much more force than the day before. Along the line, Augustus and the other tacticians had conveyed the same message to their own charges: *'Push with all your might as soon as the enemy wall is a sword's distance away.'*

Consequently, the British line was able to hold when the impact came. All along, arrows splintered into shards (for the enemy shields resembled pincushions after the assault by Dominic's archers) as men screamed their fury at men.

Smala stood behind a shieldsman named Oswine—a fisherman from Husum in Angeln. Having seen the size of Guertepir's forces, he had considered deserting on the first day, but in the end had decided the ridicule he would endure back home would be far worse than actually dying on the battlefield.

Now he wasn't so sure, as his opponent—a leathery Hibernian with stinking breath and mad eyes—attempted to swipe under his guard with his mattock. Oswine, determined not to have his feet taken away at the ankles, dropped his shield just in time to prevent his dismemberment. He stooped, keeping his head behind the shield, as instructed to do at Brythonfort. As the mattock dug into wood, the whistle of steel above him evinced that an ax-wielding man behind the leathery Hibernian had swung for his head. Oswine's hasty training had saved him for now.

Smala was quick to counter and make use of the space before him. Carrying a spear—his preference being to jab, rather than swipe at his opponents—he shoved its tip into the face of the ax man, splitting it apart. In one movement, he removed the spear and thrust it at the other—the one who had struck at Oswine's ankles. Carelessly, the man had allowed his forehead to rise above his shield. Smala's first strike took off the man's helmet, his second razored through flesh and bone. With head riven and brains exposed, the man swayed upright and dead, held vertical by the crush behind him.

A shudder went through the wall and Smala feared the worse as he twisted his head and saw that's its trueness of line had gone.

Augustus was concerned about the detritus at his feet. To push against the seven-deep enemy line was bad enough, but the dead horses and cadavers left from the cavalry battle threatened to destroy the integrity of his shieldwall. The line was disjointed in places, as men stumbled and lost contact with their shield neighbours. This could only lead to one outcome—imminent breach.

He resorted to pushing, crouched, behind his huge shield as he realised the futility of his position. Pwyll, who had stood beside him moments earlier, was now twenty paces behind. Enemy infantry had begun to pour past Augustus as the men rushed to meet the shields now at his rear. Alarmed, he noticed that only fifty shields were locked with him, and realised the time for free skirmish had come.

He turned to the man beside him. 'We need to break and fight!' he shouted. 'They're coming at us from all sides now!'

'BREACH! BREACH!' the cry went up from both British and enemy infantry as the linear lines of the shieldwalls dispersed, and hand to hand fighting began. In total, sixty British shields had collapsed at the centre, but the flanks still held. There, two opposing lines of shields, now tussled for ascendancy.

Dominic and his archers were abroad again and active in the breach where the fight raged with savage intensity. From a distance, they began to pick off enemy fighters in the centre of the melee.

Dealing with any who broke through, Arthur and his tired cavalry prowled the back of the wall. 'We're containing them!' shouted Arthur to Flint as he cut down a Saxon who rushed to him on foot. 'Our men fight like wolves and Dominic's arrows take out their extra men; and the side walls still hold!'

But Flint had frozen, his face a mask of despair as he stared ahead. 'Chariots,' he mumbled. 'No wonder Cunedda and Diarmait were nowhere to be seen, they were saving themselves for the chariots.'

Aghast, Arthur stared through the breach and down the hill.

Below, Guertepir had unleashed one hundred and fifty chariots. Beside them bounded a pack of war hounds—seventy in number. Arthur, knowing that time was precious now, beckoned his riders towards him.

'The chariots are bladed, and like the hounds are indiscriminate. They'll shred all the fighters in the breach—British and enemy! They seek to clear a hole and attack our lines from behind and so win the day! We must meet them, though I fear it will lead to our deaths.' Fey now, he raised *Skullcleft* and stood in his saddle. 'DEATH OR GLORY!' he roared. His knights, both British and Anglii reciprocated the cry as Arthur turned towards approaching hell.

But before he could spur Storm into her final glorious gallop, Gherwan's shout came from behind. 'Hold up! Hold up! Robert has come!'

Robert and Simon had heard the roar of battle when still two miles away. With them, thirty horses pulled thirty ballistae along the rutted road towards the rear of Badon Hill. After much experimentation and many failures at Brythonfort, they had managed to build the war machines, and after careful adjustment and fine-tuning, had coaxed them to fire accurately. All now had their torsion springs winched back ready for immediate use; all were loaded with either heavy dart or stone projectile.

The climb up the twisted road proved bumpy and awkward as they neared the ridge. When the cry of 'Breach!' was heard, they goaded the heavy drays into one final strenuous push up the hill.

Surrounded on all sides by Saxons, Augustus laid about him, slashing with his heavy sword. Aware his death was near, such was the disparity in numbers, he had decided to give it his all. He purposed to fight until he dropped.

His blade bit through the leg of an opponent who shuffled too close. The man went down screaming, his stump spraying blood. Another man rushed in, seeking to gain advantage over a breathless Augustus. Acting upon the opportunity, the Saxon tensed, swung back, then aimed at Augustus' exposed neck, just as a hound—snarling and crazed—took him down before he could deliver.

Augustus, astounded, turned to meet another man as the war hound went to work on the Saxon. Iron rang upon iron as Augustus blocked his assailant's sword swipe. He pushed him away. Standing a body length apart, both paused ... too exhausted to press the fight at that moment.

The Saxon, panting, looked down the hill, then at Augustus. A triumphant smile had come to him. 'You're finished, you big bastard—you and the rest of your British rabble,' he said in Saxon. 'The chariots are coming, try your big sword on them if you dare!'

Augustus did not turn. Instead, he kept his eyes on the man before him as, all around, the distant blur of fighting continued. Hounds tore and swords bit, but his world stood frozen and silent for now. *'Chariots,'* that much he had understood. *It was bleak anyway, but now it's over*, he thought as the Saxon ran from him and away from a breach soon to be filled with hurtling horseflesh and spinning blade. He looked down the hill, his eyes haunted; his unicorn shield held before him. Dogs ran and chariots sliced through the fields. Soon they would be upon him and he knew not what to do.

His first warning before the air parted above his head was a sibilant, yet powerful *'SSHHH'* that grew alarmingly from behind, then receded as it passed him by. The ballista bolt raced downwards and thumped into a knoll, throwing up an explosion of turf and soil.

He turned and saw the giant crossbow snouts of the ballistae as, one by one, the artisans pushed them into position on the crest. Behind them, sat bestride their mounts, waited Dominic and his crew of archers. The wolf man stood in his saddle beckoning for all Britons fighting in the breach to come to him. On the flanks, the shieldwalls still held and there the battle blazed.

Augustus didn't need telling twice. He lumbered up the hill, passing many who still fought. Soon, he came to Pwyll, who faced another fellow (a freeman farmer and a member of the Saxon Fyrd) whose ineptitude was only matched by Pwyll's. Both men had already made several ineffective lunges without inflicting a single wound upon each other. Augustus approached Pwyll's adversary from behind and landed the pommel of his sword upon his head. The man dropped, leaving Pwyll face to face with Augustus.

Augustus struggled to be heard above the clamour. 'Come on, man; get yourself out of here—follow me back up the hill, unless you want your head taken off with a ballista bolt!'

Pwyll wavered a moment, to stunned by the day's events to take in Augustus' words. Leaving nothing to chance, Augustus slap-grabbed his chest and dragged him away.

By now, other Britons had begun to flee from the epicenter of conflict and run up the hill, towards where Dominic's archers continued to send a shower of death downwards.

The wolf man stood in a line of forty. Behind him, two more files, each comprising of forty bowmen, stood ready. Dominic's charges loosed their arrows and the second line stepped forward and immediately did the same. These were replaced by the third set of archers, and so a continuous and unbroken flock of arrows was sent down the hill. The rotation maneuver, which had been relentlessly practiced on the training grounds of Brythonfort, progressed and knocked droves of Saxons to the ground. Many war hounds fell beside them.

Meanwhile, scores of Britons ran up the hill, until only a handful of them remained in the gap, these being men who had become embroiled within their own sphere of combat to the exclusion of all outside influence.

Snarling and fierce, having survived the arrows, the remaining dogs arrived. As they leapt, they quickly fell to spear or sword. Arthur himself fended off a hound, meeting its leap with *Skullcleft*. The hound dropped riven at his feet.

More ballistae were in position and primed for use. Arthur walked behind, casting a wary glance down the hill at the approaching chariots. Beside each war machine stood two men, strong of arm. Each pair had practiced briefly at Brythonfort, after Robert, Simon and the rest of the artisans had finally figured out the complexities of ballista construction. Proficient at ratcheting the machines to full tension at speed, the men had begun to release the death bolts.

Arthur approached Robert. 'They're on their way, Rob!' he shouted. 'Already, they've reached the lower fields.'

By now, most of the men were back up the hill, but on the flanks the shield fight continued. Two sets of opposing walls—smaller versions of the continual long wall which had existed at the start of battle—now fought without conclusion. Led by Smala, the Angle wall had fought tenaciously and managed to utilise the steep slope to their advantage and so push the allies a short distance down the hill. The other wall, though, was at deadlock, as men driven to the point of nausea, and too weak to raise their weapons, took to merely leaning on their shields such was the level of their exhaustion.

As soon as the gap had appeared, Guertepir had released his chariots. To throw them at the Britons was his big surprise. His charioteers would burst through the breach and get behind the British shieldwall and so win the day. To send them against the flanks had been unthinkable—the terrain there being too rutted and hedge-clogged for the wheeled conveyances. No … it had to be the smoother centre ground, and that could only happen if a breach occurred, and that had happened now. He viewed the battle from the elevated wall-walk of Aquae Sulis' northern face. Beside him stood Almaith—her hand to her mouth in suppressed joy as she watched the carnage play out before her.

Diarmait was astounded when the first ballista bolt flew. Beside him rode Cunedda and Abloyc, both on chariots pulled by white stallion siblings from Guertepir's stable. As more ballistae snouts appeared at the summit, Diarmait considered the wisdom of going up through the breach. To turn back, though, was unthinkable—an act of abject cowardice. And so he continued to whip his pony forward; the beast wild-eyed and snorting with fear as it weaved through retreating allies, who were frantic to escape the cascade of arrows looping from the ridge. Some, unable in their exhaustion to avoid the chariots, fell before them, or were riven or rendered limbless by scything wheel blades.

Other chariots, falling foul to jarring ground or corpse-litter, flew in tumbling cartwheels, their riders ejected and flung skywards.

Cunedda shouted to Diarmait. 'Prepare yourself, my friend! They're about to use the ballistae again!'

As if on cue, several of the giant crossbows sent forth their bolts. With an approaching hiss, the projectiles raced towards the first of the chariots, now only three hundred paces distant. The time from release to near-miss was a mere moment as one of the bolts hurtled past Abloyc. He gasped, unsure if his own decision to continue had been an error of judgment.

Behind him, several of the bolts found targets. Many ponies took the brunt of the assault. Pierced in their breasts they fell dead, their chariots careering over them in crashing arcs of destruction. Bodies took to the air and landed broken on the bloody field.

Other bolts hit the chariots, smashing into structures and wheels, and sending shards of twisted timber skywards. To make things far worse, Dominic's archers continued to fill the sky with arrows, their approaching death whisper being the last living sensations for many of the charioteers.

The first ballistae assault took out twelve chariots. Furthermore, Dominic's archers had killed or injured twenty of their drivers. Some of the surviving charioteers, now nervous and hesitant, dragged their steeds to a halt.

But Cunedda still thundered upwards, even though a chariot upended beside him. Another hiss as a ballista bolt flew past. Loaded again, the ballistae had begun to fire. A look behind, told Cunedda that chaos ensued. He reined in his pony, bringing it to a snorting standstill.

He cursed the British archers for their unrelenting doggedness as an arrow whispered its hint of death past his ear. He considered his choices. Below him, Diarmait, who now had Abloyc beside him, had signalled the others to stop. As he watched, Diarmait pointed to Aquae Sulis and made to leave the hill. Above Cunedda, the ratcheting sound of ballistae being primed for a third assault was enough. He snapped the reins of his pony, guiding the animal downwards and away from the ridge as Dominic's arrows splintered into the wood of his retreating carriage.

A cheer erupted on the crest of Badon Hill, but Arthur and his generals knew there could be no let up. In response, Robert and Simon instructed their operatives to send the third wave of ballista bolts down the hill. Dominic's arrows continued to rain death until the chariots were out of range. Twenty more of the war machines fell in the flight, victim to bolt and arrow. In total, seventy chariots lay wrecked, their sub structures adding to the dreadful litter of carnage on the battlefield. The breach was left unpeopled—a killing zone.

Guertepir's shieldwall, seeing the withdrawal of the chariots, had started to disintegrate. At first, just a few men peeled away, but soon swathes of them covered the slopes of Badon Hill. Seeing this, Guertepir's archers and cavalry ascended the hill a distance to provide cover for the retreat.

On the ridge, the cheering erupted to a new intensity and this time Arthur was happy to let his men celebrate for a while. But as the survivors from the British shieldwall trudged to the summit, Gherwan's euphoria faded. Many British lay dead below him; more than half of Arthur's force, by his guess, had perished that day.

He took Arthur and Flint to one side, away from the sounds of celebration. 'It's good that we won the day, but this is the end for us,' he said.

Arthur was crestfallen. 'I fear what you are about to tell me, but how many do we number now?'

'Eight hundred men or thereabouts for the shields, three hundred cavalry and over one hundred archers.'

'And the enemy force?'

'At a guess, still two thousand shields, even after today's heavy losses. Cavalry about the same as us—three hundred. Chariots … eighty or so.'

'But now we have the ballistae,' said Flint. 'Surely they count for something.'

'Yes, but we can't beat them with ballistae alone; the men are finished, there's no fight left in them'—he pointed towards the ridge where shieldsmen lay prone and spent—'can you really see them forming a thin wall tomorrow and lasting longer than a mere moment?'

'But surely we can keep their wall at bay with the ballista,' pressed Flint.

'If we had an unlimited supply of bolts, maybe so, but Guertepir's not stupid—he'll sacrifice his men until the ballistae fall silent.'

'But we can't give in.' Arthur's voice was barely above a whisper, such was the level of his disappointment. 'Not after all that's happened today; we just can't give in.'

Gherwan looked at Arthur, looked at Flint. He shrugged. 'No ... I don't suppose we can,' he said.

Augustus lounged beside the campfire with Pwyll and six other men—Pwyll being the only survivor from the group who had joked with Augustus the previous night. All possessed the hollow-eyed look of men who had witnessed unspeakable horror.

Pwyll slapped his palm gently against his ear as if trying to expel a demon from the organ. 'I still hear the battle as if it rages just over the hill,' he said, 'I can't get the damned noise out of my head.'

As the other men muttered their concurrence, Augustus, who had recently arrived from Arthur's war council, made to get up. 'You and me both,' he said. He placed his hand on Pwyll's shoulder as he grunted to his feet and started to walk to the rear of the hill. 'But *it will* go away eventually, Pwyll, trust me.'

He strolled to a grassy shadow that overlooked the tumble of fields leading away from Aquae Sulis. He climbed onto the hummock. Below him lay darkness and the service roads used by Arthur's forces; and somewhere beyond the fields his beloved

Modlen camped under the dark sky. Tomorrow would be his last day as a living man—he knew that now. Arthur and the rest had decided to fight on, but there was no hope. The men around the fire had nothing left to give. They were typical of all the men he had spoken to, and he had spoken to most of them. His thoughts dwelt upon Modlen and the dear children they had recieved as their own. What would happen to them? How would they cope without him? Would they even survive the storm about to blow their way? A flicker in the distance caught his eye. Torchlight? The eyes of a fox? A trick of the darkness? He did not know. Then the point of light was joined by another … and another. Augustus tensed, something was amiss. Soon, pinpricks of orange studded the night like emergent nebulae in a distant galaxy. He turned and left the hillside. Arthur needed to know.

Along the good Roman road, Modlen and Nila had travelled thirty miles in their covered wagon. After reaching the halfway point between Aquae Sulis and Brythonfort, and one hour before dusk, they decided it sensible to make camp for the night.

Titon, sniffing and exploring, had romped alongside the wagon all day. On two occasions the mastiff had set rabbits to flight, but his efforts to catch them had come to nothing. Now the dog lay prone and panting, tired after a long day of adventure.

'I'll tie him to the wheels,' said Modlen as she poked a stick into the night fire. 'Don't want him running off into the blackness; Gus'll never forgive me; he's grown so fond of the animal.'

'Gus would forgive you *anything*,' teased Nila. 'He adores your very bones, anyone can see it.' She knelt and stroked Titon. 'This fellow needs a drink. I'll get him some from the stream over there; he's not drinking our fresh water, that's for sure.'

Raedwald watched the women from a distance. Their shadows danced around the glow of their fire and, most importantly, they had tied up the dog. He intended to kill the slim woman first—the one embraced by Dominic that morning. Such a deed would crucify the bastard. Then when he, Raedwald, rejoined the Saxon infantry he would get to Dominic himself and more importantly to Withred the turncoat—the man who had killed his father.

He flinched as the slim woman left the fire. She was walking towards the stream—*walking towards him!*

Arthur stood three paces from Ffodor, seemingly unable to take in his visage. Vulture-like and stern, with his beaky eyes and bushy eyebrows, Ffodor stood in the livery of a Roman general.

He shot a look towards Flint. 'Found out it wasn't your man who shagged my daughter after all'—he gave a sideways nod to his man, Rogan—'it was my champion all along … he or the dozen others who made the *beast with two backs* with the flighty mare.'

Arthur nodded sagely. 'I told you my man was not responsible. If you had listened to me, many of those dead on the fields tonight would be returning to their farms and villages instead of lining the bellies of crows.'

Ffodor gave a self-recriminatory sigh. 'I know, you have no need to tell me. I am a stubborn man … blinkered even. But I thank the lord I have men such as Rogan, who put the security of our lands above their own safety. He was aware he endangered his head when he came to me with his revelation, but for once a dogged old man was able to see sense.'

Arthur peered into the darkness behind Ffodor. There, a great host had begun to strike camp. 'And so here you are, better late than never.'

'Yes, and I have brought you another sixteen hundred men for the shields and four hundred Rome-trained knights.'

'And chariots; I saw chariots,' came in Flint.

'Ah, yes … chariots; fifty of them.'

Arthur pointed along the ridge where many fires burned. 'My men are too tired to even come and investigate your arrival. I expected them to stand with the shields tomorrow but not much more. A night's rest and the sight of fresh men may yet get them to push with vigour in the morning.'

Gherwan arrived. 'I've walked amongst the new arrivals and all are in good shape.' He gave Ffodor a brief bow of his head. 'You keep your levy well trained, my lord. With them, we equal the enemy in numbers now; furthermore, the men of Travena are hungry for combat.' He turned to Arthur. 'Tomorrow we should assemble on the ridge and show Guertepir what we've got.'

THE BATTLE — DAY FOUR

Guertepir had thundered at Wigstan. Now, the
Saxon chief, whose spiked blond hair had fallen
into a greasy heap to sit flat upon his head, tried

desperately to defend himself against the Hibernian's tirade.

'What did you expect!' he shouted. 'Did I not say fill the shieldwall with Saxon, Votadini *and* Hibernians on the second day; but—no—you expected a quick victory.' His tone became mocking. '"*We must be prudent*," you said, "*you brave Saxons will be enough to defeat them*," you said, "*keep men back to meet the British reinforcements when they arrive*." Except they didn't come … eh Guertepir? Arthur duped you to attack him uphill, that's apparent now. And look what happened—the British lived to fight another day, and what a tremendous fight!'—he counted out on his fingers—'Cenhelm gone, Hrodgar gone, Osbeorn gone—'

'And overnight half of your cowardly force *gone*!' roared Guertepir. 'Look outside! Half of the wagons departed from the fields—no doubt driven by Saxons who changed chainmail for smocks. We now have scant advantage over them because of your cowardly fyrd.'

'Can you blame them after their chiefs were slain and Arthur began firing half-trees up their arses!' defended the Jute 'Believe me, man; it's much easier for them to return to their old lives … to milk goats and cut barley … anything rather than walk up that damned hill again.'

Diarmait, who stood with Cunedda (the two men having become close friends since their trip to Camulodunum) intervened. 'On thing's for sure,' he said. 'Allies who fight amongst themselves always end up on the losing side. Bear in mind, even with the desertions, we still hold an advantage in numbers over them, and now we know of the ballistae we can be better prepared.'

'Dahh!' Frustrated, Guertepir swiped the wine from his mouth with a cloth and tossed the rag on the table before him. 'The dawn's almost here and I've no wish to hear any more Saxon, or Jute, or whatever-you-are, Wigstan, excuses!' He turned from them, his patience exhausted. 'Meet me on the walls in the morning,' he muttered over his shoulder as he walked away. 'For now, an old man needs his sleep.'

'Sleep … he goes for a sleep, I do not believe it,' said Cunedda some moments later as he gave Diarmait a disbelieving glance. Diarmait's look to Cunedda—*we should speak now about our matter*—was not lost upon the Votadini chief. He was silent awhile before emitting a reluctant, inevitable sigh. He made his decision and guided Diarmait from the room. 'Very well, my friend,' he said, 'we will talk further.'

'Cunedda ... the sun's risen and you really need to see this.' Abloyc, who had camped beside the northern wall of Aquae Sulis overnight, bristled with urgency. 'It seems Arthur has indeed got help.'

Cunedda, alarmed, rose from the table where he had been sitting with Diarmait. 'Get Wigstan to meet us at the gates,' he told Abloyc. 'And try to drag the men from their women and get them to form a wall.'

The assembly strode from the gates of Aquae Sulis. On the summit of Badon Hill, men stood along its entire ridge, their shields displaying the osprey crest of Ffodor, their apparel and weaponry that of Rome.

Abloyc frowned and tugged at his blond chin-beard. 'I don't understand this,' he mused, 'I thought the Romans had left these isles.'

'And so they have,' said Cunedda. 'Like Arthur, these men belong to the Dumnonii. They are Britons. The Roman apparel can only mean one thing Ffodor ... like Arthur he trains his men to fight as Romans.'

Abloyc was concerned. 'This changes things,' he said. 'Before their arrival we had a tough day before us, now our position is positively shaky.

473

We've no idea how many more men lurk behind that hill … and look, they have chariots.'

Interspersed between the men on the crest, Ffodor's chariots had been driven to the fore. Diarmait and Wigstan shared the concerned expressions of Cunedda and Abloyc as they craned to see up the hill.

Irritated, Wigstan turned towards the city gates. 'Guertepir … where in hell's name is the man? Surely he's out of his bed by now. Does he think this is just—'

An ashen Kelwin, the guardian of Guertepir's purse and the man who had advised him to raid cattle from the western peninsular, rushed from the gates. His demeanor abruptly put Wigstan to silence. 'It's Guertepir,' he said, stricken. 'He's drowned in the pool. Almaith and his druid are beside him and dead in the water. It appears they tested out their new found immortality and failed.'

Two hours passed as Arthur, Ffodor and Gherwan stood upon the ridge of Badon Hill. One thousand paces below them, two shieldwalls, consisting of mainly Hibernians and Votadini had assembled. Each was two hundred men wide and four men deep. Central to them, Hibernian chariots waited. Enemy cavalry had taken to each flank.

'They seek to impress us with their strength,' said Ffodor. 'The fear of Mars must be upon them.'

'If they hope to intimidate our men, they're wasting their time,' said Arthur. 'Those that remain will not be daunted.'

Ffodor gripped Arthur's arm and pointed his long fingered hand towards the distant assembly. His vulture's eyes had noticed a movement before the enemy line. 'See ... they have sent out an envoy. A number of them ride to the fore waving the flag of truce.'

Arthur gave a puzzled shake of his head. 'They wish to *talk*?' After considering his options for some moments he turned to Gherwan. 'Get Withred and Flint ... and while you're at it, Dominic and twenty of his archers.'

'You purpose to meet with them, then,' asked Ffodor as Gherwan departed.

'Yes, why not, what have we to lose? Who knows, they might intend to stand firm below ... get us to go to them. I wouldn't blame them. Would you come up this hill against us?'

'That, I would not. One thing's for sure, though; they've pricked my curiosity.' Soon,

Gherwan arrived with the men 'Come,' said Ffodor, 'let's hear them out.'

Diarmait and Cunedda had decided to tackle the problem of Guertepir—the Hibernian king's excesses and strange behaviour having led them to question his sanity.

After learning of his atrocity at the bathhouse, both men had become deeply concerned. Going to war was one thing; blood sacrifice and an attempt at deification another. Cunedda was not sure he could trust Guertepir to keep his side of the bargain. Diarmait, for his part, was uncertain if he even wanted to serve under the king anymore.

Furthermore, the Saxons had taken heavy losses, and along with desertions now numbered less than six hundred men. Of the chiefs, only Wigstan had survived, but the Jute's dejection had considerably deepened since Hrodgar and Cenhelm had fallen in battle. As for Diarmait and Cunedda, any thoughts of a campaign into the west with such a sorry Saxon crew had become unthinkable.

'I want freedom to patrol your seaboard and you want a quiet life in Dyfed,' Cunedda had said to Diarmait after the third day of battle.

'What we are even *doing* here now is beyond me.'

'We're here because of a mad man's greed and Saxon ambition,' replied Diarmait, 'but there may be another way to deal with this.'

Cunedda, who had no need for Diarmait to spell it out, nevertheless foresaw a problem. 'Not with Guertepir alive there isn't … or for that matter his wife and druid.'

Frowning, Diarmait had rubbed his hand across the stubble of his chin as he studied the flames of the nearby, warming fire. He considered the implications of Cunedda's statement, before giving him a look of deep gravitas. 'If we kill them, it needs to appear to be an accident,' he said. 'The retribution from his wife's father in Hibernia and the more loyal of his people in Dyfed will plunge my land into chaos if foul play is suspected.'

'And the Saxons, what do we do about them?'

'Let them go home. Wigstan is already a beaten man … his followers more so.'

They left and dealt with Muirecán first. The druid was sleeping an uneasy slumber in the cellars below the temple of Sulis Minerva. Cunedda held him down whilst Diarmait pushed a woolen blanket over his face. Against

477

such strength, Muirecán's resistance was short lived and futile.

Almaith slept alone in a separate chamber from Guertepir 'I'm doing you a service, believe me,' Diarmait had whispered to her as he raised the blanket. Almaith, like Muirecán, died quickly, leaving only Guertepir to deal with.

The Hibernian king was awake, his shadow looming before the window. He sat peering outwards. As Cunedda waited, Diarmait considered the blanket, shook his head in dismissal, then let it fall to the ground. From his tunic, he took a leather throng and crept towards Guertepir. Swiftly, he slipped the ligature around Guertepir's neck and pulled upwards. But Guertepir had had no intentions of delivering his death on a plate for Diarmait. Wild eyed, he thrashed, kicked and gargled, surprising his captain with the depth of his strength and energy. Diarmait fell to the floor with him and Cunedda grabbed Guertepir's legs, restricting his flailing. He turned his head away as Guertepir defecated. A final, gurgling choke, as if spitting out one last defiant curse, came from Guertepir as his struggle finally abated. He was dead.

They pulled his corpse from the room and into the dark night. Above them patrolling the wall, three guards spoke briefly as they crossed.

'Hide him in the shadows,' whispered Cunedda. 'We must wait till the guards are away from us.'

The pair caught their breaths and dragged Guertepir (for lifting him was out of the question, such was his bulk) towards the gloom below the wall. When the footfalls from above faded, they considered it safe to move and hauled him through the shadows until reaching the stone ingress of the bathhouse. After pulling the corpse inside, they laid it in a puddle of deep shadow beneath the image of Sulis Minerva, then left to fetch Muirecán.

Thin of frame and much lighter than Guertepir, the druid was lifted to Cunedda's shoulder. Stooped, the Votadini chief trudged with him into the dark streets, while Diarmait crept ahead, alert for any who might be abroad. Muirecán's portage passed without incident. At the temple, they placed him beside Guertepir, then left for Almaith.

Heavier than Muirecán, they took her lolling form by the shoulders and ankles and weaved back through the narrow streets, chancing their luck as they stumbled towards the bathhouse.

Once there, they walked into the thermal pool with Almaith. 'Seems that Sulis approves our action,' commented Cunedda as he released Almaith's body. Her wan face rolled upwards in the water; her grey locks a swirling mass around her head.

Under the dancing light of a brand, they dragged the other bodies into the pool. Cunedda dealt with Guertepir first. 'It will hide the strangulation marks,' he commented as he slid a blade across the dead king's throat.

With no heartbeat to eject it, Guertepir's blood seeped sluggishly from him, and moments later his corpse was surrounded by a swirling fog of crimson as his body turned and bobbed in the water.

Diarmait took his own blade to Almaith and dealt with her in the same way. Muirecán, he stabbed in the guts. When he had finished, he placed the blade in the druid's stiffening grip. *Perfect*, he thought as he pushed Muirecán from him. *You offered your people to the Gods then sacrificed yourself to them.*

They climbed from the water and shrugged back into their tunics. 'Come, let's get out of here,' said Cunedda as he grabbed the flaming brand from the wall. Pausing as he peered from the doorway, he added: 'See you at first light. An interesting day awaits.'

The parties met under a clear dawn on middle ground between the ridge and the enemy line. Arthur stood with Ffodor, Gherwan, Flint, and the Anglii, Smala and Withred. Behind them, with bows primed and pointed to the ground, stood Dominic and his archers. Facing them, some fifteen paces away, stood Cunedda, Diarmait, Abloyc and Wigstan. Like Arthur, Cunedda had brought a company of archers with him to provide a measure of protection.

After a period of silence, Diarmait was the first to speak. He pointed up the hill to Arthur's line of infantry. 'Those men have no need to die here today,' he said. He allowed the gravitas of his remark to sink in a moment before turning and pointing towards his own shieldwall some quarter mile distant. 'And neither do they,' he added.

An extraordinary expression had come to Arthur's face, half scepticism, half surprise. 'Where is your master,' he asked, ignoring Diarmait's words for now. 'Why does Guertepir send his captain to speak for him?'

Diarmait's group exchanged uncomfortable glances. 'He's dead,' said Diarmait eventually,

'… along with his wife and druid. He sacrificed himself to Sulis Minerva during the night. Thought he would be reborn a God, no doubt … he wasn't … he's still dead.'

There were expired breaths within Arthur's gathering and an outbreak of hushed but frenzied conversation. Far from convinced, Arthur observed Diarmait through hooded lids. 'You lie,' he said. 'This is a trick to fool us into complacency.'

Diarmait, who had expected such scepticism, signaled to a man who stood with a horse some fifty paces behind. The groom led the beast forward. Slumped over its back was a blanket covering a shape. When near enough for Arthur's group to see, Diarmait walked to the horses and removed the blanket. Guertepir's purple, bloated corpse was revealed.

Arthur stared at the aberration a moment then turned his attention to Diarmait. 'Yes it's him. The wicked bastard's death should be celebrated, but this changes nothing. The rest of you still live and will pay you've done. Why are you even standing here, Diarmait? You said no one needs to die, but that decision was taken from you the moment you decided to kill my people and steal my city. What have you to say to that; captain of a dead king?'

'That this day can still end by seeing us walk away from this. We can pack away our tools of war and just go home.'

Arthur gave a sniff of exasperation, exchanging a look with Ffodor, who had watched and listened grim-faced to the opening exchanges. Arthur said: 'That is not how these things work, you should know that. It's too late to sue for peace now; retribution has to be exacted.'

Abloyc, who had remained silent up until then, burst out with: 'And maybe it will be Britons who die in numbers if this goes ahead. The outcome is far from certain today.'

Arthur studied Abloyc. Arrogant in manner and insolent in tone, he did not like what he saw.

'One thing *is* certain,' said Arthur as he seared Abloyc with his cold-eyed appraisal. 'I will seek *you* out personally and make you eat your words.'

Cunedda slapped his hand across Abloyc chest, restraining him as he made to step towards Arthur.

Arthur, singularly unimpressed, positively smirked at Abloyc.

Cunedda pushed the glowering Abloyc back a step. 'Forgive my hot-headed friend,' he said.

'Never was one to think before he acted.' He turned his attention to the matter at hand. 'Diarmait is right, though ... there is another way; if there wasn't we wouldn't have come to you. Instead, we would be locking shields by now.'

Ffodor, whose patience had drained as the parley progressed, stepped to the fore. His head bobbed like a feeding raptor as he challenged Cunedda. 'Then spit it out man. If you have a solution to the impossible then spit it out, because I can assure you, you're in for a fight here today—my men yearn to spill the blood of those who would take their lands. So *what have you to say*?'

'This,' responded Cunedda. 'Sometimes these things can be decided by sole combatants rather than entire armies. Providing each side lay down their conditions and they are acceptable, then each of us can select a champion to fight for their terms.'

'*Terms!*' spat Arthur. 'What happened to savage ambition—ambition to rule all the lands east of Norwic. I take it your aspirations have shrunken somewhat?'

'No Arthur, they are the same,' said Cunedda. 'We Votadini never wanted anything more than security for our people. Our alliance with Guertepir was for that purpose. As for him'—he glanced at the dead king's body—'he wanted Aquae Sulis for his wife, but his desires came to a foolish end last night.'

Arthur shook his head, far from won over. Now he jabbed his finger at Wigstan, the Jute. 'What about him?' he asked Cunedda. 'How did you get him and his murderers to join you. What did you promise them?'

'Lands to the west—your lands, I do not deny it,' said Cunedda. 'The two thousand they provided could have been the difference between defeat and victory for us, and everything comes at a price.' He shot a contemptuous look Wigstan's way. 'We were wrong, though. Many of them came thinking it would be an easy victory—more of a prolonged feast. As soon as their ale ran out and the ballista bolts started to fly they deserted in droves.'

'So why do *you* stand here now?' Arthur asked, turning his attention to Wigstan. 'Why have you not followed your cowards eastwards?'

'I am here because I'm the only one who hopes you do not accept a compromise. I am Jute and when I go home to Cantiaci, I desire my head to be held high, having done battle with you.

'Oh, it *will* be held high, man. Held high for all to see on the end of my sword.' Wigstan bristled at Arthur's remark as a soft ripple of laughter came from Dominic's archers who were within earshot. But the Jute, unlike Abloyc, had the wits to stay his hand.

'So you wish your Jutes to regain their honour and fight this day, eh?' pressed Arthur. When Wigstan gave a defiant nod Arthur turned his focus back to Cunedda. 'See! One of your captains is still spoiling for a fight. What have you to say, chief of the Votadini?'

'I say this—he will go by whatever is decided here. I have already spoken to him on the matter. He has no choice, he knows that.'

'Name your terms and name your champion, then,' said Ffodor, rather to everyone's surprise. 'I will reserve judgment until I've heard you out.' He looked to Arthur and shrugged. 'Might as well. What of you? What is your intent?'

'Seems like I'm about to listen to his terms,' said Arthur with irritable resolve. 'I'll let you know my intent when he's finished speaking.' To Cunedda, he said: 'Speak out then. What are your conditions?'

'Aquae Sulis—now we're here, we may as well have the place—and the lands north— nothing more,' replied Cunedda. 'I will have Deva as before, but with the added protection of Diarmait's forces along the western seaboard. Diarmait will take kingship of Dyfed, Guertepir's lands, and he and I will form an alliance for our mutual protection. Wigstan will return to Cantiaci with a wagon full of British gold.' He nodded persuasively to Arthur. 'So, you see, even if you lose you come out of this pretty well.'

Arthur said nothing, but turned to Ffodor. 'I would speak with you'—he pointed towards a patch of trampled scrub some two hundred paces distant—'privately, over there.' Ffodor assented and they bade their leave and left. Their conversation went on for a while, sometimes heatedly, sometimes conciliatory. After seemingly reaching an agreement, their parley closed calmly. They returned to the gathering.

Arthur got straight to the point as he addressed Cunedda. 'We will go with what you say, but listen to this: if *I* win you hand me back my city and the men responsible for the deaths of the civilians and unarmed guards of Aquae

Sulis.' His smile was sardonic as he continued. 'You see … I know what you did in there.'

He let the uneasy silence linger a while as Cunedda exchanged a barely perceptible nod with Diarmait. So far so good. Everything was going the way they had planned it to go.

Arthur went on. 'Then you return to Deva … return to Dyfed, and swear to protect my northern territory from Saxon invasion. Indeed, a garrison of men from Travena and Brythonfort will billet in your towns and ride with your patrols. In turn, Brythonfort and Travena will accept a garrison of your troop and so an unbreakable bond will grow between us. Those are *my* terms Cunedda, *my* conditions Diarmait. But do not forget, I want the men responsible for cold murder. Refuse me that and total war is between us.'

Cunedda and Diarmait walked from earshot. Their conversation was short and decisive. When they returned, Cunedda spoke. 'Accepted' he said. 'And maybe you can kill two birds with one sword.' He moved to Abloyc and pushed him forward. 'Here is our champion, now choose yours.'

Abloyc shrugged Cunedda's hand from his shoulder. Having watched Withred, Flint and the famous Gherwan in battle he was not eager to fight any of them. 'What … me? Surely, Wigstan's a better choice. I thought we had agreed before, that should Arthur—'

'*Two birds with one stone*; what did you mean by that?' Arthur's tone was bitter ice. Cunedda's seemingly throwaway remark had not been lost upon him.

Cunedda's laugh was devoid of humour. 'You miss nothing, I'll give you that, Arthur. *Him*! he said in the way of explanation as he gestured towards Abloyc. 'A killer of an infant child and slayer of the unarmed. Kill him and part of your conditions are met. I learned of his deeds when arriving at Aquae Sulis with Diarmait. And the act gave me no pleasure, believe me.'

All looked at Abloyc. Most despised him.

'Let me do it,' said Flint. All turned his way. He met Arthur's gaze and continued with a quiet rage. 'Let me be your champion my lord. Erec was my friend. His family were as my own.'

Arthur was silent a while, then said: 'Very well, Flint. So be it. How can I refuse, I know what they meant to you.'

The rules of combat decreed that Abloyc and Flint should wield identical weaponry. Abloyc had put forward the use of ax and shield—it being his preferred combination. Flint had agreed, wishing only to get at the man and exact his revenge. Both wore bronze breast plates and simple nasal helmets.

Arthur accompanied Flint, whilst Cunedda escorted Abloyc. A ring of men surrounded them, allowing a large circle seventy paces in diameter to serve as a combat area.

Cunedda spoke first. 'Let all here today hear my oath and hold me to it. I swear that I will ratify the terms of this contest should my man win; or accept the conditions of defeat, should he lose.' He outstretched his arm, fist clenched, as he awaited Arthur's response.

Arthur reciprocated the salute, and their fists touched as he repeated Cunedda's oath, word for word.

They stood silent a moment.

'Then let it begin,' said Arthur.

'Let it begin,' repeated Cunedda.

Flint assessed Abloyc as the man shook the stiffness from his shoulders and bounced lightly on the balls of his feet. With a movement of his head from side to side, Abloyc relaxed the sinews of his neck.

If unsure of an opponent's capabilities, allow him the first strike. Erec's words came to Flint as he watched his rival's elaborate warm up display. Flint had adopted a motionless crouch, with ax and shield ready as he scrutinised Abloyc's every movement. *The eyes are the clue,* Erec had said. *They betray your opponent's intention.*

An eye flicker, then Abloyc was at Flint. Three rapid blows—one overarm, two sideways—were met by Flint's shield as a roar erupted from the watching men. Flint's parry hissed through cold air as Abloyc skillfully twisted sideways and avoided the swipe.

A flurry of assaults and counter assaults ensued, the clanging of iron upon bronze filling the circle of combat with its clamour. Shields soon became battered, axes dulled, as the contest raged on, brutal and unlovely. No spectacle for the admirer of subtle and skillful engagement, the contest had become an unrelenting display of raw belligerence.

A pause occurred as new, keen axes were thrown to the combatants. Between heavy breaths, Flint found words for Abloyc. 'Killer of a child ... do your deeds not spoil your sleep? ... you dashed an infant's head against ... against a wall ... how do you live with that?'

Abloyc picked up his fresh ax. There was a sneer in his smile as he replied: 'Easily … I live with it easily … because I have killed many. The child becomes the man, and the man seeks you out for your deeds. Easier you pinch out the stem than chop down the tree.'

'And you enjoy it, don't you, bastard. I can sense your delight as you speak of it.'

Abloyc deigned not to reply; instead he repeated his stretching and bouncing display as he fixed Flint with an impassive stare.

Flint was back in his crouching stanch as he hefted his own new ax, testing its balance. His other arm throbbed from its battering behind the shield.

Again, Abloyc's eyes forewarned of his forthcoming attack. Flint's shield met the first blow, but this time he left a gap for Abloyc. His second strike was aimed at Flint's exposed neck and Arthur's man barely raised the shaft of his ax in time to parry the swipe. Deflected upon his breastplate the ax head sparked, then scraped downwards. Flint staggered, aware that death had kissed him briefly. He took three stumbling steps backwards. Seeking to press his advantage, Abloyc came at him again. Still off-balance, Flint could only defend against the overhead hack which fell upon him. The ax slid down his shield and severed one of the shoulder straps securing his breast plate.

Abloyc's momentum had taken him shield to shield with Flint. As they pushed apart, Flint's breastplate, secured by its remaining strap, swung away from him. He flung the sheet of bronze away and pressed forward towards Abloyc.

Two of Flint's ax blows fell into the Votadini shield; then two more. Abloyc stumbled and barely manage to fend off Flint's combination. As Abloyc spun away in a bent-kneed stoop, he sent an opportunistic backhanded slash at Flint. The attempt was clumsy, but the back face of the ax found Flint's ribcage. With no breastplate to protect them Flint's ribs crumpled.

Bile leapt to his throat and an agonised '*heahh*!' came from him, such was his pain. He staggered away from the next attack as his man rushed him again. His heel caught against his abandoned breastplate and he went to ground. When his arm came from his shield loop, Abloyc was quickly onto it and kicked the plate out of reach. Flint rolled. Turf and soil erupted beside him as Abloyc's ax bit the ground.

Flint's avoidance had taken him near to the breastplate. He grabbed it and held it above him as a shield. Sparks flew as Abloyc's downward hack creased the breastplate, but the armour held, preventing Flint's head being riven from forehead to chin.

Abloyc grinned as he sensed victory. Now he could finish Arthur's man, who now had no shield to protect him or weapon to wield. It would be easy to end this now. He went for Flint, but the breastplate again managed to repel his blow.

Flint rolled again, this time towards Abloyc—so near he could smell the leather of the Votadini's boots. He heard Abloyc's swiftly inhale above him as he drew back his ax for the deathblow. Flint rammed the edge of the breastplate into Abloyc's exposed shin, the strike cleanly fracturing his lower leg. Howling, Abloyc hopped away from him.

Most of Flint's energy was gone as he struggled to his feet. Abloyc, frantic to keep upright, spun on his good leg. When his balance left him, he fell forward before Flint. Grimacing, he attempted to gain his knees, but his jarring bones caused him to scream. He was defeated. He could not stand.

The circle of men had closed around them; and only now did Flint absorb the wild cries which had sounded unabated throughout the dual. He stood above Abloyc, panting but resolute.

With no need to rush, such was the level of Abloyc's debilitation and his own fatigue, Flint strolled to retrieve his discarded ax. Looking to Arthur and Gherwan he gasped: 'This ... is for our friend ... and the baby who would ... who would have become him.'

He kicked Abloyc's helmet from him. The Votadini twisted his head, his eyes glittering with hate as he spat out his final curse. 'Then what are you waiting for? Finish me you Dumnonii shit!'

Flint looked to Arthur again, and then to Cunedda. To his surprise, the Votadini chief looked untroubled by the outcome. He gave Flint a brief nod. 'Finish him. Do it now,' he said.

Flint obliged, and two hacks with his blunted ax removed Abloyc's head. With disdain, he kicked the head to one side and pushed through the cheering crowd, their praise and supplication unwanted.

Raedwald lay, locked-breathed, under the shrub as Nila approached. So near was she, he heard her sweet singing voice as she stooped to take water from the stream. He decided she would have to do for now—the other hag could wait until she strayed from the protection of the dog. Knowing he had only seconds to act, he crept from cover and approached Nila.

Modlen took Titon's jowls in her palms and gave them a spirited shake. The dog, ever glad of human attention, gave out low yelps of pleasure and playful growls.

'No you don't,' laughed Modlen as the canine stood on its hind legs in an effort to lick her face. 'I knew I shouldn't have encouraged you. Get down you great—'

A curtailed shriek stopped Modlen dead. The noise had to be Nila. Something, beast or man, had caused her to scream. She untied Titon and moved falteringly towards the stream.

The falling light had rendered the scene monochromic, so that Nila's blood ran as a black flow into the water. Raedwald turned, his eyes ablaze and his knife bloody as he sensed Modlen's approach. At his feet Nila bled out, her throat agape. He flinched and considered his options as he beheld Modlen. The woman—too stunned to act for now—merely stared at him, but she had brought the dog. Raedwald's gaze fell to his knife, then turned to the animal. He considered whether to run or fight. A malevolent growl from Titon served to make up his mind and Raedwald left.

All went well for him at first—his own panting breath and rushing footfall the only sounds breaking the blanket silence of the wooded grove through which he ran. He reached the edge of the spinney. Beyond the trees was scrubland—uncultivated and wild. He pushed through stiff broom and juniper looking for a place to hide. He counted out his steps, one hundred should be enough, then he would be safe. The shrubbery thickened and Raedwald began to relax somewhat. A growl: low, menacing and gathering in intensity, was his first warning; the rapid rush of paws upon leaf litter—his second, as the mastiff closed on him.

Trained to chase, then kill, by his past master, Titon had bounded away from Modlen as soon as her trembling hand had dropped its leash.

After crashing to ground, such was the forcefulness of the dog's leap, Raedwald rolled over and fished for his knife. His hand found only an empty sheath. 'No—no, go ... off, away with you.' In shock, he chattered and batted at the animal as it rammed its nuzzle into his midriff.

497

Titon pulled its bull neck backwards and jerked Raedwald's tunic from him, exposing his bare torso. Again, it bit and pulled, this time bringing away skin and muscle. Raedwald's screams emerged high-pitched and reedy as the mastiff, oblivious to the blows Raedwald rained upon its head and body, attacked a third time. Now the dog went for the youth's glistening entrails, pulling them in strings from the ragged tear in his gut.

As he scrabbled for his innards, Raedwald implored Titon for mercy—his babblings serving only to spur the animal to a higher level of frenzy. Twisting its neck from side to side as if shaking the life out of a rabbit, the mastiff jumped into the air with a mouthful of the Saxon's twisted viscera.

Upon landing, Titon turned its attention to Raedwald's head, attacking it with meat-rending bites as it snatched and pulled, snatched and pulled; stripping him of his features until only the musculature of his face and exposed, veined eyes remained. His mouth, stripped now of its lips, continued to move in a parody of speech, as a froth of gargled blood emerged. His demise dragged on, prolonged and dreadful, his whimpering continuing until Titon finally grabbed and pulled at his throat.

Modlen wept as she hugged Nila's limp form to her breast. Her friend was dead, She knew that now. Killed by a shadow in the night.

CHAPTER TWENTY-TWO

Cunedda and Diarmait took to the northern road and reflected upon the success of their plan. As early as the second day of battle, both had come to realise that the conquering of Arthur's lands would not be possible. Saxons had fallen in droves, their chiefs dead and their resolve weakened.

Furthermore, they were aware that a prolonging of the war was contrary to their personal ambitions—Cunedda's being the long-term security of his people; Diarmait's the removal of the mad king, Guertepir. Mindful they could not just walk away, and that a straight surrender might come with too many conditions, they had decided to press Arthur for the fight of champions, knowing the terms attached to such a contest would be far less severe.

Cunedda and Diarmait's meeting on the third day had been brief and decisive. Both stated their intentions, aired their views, and reached an agreement. It was decided that Guertepir and Abloyc (two men far too disruptive and unpredictable) needed to be eliminated. They took the deal to Wigstan, prepared to kill him too if the need arose. Fortunately, the Jute, who had few options left, had reluctantly agreed.

As for Cunedda and Diarmait, neither desired Aquae Sulis—its inclusion in the conditions of combat serving only to give the fight of champions a degree of credence. Their plan had been brilliant in its simplicity and the war had ended with minimal bloodshed on its fourth day.

At Corinium they parted; Diarmait, now the lord of Dyfed, went westwards to his coastal ring fort; Cunedda went northwards to Deva.

Arthur and his army were lauded as heroes as they journeyed back to Brythonfort. Bedecked by garlands of evergreen (man *and* horse), their trip was tinged with both joy and sadness. Many of those who had ridden to Aquae Sulis to wage war were now absent. Of the one thousand men of Arthur's levy, only three hundred had survived. Seventy knights and thirty-three bowmen had also perished. Smala and his Angles had fared little better, losing a respected leader in Hereferth, as well as twelve hundred of their levy and over three hundred knights.

As the army passed by village and farmstead, hope would collapse to despair when folk learned of their losses. Others—the

501

lucky ones—greeted their men with displays of joyous relief.

Ashen with pain, Flint rode aslant in his saddle as Brythonfort's gates loomed before him. Beside him were Dominic, Augustus and Withred.

'Nothing like a few broken ribs to put colour in a man's cheeks.' Augustus attempted to bolster Flint. 'And I should know; I rode all the way from the eastern forest with six of 'em broken after being ridden over by that bastard, Ranulf.' He tapped Flint on the knee. 'It's nothing that Rozen can't put right, though. She and her herbs work wonders.' Giving him a knowing wink, he added: 'Thought about asking her for something to make my cock stiff but my Modlen reckons it's all right as it is.'

Flint chortled out an explosive laugh and immediately wished he had not. Grimacing and grinning at the same time, he berated Augustus. 'I've told you to keep quiet. Every time you speak I end up like this. I can't wait to get out of this saddle and away from you.' A huge crowd had gathered at the gates of Brythonfort. Flint scanned the horde looking for his mother. 'Ma should be waiting,' he said. 'I'll be relieved to see her.' He gave Dominic a sideways, crafty glance. 'What say you, Dom? Will you be glad to see my mother?'

Flint knew! Dominic had read the look. He replied with some discomfort. 'It seems you already know the answer to your own question. Flint ... listen ... this was not something either of us—'

'You've no need to explain, it's fine by me,' smiled Flint. 'I've recognised it for weeks anyway. I noticed the way you looked at her; the way she looks at you, these days.'

'Thank you,' said Dominic. 'You have no idea what—'

'Here's my Modlen!' shouted Augustus who had been riding ahead. He jabbed his horse into a trot towards her.

Modlen waited with her orphans: Cate, Ula and Art; and their latest addition, Cara. Martha—Murdoc's widow—stood with Simon. She held Ceola. Titon sat at their feet, his stump of a tail banging against the earth as he waited for Augustus. Ula and Art jumped into Augustus' arms as the dog, unable to wait any longer, bounded and barked around them. He spun with them a moment before settling his concerned gaze upon his wife. Something troubled her, he could tell. Her red eyes and folded arms were indicative of impending bad news. He knew her too well.

Modlen went to him then, and poured out her sorry tale.

Wild cheers erupted as the main body of Arthur's army, led by the great lord himself, reached the gates. Amidst the clamour, stricken and weeping now, Augustus turned to meet Dominic and Flint, his sorry countenance warning them of forthcoming ill tidings.

'Your mother, Flint'—Augustus swiped his sleeve across his eyes as he fought to gather himself—'she didn't make it back. Murdered, she was, by a Saxon renegade.' He pointed to Titon. 'My dog took the killer, but it was too late for the poor woman.'

Flint slumped against the neck of his horse. 'No—no—not this,' he muttered. 'Please not this.'

Dominic went to Flint as the knight crumpled. He embraced and rocked him, unmindful of his own devastation.

Augustus stood with Withred. Both were silent and sad. After a moment, Augustus remembered something. 'These were found on the Saxon,' he said, as he held out the necklace for Withred to see. 'They must have belonged to Nila.'

Withred drained of colour. 'Let me see it,' he murmured.

Augustus handed him the beads.

Withred looked skywards, his eyes stinging as he clutched the necklace. 'Raedwald,' he wept. 'The murderer's name was Raedwald ... son of Egbert ... he killed my aunt, also. These belonged to her.'

Time passed as the roar of cheering crowds engulfed them. Eventually, Dominic slid from his mount as Augustus led a slumped and wretched Flint towards the gates.

Martha and Simon came to Dominic, and they hugged and wept. Wept for Murdoc; wept for Nila; wept for the nature of man and his shattering wars.

CHAPTER TWENTY-THREE

Weeks passed and the western lands became settled again. The war had secured relief from Saxon invasion and engendered a peace that would last for decades.

Withred travelled northwards with Smala and a large host of Anglii folk who had recently arrived from the continent. All intended to settle north of Hadrian's Wall in the lands vacated by Cunedda. With Withred's group were Augustus, Flint, Arthur and Dominic.

Arthur (who rode with an accompaniment of thirty of his knights) had decided to visit Cunedda and Diarmait at Deva and Dyfed; his purpose to cement the newfound alliances made after the battle of Badon Hill.

The abandoned fort at Venonis, at the crossroads of Watling Street and the Fosse Way, marked the parting of the ways for many of the group. Here, Arthur, Flint and the knights, made ready to take to Watling Street and follow its northwestern course to Deva.

Arthur went first to Withred, embracing him. 'You're role in securing the future of this isle is immeasurable,' he said. 'Who could have imagined a man who came here as a mercenary, would become one of Britannia's greatest heroes.'

'No, lord,' Withred's laugh was laced with modesty. 'I only did what any decent man would have done.'

'And in doing so, you lost a woman precious to you.'

'I *will* see my aunt again one day,' said Withred with conviction. 'Together we'll walk through fields of barley with mother and father, and feel the warm winds of Elysium upon our faces.'

'And what now, Withred. What will you do now?'

'Go with my people and help secure their future beyond the northern wall.'

'As ever, you do what's right,' smiled Arthur.

As they spoke, Flint and Dominic also prepared to part their ways. United in their grief, their bond was tight, their sentiments sparing yet poignant.

'Keep strong,' said Dominic. 'Your body has healed, but your eyes tell me your heart has not.'

'So says a man with the most despairing eyes I have ever seen,' said Flint sadly. 'We are both damaged, Dom, and need time to settle.

After they imparted their final words they embraced, then Flint took to Watling Street with Arthur.

Dominic rode beside Augustus and Withred. Ten miles north of Venonis, the ancient forest of Sherwood abutted the western edge of the road.

'Did you notice that Arthur did not say goodbye to you, Dom,' said Augustus as the tracker swung from his saddle and examined the earth at the side of the road.

Crouching as he rubbed soil through his fingers, Dominic squinted up at Augustus. 'Yes, I did. Refuses to believe I'm not coming back. Said at Brythonfort before we set out, that he wouldn't curse our parting with a farewell.'

'And I should do the same,' said Augustus, close now to tears as he sensed Dominic's imminent departure. 'That, or pick you up, bundle you with ropes, and take you back with me to Brythonfort.'

Dominic stood and went to Augustus' horse. He patted the charger and looked up warmly at the Briton. 'A big horse for a big man,' he said. 'And a man with a heart bigger than the forest I'm about to walk into.'

Augustus looked at Dominic; at his two ponies, one of which was loaded with extra gear. He pulled himself from his saddle and dropped down to him. Withred joined them as Smala and his people made their slow progress up the Fosse way.

'What does the earth say,' asked Withred as he glanced at Dominic's soiled hand. 'It's told us much in the past, my friend ... saved our lives and guided us through territories unknown. This time I hope it tells you to get back on your mount and ride with me to the northern lands. There, you can help us settle.'

'No, it tells me I'll be having game for my supper before this day's out.' He nodded towards the brooding forest. 'In two days I'll have established a camp in there; in two months a permanent base.'

Augustus, exasperated and upset at the same time, burst out with: 'And do what, man! You don't even know these woods; have no idea what lurks within them.'

'One thing *is* for sure, though,' said Dominic. 'No Saxon will enter the forest, not this far north.'

Their pleas went on a while longer, but they knew Dominic too well ... knew his will was unshakeable once his mind was set. Eventually, he embraced them both and turned away.

'I'll see you again, Dom!' shouted Augustus, as Dominic led his ponies to the forest edge. Augustus dragged his sleeve across his face as Withred placed an arm over his shoulder. He shouted again to Dominic. 'If I have to search for you for months, I'll find you and rake your bald head with my knuckles! You just see if I don't!'

Dominic, smiling, turned and waved to them.

'You tried, Gus,' said Withred. 'All this way to persuade him not to leave but at least you tried. Now you must return to Modlen and your children.'

Augustus slumped down sulkily at the road's edge; his fisted hands pressed to his temples. 'And start my life again without so many dear friends,' he said, staring at the ground. 'And Tomas … he doesn't know. Dominic couldn't bring himself to tell the lad. That's something else I need to do when I get back.' After some moments, he turned his attention to the sky, then got to his feet. His tears had dried. 'You're right I need to start back while most of the day is before me. And you'—he jabbed a thick forefinger at Withred— 'I *will* see you again and soon.'

They embraced and exchanged their final words. Soon the road was empty as Withred rode north and Augustus took the trail back to Brythonfort.

As Dominic watched them go, he thanked the Gods for bringing such people into his life. Then he cursed the same Gods for allowing him to love them. To love was to be let down; to be hurt; to be left a shell. His love for Murdoc and Nila would be with him to the grave, but they had gone now.

Behind him, the forest whispered her siren's call. She would accept his love, but never curse him with her death … never leave him alone. He sighed and entered the wilderness.

The End

Made in the USA
Lexington, KY
29 July 2015